Nepantla Familias

The Wittliff Collections

Wittliff Collections Literary Series
Steven L. Davis, General Editor

NEPANTLA FAMILIAS

**An Anthology
of Mexican American
Literature on
Families
in between Worlds**

Edited by Sergio Troncoso

Texas A&M University Press
College Station

This paper meets the requirements of ANSI/NISO Z39.48-1992
(Permanence of Paper).
Binding materials have been chosen for durability.
Manufactured in the United States of America

Library of Congress Cataloging-in-Publication Data

Names: Troncoso, Sergio, 1961– editor.
Title: Nepantla familias : an anthology of Mexican American literature
  on families in between worlds / edited by Sergio Troncoso.
Other titles: Wittliff Collections literary series.
Description: First edition. | College Station : Texas A&M University Press,
  [2021] | Series: Wittliff Collections literary series | Includes
  bibliographical references.
Identifiers: LCCN 2020052162 | ISBN 9781623499631 (cloth) | ISBN
  9781623499648 (ebook)
Subjects: LCSH: Mexican Americans—Ethnic identity. | Mexican
  Americans—Cultural assimilation. | Mexican American families. |
Mexican
  American families—In literature. | Mexican Americans in literature. |
  Group identity in literature. | Mexican-American Border Region—In
  literature. | LCGFT: Essays. | Poetry. | Short stories.
Classification: LCC E184.M5 N35 2021 | DDC 973/.046872—dc23
LC record available at https://lccn.loc.gov/202005216

SOURCE CREDITS

"All the Pretty Ponies" by Oscar Cásares first appeared in *Texas Monthly*,
2014. Reprinted by permission.

"Mujeres Matadas" by Daniel Chacón first appeared in *Hotel Juárez: Stories,
Rooms, and Loops*, Arte Público Press, ©2012. Reprinted by permission of
Arte Público Press—University of Houston.

An excerpt from "Losing My Mother Tongue" by Reyna Grande was
previously published on LitHub.com, 2019.

"Self Portrait in the Year of the Dog" by Deborah Paredez first appeared
in *Year of the Dog*, BOA Editions, ©2020. Reprinted by permission of The
Permissions Company, LLC on behalf of BOA Editions, Ltd.

"Mundo Means World" by Octavio Solis first appeared in *Catamaran
Literary Reader*, 2016. Reprinted by permission.

"Life as Crossing Borders" by Sergio Troncoso first appeared in *New Letters*,
Vol. 85, No. 4, 2019. Reprinted by permission.

Contents

FICTION

Nepantla Familias

Introduction

As a child in the Ysleta neighborhood about a quarter of a mile from the US–Mexico border, I had a strange recurring dream: I would be suspended in the clouds or fog, on a beam, gently falling into oblivion to one side and then falling to the other. I would never feel any pain or terror, and I would never know what happened after I fell to one side of the beam or the other. In the dream, it was the falling that mattered, somehow, the movement, and it was sitting on the beam for a few seconds before inevitably I would sway and fall to one side or the other.

Over the years, after I left childhood and El Paso, Texas, after I left the border and returned to it, I would interpret this dream of the "middle ground" in many ways. Living between Spanish and English. Being Mexican yet also American. Choosing values I inherited from my parents while also choosing values I created for myself. Living in many worlds in a single day—the worlds of the past and the present, the worlds of cities and rural areas, and the worlds of different languages and cultures. I believed the dream image even applied to my feeling of being in between the outsider who is ignored or attacked and the native who inherently belongs in the United States. Lately, as I have gotten older, I think about this dream in another way, as living on the border between life and death, with the many questions to be answered about the "undiscovered country" all of us will visit, but also about how those very questions change the life I live today. Strangely, falling to one side helps you to understand your falling to the other side in the next instance.

So the middle ground or borderland that defines *nepantla* has been with me, in one way or another, all my life, and the essays, poems, and short stories in this anthology reflect the diversity and variety of experiences that might explain, reveal, and mysteriously explore this liminal land that is so essential to the Mexican American experience, particularly within families. Because it is through our families that we live nepantla, that we negotiate it, that we have questions about our identity and choices, that we are convinced to fall one way or another, or even to balance perpetually between many different worlds. Through our families, we understand better "the other side," even if we perhaps fall more to a side different from our ancestors.

This Mexican American experience of living between two worlds has been—and will forever be—essential and important to the United States for at least three reasons. Of course, the first reason is the proximity of Mexico to the United States and the growing numbers of Mexican Americans who are citizens of the United States. But the ability of at least some Mexican Americans to go easily back and forth, between countries and languages, gives this first reason a continuing vitality that does not exist for other immigrants to the United States. And that many non–Mexican Americans not only regularly travel to visit our southern neighbor but also live and retire in Mexico has created another version of nepantla that in a way dovetails the "Mexican American nepantla" of this anthology.

The second reason Mexican American nepantla will remain at the forefront of our culture and society is what it reveals: the wounds of our history. The wounds of Mexicans feeling like outsiders in a land that was once theirs. The wounds of leaving Mexico for opportunity in the United States and then often feeling a step behind in language, knowledge, and power. The wounds of leaving home for some place better that you also want to make into a home. Some of these wounds heal permanently, and some heal for a moment, only to be ripped open again later. Many of these wounds may haunt us even as we appear polished, accomplished, and well integrated into our communities in the United States. These wounds in many ways define us, and should define us, not only for the pain they have caused us, but also for what we have endured and overcome. In moments of peace, these wounds may even be a source of our tragicomedy and laughter.

That brings us to the third reason why I believe nepantla will remain a vital experience in the United States: as much as nepantla helps to understand Mexican Americans, living in a middle ground—with its uncertainty and questioning of the self—is also a deeply *universal* experience. But to appreciate this, a reader has to open these pages, experience these essays and poems and short stories, and cross her own borders. Toward empathy. What this reader will discover is new possibilities for understanding the Mexican American experience of nepantla. Most of the literary work in this anthology is appearing for the first time anywhere. Of the thirty literary works in this book, only five have been previously published as of this writing.

That is my hope, at least, as the editor. Anyone who has left their home and tried to find a new one in a strange place—at times welcoming and at times hostile—they should find themselves in these pages. Anyone who has felt stymied by ancestors and their demands, yet also emboldened by their sacrifices and forgotten values—they should find themselves in these pages. Anyone who has forged a self from pieces of many worlds, to fit and not fit in a new home, who has balanced on many beams to understand different sides—yes, they should find themselves in these pages. Anyone who has loved another from a different world—they should recognize a version of themselves in these pages. And anyone who has crossed any border to create who they are, rather than to take who they are for granted, rather than to assume a place belongs to them—and suffered the consequences for it—they will find their fellow travelers, their kindred spirits, in these pages.

This is where I also hope this anthology not only reveals the Mexican American experience of nepantla to Mexican Americans but also becomes a bridge for those who are not Mexican Americans to understand another community as well as to understand themselves. To understand and write from the perspective of a particular community—to be deeply *proud* of that community—does not inherently mean that you cannot understand others outside your community. The either/or proposition that forces you to choose between your community and, say, your country has never been true. The very skills we learn to cross borders within ourselves help us to cross borders toward others outside our community.

Nepantla Familias: An Anthology of Mexican American Literature on Families in between Worlds. Nahuatl. Spanish. And English. The title itself contains the many worlds Mexican Americans have traveled. It also conveys a balancing among these worlds that points to a new self for a new world.

—Sergio Troncoso
May 20, 2020

 Nonfiction

Here, There

David Dorado Romo

Liminal zones are unexpected thresholds. They're passageways that you enter, sometimes without having the slightest clue how deeply they are going to transform you. They take you to other worlds you didn't even know existed. Sometimes you don't realize you entered liminal zones until many years later.

I grew up in El Paso, Texas, less than a mile away from the US–Mexico borderline. This part of the world—in the middle of nowhere and in the midst of everything—is full of liminal zones.

Juan el Predicador used to stand on a corner of Oregon and Fifth Street in El Paso's Segundo Barrio and denounce the generation of goddamned snakes and the sinful world that doesn't give a shit for pobres locos like him. He would sing church hymns while holding a Bible on one hand and pointing to the sky with the other, praising the Lord and then cussing out the pinches culeros who sent him to fight a war long ago in a foreign land, where he left behind a huge chunk of his former soul. People said Juan el Predicador didn't come back the same from that war. During his street sermon he would punctuate each phrase with a compulsively repetitive, "Here, there, here, there."

And I always figured he said that because he was neither here nor there, or maybe he was both here and there simultaneously. Like almost everything and everyone on the border, including me. Here. There.

When I was a boy I used to visit my great-aunt Adela Dorado, who lived in one of the Oregon Street red-brick tenements, a few yards from the corner where Juan el Predicador would later preach. I don't remember everything about my tía Adela, but there are certain details that will never leave me. Every morning she would make me fresh-squeezed orange juice. She would scratch my back when putting me to sleep at night, and I will forever associate back-scratching with acts of great love. I remember the Pentecostal church songs she would sing to me while I accompanied her on plastic guitar with rubber-band strings. I vaguely remember some of the lyrics. "Mis amigos no me quieren porque yo ando con el rey!" I remember her stories about being abducted at the age of twelve by a Mexican federal officer during the Mexican Revolution. About his cruelty. About how he tied her with a lasso and she had to walk behind his horse. About how she later escaped from him and took a train to Ciudad Juárez and then later to El Paso. She would cross back and forth between the two cities when she worked as a maid on the American side of the line.

I remember she first introduced me to a liminal zone called the Santa Fe international bridge, where millions of people have been subjected to strange rites of passage. I remember she told me how her shoes melted when she put them in a large steam dryer at a quarantine plant at this border crossing, where vampires in uniforms would delouse her and the other people with brown skin. They would go into a room and be sprayed with a white powder, and when they would come out on the other side their bodies would be all white.

I didn't always believe my tía abuela's stories. Sometimes they sounded too strange to be true. Or too painful. And I don't remember all the details. Just the feelings.

Not all my memories about the Santa Fe bridge are bad. For instance, that's where Elizabeth, my God-fearing Pentecostal girlfriend, and I lost our virginity. Partially. In Hebrew, *Elizabeth* means "house of happiness." We were both in high school, and we were returning in my car from Juárez to El Paso. The line of cars waiting to be inspected was long and slow. It happened on top of the bridge, right in the middle, where you can see the lights of both countries.

The sixteenth-century Aztecs already had a term for a liminal middle ground. It's *Nepantla*, which in Nahuatl literally means a "mutual place." It forms part of the verb *Nepantlaçotla*, meaning "to love each other mutually." Sometimes a liminal zone can also be an erogenous zone.

The Assembly of God church I attended as a teenager was another one of those entryways into unexpected worlds. It was an unpretentious church named after the garden on the Mount of Olives where Jesus prayed the night before his death, when he asked his father to spare him from the torturous death that awaited him, sweat pouring from his forehead like drops of blood, but his father remained silent. Gethsemani was located on Alameda Street between a funeral home and an old movie theater, once called the Teatro Alameda. That Teatro Alameda showed the first Mexican American movie in the history of the United States, *La venganza de Pancho Villa*. The film's Spanish intertitles would say one thing, and the ones in English would sometimes be deliberately mistranslated and say the exact opposite.

The Pentecostals of Alameda Street, like all Pentecostals around the world, are a Protestant denomination known to the outside world for their peculiar custom of praying in unintelligible tongues. The hermanos and hermanas of Gethsemani would leave their pews and walk up to the front of the church facing the preacher's podium, and suddenly they would begin to shake uncontrollably when the spirit of God would descend on them; tears of joy would pour from their faces, and their hearts would overflow with the force of a thousand rivers. And the people would forget their own language as well as all their troubles and failures and begin to speak directly to the great universal force with rapturous words and syllables and utterances they never learned. Ecstatic glossolalia, they call it. Like the euphoric waves of sound that used to pour out of John Coltrane's saxophone that carried his audiences to the higher realms during his improvisations on the musical psalm "A Love Supreme."

On Sundays the young women of Gethsemani would wear their prettiest dresses to church, and the pastor would preach about the different kinds of love. There's *agape*, from the Greek word meaning divine love, the selfless kind that gives everything away and expects absolutely nothing in return. Then there's *philos*, the kind of love you feel for friends and family. And finally there's *eros*, as in erotic sexual love, which in my Spanish-speaking Pentecostal church was forbidden except within the confines of marriage.

I meditated on the preacher's sermon when Elizabeth and I made out on top of the Santa Fe international bridge. I wasn't supposed to love Lizzy the way I loved her, but I did. And it felt so good to be sinful. "If loving you is wrong, I don't want to be right." My hands trembled as they caressed her body and gradually descended into a place they had never been before. Outside while the cars waited to cross into another country, the street vendors sold paletas de limón, mazapanes, and cacahuates garampiñados.

I can still remember the fragrance of her perfume when I kissed her neck. Years later, when I lived in Jerusalem, I sent Elizabeth a bottle of perfume labeled Bathsheba. Bathsheba was the name of the woman King David killed for out of love and lust.

I was sixteen years old when my Uncle Ruben, a Pentecostal preacher from Nuevo Laredo, took me on a Holy Land tour, and I knew immediately that I had to return to Israel and find a way to stay there for a longer period. So as soon as I returned to the border that summer, I enrolled in Hebrew language classes at the Jewish Community Center in El Paso. As I look back, I realize there were two main reasons I wanted to learn that ancient Semitic language.

First, I wanted to read the Bible in the original tongue. I figured much of what I knew about it had been lost in translation, and I was right. Take, for instance, the first verse of Genesis: "In the beginning God created the heavens and the earth." A multitude of the nuances and ambivalence of the original Hebrew are lost in the English version. To begin with, *Elohim*, the Hebrew word for God in this verse, is plural. The word for create, *barah*, means to form or mold, as a potter might form an object out of clay. There are alternative grammatical interpretations of the phrase *bereshit*, meaning "in the beginning." The original Hebrew could also be translated as, "When God began to mold the heavens and the earth." This reading would suggest that the verse is not describing the very beginning of the universe itself but rather the moment that God(s) is/are molding preexisting materials and energies.

I wanted to go to the root of things, to the origins, but the more I studied Hebrew, the more I realized that almost every verse of the original version of the scriptures had potentially alternative meanings and interpretations. Nothing was as simple and unambiguous as I had been taught in my church in Central El Paso. My new knowledge made me feel that perhaps everything I thought I knew was based on one kind of mistranslation or another.

The other reason I wanted to learn Hebrew and live in Israel was that even as a young student, I already intuited that I needed to get as far away as possible from my home in order to understand where I was from. I studied the language for a total of four years, first as an undergraduate at Stanford and a year later at the Hebrew University of Jerusalem. In Israel, I rented an apartment in Abu Tor, one of the city's oldest Palestinian neighborhoods. Today, the Arab neighborhood is right up against the wall that divides the Palestinians from the Israelis. I felt very much at home in my new environment.

For me, the divide between Arab East Jerusalem and Jewish West Jerusalem was not too different from the partition between El Paso and Juárez back home. The streets in Abu Tor were unpaved, and in the mornings an elderly Arab man with a donkey would sell kefir milk to the neighbors. This also reminded me of similar scenes I witnessed as a child in Juárez. While I lived in Israel I was romantically involved with Lucia, the daughter of the Palestinian landlords who lived in the house next to mine. She was a Greek Orthodox social worker who invited me to her home for tea while her parents were away, through a back gate that connected her home to mine. We had to meet surreptitiously because public dating was frowned upon by her conservative Muslim neighbors, although her own parents were slightly more liberal regarding social mores. It didn't stop us from doing in secret the things lovers do everywhere. In El Paso, when young couples want privacy, they go to Scenic Drive or Transmountain Pass to make out. But in the Holy Land, Lucia and I parked on top of the Mount of Olives, a few hundred yards from the Garden of Gethsemani, while we kissed and caressed each other passionately. From our car, we could see the lighted stone walls, gates, and towers of Old Jerusalem at night. Had I never set foot as a teenaged boy inside Gethsemani church, on El Paso's Alameda Street, I would have probably never ended up in the original garden of Gethsemani, in the birthplace of three of the world's major religions, where Jesus prayed the night before his crucifixion. Funny how sometimes everything seems to be tangled up together in the strangest ways across space and time.

I was twenty years old and had a lot to learn. When Lucia shared personal stories with me about living under Israeli occupation, she opened my eyes to a world of global political complexities I was not aware of before. I began to realize that the Palestinian communities living in a militarized zone under constant surveillance were not too different from my own fronterizo communities back home.

When I would cross the checkpoints that separated the Jewish from the Arab sectors, the Israeli soldiers at the checkpoints asked those of us deemed suspicious the same kinds of profoundly existential questions the customs agents do at the El Paso–Juárez bridge—except in Hebrew. *Mi eifoh atah?* ("Where are you from?") *Lama atah kan?* ("Why are you here?") *Lean atah noseah?* ("Where are you going?")

They are the kinds of questions that are very difficult for essayists with history and philosophy degrees like me to answer in five hundred words or less.

Where am I from? On my maternal grandfather's side, my indigenous ancestors were Huicholes, or *huirrarika*, but I'm not exactly sure where all of my other indigenous ancestors originally came from. The popular theory is that they arrived through the Bering Strait more than fourteen to twenty thousand years ago. But based on ancient oral traditions and codices, many Original Peoples believe they came from the south, which seems to be supported by some linguistic analysis of early native languages in the Western Hemisphere, which shows that the oldest languages of this part of the world originated in the southern hemisphere then moved north. All I know is that some of my ancestors have been in lands now called the Americas moving and migrating back and forth, north and south, and vice versa for so long, we are no longer exactly sure where we started.

Where am I from? I'm from here. I'm from everywhere.

But of course I know that's not what the armed gatekeepers at borders want to find out when they interrogate you. As fronterizos, we know exactly what they want. We internalized the unwritten rules for the border crossing rituals a long time ago. We know to keep our answers short, simple, and unambiguous; to make eye contact but not too much, because it might be interpreted as defiance or contempt; and finally to avoid humor. At border crossings, all jokes are taken seriously.

Crossing borders in a war zone is particularly hazardous. The tension of living in a constant state of war seeps into your body almost unconsciously. It is like walking in an unmarked minefield. At any moment an explosion could go off. Guns are everywhere in Israel. When you step into a city bus you often have to sit beside soldiers with Uzi machine guns strapped to their shoulders. When they nod off beside you, sometimes the barrel of their weapon points right at your face, and you have to gently point it elsewhere.

You get used to it. It almost becomes normal that people get shot and blown up on a regular basis. You read about it in the newspaper; you hear about it from your friends; and sometimes it happens to people you know. A friend of mine, a fellow student from Texas enrolled at the Hebrew University, lost a foot and part of his leg while camping in a desolate forest area. He and his American friends jumped over a fence without reading the warning signs in Hebrew. What they thought would be an ideal site for a picnic turned out to be a minefield. When he stepped on the explosive device, his foot flew several feet up into the air. After a while, the precariousness of living in a war zone takes its toll.

I returned to El Paso after two years of living in Israel, but the tension did not go away. I brought the war home with me. Or maybe there had always been a war here and I just hadn't seen it before. The concrete barricades at the Santa Fe Street bridge. The barbed wire. The Border Patrol checkpoints. The surveillance cameras and sensors along the river levee. The hovering helicopters. The floating bodies in the Rio Grande. Before, it had all seemed so normal to me that I hardly noticed. But I had come back with new eyes and now understood how abnormal everything was.

Gethsemani was no longer located on the gritty and lively Alameda Street. The Assembly of God church had relocated to a slightly more affluent section of East El Paso, not far from Cielo Vista Mall. The church services had changed. Things were more subdued, more Americanized. Fewer people received the gift of tongues. When the preacher spoke, I was much more critical. It bothered me that his emphasis was on personal moral failings, on individual sins, and hardly at all on collective matters of social injustice. I often cringed at the authoritarian oversimplifications coming from the preacher's mouth. His Spanish-language sermons, mixed with a few phrases in English, made it sound as if God were some kind of conservative Hispanic politician. It didn't at all sound like the *Elohim* of the original Hebrew. In short, I no longer believed as I used to.

Elizabeth and I continued to see each other occasionally when I returned. Her religious beliefs were as strong as ever, unlike mine. She never stopped seeing our erotic encounters as an expression of moral weakness. In the past, the feeling of transgression and the guilt merely increased the passion for me. But I no longer thought we were doing anything wrong. Quite the opposite. Erotic and divine love were merely different flames of the same fire. Elizabeth didn't understand how I could have changed so much. She hadn't uprooted herself as I had.

She was right. I didn't come back the same. Before leaving for college and before my travels to the Middle East, I had felt comfortable and relatively well integrated within my El Paso community. While I was at Jefferson High School, or La Jeff as everyone called it, I used to be on the swimming team. After practice at the Washington Park pool, my happy-go-lucky friend Art and I would hang out at Chicos Tacos and talk about everything and nothing under the sun. That was the thing to do.

On Saturdays, I used to hang out at Cielo Vista Mall, one of the local temples to American-style capitalism. It's not at all what comes to mind when talking about a transformative liminal space. But somehow, as I look back, that's exactly what it turned out to be. In Spanish, Cielo Vista means Sky View. On August 3, 2019, a man armed with a Romanian AK-47 and a white supremacist manifesto walked into this same shopping strip and massacred twenty-three fronterizos. One of the people who lost their lives that day was Art Benavidez, the good-natured kid from La Jeff who used to talk to me about everything and nothing.

There was a movie theater inside the mall where I watched the first *Star Wars* movie. There was also an arcade with video games where you got to shoot down alien invaders for a quarter. Cielo Vista was the only place in town during my youth with a bookstore, Walden Books, where I bought my first collection of works by Hemingway, Freud, Plato, and Nietzsche. These and other books planted the seeds for my lifelong love of literature and philosophy.

For me, reading has always been an act of transgression. I've been a voracious reader from an early age. During my elementary school years my mother would bawl me out for spending so much time locked up in my room by myself devouring book after book. "You're acting like a girl!" she would scold me. "Why don't you go outside and play with the other kids?"

Although he never told me directly, my church pastor also didn't approve of my intemperate reading habits. From the pulpit, he would regularly preach against the pride and arrogance of intellectuals who think they are above the rest of the flock. "Be careful what you put into your mind," he would warn his parishioners. "What you read can make you lose your faith."

I felt guilty about it. So I would try to keep my reading material within the fold. I read theological works by Calvin and Erasmus discussing free will and predestination, commentaries about the Jewish Talmud, and philosophical treatises by Søren Kierkegaard about the teleological suspension of the ethical. I would ask my pastor question after question during Sunday School, which he usually couldn't answer to my satisfaction. I could tell he was annoyed by my incessant inquiries. I began to feel that his preachings about the pride of those who depended on their intellect rather than their faith were aimed specifically at me. I was like

Adam and Eve, who weren't satisfied with living in the Garden of Eden but preferred to disobey God by eating from the Tree of Knowledge because they foolishly wanted to be gods themselves.

After a while I stopped going to church. I lost the Pentecostal faith of my youth, and I disconnected myself from my old spiritual community. But in a way, I never stopped speaking in tongues. I also never ceased asking foolish and annoying questions. I couldn't suppress my drive to dig deeper into things. That's what led me to Israel to study Hebrew, Greek, and Aramaic. It was that same search for ancient wisdom that would later motivate me to visit indigenous communities in Mexico to study native languages including Rarámuri, Nahuatl, and Huirrarika (Huichol). They say that when you master a new language you take on a new soul. Your new tongue seeps into your unconscious, and what emerges is not only a different way of communicating, but also a new way of being. Maybe I lost my old faith, but found a new one.

For me, submersing myself in a new language was the first step in entering those stages of personal transformation described as liminal. The term *liminal* comes from the Latin word *limen*, meaning threshold. Anthropologists have used it to describe an in-between stage between a previous social order and a new one during rites of passage. The unstable nature of liminality makes it alluring, sacred, and dangerous. It's simultaneously destructive and creative and paves a way for understanding both sides.

And sometimes even a simple question leads you to enter those liminal passageways that change your life.

In Nahuatl, to inquire about someone's name you ask, "Quen timo-teca?" meaning "How were you planted?"

I realize that for many years, no matter how far I traveled my intention was to return to that place where I was planted. It's a place that I left a long time ago that is neither here nor there, or perhaps it's in a middle ground that is simultaneously here and there. Maybe it's a place that never left me. In Nahuatl, that place is called Nepantla.

Life as Crossing Borders

Sergio Troncoso

I grew up in Ysleta, a colonia on the eastern outskirts of El Paso, Texas. A shantytown right on the border. To paraphrase Tina Fey as Sarah Palin, "I could see Mexico from my house." When my parents moved from Juárez, Mexico to El Paso in the early 1960s, we had no running water for the first couple of years in Ysleta. We had an outhouse in the backyard. The city of El Paso was about to annex Ysleta. I remember arriving at our half-built adobe house with plywood sheets covering the windows: tirilones, hoodlums, had stolen our copper plumbing. We needed to move in to protect the little we had. We used kerosene lamps and stoves. My mother stomped dead any scorpions that scurried from the recesses of the adobe. An irrigation canal was where my brothers and I would escape to burn tumbleweeds, search for cangrejos, crayfish, or target beer bottles with our BB guns. Everyone in Ysleta was poor, everyone was Mexican (and I don't mean "Hispanic," I don't mean "Mexican American"). I mean mexicano. Everyone had just crossed the border. Everyone was working room by room to build their homes, exchanging work with neighbors. One street away, Don Chencho, the mason, for example, built our rock wall in the backyard, while my father, the draftsman, drew the blueprints for new bathrooms or family rooms and submitted them to the city for approval.

As Ysleta morphed from a colonia into a working-class suburb, our neighborhood had gang fights on many Friday and Saturday nights, Barraca contra Calavera. Barraca was our side, which meant "shack town." Calavera was next to a cemetery on the other side of an irrigation canal for cotton fields, where the old Ysleta Mission has been for centuries. That was "skeleton town." Two doors from our house on San Lorenzo Avenue was the house of one of the leaders of Barraca: I knew him only as El Muerto, the dead. His sister was in my grade at South Loop School. I would guess that at least half a dozen kids in my neighborhood died before they turned twenty from gang violence, drunk driving, or drug use. I remember the names of many characters from Barraca: Joe, Willie, Sonia, Robert, Pablo, Ismael, Carlos, Ramon, Glenda, Letty, Johnny, and Mundis. In Latin class at Ysleta High, I helped Willie roll joints in the back of Mr. Rittman's class: I never smoked pot in Ysleta (I did at Harvard College), but I knew how to make friends with these tough characters—I helped them with their homework—and they protected me, or at least they left me alone. Willie often hid a switchblade in his boot pocket, and God help you if you crossed him.

The reason I tell you this first story about my childhood, of course, is to open your eyes: if you have never been to a place like Ysleta and just happened on it (or you met someone from a place like Ysleta), you might tend to dismiss the place, and say, "Oh, it's a poor Mexican neighborhood on the border, where nothing good comes out of it, and of course, the people there have nothing to teach me; they have nothing to offer the world." An attitude like that guarantees that a place like Ysleta will be ignored. Writing about that neighborhood and getting others to read those stories, however, counteracts stereotypes and lazy generalizations.

In the story "A Rock Trying to be a Stone" from my first book, *The Last Tortilla and Other Stories*, I wrote about three tough characters and a dangerous game they are playing. What the story reveals is that the character who looks the worst—the cholo, the maldito—ends up being the one who sacrifices himself to try to save one of his friends. Appearances can be and *are* deceiving, and one who looks like he might kill you might also be the same one who possesses *true character*, as Aristotle defines it: the ability to act right, even in a dangerous situation. A stereotype also misses the variety and nuances and possibilities of characters within Ysleta, even within the same *family*. Joe, for example, was tougher than even Willie, but Joe's sister became a school principal, la Mary Lou. Good storytelling seduces you into looking beyond stereotypes. Even if everyone is poor, even if everyone is Mexican, even if everyone lives a ten-minute walk from the border, the culture and characters vary from family to family and even within a family. So stories, my stories certainly, seek to expand your empathy, to make you look at characters you might ignore in real life, and also to explore how their struggles might affect you as a reader.

Let me tell you another story. When people find out how I grew up and where I grew up, they invariably ask, "How did you get from a place like Ysleta and the US–Mexico border to Harvard and then Yale?" The short answer is that I translated the Mexican immigrant values of my parents into values that would help me succeed in education and writing. That short answer, of course, misses the uncertainty, the failures, the adaptations on the fly, the stupid choices, how I learned to persevere, the grit my parents gave me, the accountability they demanded of me.

The longer answer is another story. After school at South Loop School and at Ysleta High School, my brothers and sister and I had to work. Why? Because my parents Rodolfo and Bertha Troncoso believed we would get into trouble in our neighborhood if we were idle. So on a Saturday, instead of going to the mall, my parents handed us hoes and shovels and a wheelbarrow to clean the irrigation canal behind our house. Now, we didn't *own* the canal, but my parents thought it would be "good for the neighborhood" to keep it clean. We cleaned the street in front of our house; we pulled out weeds from the sidewalk; we trimmed the trees in our yard; and we carried the debris to the dump. Other Saturdays and Sundays, we carted brick to build our patio, or loaded lumber from Cashway to add another room to our adobe house, or shoveled gravel and mixed cement to build a small basketball court in our backyard. As my mother would say repeatedly to us, "There is no tired in my house."

You might ask, "How did this work-until-you-drop mentality help you with education?" Well, as a kid I got sick of working for my father. I called him our Mexican Stalin: He took our family from an agrarian lifestyle and a patch of dirt in the Chihuahuan Desert to an industrialized lifestyle and a lower-middle-class life. How? With our slave labor. By blood and sweat. By using our work to create value for our family, value in our home, value in the old, dilapidated apartments he bought (and *we* renovated), on which he would work after his forty-hours-per-week job as a draftsman. My mother was just as bad. Both of them duros, disciplined, and determined. Mr. and Mrs. Joseph Stalin Troncoso. Once I convinced my brothers to strike and rebel from our back-breaking work at los departamentos, to get my father to pay us the grand wage of twenty-five cents an hour. School was my only escape from my parents. To do well in school so that I didn't have to lug more cinderblock or drive another truckload of escombro to the dump, I had to work, but this time with my mind.

Teachers, of course, became instrumental in translating this discipline and work ethic into mental work that would help me in school.

None were more important than Pearl Crouch and Josefina Gutierrez Kinard, my high school journalism teachers. Mrs. Crouch reminded me of an Anglo version of my tough abuelita, Doña Dolores Rivero, who survived as a teenager during the Mexican Revolution. Mrs. Crouch would dissect every lead I wrote, tear apart my news stories, and show me where they were lacking in clarity or substance or where I needed to go back and ask more questions to find out more details. What she was teaching me was how to look at my own work from afar, as an editor: how to dissect it so that a reader would be transported and informed and maybe surprised, all in the same news story. La Gutierrez was kinder than Mrs. Crouch, but no less demanding. Rewrite after rewrite after rewrite. That's how you become a good writer, with this critical, in-the-trenches, sentence-by-sentence literary spadework. But you need to sublimate your ego, you need to be ready to work, and you need to appreciate that what matters is what's on the page (or what's not on the page) and *not* how tired you feel about the process.

I responded to Mrs. Crouch's demands by working harder, and she responded by giving me opportunities. This is a simple lesson that I learned from her and that I apply to my own students at the Yale Writers' Workshop: "I will give you work, and I expect you to work as hard as I do, and I expect you to finish this work, and if you don't, if you come up with excuses, or complaints, I don't want you in my class. There's the door."

When I had not yet been to the fancy neighborhoods of El Paso, Mrs. Crouch took me to compete in scholastic writing competitions in San Francisco and New York City. I saw my first Broadway play with her, *A Chorus Line*. We ate at the famous restaurant Sardi's, and she told me, "Sergio, you don't have to stay in El Paso, you can apply anywhere, go to Columbia University." Mrs. Crouch told me about the Blair Summer School for Journalism and the scholarship I would eventually win to attend BSSJ in New Jersey. She also introduced me to her friend Ron Clemons—Blair's associate director from Independence, Missouri. When Irma Sanchez, another mentor who was also my high school guidance counselor, suggested applying to Harvard, Yale, Stanford, Princeton— and other schools that were just names on a page for me, before the Internet, before the Common App—I applied because I didn't know any better. I didn't know what I was getting myself into. I had never heard of the Ivy League. When I received my acceptances, I chose Harvard because my mother revered John F. Kennedy—the first Catholic president of the United States—and she said, "If President Kennedy went there, then it must be a good school."

Having never visited the state of Massachusetts or the school, I arrived at Harvard by myself, wearing Led Zeppelin T-shirts and bell-bottom jeans. As the cab driver from Logan Airport drove into Harvard Yard, I nervously asked him why he was taking me to a park. I was secretly worried I might get kidnapped, as sometimes happened in Mexico. He said, laughing, "This is the school. This is not a park. Harvard's all around us."

In many of my short stories and novels, the protagonists are outsiders, people who don't know the rules, people just trying to survive day to day, observant individuals who pick up every detail and can learn quickly on the fly. That was me my first year at Harvard. Every day of that first semester I wanted to quit. I didn't know how to write a real term paper, what the structure should be. My English was ungrammatical, basic, stilted. More than those technical problems, I felt alone, fearful, culturally at sea. When I called my abuelita in El Paso that first week and said to her that I wanted to quit and return to El Paso, la revolucionaria whose family fought with Francisco "Pancho" Villa in Chihuahua, let me have it: "Sergio, don't come back with your tail between your legs. This is what you wanted. *Show* them who you are!" Doña Dolores never had more than a third-grade education, and she didn't know what Harvard was, but she knew how to fight. That *grit* was what propelled me through that first semester. When I scored my first A- in Expository Writing freshman year, I knew I could do as well as the prep school kids. Every day that first year, I stayed until Lamont Library closed at midnight: I knew how to work until my back ached. I knew how to lose myself in my work, and I would rather drop dead from exhaustion than fail and disappoint my family. That was my kamikaze mentality.

The other two keys to my transition from Ysleta to Harvard are these: first, educate yourself about who you are and where you are from (that will give you the powerful reasons for your education), and second, use Spanish or any foreign language you know and whatever small advantages you have to advance your education. Let me explain. I arrived at Harvard, and suddenly I was brown against a white background. I had never been the minority in Ysleta or El Paso: mexicanos have for generations been the majority in El Paso. Many at Harvard said, "You don't act like a minority." Years later I pondered what that meant. Did it mean I didn't act sheepishly enough, or did I not think of myself as less because of the color of my brown skin? I was scared, but that didn't mean I expected to be defeated. I didn't know who I was, and who I was suddenly became the most important question at Harvard. Part of me was still in Ysleta, while another part of me was fighting to survive at Harvard: I was living between two worlds. So I began to study Mexico and Latin America, to understand the culture and history and politics that I had not been taught in Texas high schools. I wanted to fill that gap. If I was indeed a Mexican American or a Chicano, what did that mean in the context of history? I had *a passionate reason to know* and an urgency to bring together these disparate worlds and my divided self.

So my college courses were more than just dry academic subjects to me: they were filling in a part of myself that I saw as empty. I put in more ganas—effort and hard work—into my Latin American studies because I was finding out who I was within the grander schemes of history, politics, and economics. Meaning is everything for ganas. Only in 2018 did the Texas State Board of Education approve the first-ever course on Mexican American studies for high school students. So perhaps in the future, fewer sons and daughters of Mexican immigrants will have to knit themselves and their histories together as haphazardly as I had to.

Spanish was also the only advantage I had at Harvard: that I was bilingual. I could conduct research in Spanish with John Womack the chairman of the history department, who wrote the classic *Zapata and the Mexican Revolution*, and with Terry Karl, who later became head of Stanford's Center for Latin American Studies. Professor Karl was my thesis advisor senior year. These professors and mentors taught me about my history while I dug into Widener Library and unearthed monographs and research articles in Spanish (as well as English).

I won a scholarship from Harvard to conduct interviews in Spanish in Mexico City for my senior thesis. That summer after my junior year I took a twenty-four-hour bus ride from Juárez to Mexico City, through long stretches of desert and over mountains, with the bus often a few feet from the edge of mountain passes. Several times people boarded the bus with chickens. I had never been to Mexico City, a sprawling, chaotic metropolis of fifteen million people (back then). The Spanish in the Federal District had a strange singsong cadence and was quicker than the border Spanish I knew, but I again adapted after crossing the border south. With letters of reference from Professors Womack and Karl, I knocked on the doors of government officials, bureaucrats who had data I needed, professors at the National University and El Colegio de México, and other researchers who I hoped would open their doors to an American college student they had never met before. My determination and border Spanish were the only real advantages I had at Harvard. So it is important never to disparage someone's bilingualism, but instead to demand that they improve their Spanish or mother tongue so that they can speak and write it beautifully. Improving my Spanish was also a way to reclaim and understand who I was.

Whenever I was back in El Paso, I also paid attention to the oral storytelling of my abuelita, Doña Lola. My grandmother would recount violent, exciting stories about El General Villa and his men riding into their hamlet, El Charco, and taking over the stores, conscripting the men by force, and even taking over the women if they could. Villa would hang lawyers and bankers by the wires of telegraph posts. It was a bloody affair. As I said to my young sons in New York City years later, listening to my abuelita tell her stories was like *Call of Duty*, Mexican style. The family lore was that Doña Lola had shot and killed two men who attempted to rape her during the Mexican Revolution. I loved listening to my grandmother's stories, and I learned many lessons about life by paying attention to them. One of the greatest regrets I have about going to the Ivy League was that Doña Dolores died while I was there. I still remember the last time I saw her on her steps of her apartment building, with her cat-eye glasses and favorite marbleized blue blouse. I know she wanted me to go and fight for myself. She asked me to promise to come back as soon as I had the chance. Thinking and writing about her have been my way of trying to fulfill that promise.

After Harvard, I was accepted to a few excellent law schools, but I did not have a real reason to be a lawyer. I somewhat hated myself for what I had become, a competitive Gov jock in the Ivy League. I wanted to keep exploring who I was, and I vaguely wanted to write. I was desperately fighting to keep that space open to pursue an artistic dream, with no money; no support from my hardworking parents, who didn't understand anything that wasn't practical; and no time left. My experience at Harvard had opened up something within me that many who are well-to-do, or those who are exposed early to excellent opportunities, take for granted: the possibility of making yourself, rather than necessity of being what circumstances required. I was desperate not to turn away from that glimpse of who and what I could be; I just needed more chances to achieve that dream. What saved me was winning a Fulbright scholarship to Mexico at the end of senior year. I suddenly had money, and I would be in Mexico City for one year.

In Mexico City, I did my official work of researching the Mexican political economy, often focusing on those dispossessed by colonialism and corruption, but I also started reading Latin American and Russian writers, German and French philosophers. I wrote in my journals about experiencing Mexican society and culture as a Mexican American. I lived frugally and saved over half of the money I won from the Fulbright. I was indeed attempting to cross another border. The easy thing would have been to stay where I was, to become a Latin Americanist, to stay in the box I adopted at Harvard to survive. But that box was to be a launching point, not my end point.

At the end of the Fulbright, I was accepted to Yale's master's program in international relations, which I chose because it was multidisciplinary and allowed me to keep crossing that border I began crossing in Mexico City. Little did I know how much this program would help me create this nascent self. Professor Colin Bradford, the director of the program, was that affable, flexible leader who allowed me to do what I wanted to do, as long as I met my requirements. So I took the regular four graduate classes in politics and economics and history at Yale and added a fifth graduate class in philosophy every semester. It was an enormous academic burden, but I knew how to work. That was how I created the time and space to stay on that intellectual journey I had started in Mexico City. Yale also charged graduate students tuition by semester in attendance, not by how many courses one enrolled in, so I did not go deeper into debt with my extra course load. I also earned money as a work-study student in the libraries for about ten hours every week. For a reduced rent from the Yale epidemiologist who owned the building, every week I swept the three floors of the townhouse where I lived in an attic studio. The burden was on me, and that's how I wanted it. I had been el terco in Ysleta, and my latest academic doggedness was just another iteration of who I had long been. All immigrants who have risked everything for the chance of a new home and a new self, like those refugees known as the Pilgrims, would understand this will to power in their blood.

When I finished the master's in international relations, I applied and was accepted into the doctoral program in philosophy at Yale. I still lived an ascetic lifestyle. My bed on Orange Street was a thick foam pad over a piece of plywood on top of cinderblocks I had found on the streets of New Haven. My girlfriend Laura (who later became my wife) said I lived like a monk. The distance from where I had begun in Ysleta to where I was in philosophy seminars at Yale's Connecticut Hall and in Vienna learning German (on a summer scholarship from the Austrian government) was greater than it had ever been. What few will tell you forthrightly is that if you cross enough borders, if you allow your mind to take you where it can, even to remarkable places, you might also start to lose who you are and what you originally had wanted to do.

I had become a different person from that stubborn, adventurous young man who left Ysleta on the fly. I became a teaching assistant for phenomenologist Professor Maurice Natanson in his course Philosophy in Literature and also for Professor John Hollander in his Daily Themes course in the English department. Again, teachers showed me the way: instead of demanding any kind of academic orthodoxy or enforcing their vision on my work, they encouraged me to mix philosophy with creative writing, to create something uniquely mine. Today I tell my own students that I want the outsiders, the unusual perspectives, the storytellers who tell the truth slant, the experimentalists: these writers will always find a home in my workshop. I am only repaying the biggest debt I owe.

I wrote my first short story out of a sense of loneliness, as a graduate student in philosophy at Yale, because I wanted to create a new home: to connect the ideas I was exploring in philosophy—specifically from German philosophers, such as Nietzsche, Heidegger, and Wittgenstein—with characters back on the border and the people I loved from El Paso, Texas. I wanted to make my philosophical questions relevant to my borderland community and to bring this marginalized community and their questions into the debates of literature. Why did this matter? You cross a border because you are searching, because you want more, because you want to match where you are with who you are, because you want to test your place. Maybe because you want to *expand* your sense of place. You are searching for something that may as yet be indefinable. A border crosser questions the very idea of home. I wrote my first story, "The Abuelita," with the protagonist as a version of my grandmother, who in the story is arguing with her grandson at Yale as he is explaining to her Heidegger's philosophy of being-towards-death. My aim was to break the stereotypes of what Chicano literature could be, to show Mexican Americans as thinkers, and to bring to life on the page an abuelita on the border who would have essential lessons to share with the wider world about how to live life. In a sense, I was trying to create a new "home," where characters from the border, American literature, and philosophical questions all belonged together in one place.

Would the wider world ignore the border or keep stereotyping it with prejudiced images? Would white audiences far from the border read writing from a Mexican American writer and appreciate that he is at once writing about his people and also exploring how we are all together facing these dramas? Can more Mexican American writers, without sacrificing their voices, break into the too-white world of New York publishers, be promoted by them, and change stereotypical views about Mexican Americans in books read not only on the border but beyond it? The answers to these questions will keep arriving long after I am not here to ask them. I am as often hopeful as I am hopeless, but these waves of optimism or pessimism never push me off course. I cross borders, because I believe that's how you respect the truth in writing and living. I cross borders, because I believe that's how you find who you are and how you discover your true kindred across cultures and peoples. I cross borders to break open a new landscape for American literature. And most important, I cross borders to include in the greater discussions of culture, literature, and politics those who have been previously excluded. I cross borders to give a voice to outsiders.

Young writers—and the teachers who teach these writers—should embrace the truth of crossing borders. The power of the word is not just to write about how a majority can oppress and demean a minority. That's powerful enough. The power of the word is not just to write about a forgotten or vilified community from that community's perspective. That's powerful enough. The power of the word is also to write about what is *unsaid* in those communities, what is *taboo*, what makes people (even your family) angry about what you are writing.

In my collection *Crossing Borders: Personal Essays*, I wrote an essay, "This Wicked Patch of Dust," that tried to make sense of a fight I had with my father one Christmas in Ysleta. It was really an essay about my arguments against machismo, this authoritarian, patriarchal attitude within our family, even though I learned and admired many other lessons about life from my father. I've written about my ambivalence toward the Catholic faith, so adored by my mother; I've discussed undocumented workers and the American hypocrisy of using and abusing them, homophobia, interfaith marriage, gender roles, racism within the Mexican American community, Chicana Muslims, sex on the levee of the Río Grande.

So embracing the truth in fiction and nonfiction is not about salaciousness or provoking controversy for its own sake, but about honoring the authenticity of who you are as a free thinker. Every political side—liberal or conservative or anything in between—creates taboos. Every community creates topics and areas in which they hang a sign that says, "Do Not Touch! Do Not Discuss! Do Not Cross!" When they do that, thinking stops. The abuse of power more easily blossoms. That community stops advancing. As I've told my students many times, the greatest censor for any writer is often herself or himself. In this country, not enough of us are crossing borders: We are not a We anymore. This is the central problem our country will have for the next fifty years. If we overcome it and create a new America, we will have many more good chapters of history together as a community. If we don't, we will begin and accelerate a decline in our country, with ramifications that could unfold over many nightmarish scenarios.

What does the improvement of reading and writing skills accomplish for a burgeoning but often disadvantaged group such as Mexican Americans in Texas or any other immigrant group? It gives them a voice. It allows us to receive complex stories and essays from *within* this community. When you give outsiders a voice, the mainstream community has to respond to these outsiders and consider them more seriously as citizens. So even what is mainstream, what is included as American, begins to change as these voices are added to the whole. *Who* these immigrants are and *how* their community evolves will change if this writing and reading also stirs them to self-analysis, to extol the best parts of their community, and to reform what they want to change. I titled this essay, "Life as Crossing Borders," but it could easily have been titled, "Life as Empathy through Reading and Writing," or "Life as Having a Voice." The work to develop the voices of immigrants right now—as well as the work with other disenfranchised communities throughout the United States—is what will build our community and forge it together to create a new We. One in which we all belong. One in which we all have a voice. One in which we all listen to each other while working together.

Losing My Mother Tongue

Reyna Grande

When I crossed the border at nine years old, I didn't know that in addition to putting my life at risk, I was also risking the loss of my mother tongue. My journey toward learning English was so traumatic that, to this day, I'm still dealing with the repercussions, not only in my career as a professional writer but also in my interactions with my own family—especially my mother and my children.

To my misfortune, the local elementary school I was enrolled in when I arrived in California didn't have a bilingual program or English as a Second Language (ESL) classes. Although I lived in a mostly Latino neighborhood in Los Angeles, my school lacked the necessary resources for immigrant children like me.

On my first day of school in September 1985, on realizing that I didn't speak a word of English, my fifth-grade teacher pointed to the farthest corner of her classroom and sent me there. She ignored me for the rest of the year. I sat in that corner feeling voiceless, invisible, and deeply ashamed of being a Spanish speaker. The trauma of realizing that the language used in school was the one I didn't know led to debilitating thoughts such as: *I am not enough. I am insufficient.*

I sat there thinking *I* was the problem—*my* lack of English was the problem. It didn't cross my nine-year-old mind that perhaps it was my school that was the problem, that my teacher's failure to be sensitive to my needs was the problem.

The message I received from my teacher was that if I wanted to be seen and heard, I would have to learn English. As long as I spoke Spanish, I would be ignored and put in a corner.

Halfway through the year, my school had a writing competition for which all the students had to write a story. I wrote mine in the only language I knew. When my teacher collected the stories to choose the best one for the competition, she put mine—and those of the few other non-English speakers—in the reject pile because it was in Spanish. My teacher's rejection of my story hurt me deeply. To me, she wasn't just rejecting my story—she was rejecting me. I felt ashamed to be an immigrant and a Spanish speaker.

This and other similar experiences made me feel ignorant and led me to believe that whatever academic concepts I understood and intellectual skills I possessed in my mother tongue were irrelevant; they were in the wrong language and, therefore, useless to my ability to function and be accepted in my new school and beyond.

Two years later, when I was in junior high, I was enrolled in my school's ESL program. Although I was happy to finally be in a self-contained class full of English learners like me, it was humiliating to be in those classes. They were located in the bungalows farthest away from the school grounds. Everyone knew that the students who took classes in those bungalows were the immigrant kids, the ones who didn't have "papers" and who spoke with a "wetback" accent. I worked hard to learn English so that I would no longer have to go to those dreaded bungalows and could rid myself of the stigma of being an ESL student.

Also, my ESL program was a transitional model—its purpose being to reclassify the students as soon as possible from English deficient to English proficient, but not necessarily as bilingual or biliterate. I don't remember my teachers ever encouraging me or the other students to nurture and retain our native language. We weren't praised for being bilingual, nor were we taught the value of bilingualism. Not once did anyone say speaking two languages was an asset, especially in a diverse country like ours. We didn't read literature in Spanish or do any kinds of activities where we could continue to improve our Spanish skills. Perhaps they saw schoolwork and literacy in Spanish as a waste of time since the goal of the program was to have us function exclusively in English-only classrooms.

My Spanish remained at the level up to which I had studied in Mexico—third grade. UNESCO defines a second language as "a language acquired by a person *in addition to* his home language." But in my ESL program, instead of addition, subtraction took place: little by little, my third grade Spanish was replaced by English until I began to think and dream and write only in that language.

Years later, I would learn the term for what had happened to me: *subtractive bilingualism*—the removal of my mother tongue, the psychological violence of tearing out a piece of my being.

In eighth grade, my junior high school had a writing competition similar to the one at my elementary school. By then I had graduated from the ESL program and was in mainstream classes. I forced myself to write a story in English and enter the competition because I wanted to be judged on the same terms as everyone else.

I got first place and won a prize.

Although winning that competition would help me gain confidence in my writing skills, which later led to a career as a professional writer, it further destroyed my relationship with Spanish. What I learned from that experience was this: *If I write in Spanish, I will be rejected. If I write in English, I will be celebrated and win prizes.* The underlying message was that English would lead to success in this country.

It was here, in this moment, that my complicated relationship with my mother tongue truly began.

Unlike my parents, who arrived in the United States as adults with their Mexican identity fully formed, I crossed the border at nine years old. My identity was still being created, and not long after I arrived in Los Angeles, I began to question who I was and where I belonged. "Do I belong here? Do I belong over there? Do I belong anywhere?" I asked myself again and again.

Although I tried to hold on to my memories of Mexico, to its customs and language, my heart began to cleave. As a 1.5 generation immigrant—born in Mexico but raised in the United States—I was forced to make sacrifices and compromises that my parents never had to make. They were impervious to assimilation because of their *certainty* in knowing who they were: Spanish-speaking Mexicans. Whereas I, a young immigrant coming of age in the United States, had no protection against the message given to me by the dominant culture: that in order to be considered "fully American," I must speak English, or else I'd risk being forced to live on the margins of society. If I wanted to be accepted and included, I knew I would have to do what my parents never asked of themselves—fight the long, difficult battle to conquer English and offer up my mother tongue as a sacrifice.

When our relationship with language is compromised, so, too, is our self-image. One area where my complicated relationship with Spanish affects me is in my writing career. At my book readings across the country, a question I am frequently asked is this: *Do you write in English or Spanish?* When I respond that I write only in English, people look at me in shock, with a mixture of confusion and sometimes criticism.

They don't say it aloud, but I can hear their unspoken questions: *Why don't you write in your mother tongue? What kind of Mexican are you?*

The kind who can't write in Spanish, I want to say. The kind who was so traumatized by her language acquisition that the term "English dominant" took on a more sinister meaning: I don't dominate English; English dominates me.

Although I didn't lose my Spanish completely, subtractive bilingualism led to me writing solely in English, beginning with the short story in eighth grade that won first place in the writing competition. For the past thirty years, whenever I put pen to paper the words that come out are in English, with a sprinkling of Spanish words for flavor. There have been a couple of times when I've tried to write in Spanish, but it is a painful experience. The words don't come; they remain so buried beneath the English words that it takes a tremendous amount of effort to dig through my memory and unearth them. I end up picking up the dictionary more times than I can count. I get so focused on the words that the characters I wanted to write about walk away and won't return until I switch to English. Only then do the words flow without much thinking on my part, and I'm able to give my characters all the attention they require without language getting in the way of the story.

Because I am ashamed to write solely in English, some years ago I attempted to translate my books into Spanish myself. It was a difficult and painful process. There were so many words I'd forgotten or never learned. I wasn't qualified to do translations, but I wanted to use my mother tongue in my writing, so I did the best I could.

To my delight, Jorge Ramos, our beloved Univision news anchor, invited me to his show Al Punto to discuss *La distancia entre nosotros*, translated by me. While the cameras were rolling, my anxiety turned my tongue into a hand-cranked clothes-wringer, and it took so much effort to squeeze the Spanish words out. Ramos gushed about the story I'd had written, but as soon as the cameras were turned off he turned to me and said, "No hablas muy bien el español, verdad?"

I left the studio feeling more insecure about my Spanish than ever. But it didn't end there. Through the years, I've gotten emails from readers sending me a list of errors I made in my translation: accent marks I missed, verbs I conjugated wrong, Spanglish words I used such as la yarda instead of el patio. They are so concerned they even send me the page numbers, too.

I usually ignore the emails, but one day I received an email I couldn't ignore. It was from Sandra Cisneros, my literary madrina, the writer whose work inspired me to become a writer. Sandra mentioned that she'd given a copy of my memoir to a friend of hers in Mexico, and the friend was annoyed. "Your Spanish version has some typos or errors. Were you aware? Did it get proofed by a Spanish speaker?" Sandra wanted to know. She was disappointed, too, because she'd wanted to share my story with her friend. "But my colleague, a Mexican national writer, will never finish reading your great book because she can't get past the errors," Sandra said.

I was humiliated, but I understood why Sandra was concerned. We are both professionals, after all. Our work must be top-notch. I didn't tell her that when my editor asked who should translate my book, I had insisted that I be allowed to do it for two reasons: (1) the thought of seeing a translator's name on the cover of my book was humiliating, and (2) how could I claim Spanish as my mother tongue if I required the services of a translator?

I knew my translation was not perfect, but it was mine. By translating my own work, it allowed me to reclaim my Spanish and use it in my writing. It allowed me to look at my book and see only my name on the book cover, not someone else's name. It was my way of saying, "Yes, I know I am married to English now, but Spanish was my first love."

Two years ago, when I finished my new book, *A Dream Called Home*, my editor brought up the Spanish translation. I wanted to do it, but I was afraid to ask. I thought about Sandra's email and all the other emails I've gotten from readers offended by my errors. My editor and my agent thought it best I not do the translation this time. "You should focus on your next book," they suggested. I didn't put up much of a fight. I felt insecure and ashamed. They were right. I should let a professional do what I could never do—a perfect translation.

My editor hired a translator based in Mexico City, and that was that. I felt disappointed, but worst of all I felt as if I had once again betrayed my mother tongue. A few months later I was reunited with my book, except that it no longer felt as if it belonged to me. I could not recognize my own story. The voice was so foreign to me, the language so difficult to decipher, I once again resorted to the dictionary, though for the opposite reasons: I was looking up words in Spanish and finding their English translation to understand their meaning. I was haunted by words such as beneplácito, rutilante, urdido, aspeado, edredón, contubernio, apabullante, escudriñar, acérrimas, fehaciente, engullido, féretro . . . I couldn't sleep at night, tossing and turning from a tremendous sense of loss.

These are the words I do not know; this is what I lost when I immigrated.

I imagined an alternate universe where instead of immigrating to the United States I had stayed in Mexico and had gone to school there, all the way to college. *Those words would be mine if I had stayed*, I told myself. But then I gave myself a reality check. The truth was, that even if I had stayed in Mexico, those words still wouldn't be mine. My family was so poor in Mexico, there was no way I would have ever made it to college. Instead of being a best-selling author as I am today here in the United States, I would be a maid in Mexico earning five dollars a day.

I spent over 200 hours revising the translation and adding my voice to it. My editor was afraid to allow me to make changes because I was going to insert mistakes. But I realized that I didn't want a perfect translation. What I wanted most of all was a book that *sounded* like me. My Spanish is imperfect, and perhaps now my book is, too, but I can live with that. What I cannot live with is not trying to reclaim what I once lost—my first language, my first love.

Besides impacting my writing, my language loss has also affected my relationship with my family. Mostly, it created a distance between me and my mother, who never learned English. In the 1980s, my mother worked at a garment factory. Later, she quit that job and became a vendor at local swap meets selling Avon products and cheap plastic sandals. She supplemented her income by picking cans and bottles out of the trash and taking them to the recycling center. By then, my siblings and I had bought into the belief that to succeed in this country you had to assimilate—learn English and give up your cultural identity. Whenever we encouraged our mother to go to adult school and learn English, she was scared of our suggestion. She would shake her head and say, "El inglés no se me pega." English doesn't stick to me.

"We aren't talking about English as a piece of chewing gum," we'd say.

My mother sought refuge in her immigrant enclave and stayed out of reach from the dominant culture. Unlike me, she never had an identity crisis, she knew she was, and would always be, Mexican. It took me into adulthood to understand that my mother's certainty in her identity made her immune to the insidious ways of assimilation and acculturation. But as a newly "Americanized" girl, I saw my mother's refusal to learn English as a weakness and a failure. She was everything I didn't want to be—a woman who didn't make it past elementary school, who went from being a factory worker to making a living recycling cardboard and cans and bottles, a woman who lived in the margins of US society.

Our relationship worsened when I left my Latino neighborhood and went to study at a university where only 13 percent of the student body was Latino. I come from a family that had no educational opportunities. In Mexico, my father only made it to the third grade, my mother, the sixth. My maternal grandfather was illiterate. When I was twenty-three I became the first person in my family to walk across the stage and receive a university diploma. My degree opened doors that had never been opened for anyone in my family. It led me to a successful career as a writer, a teacher, a public speaker. It gave me the American Dream but, more important, the *certainty* in knowing that I had earned my place in American society.

The price I paid for my successful integration into the dominant culture was my relationship with my mother. Spending time with her became more and more awkward. There was so little we could talk about, so little I could share with her about my English-speaking American life, and through the years it became harder and harder to find common ground; even finding the words in Spanish to tell her about my world became a challenge. When I was at the university, what could I tell my mother about the books I read in my literature courses, the rising cost of tuition, the exams I had to study for? When I became a writer, what could I tell her about my struggles of figuring out the structure of my novel, my fear of not being able to find an agent, or—once I was published—the pressure I felt at living up to my readers' expectations? When I became a public speaker, what could I tell her about the anxiety I felt about a keynote speech I had to deliver at an upcoming education conference, my exhaustion of traveling from city to city to bare my soul in front of strangers, the responsibility I felt at having to represent and advocate for my Latino community everywhere I went? My mother knew nothing of those things, so I said nothing. Instead, she and I would talk about the market price of cardboard, our relatives in Mexico, the cost of tomatoes, or when we ran out of things to say, we'd just talk about the weather. It was all small talk, as if she were an acquaintance I'd run into by chance, instead of the woman who delivered me into this world.

One day, while I was in Los Angeles doing a book presentation, I picked up my mother to take her to lunch. She lives in Pico-Union, one of the last remaining immigrant communities next to a gentrified downtown Los Angeles. She lives less than a mile away from a four-star hotel, the Staples Center, L.A. Live. But those places could just as well be as far away as another galaxy, not on the other side of the 110 freeway. As I was pulling up in front of her house, I was shocked to see all the homeless people camped out across from her house, under the freeway overpass. A homeless person was refilling a gallon of water at the fire hydrant on the corner. Then I saw my mother. She was waiting for me at the curb, which was lined with all kinds of trash.

My mother can't afford to live anywhere else. The little money she makes recycling cardboard and cans and bottles is barely enough to pay the rent for her one-room studio. Though my siblings and I have offered to take her into our homes, she refuses. She is not at home with us.

She got in my rental car and handed me a book. "I thought you would like this since you like to read," she said with a smile. I was touched by the gesture. My mother has never once gifted me a book, not even when I was a young voracious reader growing up in a home without books. But when I looked at it, my excitement disappeared—it was a sixteen-year-old travel guide to Mexico.

"Where did you find this?" I asked, holding the tattered and stained book in my hands.

"In a dumpster," she said, "while I was looking for cans and bottles. I don't know what it's about, but it says Mexico. Do you see?"

"Yes, I see."

If she could speak English, would she have known that she was giving me a useless travel guide? I wondered. When I dropped her off after lunch, I tossed the book back in the trash where it came from. *She's trying to connect with you,* I told myself as I drove to the airport to catch my flight back home, but I couldn't help feeling bad about what her gift meant, of what it said about our relationship. I couldn't stop thinking about how dirty I felt holding the book, even after I'd washed my hands.

Another question I get at book events is this: *Do your children speak Spanish?* This is yet another source of shame for me because the answer to this question is "Yes . . . and no." Because I think, speak, and write in English, I failed to teach my son and daughter Spanish. Speaking to them in Spanish required too much effort. I had to remind myself to speak in Spanish before I opened my mouth, but by the time the right part of my brain received the reminder, I had already blurted out what I needed to say to them in English. I found that the only time I ever spoke Spanish to my children was when I was angry and yelled at them. "¿Qué están haciendo, chamacos?" Perhaps because I grew up being yelled at in Spanish by my parents, yelling in Spanish comes much more easily to me.

My son is in eleventh grade and does not speak Spanish beyond level one. Unfortunately, the area in Los Angeles where we lived when he was in elementary school did not have a bilingual program, although 70 percent of its student body was Latino. Bilingualism was a gift that I could have given him, but I didn't realize, until too late, the importance of this gift. In the United States, his lack of Spanish has been of little consequence in his everyday life, except when he interacts with my mother. He can't speak to his Abuela Juana without the help of Google translate. When we go to my hometown in Mexico and he can't speak to any of our relatives or neighbors, especially the kids his age, he gets frustrated and tells me that he doesn't want to go back anymore. A year ago, I got him to go back to Mexico because it was to San Miguel de Allende, where I had been invited to give a talk for PEN America. There are so many expats living there that his limited Spanish wouldn't be a problem, I promised him. In fact, to my chagrin, the presentation I was asked to give in my own native country *had* to be in English. So he came along and sat through my presentation, where I spoke English to the gringos in the audience— including my own son. After the talk, we went out to dinner with the PEN members, all of whom could speak English. But there was a teenaged girl in attendance who spoke only Spanish. She sat next to my son, and throughout dinner my son texted me his complaints. "Mom, why didn't you teach me Spanish? I'm sitting next to an angel and now I can't talk to her!" I have single-handedly ruined my son's love life in Mexico, and the next time I asked him to come with me, he refused.

My daughter's Spanish was as limited as my son's. Fortunately for her, in January 2016, we moved to Davis, California, where the local school has a two-way Spanish immersion program even though the city is 70 percent white. My daughter didn't want to be enrolled in that program, but we gave her no choice. I promised her that one day she would thank me. Since she was entering halfway through second grade and not kindergarten, she was given a placement test. She barely passed it. She couldn't say sentences, only individual words such as agua, abuela, mamá, papá. She was put in a class where half of the students were English dominant and the other half Spanish dominant. She had two teachers, and every day the class spent half of the day with the Spanish teacher and the other half with the English teacher. She was in a class that had books in Spanish and English and was encouraged to read from both. I didn't know whether she was learning or not because even though I made the extra effort to speak to her in Spanish, she would always answer me in English. "Háblame en español," I demanded. But no Spanish words came out of her mouth.

Six months later, I was invited to visit her classroom to see my daughter's final project: a twenty-minute PowerPoint presentation about thorn bugs—in Spanish. In six months, my daughter had become completely bilingual, with no loss to her native tongue and, better yet, no trauma! And she is not only bilingual, but also biliterate. Currently, my daughter is in sixth grade, and her reading level is eighth grade in English and sixth grade in Spanish. I am grateful to have found her a bilingual program that is encouraging her to learn in two languages. She has greatly benefitted from additive bilingualism. And although I expected her to one day thank me for enrolling her in a bilingual program, her gratitude came much sooner than expected.

When I took her to Mexico to visit my relatives over the holidays, she was so happy to be able to speak to everyone there, including her own grandmother, whom I had invited to join us on the trip as a way to reconnect. There we were—my mother, my daughter, and I speaking Spanish together. "Thank you, Mommy, for putting me in that program," my daughter said on the day we arrived. The best part of the trip for her was teaching my cousins' children the Spanish Christmas songs she had learned in class.

My daughter's journey to learning a second language was the opposite of mine. She was never asked to sacrifice, subtract, or replace anything about herself. It took years for me to understand the beauty of being bilingual, but my daughter learned it from the start, because the most important thing her bilingual program has taught her is this: she is now more, not less, than who she used to be.

I am still dealing with the damage caused by educational and social institutions that shamed me into speaking only English. I haven't finished taking stock of the effects of my language trauma, of how it impacted my identity as an immigrant, a daughter, and a mother. But I am slowly reclaiming what I'd been forced to give up—my connection to my mother tongue and, with it, my relationship with my own mother. Little by little I will rediscover what I once lost, one word at a time.

Día de Muertos

Stephanie Elizondo Griest

When my mother called me back to my father's sickbed, I was at a dinner party 550 miles away. Another guest took one look at my shaking shoulders and offered to drive me there. It was nearly 10 p.m. by the time I had thrown mismatched clothes in a suitcase and locked up the house where I'd spent the previous two weeks at a writing retreat.

As we peeled out of Marfa, Texas, the night air filled with skunk. I breathed it in deeply, as Dad would do. Once, when he was a little boy, his dog got sprayed while they were romping around the park. He claimed to love the stench afterward, as it induced that and other memories of his Kansan childhood: watching his mother mash potatoes in the kitchen, riding sleighs with his brother at Christmas, pounding the beat in the high school marching band, delivering newspapers under the rising sun.

The Mexican in me knew this skunk was a sign, then. I spent the next 545 miles trying not to interpret it.

* * *

If I were a proper Mexican daughter, there wouldn't have been any frantic driving through the night. I never would have left home in the first place. But wanderlust is a Griest inheritance. My great-great-uncle, Jake, was a hobo who saw all of America with his legs dangling over the edge of a freight train. Dad won a seat with a US Navy jazz ensemble as soon as he graduated from high school and spent 15 years drumming for admirals and presidents on aircraft carriers around the world.

One night, while Dad was performing at a nightclub in Corpus Christi, a beautiful young Tejana walked in. He introduced himself at intermission by accidentally spilling his Coke all over her shoes. He led her backstage and gently wiped them clean. They got married three months later. His next gig was Mardi Gras, and the only way her parents would let her accompany him was as his bride. Tía Benita stayed up all week sewing the white satin dress.

Mom's family had migrated from the foothills of Tamaulipas, Mexico, to a cattle ranch in South Texas in the late 1800s. Among the ancestral traditions they retained was the one tasking the youngest daughter with eldercare. Tía Alicia was so devoted to Abuela, she never even had a family of her own. So Mom caused an escandalo when she absconded to the northeast with Dad for eight years before landing a job at IBM back in Corpus. She then broke not only Mexican but American conventions by becoming the family breadwinner while her husband stayed home with their two little girls.

Dad turned us into travelers early, buckling Barbara and me into the seat on the back of his bicycle as soon as we could hold our heads up straight. After school, he would whisk us off to Port Aransas to see the porpoises or to Rockport to climb on the jetties, and every summer he packed up the van for a road trip to Mesa Verde, the Redwood Forest, or the Grand Tetons with John Denver crooning through the tape deck. When we started developing interests of our own, he always offered to be our chauffeur. He once drove my friend Shea and me 240 miles to a U2 concert—"Achtung Baby" blasting through the speakers—waited in the parking lot for four and a half hours, and then drove us 240 miles home. By the time I reached college, my wanderlust was raging. I majored in the language of the farthest country I could fathom—Russia—and jetted off to Moscow to become a foreign correspondent. Since then, I have explored nearly fifty countries and lived in fifteen different cities.

If I thought about it from my (Griest) vantage point, then, it was weirdly appropriate to be eight hours away when Mom called me home. There was nothing Dad loved more than a drive.

Racing into the dark night, though, I felt wholly Elizondo and regretted every mile.

* * *

Our last big family trip was in 2010, to Dad's bucket list destination: Alaska. That's where I first started noticing his happy-go-lucky personality was changing. He demanded to be in bed by 5:00 p.m. each night, not because he was tired, but because he deemed the rule unbreakable. We couldn't convince him otherwise. Ditto with his insistence on arriving to places before they even opened. And he kept asking the same questions again and again and again.

One afternoon, we spontaneously decided to have a cookout at a campground near Seward. It was raining by the time we found a store that sold hot dogs and marshmallows. Huddled around the grill, I realized that everyone was wearing the same color rain jacket—royal blue—except Dad. His was white. With his white hair and white beard, he looked like a cloud in our family sky. I breathed in the serenity of being surrounded by everyone I loved most.

Then I noticed that my twelve-year-old niece was showing Dad how to turn his stick into a spit. This man who had provided every meal of my childhood seemed mystified by the concept of roasting. After lunch, we set off for a nearby waterfall. As I lingered behind to take our photograph, I saw how difficult the trail was for Dad to navigate. This man who had played tennis five mornings a week for half a century no longer knew where to put his feet. Mom finally grabbed him by the elbow, because this man who had driven us hundreds of thousands of miles across America now needed steering. I exhaled the first of the infinity of losses.

* * *

Barreling down the county road that curved along the Mexico border, it occurred to me that my impromptu driver bore a passing resemblance to Dad. They had the same beard and penchant for wearing denim shirts. They also shared a remarkable stamina for driving. In 550 miles, he stopped only twice, both times for gas.

Mom had warned us this could be a fire drill. One of her cousins had recently flown from Seattle to Corpus five times on a moment's notice, only to witness her previously comatose mother revive. Mom predicted this would be the case with Dad, too, especially since his Aunt Maude spent more than a decade in a vegetative state before succumbing to the disease they shared: Alzheimer's. I personally doubted he'd make it to 2020, but was reasonably optimistic he'd endure the summer. I last saw him on Father's Day weekend, prior to departing for Marfa. I spoon-fed him his favorite soup—asparagus pureed with sour cream and lemon—before entertaining him with YouTube videos. It had been a while since his last coherent sentence, but he said, "That's so cute," at the sight of a baby panda bear trying to climb out of a trash can. Efforts to engage him in further conversation went nowhere, though, and he soon fell asleep.

The next day, Mom and I wheeled his chair onto the patio, where I announced it was time for music. Grandma Griest had discovered eighty years earlier that if she gave Dad a wooden spoon, he would happily whack a pan for hours. Besides his childhood paper route, he had never earned a paycheck for anything besides his music. Alzheimer's had transformed his drumming from a livelihood to a lifeline: as long as he could find the rhythm, we knew he was still there.

Dad's hands had curled into fists weeks ago, but there seemed to be enough room for a drumstick. I slid one in until it felt secure, then raised up a book beneath it. Nothing happened. I tapped the drumstick for encouragement. Still nothing. And then he closed his eyes. Mom and I looked at each other and sighed.

Growing up, she was the one with whom I had struggled to communicate. Every morning as I waited for Dad to fix my breakfast, Mom would swoop into the kitchen wearing a power suit with shoulder pads, gulp down some Folger's, and dash out the door in high heels. She didn't return until nightfall, and we all knew not to bug her until she'd completed the crossword puzzle. If one of her relatives called, however, she'd smile with her entire being. She always took the phone out onto the porch, but her laughter rang out above the TV. Spanish sounded like the ultimate comedy show, only the rest of us weren't in on the jokes. That's because Mom grew up in an era where teachers would shove a bar of soap in your mouth if they caught you speaking Spanish in the classroom. Then she married a gringo who knew only two words: *taco* and *vámonos*. She never taught Barbara or me how to speak her native tongue, since she didn't want to linguistically divide our home. Whenever we visited Abuela, we sat around mute—until it was time to eat or go.

Just then, I remembered the chant Dad used to teach his beginner drum students. "BOOM get a rat trap/bigger than a cat trap/BOOM!" I sang out. His eyes fluttered open. A long moment passed. Then he faintly tapped back.

* * *

We pulled up to the care facility at 5:44 a.m. My impromptu driver stepped out to give me a hug, accepted the only thing I had to give (bruised bananas), and then drove 550 miles back to Marfa.

"Daddy, I'm here," I called out as I entered his room. His expression did not change, but there was movement beneath his blanket. I lifted up a corner, and his fist rose in greeting. I wrapped one of my hands around it, then caressed his skeletal face with the other. His indigo eyes were wide open. Peering into them, I chanted words of love and gratitude. At some point in the four hours that ensued, Barbara—who'd taken a quick nap after driving in from San Antonio at midnight—took the place of Mom, who'd been keeping vigil for twenty-four hours and wanted a shower. Holding our dad in our arms, my sister and I played his favorite songs. John Denver's "Rocky Mountain High." Judy Garland's "Somewhere Over the Rainbow." Frank Sinatra. Then I cued up the song we loved to sing while Dad played the piano when we were little: Simon and Garfunkel's "59th Street Bridge Song." Moments after the chorus had ended—"Life, I love you / All is groovy"—a nurse walked in. I peeled my eyes away from Dad's to ask how much time we had. A couple of days, she said. His skin wasn't mottling yet. His legs were warm. His vitals had stabilized. There was still—

Barbara gasped. I looked down. Dad was gone.

* * *

Two nights before Mom called us home, I was sitting on the porch with a glass of white wine, enjoying a desert breeze after a long day of writing, when I saw movement in a cluster of nopales. First one, then two, then three little bodies bounded over, a blur of black and white. Skunks! It wouldn't have been more surprising if they were wolverines—and they were headed straight toward me. Without thinking, I stood up and greeted them.

"Well hello there!"

Immediately they halted. We stared at each other for half a second before they made a collective U-turn and scampered off in the opposite direction.

* * *

I wanted to stay with my father until his body had turned completely cold. When informed I could not do that, I started wailing. Promptly, I was silenced. Seven other residents were on the other side of the thin walls. I must not frighten them. *Okay*, I gasped. I stifled my cries until we had stepped outside the care facility, then let loose. But no: the facility was located in a residential neighborhood. I had to be quiet there, too, so as not to wake the neighbors. *Okay.* I waited until we pulled into the driveway behind our house. Dad had turned the garage into a man cave before that term was even invented. A train set ran around the ping-pong table. Sinatra posters plastered the walls. Hot-air balloons dangled from the ceiling. The sight of Dad's drum set is what buckled my knees, though. For the third time, I started wailing. But this was deemed inappropriate, too. Someone lifted me by the shoulders and steered me inside the house. By the time I made it to the living room couch, where wailing presumably was permitted, I couldn't. My cries were stuck inside me.

*   *   *

Eight days after burying my father's ashes, I unlocked my condo in Chapel Hill, North Carolina, and anxiously unzipped my suitcase. To my relief, his old snare drum had survived the flight. It had hung in the garage for decades, and when we pulled it down after the funeral, Mom and I were surprised to find the remnants of a bumper sticker that said "MIDWESTERN MUSIC AND ART CAMP 1954" in faded script. Dad would have been seventeen then, preparing for his audition for the Navy. I placed the drum in the corner of my office then continued unpacking until I came across his dog tag. We had found enough of these engraved tin plates in Dad's dresser for each family member to take one home. Where should I put mine? I circled my house a few times before setting it atop the drum for safekeeping. Ditto with my eulogy, which I rolled like a scroll. Then a neighbor knocked on the door, proffering a bag of my mail. Sympathy cards awaited inside, so lovely, I couldn't just toss them into a box. I stacked them atop the drum, but that wasn't right either, since only the top one was visible, so I fanned them out in a half-moon around the drum. This made my eyes sting. I went to the kitchen to brew some tea, then halted at the cabinet. I had celebrated my birthday before flying down to Texas and hung the roses I'd received upside down from the cabinet's handle. *Dad sent us roses every single Valentine's Day of our lives.* Grabbing the dried flowers, I hurried back to the office and laid one between each card. Then I took the large framed photograph I'd been given by the funeral home—Dad in a denim shirt, smiling on the Alaskan railroad—and propped it atop the drum, along with votive candles.

This was not a ritual I had observed in childhood. Mom kept photos of family who'd died atop the piano, but that was the extent of ancestral veneration in our home. Like many Mexican traditions I now uphold, I learned about altars from books by Laura Esquivel and Gloria Anzaldua, from college courses like Chicano Politics and The History of Mexican Americans in Texas, and above all, from my travels. I briefly wondered if it was appropriate to honor Dad this way, given his ambivalence to Mexican culture, but before I knew it, I was talking to his photograph. This made me laugh. A year before Dad entered the care facility, Mom told me that she'd overheard him chatting away in his bedroom one night. At first, she thought he was on the phone, but then she remembered he had forgotten how to use it long ago. When she opened his door to ask what he was doing, he said, "Talking to Stephanie," then tapped my framed photo.

* * *

Mexico bewildered me when I was little. I couldn't understand why the landscape changed so drastically when we walked across the international bridge from Laredo to Nuevo Laredo. Suddenly, the sidewalk broke apart. There were blind men strumming guitars on the street corners. Women pushed heavy carts of candied fruit swarming with bees. Barefoot children sold boxes of Chiclet. By the time we reached our first stop—Marti's, Mom's favorite department store—I had already distributed my allowance into a succession of outstretched palms. By high school, Mexico was the place where I bought Retin-A for my acne and sneaked sips from Mom's margarita when she wasn't looking. Boys at school teased each other about getting laid there. They swore prostitutes had sex with donkeys there. That—coupled with the fact that we were never taught anything about Mexicans in school besides their murdering of Davy Crockett at the Alamo—made me leery of my ancestral land, indeed.

Once I started traveling around the former Eastern Bloc while based in Moscow, however, I learned that you cannot judge a nation by its border towns (or, equally enlightening, by how it is portrayed in a Texas public school). Russia is also where I learned that many Soviets so revered their native culture they had risked being banished to the Gulag for their efforts to preserve it. Soon after returning to Texas, I enrolled in an intensive Spanish course, then invited Mom on a trip to Mexico City, my first to the interior. Beholding its glories—the Mayan codices at Museo Nacional de Antropología, the splendor of La Casa Azul, the murals of Palacio de Bellas Artes, the Aztec pyramid bursting through the zócalo—committed me to maintaining our family's ties there, especially when I met our last living relatives in Monterrey. They were in their seventies and had just two grandsons, both of whom pined to live in El Norte.

By the time I turned thirty, Mexico was the subject of almost everything I wrote. I spent much of 2005–06 bouncing around from Queretaro to Oaxaca to San Cristobal de las Casas, trying to decide which city I loved best so I could move there. But then, in 2007, the United States' insatiable hunger for drugs plunged Mexico into narco war. Nearly 300,000 Mexicans died or disappeared in the decade that ensued. The violence slashed countless dreams, mine included.

In my forties, though, my own life imploded when I got diagnosed with ovarian cancer. The first place I flew when my oncologist promised it would no longer compromise my immune system was Mexico. It healed me in ways that chemo could not. Which is why, seventeen days after burying my father, I booked a flight to Oaxaca for Día de Muertos.

* * *

I arrived to Oaxaca late at night in the driving rain. When I awoke the next morning, the city was gleaming with cempasúchiles. The orange-gold blossoms had been strung on ribbons that cascaded from rooftops, arched above doorways, and dangled from trees, and the rain had scattered their petals across the cobblestones, so that every road was golden. I bought an armload from the first seller I encountered and hurried back to the room I had rented. After pulling off each blossom, I lined them along the dresser, across the windowsill, and inside each of the shelves, then sprinkled a handful of petals atop the photo I'd brought of Dad, along with his dog tag.

From what I had read, a pueblo called Xoxocotlán was renowned for Día de Muertos festivities on October 31, so I booked an excursion from a pop-up travel agency downtown. One of the many options the agency offered was a "concurso de altares." Misinterpreting this as a lecture on altar-making, I plunked down an extra one hundred pesos. Instead, the concurso entailed trotting alongside a massive comparsa—or Día de Muertos parade of twirling puppets, marching bands, ladies dancing with pineapples, and teenaged boys launching bottle rockets into the sky—for five and a half miles until we reached the shuttle that took us on to Xoxocotlán. We arrived at 10:00 p.m. to a mob scene. Día de Muertos fell on a weekend that year, so tens of thousands of Mexicans had sailed in from throughout the country, while the smash-hit movie *Coco* had reeled in tens of thousands of foreigners. Seemingly every last one had painted their face like a skull, complete with rhinestones around their eye sockets and a black-tipped nose. Our tour guide cast us into the ghoulish sea, saying she'd wait for us by the stage, where a concert was underway. Before I could verify a time, I got caught in a wave that beached me at the cemetery gate. Walking across the threshold, I gasped. Every single tomb was outlined with flickering candles. Amid the trails of cempasúchil petals, the cemetery glowed like a city of gold—albeit, one on the verge of siege. Bands of drunken skeletons stopped at every tomb to snap a selfie, despite the fact that a bereaved family had gathered there, the widows draped in black rebozos, the children clutching pan de muerto. The graves were so close together, many were getting trampled. It felt so disrespectful that I tried to leave, but the crowds propelled me forward, forward, forward, until I finally veered off at a tomb surrounded by an especially large family. The matriarch looked up from what might have been her husband's grave. Reaching into my backpack, I pulled out the bag of pan de muerto I had brought from Oaxaca and handed it to her. "Just one?" she asked.

"It's all for you," I said, then hailed the next wave toward the exit.

* * *

Traveling in Mexico had taught me that the schizophrenia of being biracial, of straddling two worlds but belonging to neither, might be the most Mexican thing about me. Mexicans have been struggling to navigate their blending of indigenous and Spanish bloodlines for five hundred years now. The single most uniting fact of our Mexicanidad is that it is a negotiation for us all. Some aspects of our identity, we inherit; others, we must pursue.

That, at least, was how I tried to rationalize spending sixty-seven dollars on a "Day of the Dead Ceremony" I found on Airbnb. Yes, it made me feel like a fraud. But what was my alternative? Our last remaining family member in Monterrey had died three years prior. We weren't in touch with her grandchildren, so I couldn't go spend the holiday with them. I had also lost contact with the Oaxaqueños I'd befriended on earlier visits. Besides, this was how I had learned many aspects of my culture: if not from a trip, then a class. If not from a film, then a book. How will we ever recover from colonization, but to reclaim what we can, where we can, how we can, with hopes that our culture might better reauthenticate in the next generation?

It proved to be surprisingly moving, joining nine strangers around an altar inside the home of a Mixtec curandera—especially when two turned out to be Chicanas like me. Together, we wrote down the names of those we mourned on slips of paper, placed them on an earthen tray, and breathed. Sprinkled cempasúchil petals and breathed. Lit candles and breathed. Burned copal and breathed. Drank from a gourd of mezcal and breathed. Dunked pieces of pan de muerto inside mugs of hot chocolate and breathed. Listened and cried and told stories and laughed and breathed.

By the time the ceremony had ended, I was emotionally spent yet rallied to join the Chicanas on an excursion to Oaxaca's main cemetery, Panteon San Miguel, anyway. I braced myself for another mob scene, but the only crowds were the families who had come to grieve. They encircled the graves of their dead, scrubbing down the crypts with sudsy water and stringing papel picado from the trees. Every tomb had been decorated with photographs as well as treats—bottles of mezcal, packs of cigarettes, chocolates, tamales wrapped in banana leaves, jars of mole—plus row upon row of cempasúchil blossoms. One extended family was blasting ranchera from a boom box. Padres were dancing with hijas, tías with tíos, primas with primos, mamis with each other.

For most of my life, Dad said he wanted to be buried in his hometown of Minneapolis, Kansas. He even bought a plot there, right next to his parents, and inscribed the headstone with his and Mom's names and birth dates. Over the years, however, he seemed to realize that Barbara and I would visit more often if they were buried in Texas, and then Corpus opened a new veteran's cemetery. Ever a fan of a 21-gun salute, Dad reserved a plot for Mom and himself, and that is where we buried him. Though heartened my parents would be easier to visit, I was crushed to read the cemetery's regulations. Only flags and flowers were allowed as devotional items, and none could be taller than the (identical) headstones. Never would I be able to decorate my parents' graves as lovingly—which is to say, as Mexicanly—as all the families were doing around me.

Something pulled inside my chest. Bidding farewell to the Chicanas, I slipped into the crowd. The cemetery was labyrinthine, but I could see a back wall beyond the roving mariachis. I was side-stepping a crypt when my phone vibrated. I looked down to see photographs from Kansas flickering across the screen. It took a moment to remember that Barbara and her husband were driving to Iowa for a conference that day and had planned to visit Minneapolis along the way. One photo was of the store where Grandma Griest bought Dad's drum set some sixty-five years before.

Nearby was a slab of abandoned concrete. I plunked down just in time before the long-stifled wail came surging out. It soared above the dump where everyone was tossing the stems of decapitated cempasúchiles, above the water spigot where mamis filled their scrub buckets, above each and every crypt. No one minded, for if there was ever a time or a place to bawl in public, it was November 2 at Panteon San Miguel. And so I sobbed until my eyeballs threatened to slip from their sockets, until I felt faint from exhaustion, before staggering away from my perch.

Maybe twenty feet away was a tomb presided over by a man with a slicked-back shock of white hair, wearing a guayabera. He was holding onto the top of his cane so that he could sit upright, and his family was gathered around him. When my eyes met his, he solemnly nodded. He could tell my heart felt a little bit lighter. And suddenly, it did.

Calle Martín De Zavala

Francisco Cantú

My mother and I arrived in Monterrey, Nuevo León, with a handful of photographs and place names connecting us to a long-buried family history—records of ancestors and landscapes almost as obscure to us as ghosts. On the morning of my thirty-fourth birthday, we walked through a quiet neighborhood just outside the barrio antiguo along Calle Martín de Zavala, a street that, after carrying many names through the centuries, now bore that of an early colonial governor. As we walked past homes with newfangled exteriors and cinder block additions, it was hard to imagine that we were in fact walking along the same street where our forebears had lived before their eventual flight to the border, the same street where my mother's grandparents celebrated their wedding at the turn of the last century, and where her father was born on the eve of the Mexican Revolution.

My mother has few memories of her father. After her parents' early separation, she moved with her Midwestern mother from San Diego to New York, abruptly leaving her father behind in a way that would forever ripple through their lives. Growing up, she possessed a single photograph of him as a young man dressed as a Mexican charro, squinting under a broad sombrero with a pencil-thin mustache and a cigarette hanging loosely in his fingers. When she finally returned to San Diego to knock on his door at age seventeen, she could barely believe that the portly man who stood before her was actually him, the man who helped breathe her into existence. Their meeting did not portend a new understanding of one another. My mother wanted to travel the world, to live her life outside. Her father, on the other hand, spent his days indoors sorting mail for the postal service, rarely leaving the neighborhood where he lived just minutes away from his brothers and sisters. As my mother grew into adulthood, as she began a career and took a husband and became a mother, she would try again and again to clear the air with her father, to break through the distance that had separated them since the time she was a smiling, brown-eyed toddler. But for her father, it remained easier to not speak of the past, to not leave oneself vulnerable to what had long ago been left behind, unchangeable and impossible to explain.

For my mother, who lived most of her life devoid of any stories of her Mexican family, a trip to Monterrey was a chance for reclamation, an opportunity to see the birthplace of her father and commune with a history she never had access to. My mother and I hoped to find, somewhere on Calle Martín de Zavala, the facade of a building that might still resemble the pocket-sized photograph we had of the family home taken in 1912, a crooked image of a two-story Spanish-style row house with wrought iron window bars and balcony railings. Under the early October sun we made our way past countless homes searching for matching features, but few of them maintained any of their historic traits. After nearly half an hour of walking, we stopped at an impromptu taco stand erected on the doorstep of a neighborhood home. Pasen a comer adentro, a woman called to us from inside, para que no les pegue el sol.

We took a seat at the woman's dining room table as she began heating tortillas on her kitchen stove, listing the various guisos we could choose for our tacos. As she prepared our order, we told the woman that we were walking this street looking for the house where my mother's father was born. We handed her the black-and-white photograph. She squinted and then quickly passed it back to us, waiving her hand dismissively. All the viejitos who remember what things looked like back then are long dead, she told us. Oh, we said. Of course. The woman asked for our surname and thought for a while as she scooped adobada and nopal onto our plates. Her tía used to talk about an old man named Cantú who lived a few blocks down, she offered, but he died decades ago. His name was Rubén, or maybe Raúl. My mother and I looked at each other and shrugged. We doubted there was any connection—our entire family had left during the Revolution. The woman laughed. In Monterrey you'll find Cantús everywhere you look. Hay bastantes.

My mother and I ordered another round of tacos and the woman began to tell us how she had inherited her home. She wasn't from Monterrey but had come to this street to care for her tía when she became immobilized by old age. She had grown up high in the sierra, she told us, in a town called Rayones. In the winters of her childhood she came to know true cold, learning to live with cutting wind and snow. I used to hate the cold more than anything, she said, but now, down here in the city, somehow I miss it. She told us how her father used to work in the pecan orchards and how her mother sold bread and sweets made from the nuts—pan semita, nogada de nuez, bolitas de leche quemada. As she became older, her family slowly began to come down from the mountains to work in the citrus fields of Montemorelos. Eventually, many of them moved on to Monterrey, abandoning forever the mountain passes, the pines, the clean air, the towering spires of limestone. Never in all of my years did I think I'd end up on a street like this in the middle of the city, she told us—pero uno nunca sabe donde va a caer.

It wasn't until several days later that I would realize how this woman had shared with us, over two plates of tacos, more about her life and the place she came from than my grandfather had ever shared with us about his own. In the coming days, my mother and I went on to visit the outlying towns where her father's parents were born, stepping foot in the same parish churches where they were baptized and where generations before them had kneeled to pray. These moments, however, were always underlain by a sense of remoteness, by a growing awareness of how little we actually had to situate or guide us. My mother, having inherited so little from her father, was being made to search for him through a haze. After all, when ancestors fail to share their stories with us, we go looking for them nonetheless.

My mother and I finished walking the entire length of Calle Martín de Zavala without ever finding exactly where her father was born. Instead, we passed by, without knowing, the home that had first offered him shelter, by the place where he spoke his first words and took his first steps, by the place where he learned, slowly, to make sense of the world.

The Wonder Woman T-Shirt

Rigoberto González

It was mine first. I had picked it out from one of the large bins at the Goodwill Thrift Store, where my family went on weekends to buy secondhand clothes. I wouldn't step into a mall selling new clothing until my freshman year in college. So for a fifteen-year-old kid, this was quite the find: a T-shirt in very good condition with one of my childhood idols—Wonder Woman. I didn't know her as Wonder Woman, however. I knew her as La Mujer Maravilla. Watching television in Michoacán meant that we were sometimes a decade behind American TV shows and current on others. So it was my great fortune to have powerhouse programming from the 1960s and 1970s—*Hechizada* (*Bewitched*), *Mi bella genio* (*I Dream of Jeannie*), *La mujer biónica* (*The Bionic Woman*), and *La mujer maravilla*—all at the same time.

I didn't think anything of the fact that all of these shows had female leads. They were all blonde also, except for Wonder Woman, played by a brunette. Lynda Carter had Mexican ancestry. But I didn't find out about that until I was much older, which made her all the more meaningful. Women at the center of the stories were not uncommon in Mexican TV, but it was mostly in telenovelas, where they suffered their way through a number of heartaches before finally getting married at the conclusion of the series. The realism of telenovelas and even comedy shows didn't appeal to me. At seven years old I wanted fantasy. I wanted escape. And Samantha Stevens, Jaime Sommers, Jeannie, and Diana Prince delivered.

The use of special effects in these American programs was mesmerizing, and nothing compared to their use in Mexican TV. But the real revelation came when I found out these shows were filmed in color. My grandparents' small television with the awkward antenna had a black-and-white screen. My parents didn't own a television. So any chance I got, I'd walk to my grandparents' house and watch my shows with my aunts, who were also fans. Abuela Herminia, my mother's mother, would sit in the corner doing her knitting and once in a while look up and declare that we should stop watching brujería—witchcraft. But it was spoken more out of a sense of duty than with conviction.

When one of my schoolfriends, who lived across the street, invited me to her house to watch *La mujer biónica*, I was pleasantly surprised by how much more magical the show appeared in that large color TV. I had started to make a habit of going over to watch all four of my favorite shows until my younger brother Alex started tagging along. At one point, in one episode (I can't recall which show), a woman with a large belly appeared and my brother pointed and said, "That lady's pregnant."

Apparently, the neighbors were horrified. My friend's mother asked us to leave. I didn't know that we had been banned altogether until my mother forbade us to go. I protested and whined until she told me that the neighbor had been offended by something we had said and that it was best to keep our distance. "They're very religious," my mother added.

From that moment on I went back to the black-and-white versions, but I was with my aunts, who were very expressive whenever Jeannie turned to smoke and got sucked back into her bottle, or whenever Samantha's mother, Endora, popped in and out of the Samantha's living room. Watching with this audience was part of the fun. From her big chair Abuela Herminia mumbled, "Brujerías." I had to imagine, however, that Jeannie's smoke was pink and that Endora's gown was green.

I knew not to beg my mother for a TV. Even as a boy I recognized that we were poor and that I shouldn't ask for much. And by the time my father came back from the north and bought us a color TV, his pocket heavy with dollars, I had become less interested in the women and more interested in the men, such as *El hombre nuclear* (*The Six-Million Dollar Man*). I was drawn also to the handsome leading men in telenovelas, their names a mouthful like Victor Alfonso or Francisco Xavier, their dress shirts opened too far down the middle of their chests, sometimes hairy, sometimes smooth and golden as honey.

At school, I was teased for my mannerisms. I smiled too much; I joined the girls in their circles and made faces at the boys. I didn't realize any of these habits about myself until they were pointed out, repeatedly. "You're going to grow up to be a woman if you don't stop lisping," one of them called out as I walked home with my book bag. I had to learn to walk forward without stopping to respond, even when the boys threw lumps of earth at my legs. Nearby, the men digging ditches simply laughed, which encouraged the boys to keep throwing.

Then, shortly after I turned ten, our family decided to relocate to California, my birthplace in a country I had no memory of. I didn't like the idea of getting torn away from Michoacán, but the prospect of starting over without the sissy reputation that had haunted me all of these years became appealing. I could reinvent a better me.

For a brief period, however, before my mother and father could cross the border, Alex and I were sent to live with our father's parents, Abuelo Ramón and Abuela María.

From the moment we were picked up by Abuelo I knew it was not going to be an easy situation. What began as excitement at the beginning of a new adventure quickly took a turn when I kept pointing at the livestock and asking Abuelo questions: "Are those cows for milk or for meat? Do they take those sheep up a mountain? Is there a mountain close by? Where are the shepherds? There isn't much grass around here. What do the animals eat?"

Exasperated, Abuelo barked at me without turning his head: "Stop asking stupid questions! And if you're going to ask questions, ask them like a man! You sound like a girl!"

Abuela didn't turn around either. It was as if she hadn't heard anything at all.

I sunk back into my seat. That familiar taunt from my schoolmates back in Michoacán had crossed the border with me.

In an American school, it was easy to become invisible. I didn't speak the language, I couldn't communicate with most teachers, and there were so many kids that only the ones who misbehaved received any attention. I learned to keep my mouth shut and to keep all expression off my face; otherwise I would give myself away. But this tactic failed when I began to develop crushes on boys—boys who would respond sometimes violently if I tried to come near them.

"Get the fuck out of here, joto!" I'd hear over and over again. But I couldn't resist this affinity I had for Mexican boys who spoke two languages and called themselves American; boys who made comments from the back of the classroom that everyone laughed at, sending the teacher into a tizzy; boys who demanded to be team captains and who scored the most points in soccer, basketball, baseball, and football; boys who were the center of the cafeteria ruckus and took liberties stealing food from other boys, usually me. I admired the power of their confidence. Wherever they stood, that's where they belonged. In the world of Americans and in the world of men, I felt out of place.

At home, I gravitated toward Abuela María. She wasn't affectionate, but she was kind. Though at times she would have fun saying my nickname over and over again, Estuche de Oro, her coffer of gold, which she pronounced "Estuchi" and then shortened to "Tuchi." My brother was Beni, short for Beneficios, as in government benefits. These terms of endearment had to substitute for hugs or pecks on the cheek, which we never got from her.

Displays of affection were not a practice in Abuelo's household. Relatives who visited simply said, "We're here!" when they arrived and "We're leaving!" as they left. The closest I ever got from Abuelo was a pat on the back, when he was pleased I had done something he approved of, which was seldom. More common were the scolding, the insults, and reprimands about not doing things the more masculine way. Like cursing.

"You have to cuss like a man," he said after I yelled when I accidentally stubbed my toe. "Say 'Ay, cabrón' or 'Ay, güey,' not just 'Ay,' like a wimp."

I never liked cussing because my mother wouldn't permit it. Cussing was not allowed in Abuela Herminia's house either. And any other displays of vulgar behavior, such as belching or crotch adjusting, were quickly met with disapproval. In Abuelo Ramón's table, a belch got a good laugh. So did farting and blaming Abuela María for it. And he had no qualms about adjusting himself as he walked out of the bathroom, the rest of us sitting in the living room, watching TV. His antics were so common they became unnoticed. Except for his habit of not lifting the toilet seat when he went to the bathroom. That habit wasn't addressed until many years later, when my father came to visit.

"Apá," he said to Abuelo. "I'd like to ask you a huge favor to please lift the damn toilet seat!"

My brother and I were mortified yet relieved that this issue had finally been voiced.

Abuelo kept his gaze fixed on the TV as he said, "Tell your boys, too. They do it also."

I knew that Abuelo's disdain of my mannerisms was less about his homophobia and more about the fact that he looked at my brother and me as burdens. Alex gave Abuelo plenty to get angry about: failing grades, fighting, skipping school to hang out with our cousins—young men who Abuelo never saw as anything but troublemakers. But I was the good boy. So he had to find something to criticize, and, as with my school bullies, my feminine nature was an easy and convenient target.

Not long after our parents joined us, they moved in with Abuelo as well, and this only seemed to exacerbate his rage. There was never enough money. There was never enough food. There were too many mouths to feed. Our uncle had also moved in with his wife and three kids. And so did our aunt, with her brood of five. "And your boys eat like hogs," he'd complain to my parents as he tossed spoons and slammed shut cupboard doors in the kitchen. "That Estuche, he's even beginning to look like a hog."

When I heard this, I blushed even though there was no one in the room with me. I sat hidden behind a book in the living room. When I read, no one bothered me. It was true that I had always been a chubby kid. My baby fat had followed me into adolescence. Still, I got teased for being a sissy a lot more than for being overweight. Acting like a girl was the bigger offense.

The breaking point, however, was when my mother discovered Abuelo had become violently physical with me.

"What is that?" she asked when she discovered a bruise on my leg. "Who did that?"

"Abuelo," I said.

"Is this the first time he's done that?"

"No."

"Since when has he been doing that?"

I paused for a bit, trying to remember the first time Abuelo hit me. Yes, it was soon after Alex and I arrived. Abuelo had asked me to help bring in the groceries. The bags were heavy but he handed them to me anyway. I wanted to show Abuelo that I was a strong boy, that I was a helpful boy, the boy who could follow directions. I was a good boy. But before I stepped inside, I tripped and the cans of tomato sauce came spilling out.

"Look at what you've done, useless! Pick them up before something gets lost."

I wasn't picking up the cans fast enough. It was getting dark, I became anxious that I had failed the first test of my worth. Not to mention the first clear demonstration that although I sounded like a girl, and acted like a girl, I was indeed, without a doubt, a boy.

Everything was back in the bags, or so I thought. I grabbed them tightly this time, unafraid of their weight. But as I walked inside the well-lighted living room, Abuelo called out to me.

"Here, you forgot one."

A can of tomato sauce came flying at me and when it struck my head I let go of the bags once again.

I couldn't tell my mother the whole story, but she wasn't asking for it. She only wanted an answer to her question, "Since when has he been doing that?"

"Since I arrived," I said to her.

Not long after, my father moved our family of four out of Abuelo's house. And so did my uncle flee with his family, and my aunt with hers. Abuelo and Abuela moved to a smaller house across from the post office and then later qualified for subsidized housing at the Fred Young Farm Labor Camp two towns away. Not long after that, my mother died, and back we were with Abuelo, only three of us this time. My father promised us that things were going to change, and they did somewhat. Abuelo never laid a hand on me again, and I was determined not to give him an excuse either. I withdrew into a dark corner of the room, unheard and barely seen in my sadness. The only saving grace was that I had to enroll in a different school. It was a fresh start. A chance to reinvent myself all over again. This time I was determined to succeed.

Though Abuelo kept his promise to my father, I was careful not to slip. The best way was to simply not speak. Abuela commented on this to Abuelo as they sat down to eat roasted peanuts. I was in my corner, reading a library book. "Look at Tuchi over there," she said. "He doesn't make a sound at all."

"As it should be," Abuelo said. There was no malice in his voice. It was more like a statement of victory. After all these years, I had been tamed.

The only time I ventured outside was when Abuelo dropped Abuela and me at the Goodwill Thrift Store. We spent hours rummaging through the bins of clothing, moving items on the crowded display shelves, and poking fun at the eccentric older ladies who walked in to try out hats from another era and coats that looked like fur but felt thorny like a cactus. I went back and forth between joining Abuela to make comments about the other shoppers and browsing the bookcases at the back of the store, packed with mass paperbacks.

During one of these visits, I discovered the Wonder Woman T-shirt.

Suddenly, I was reminded of my days in Michoacán, sitting with my mother's sisters, who giggled and cheered whenever Diana Prince spun and spun until her bun came loose and after the flash of lightning, when Wonder Woman stood in her skin-tight superhero outfit. A few seconds later she was bending steel rods or tossing crates or lifting cars or leaping from the ground to the top of a building. Invincible and unstoppable, she had arrived to save the world, to save us all.

But what really convinced me that this was the version of Wonder Woman that I needed was her picture: slightly turned to the side, ready for battle with her magic lasso looped around her hip, smoke in the background suggesting that she had just completed her transformation from a prim and proper intelligence officer to Amazon warrior. There she was, my childhood idol, in black and white, exactly as I had learned to appreciate her in that black-and-white TV.

"Can I get this, Abuela?"

Abuela lifted the bottom of the white T-shirt to inspect the image closely. "Who is this woman?" she asked.

"La mujer maravilla," I responded.

"La mujer maravilla?" Abuela looked at it with disinterest for a few more seconds before saying, "Put it in the cart."

I wasn't intending to ever wear the T-shirt. It was more like a memento, a photograph, a small reminder of the happiness I once felt long before I was moved from one country to another, torn away from my mother's family to live with my father's. I must have stored it in a safe place to keep it a secret, so well hidden that I completely forgot about it when, a few years later, I moved out of the house for good to enroll at the university.

College was yet another new beginning, though this time I was not going to be what the bullies wanted me to be—I was going to be myself. And for thirty years I managed it. Mine wasn't a smooth journey, but it was mine exclusively: bad decisions, good decisions, failures, and triumphs. I didn't receive much news from home except when somebody passed away. Abuelo died in 2004, Abuela in 2011.

Then one evening, scouring Facebook out of curiosity to see pictures of the relatives I had left behind decades ago, I came across a photograph of Abuelo and Abuela posing with their youngest son and his two daughters, the oldest almost as tall as Abuelo. Abuela wore one of her aprons, this one pink, but Abuelo stood proudly in my Wonder Woman T-shirt. Except that he had cut off the sleeves to expose his shoulders and thin biceps. He did this to all of his T-shirts because he believed it made him look manlier.

I had expected to feel outrage at the defilement of what was once an important connection to a better period of my life. But seeing him looking frail and harmless after all these years awoke a soft spot I didn't know I had inside. It was a kind of tenderness tinged with sympathy and perhaps nostalgia that I'm certain all middle-aged men develop for their adolescence, when everything seemed terrible but with the passage of time now didn't seem as painful as all that. Or maybe that was what coming to terms with the past did to a person. It was closure, letting the wounds heal and arriving at this miraculous new place called forgiveness.

In(toxic)ated Masculinity

Alex Espinoza

I was seven years old the first time I got drunk. This was in the late 1970s, before childproof locks on cabinet doors, when we'd ride around the back camper of my uncle's van without seatbelts, before toys came with choking hazard warnings. My mother kept bottles of Thunderbird and Night Train—cheap fortified wine that tasted like paint thinner or gasoline—in the cabinet beneath the kitchen sink. She would shove them behind jars of glass cleaner and boxes of powdered dish soap. My siblings and I would often catch her taking swigs now and again throughout the day and sometimes in the evenings. I asked her once what the bottles were.

"Furniture polish," she replied, closing the cabinet door.

It started out as a game, a way for me to impress my brothers and sisters, a way for me to be the center of attention in our large family. When our mother, or any other adult, wasn't around, I'd go to the kitchen, reach into the dark well of the cabinet, my small arm stretching past fragrant solvents and cleansers, until I touched the cool smooth glass bottle of cheap booze, unscrew the cap, and take short sips, much to the delight of my siblings who watched on, daring me. One afternoon, when we were home alone, during a brief period when my mother worked at a factory in Monrovia, California, my brother decided to fill a glass tumbler with the foul "juice." My siblings stood around me in a circle, watching as I gulped it down in one long and continuous swig. I can't remember now what it felt like to be that drunk at such an early age. I remember that my brother received a stern scolding from our mother, but nothing more, and that the incident became part of our family lore, a story that my siblings and my mother often loved repeating. As I grew up, I quickly learned that alcohol not only provided me with an opportunity to be the center of attention, but also gave me a chance to assert my masculinity. The way the men in my family showed that they were men was through drinking and smoking. So, I kept taking swigs from my mother's bottles of cheap wine even after I got wasted. She didn't hide them away. She kept them in the exact same spot. When my older brother came home from his factory job, he'd sit on the couch, crack open a beer, and chain-smoke cigarettes. It was not uncommon to see me taking sips from his can and puffs from his Marlboros.

During large family gatherings at our house in La Puente, my aunts and uncles and our endless stream of cousins descended on our house on warm summer evenings. There'd be music and carne asada, or, if the event was truly special, my father would string a live goat from the branch of our lemon tree, slit its throat, and prepare the animal for birria. There were ice chests full of beer and enormous amber-colored bottles of hard alcohol that glowed warm and menacing under the kitchen's fluorescent lighting. My uncles and older brothers would congregate in the garage, where they'd stand around the cooler, pulling back tabs from can after can of beer, drinking until everything was gone. They'd then move on to the hard alcohol, to shots of tequila or vodka. They talked about ex-girlfriends with supple thighs, soft lips, big breasts, sex in the backseats of cars, accidental pregnancies, and secret abortions. I always remained in the background, at the edge, at the periphery of this circle, watching this aggressive show of toxic masculinity. It was both fascinating and disturbing to listen in. I learned things about sex and bodies that a boy my age shouldn't know.

Getting completely wasted for the first time was viewed as something of a rite of passage among my brothers and their friends. As I got older, the innocent clandestine sips here and there from my mother's liquor bottles started feeling silly, almost amateurish. My brothers, now young men in their late teens and early twenties, always woke up hung over on Sunday mornings and talked about partying with their friends the night before. There were references to fights, making out with girls, and puking in bushes. There was a boy I knew, only a year older than me, who'd started hanging out with my them and their friends. They admired his ability to drink so much and not lose control. They said he was a "bad ass" despite his age.

I grew jealous of this boy. I craved that same respect from my brothers. I imagined myself partying with them, getting cheered on and patted on the back as I chugged beers or took shots. I wanted to be a "bad ass" too. Never one to be overshadowed by anyone, and always the consummate attention-seeker, I knew that as my fifteenth birthday approached, I would have to prove to everyone around me that I was truly a man. One night, I got drunk, I mean *really* drunk, at the home of a family friend. That evening was a blur of beers and fragmented conversations, of stumbles and falls down a flight of stairs, of vomiting all over the carpet of our friend's apartment. None of my brothers were there, though. They'd missed the entire spectacle.

It turned into an impulse, an itch, a need to prove to those around me that I belonged, that I was a man, that I could hang with the big boys. Alcohol gave me confidence, and it deflected attention away from my internal struggles with my own sexuality and with a physical disability that left me feeling inferior. This disability hindered my ability to participate in sports, something my brothers loved, something they were especially good at. It kept me away from the football field, the baseball diamond, the basketball court, and the boxing ring. I couldn't do the things they did with their bodies. I was always being poked and prodded and examined by an endless stream of doctors. After so many hours listening to them pick me apart, dissecting me like some science experiment, I began to believe there was something seriously wrong with me. What other explanation could there be, after all, for my disability, my homosexuality, and my debilitating hair loss (another serious condition I suffered from)?

As I grew older, I watched my brothers develop dependencies on alcohol and drugs. As they fell deeper and deeper into a world of booze, pot, and harder substances, I found solace in books and poetry. I began writing stories, using my imagination to escape, to transport me to far-off places. I created worlds where someone like me belonged, where I was accepted, where I didn't feel so alone. But my creativity and imagination had its limits and couldn't protect me from the brutal realities I found myself trying to avoid.

It was best to stay quiet and hide one's sexuality back then. In the late 1980s and early 1990s, being gay was largely frowned upon. AIDS was still a very real and frightening phenomenon. In my working-class neighborhood, in my hyper-masculine and hyper-Catholic family, such a thing was absolutely forbidden. I suppressed it, buried it away, tried acting "normal." Just as I hid my disability and hair loss with long-sleeved shirts and caps, my sexuality was something I learned to suppress. I formed a friendship around this time with a high school classmate, an overweight boy with bulging eyes who chain-smoked cigarettes he stole from liquor stores. One evening we confessed to each other that we were gay. It was the first time I remember saying that word out loud. I breathed myself into existence then. As affirming and empowering as it was, I also recall feeling incredibly terrified. That friend and I made a promise to keep each other's secret, to stick together, and to always be there for one another. We found others like us, other closeted Mexican boys, and we all began to hang out together. When one of us was old enough to drive, we found ourselves heading into West Hollywood on Friday and Saturday nights to hang out at the gay clubs. Among that circle of friends, I felt myself the most unattractive because of my hair loss and my disability. The pressure to belong and fit in was just too much. I'd walk into those places in my frumpy, baggy clothing and my silly-looking hats, and the dark walls and the dance floors would be packed with guys in hard bodies and tight shirts. As my friends danced, I waited on the side, watching them move and gyrate. The house and techno beats were new to the scene back then. I remember Technotronic, C+C Music Factory, and Inner City, those thumps reverberating through my body. I remember wishing that sound could loosen me out my flawed skin so that I could fly far, far away from all of those men and their eyes that would size me up before quickly moving on to someone else.

That was when my drinking habit became something else entirely. Just like the innocent sips from my mother's booze bottles, or the one-off incident at our family friend's house, those moments were meant to show we'd transitioned into manhood. I could hang out in the garage with my brothers and their friends and, away from my mother's influence, I could sneak swigs of beer and belong. It bound me to my brothers and their friends. But when I started hitting the clubs with my own friends, my drinking changed. It became a way for me to stave off the fear and insecurity I felt being around other gay men. I remember gulping down tumblers full of Bacardi and Coke in the parking lots (or anything else we could get our hands on). Other drinks of choice among me and my friends included Night Train (a drink I was all too familiar with, thanks to my mother), Boones Farm wine, cheap vodka mixed with orange soda, Colt 45, wine coolers, Cisco, generic-brand tequila mixed with anything, Captain Morgan Spiced Rum, premixed "Club" brand drinks with flavors like "Sex on the Beach," "Fuzzy Navel," and "Screwdriver." I won't lie. I drank some pretty foul shit. I built up a tolerance for alcohol early on in my life, and this became a badge of honor for me. If pounding beer after beer or taking shot after shot and still being able to hold one's own was a sure sign of strength and manliness, then I was good. I don't think I ever walked into one of those gay clubs completely sober. I never could. I had to be extremely drunk, and even this didn't always work to dampen the fear and intimidation I felt. So pervasive and intense was this apprehension that it often made me lightheaded and tremble uncontrollably. Why did I continue going then? Why didn't I just tell my friends the truth: that the club scene made me feel flawed and imperfect? I couldn't risk being ostracized from them. This was the first real gay community I had established with anyone. My friends were catty, snarky, prone to capriciousness and unreliability. But they were my only gay friends, the only people I could be myself with. The last thing I wanted to do was break ties with them. If that happened, who would I turn to? I'd seen *Psycho*. I imagined myself Norman Bates, a "mama's boy," running around the house in a wig and a dress. A repressed maniac. A loser.

Some of those friends eventually developed addictions to harder things, such as cocaine or meth; others were able to completely repress their sexuality and married women and had children. My first gay friend, the one I'd originally come out to, ended up a kleptomaniac; so serious was his habit that he was arrested and thrown in jail for stealing credit card numbers from customers when he worked at a Gap, charging thousands of dollars of merchandise he stole before being caught. I still remember when he called me from jail, crying, begging me to help bail him out. I kept drinking, even as I lost touch with that insensitive and superficial lot, even as my brothers started families of their own and slowly, but surely, sobered up.

I kept at it, though.

Nothing would stop me. I still had a lot to prove. Or so I thought.

I knew why I continued maintaining this unhealthy relationship with alcohol, sneaking cans of beer into my bedroom and hiding them from my mother, who I still lived with. I hadn't come out to her. My sexuality was a dirty secret I buried deep inside my sock drawer along with those bottles and cans. The society, the culture I'd been born into, the religion I practiced, led me to believe that my desires were wrong, inferior, perverse. I felt too weak to control the temptation, though. No amount of praying could quell the desires that stirred inside me; nothing could stop me from seeking out sexual encounters with men in parks, alleys, and adult bookstores. I used alcohol back then as a way to justify these actions. It was easier to blame this behavior on booze.

When an opportunity to finally move out of my mother's house presented itself, I jumped at the chance. Maybe living on my own, away from my family's influence, would free me to live my life openly and proudly. Maybe I wouldn't feel like I needed to use alcohol as a crutch, as an excuse for my subversive ways. I moved to the heart of Hollywood. There, in the midst of so much temptation, not far from the clubs I used to go to with my friends, my wild tendencies only intensified.

It's late, around one in the morning, I think. I'm driving east on a freeway, clocking about ninety miles an hour in my car. My windows are rolled down even though it's the middle of winter; the night air is keeping me awake. I'd spent the evening partying around L.A. and West Hollywood with a friend of mine. Everything before this moment is a blur of bars and cocktails. The Viper Room, the Dresden, Rage, Union. I rattle off the names in my head to stay alert as I swerve past semis and utility trucks. Drinks. I've had drinks. I can taste their remnants in my mouth—beer, vodka and cranberry juice, tequila and salt. Tomorrow I will be hung over. Tomorrow I will have to crawl out of bed, shower, dress, try to eat something without getting sick, and make it to work. I will spend my shift as assistant manager of a trendy, high-volume furniture store on the Third Street Promenade in Santa Monica nursing a headache and a queasy stomach as I go over fabric swatches with rich housewives from Malibu and Pacific Palisades, as I count change and balance out registers, as I try calming irate customers down on the phone when I break the news that their dining table is on back order for another six weeks. But, right now, careening down the freeway toward the windswept fields and arid hillsides of the Inland Empire, none of that shit matters. I've got a good buzz going, and I'm chain-smoking cigarettes. Off the freeway, I follow a line of refrigerated big rigs down a bumpy street pockmarked with potholes. Loose gravel pings against the side of my car, and it almost sounds like it's raining outside, but there isn't a cloud in the sky. The moon hangs bright and low in the chilled air, drifting above the shadow of a smokestack from one of the many abandoned factories in west Fontana. I shouldn't be driving this late, this drunk. I should be back in Hollywood, asleep in my bedroom in the apartment I share with my best friend. Instead I'm sitting alone in my car. I reek of cigarettes and booze, and I can hardly keep my eyes open. As the light turns green, and the semis lunge forward into the intersection, I trail behind and pull into the parking lot of an adult bookstore. Through the fog of my inebriation, one thing is clear, though: I'm here to cruise. The video arcade is a dark maze of narrow hallways as I make my way around, grasping at the flimsy plywood walls to brace myself in case I fall over. The sounds of coins dropping inside slots mix with the artificial moans coming from the private video screens. Some patrons keep their doors closed and locked while others leave them open. Even though it's cold outside, in here the air is warm, ripe with the raw scent of male sex and sweat with a hint of bleach; along the wall, next to a display case showing the movies playing on each channel, I see a mop and bucket.

I don't know why I keep coming back to these places, I tell myself. I don't know what I'm looking for. And why all the way out here? So far from L.A.? Why didn't I just stay in the city? Find someone to hook up there? Maybe I miss home. I think about my mother's house, a few miles east on Valley. She's likely sound asleep, wrapped in the blanket I gave her last Christmas. There's an overwhelming sense of urgency (need, perhaps) that is so strong, so palatable that it cuts through the haze of alcohol and keeps me there waiting for something to happen, for someone to sidle up to the booth next to mine, offer a knowing glance, then kneel before me as I unzip my pants. Experiences like these no longer leave me satisfied as they did when I was younger. There is a deep emptiness that takes root inside, and I cannot shake it no matter how hard I try.

The guilt is there the next morning, along with the headache, the nausea, and the cold, clammy skin, as I drive to work. Leaving the darkness of the parking structure and walking into the intense morning sun, I'm struck by the brightness, the vivid blues and reds of the sky and the buildings around me. Maybe the colors, maybe the light, maybe the scent of ocean air will sober me up, polish me back into shape, and the headache and nausea and the guilt will magically go away. But no. It'll trail off eventually, though. I know that later in the day, as I'm wrapping up my shift, my friend will call me from a crowded bar and invite me out for drinks.

"It's Two-Dollar Chardonnay Tuesday," she'll remind me. "Let's meet up at 5."

I know that, against my better judgment, I'll agree even though I should go back to my apartment and rest and get ready for another early-morning shift the following day. I will drink way too much, spending money I don't have. I will be out at all hours of the night again. And again, I'll get behind the wheel of my car with the expressed intent to go home and sleep it off.

But I won't. This I know. This I'm certain of.

I'll end the night behind an alley or inside a dark public bathroom at a nearby park or at a sex club or adult movie theater. Hours will pass before I will finally stumble out to my car, the inky darkness of night fading fast as the sun rises in the blue-black sky. Somewhere in the distance, a lone rooster will crow.

Between the hangovers and dwindling funds, I vacillated between feelings of excitement and curiosity one moment then guilt and remorse the next. It was anxiety inducing, and the whole thing left me feeling exhausted and unable to deal with the day-to-day demands of my life and my job. But there was also something so alluring about living such a complicated reality, my identity split between my normal life of work and bills and this nocturnal one of trendy bars, pricey cocktails, sex clubs, and public bathrooms. Despite the thrill of it, I struggled to make sense of my behavior around this time. But whose motives are clear when they are in their twenties and away from home for the first time? I would often think. Maybe if I quit drinking this would prevent me from engaging in casual hookups. I thought about my father, who had died when I was a junior in high school, and his insatiable appetite for alcohol. Booze made him do bad things too, like fight with my mother and spend all our rent money at the bar, buying beer and alcohol for strangers, handing out crumpled wads of twenties and fifties to anyone around. He tried quitting a couple of time, especially when he was diagnosed with diabetes. But he always fell off the wagon.

My own efforts to stop drinking would last a few days, and I'd eventually find myself in the same spot; only this time the guilt would weight heavier on me than the previous times. Still, driven by a desire to understand where my impulses were originating, I tried finding answers in books. I spent hours after my shifts at a bookstore just a few stores down from the one I managed. There, with a strong cup of coffee in my hand, I browsed the self-help section for books on controlling addiction or combating guilt. I took quizzes to determine whether I was an alcoholic ("Have you ever experienced blackouts?" My answer to this was yes) or a sex addict ("Have you ever put yourself in a dangerous situation in your pursuit for sex? Has this led you to have sex with people you would not normally choose?" Answers here were yes and yes). Everything I read told me that if I answered yes to any of the questions provided or if my behavior was placing me in danger, I should SEEK PROFESSIONAL HELP IMMEDIATELY. The only thing was that I didn't know who to talk to. I had no medical insurance. I couldn't ask my mother or any of my siblings for help. I imagined the phone conversations ("I think I'm an alcoholic and addicted to sex because I drink so much I black out, and I've spent hours driving around and around the same park looking for someone to give me a blowjob."). That would not go well. I tried accepting my fate, tried reconciling with the fact that maybe I just was some horny booze hound who loved sex and debauchery.

Maybe it was inescapable. Maybe it was my destiny to live such a dangerous lifestyle. Maybe I would die young, my car wrapped around a streetlight along an unassuming stretch of freeway. Years later (not until I started seeing a licensed therapist) I learned how to confront my demons and came to the realization that my relationship to alcohol would never be simple. By this time, my mother had passed away, and I had settled down with my partner. I used to laugh when I'd imagine my mother's expression if she knew I was paying a white man in a shirt and tie to listen to me as I aired all our family grievances, week after week.

"You're telling all of this to some stranger?" she'd say, aghast. "Have you no shame?"

It was shame that made me develop an unhealthy dependency on alcohol. It was shame that made me hide my sexuality. It was shame, and fear, that kept me from ever revealing to her and to those around me who I really was. It was shame that prevented me from seeing the ways in which my culture distorts the notion of masculinity, the way it buys into this idea that men needed to behave a certain way in order to be considered men, that things like alcohol were the elixir of courage and bravery and virility. Yes, I had plenty of shame, but I know better now. I don't have anything left to prove to anyone.

There's nothing left to lose.

Not anymore.

Piacularis

Domingo Martinez

I don't know how he found me, but it started with this stoner guy, Tony Garza, who introduced me to the sort of lifestyle that I had been told to avoid while growing up.

Tony had been in high school longer than I had been alive, it seemed. He had been a freshman when my oldest sister was a junior at Homer Hanna High School.

When I met him, I think she was graduating from college in Kingsville, Texas.

Tony was a curious combination of bad news and the Good Son. Tony skipped like a scratchy Goodwill record, attempting to "trip" on anything he could get his hands on.

"Hey, Domingo," he said, "I remember your sisters here, man. Whoah! Could those girls party! Ha, ha; right on." And then there was a raised eyebrow or some other insinuating challenge to my sisters' collective chastity, which I was fairly immune to by age fifteen. Hell, by fifteen, I participated in the exchange. "Oh, yeah? They do you, too?" I am terribly ashamed of that sort of stuff today. That need to be accepted at any cost.

Tony was a tall, good-looking kid, if a bit hairy, like an Old Testament seductress. Then again, he was nineteen and had shed the baby fat that clings to most of us at that age. Dark hair, depleting acne, middle-class parents, and he wore all right clothes, even if they were bought by his mother: Tony seemed like he had it together. By the time I had made it to high school, Tony had figured out every angle to skipping class and getting his absences excused. Well, so he said and tried. He was, remember, in the tenth grade at nineteen.

"Arr, that," he'd say dismissively when his age and status came up. "I was a really smart kid and they accelerated me through two grades, and

I'm where I belong now. I just wanted them to catch up."

We all said "Arr," after a while, all of us who hung out with Tony. We were like a band of pirates, crammed into a smoky car. Tony would say something asinine or absurd, and we'd answer "Arrr," in a sort of call-and-response. "Hey, check out that guy. That dude looks like a Mexican John Travolta."

"Arr."

"Like your mom."

"Arr."

"Or yours."

"Arr."

"Right on."

Tony first approached me when I was a sophomore. I would have been hanging out with him as a freshman, but we didn't know each other then. Then, I was still living in the shadow of a football cast by my older brother Dan, who was a varsity player as a sophomore. Dan was always big for his age. I was always small. I hated football. But I played it.

Anyhow, it was during a street game of football that I broke my arm and was demoted to "manager" of the football team, which was fine by me.

And it was when I had my arm in a cast that I smoked pot for the first time. It was with this set of twins, Chad and Corey, who owned a five-year-old red Ford Tempo. I was begrudgingly invited along to smoke a joint with these tennis-playing geeks one afternoon, after Tony had sold it to them for five bucks, though he'd only paid one. They were on the tennis team, juniors, and contemporary with my brother and sister, and I heard them talking about it. So I insinuated my way in by invoking my older brother's name, of whom Chad and Corey were clearly frightened. We drove away from school and pulled into a soon-to-be developed subdivision "circle," a cul-de-sac in the Brownsville Country Club. We parked in a dry, brown, borrowed seclusion, the overgrown and parched grass hiding us from every direction.

We could hear traffic and the strip mall nearby.

"Here, light this end," said Chad or Corey.

"No, you idiot, over here," responded Chad or Corey, taking it out of Chad or Corey's mouth and flipping it over to expose the exact replica of the other end.

"Aren't you supposed to wet it down or something?"

Me, definitely. I had seen Tony showing them how to light it, when they'd bought it.

"Here, like this," Tony had said, showing either Chad or Cory.

He licked his lips and made an "O" and then stuck the joint in his mouth, simulating one quick stroke of fellatio. I was about to comment on this correlation but appreciated instead the male sincerity of the ceremony and kept quiet.

"What? No. How? I mean, What do you mean?" said the other guy.

I think it was named "Jeff."

"I don't know—I saw some guy smoking it once, and he stuck it in his mouth and put spit on it to keep it from burning too quickly or something," I said.

"Forget that," said Chad or Corey, dismissing my concern.

"Just spark it up, dude," said Chad or Corey, the one who hadn't spoken earlier.

And then it went.

I watched him suck, suck, suck until the cherry was lit.

Then it was cough, cough, cough from the gagging fit.

Chad or Corey went next, and then he coughed and coughed.

The other guy, "Jeff," took his turn with the same result.

Then I got it. I tugged slowly, preparing to gag like I did on cigarettes, and tried to force myself not to swallow it down into my stomach, like I usually did when I pretended to smoke.

But I didn't gag.

So I tugged a bit more.

No gagging. More tugging.

Then a huge coughing fit.

"Ha, ha," said either Chad or Corey, and then he coughed until he was purple.

This went on until the joint was just an excuse of its old self, and then we all crammed into the car and drove to Sunrise Mall for a slice of pizza.

I wondered if I was finally a "teenager."

"Dude, are you high or what?" said either Chad or Corey through a wide grin, the one driving. "Dude, I'm feeling it!" said either Chad or Corey, in the passenger seat.

"Yeah, man; I think I'm high," said "Jeff," next to me.

Me, I wasn't so sure.

I think I felt something, but I wasn't certain. Studying myself in the reflection in the window. Glad they have air conditioning in the Tempo. Am I high? How do I know? I don't feel any different. I'm not giggly. Or am I? Maybe I just haven't heard anything funny. Maybe a joke is in order.

"Anyone know a joke?" I asked. I was thinking out loud.

"Dude, what are you talking about?" said either Chad or Corey, whoever wasn't driving.

"Nothing," I said and turned back to my reflection. How do stoned people feel, I wondered? How do you know you're high? Isn't something supposed to change? Aren't you supposed to feel any different?

"Hey, how do you know if you're high?" I asked. This brings the car down.

"Dude, if you have to ask, you aren't!" from the idiot next to me.

Wisdom from this "Jeff," in nightmarish experimental Nazi braces.

His retort brought on more laughter from the front seat.

Fuck's sake, I thought. The things you have to suffer to get a lift in this town.

I started thinking about being in this car and being so disparate from these kids. Man, you really can't tell the difference between these two guys in the front seat. What's that like? They're really just one person. One finishes the other's sentences. Halves of a single personality. That must be fucked up. Double the white guy. This other guy, "Jeff," next to me, he clearly doesn't like me. Stupid rich fucker. Must be British, with his teeth needing so much work. Should smash him in the mouth, with all that metal work. Would rip his mouth to hell in one punch. Ha. Just don't feel like it, though. Just kinda calm and shit. Jesus, what's that on the radio? These guys can't like Bon Jovi? Are they really listening to Jon Bon Jovi?

"Dude, are you listening to Bon Jovi?" I asked Chad or Corey, and Chad or Corey.

"Shit yeah, dude. That's the jams," said Chad. Or Corey.

That's fucked up. Grown boys listening to Bon Jovi. I thought only girls liked that stuff. Maybe Chad and Corey are gay. Would they be gay together? That's like masturbating, kind of. If you think about it. Having sex with yourself. In another body. I bet the Catholic Church has a tax for that; they're pretty on top of all sorts of loopholes, with sex. Man, this music sucks. I could go for some of the stuff Dan likes right now, you know? Maybe some Bad Company. Or the Scorpions. Or Cheech and Chong. Ha, ha. Cheech and Chong. I wish I could get high and maybe listen to that with no one bugging me about it so I could really study it. I like radio plays. That's when you're SUPPOSED to listen to it, you know, when you're high. Maybe that's what it's like to be an "adult," right? Be all in charge and shit. Just smoke some pot and play *Cheech & Chong's Greatest Hit*. Ha. But that's crap, man. I mean, it's just not clever, you know? Cheech just plays the stereotype, and they always go for the easy joke. It's dumb. For dumb people. But it's stoner shit. Stoners need reassurance that what they're doing is OK. That's why they listen to stoner music, like Pink Floyd: more for the validation, certainly not because it's any good.

"Hey, are we going to the mall?" I asked.

"Yeah," said Chad or Corey. "We're going to get a slice of pizza before we get back. I think Denise and those chicks are there, ha ha ha."

Denise and those chicks. Those are rich white tennis chicks, out of my league, I thought. I got nothing to do with them, maybe. They're better off with these guys. Though Denise looks like a pornographic fantasy, in her white miniskirts, in our biology class. Ha. "Biology" class.

"Hey, I don't think I got high," I said.

The car broke up laughing.

"No, I mean, what if I am high? How can I tell? I mean, how do I interact with like, you know, the public and shit?" I said. As an example of whom I meant, I poked the window with my fingertip.

"Dude, you're high," said Chad or Corey, the one driving.

So if one's driving, does the other one have to be there? Maybe one can't function without the other being around? Since they're part of the same egg? Anyhow, they all kinda look alike, anyway. White guys. They dress alike, wear the same haircut. The baseball hat turned backward in the same way.

"No, I don't think I am high," I said.

The car was still laughing around me.

We were parking. Chad or Corey turned the radio off, and it went quiet. The abrupt silence was suddenly suffocating, as I realized I had only a single dollar on me. One of the guys cleared his throat and then opened the door to spit out a viscous glob of something. I decided I didn't want to get out of the car. Didn't want to talk to anyone.

"Dude, I don't think I want be out there," I said to Chad or Corey. It started laughing, in unison.

"Hey, just get me a slice," I said, "The $1.10 special," and I handed him my dollar.

"Dude, your family's all poor," said Chad or Corey, and it started laughing again, with the other guy, "Jeff," laughing so hard that he was drooling. My humiliation was amplified by the marijuana. I was mortified and thoroughly certain I should do something about this. But yet, I was totally lethargic. Someone's head needs to get knocked in, I'd been told. At some point. But whose?

"What?" I asked. I felt my Dad say, *"No te déjes, Yunior!"* somewhere in my lower back. It's a slogan from the dictionary of macho: Don't give it up. Your honor. Your integrity. Your masculinity. Your sense of yourself. Your ass, mostly. *No tienes vergüenza?* That cocktail of shame and anger was back.

"Ha, ha," said Chad or Corey. "Nothing."

I missed something, I was sure. And now I was mad. But I didn't know why. *Me dejé*, I felt, somehow. Honor was besmirched.

"Just leave me your keys so I can listen to the radio," I said.

I can do without food. I've done it before. Wait; wasn't this something about a slice of pizza? What did that fucker say to me? Shit. When they were gone, I sorted through Chad and Corey's tape selection hidden under the armrest in the center console with my left hand, my right arm holding onto the handle over the door because it was swelling, in the cast, in the heat. They had Christian music, it looked like, Guns N' Roses' *Appetite for Destruction*, Def Leppard's *Pyromania*, and some Anne Murray. I played the second side of *Appetite for Destruction* but then remembered how much I secretly liked Anne Murray and played that next, thought about how much I didn't want to be around these guys, how I didn't want to be here. And then I saw them coming back, laughing, slugging each other all Chinese-eyed and inclusive, without pizza, and they all looked at me at the same time, in the car, and I looked back at them. I wish I could say that I felt somehow superior as they kept coming closer, but the look that crossed their faces as they registered me, in their car, waiting for the lift back to school, and how their faces all fell in unison, Chad and Corey and this guy "Jeff," how they looked at me like, *Oh, yeah. HIM*, I have to tell you, it made me feel very small, very Cheech, very dirty, and like I wished I could be stoned and stupid and guaranteed, just like them.

All the Pretty Ponies

Oscar Cásares

I won't try to convince you that two dollars a day was a lot of money to earn in 1972, though it was if you happened to be eight years old and had no money of your own because this was your first job. Saturday and Sunday, noon to sundown, we were hired to place little kids on Shetland ponies and guide them in a big loop around an empty field, which sat across the street from the Pancake House. One loop cost a quarter.

The four ponies—Red, JoJo, Happy, and Whitey—belonged to Mr. De la Rosa, who kept them in a corral just down the alley from his trailer home. My father had gotten me the job. A tick inspector for the USDA, he used a quarter horse to patrol the banks of the Rio Grande looking for any livestock that might cross over from Mexico. My father rode his horse five days a week, in all kinds of weather, even after his back surgery laid him out and it was a year before he could ride again. His work also involved issuing permits for livestock kept within the county, which is how he met Mr. De la Rosa, who was in seventies and retired, except for his pony business.

The best part of the job was when there weren't any customers and Mr. De la Rosa would leave to run an errand. It felt good to know he trusted us to watch his business for a few minutes, that he had that much confidence in us. Then again, he was leaving four ponies with four boys, none of us over the age of ten, and it was only a matter of time before we started acting our ages. After seeing who could get Red, the fastest of the bunch, to circle the field in less than thirty seconds, we'd moved on to trick riding. Balanced on his saddle, I managed to get around the loop standing on Happy, the brown-and-white pinto who clomped along with his eyes half shut. Later we took turns leapfrogging onto the saddle as we'd seen cowboys do on TV. But we were also smart enough to keep an eye out for the old man's green truck.

One night, as my father drove me home, I mentioned that I'd made it around the loop faster than all the other boys, thinking he might be impressed.

"That's not what the man is paying you for," he said, "to be playing games with his animals." He kept his eyes on the road.

"It wasn't just me," I said.

"You're the only who's in this car."

I felt stupid, not for what I had done but for telling him, for thinking he might understand that we were just having fun. I hadn't even mentioned the trick riding. It made me not want to tell him the good news, that Mr. De la Rosa had asked us to ride the ponies in the Charro Days parade. Then I remembered that my father, because of his work, already knew the ponies would be in the parade, along with all the other horses he'd signed permits for.

Everyone I knew had been in, or wanted to be in, the parade. Charro Days was the biggest, most special thing that happened in Brownsville, an annual celebration, since 1938, of our cultural ties with our sister city across the border, Matamoros. Like a second Christmas only two months after the first one, we couldn't wait for it to come around. Men and women, boys and girls, young and old, we showed up in thousands, many dressed up as the Mexican cowboy that the four-day festival was named after. Regardless of where you were from or how long you'd been here or how well you spoke Spanish or what your last name happened to be, it was the one time out of the year that everyone in Brownsville was Mexican. On the first day, city officials from Brownsville and Matamoros stood on their respective sides of the international bridge and, at the appropriate time, belted out a grito, the legendary call of the cowboy. The bridge then stayed open for everyone to pass back and forth and the party to continue on both sides of the river. Classes were canceled Thursday and Friday, kids performed traditional Mexican dances dressed as campesinos and señoritas, and the carnival came to town, which for most of us was about as close as we were going to get to a real amusement park.

I knew people who had been on floats in the parade but no one who had ridden a horse down the middle of the street. After the dancers, the marching bands, the Shriners honking their horns, and the politicians waving from the back of convertibles, it was the horsemen, los charros, who closed the parade. These charros were like the ones we'd seen on TV and up on the screen at the Grande Theatre, over on Washington, their images blazing across the screen and into our imaginations. These were the charros whom mothers would dress their children like every year, making sure to draw proper mustaches on their little boys. These were the charros whom fathers would lift their girls and boys to see as they passed in the parade, saying, "Someday that'll be you."

On the day we were to ride the ponies, we showed up two hours before the start of the parade and, together with the other riders and their horses, waited in a lot next to the stadium. Through the chain-link fence, I could see two pretty girls sitting on a float, also waiting. They posed for a last-minute photo, one of them adjusting her rebozo, the other fanning out the vibrant flowers embroidered across her china poblana skirt.

Mr. De la Rosa had bought us wool poncho vests, sombreros, and giant red bow ties that clipped onto our white shirts. He would be walking alongside us wearing the same outfit, but his white hair and brow-line glasses made him look more dignified, even debonair, as if he were only out for a stroll with his muchachos. The other horsemen, twenty or so of them, were dressed like real charros, with immaculate sombreros, silver spurs strapped to their botines, and embroidered pants and jackets, some adorned across the back with Mexico's iconic eagle and snake, others with fighting cocks. A few were dressed more modestly, with chaps and sheathed rifles that made them look like rancheros who had just pulled up to water their horses.

Most of these men knew my father, who was also there, in his work clothes, checking the final animal permits. That morning, over breakfast, he had said he needed to take me to the farm where he kept his horse. When I asked him why, he said that someday I would be riding his horse in the parade. "You should start practicing now," he said. He looked at me, and all I could do was nod. To ride a real horse was something altogether different, something I hadn't considered or thought I might be ready for.

It was time to line up for the parade. One of the charros decided that the four boys riding the ponies and Mr. De la Rosa should be the first to exit the gate, followed then by the three horsemen holding up the Mexican, Texas, and American flags, then the rest of the charros. Today I would be leading the men; maybe next year or the year after, when I turned ten, I would be holding a flag.

But as we turned us toward the main gate, the wail of a police siren spooked Red, and I was thrown backward. I had been holding the reins loosely, and now they slid down, past the edge of the saddle and beyond my reach. My right boot tangled with the stirrup before I landed on my back in the dirt. I looked up in time to see Red galloping away.

At the far end of lot, my father raised his hands chest high and calmed the pony, until it trotted and finally came up to him. The charros and I watched as my father clutched the reins and walked toward us, his gait favoring his left side. He stopped in front of me.

"Are you going to stand up?" he said. He wasn't reaching down to pick me up; he was only asking.

Nothing felt broken. The sombrero had probably softened my fall. What I felt was not pain. It was the shock of being thrown. It was the shame of lying in the dirt with my poncho vest and red bow tie that had managed to stay on as the men, on their horses, loomed over me. It was not knowing if they wanted to laugh at me and weren't, out of respect for my father. A sob caught in my throat and I felt myself clenching my teeth as if I had a bit in my mouth.

"¿Entonces qué?" he said.

He held out the reins and waited for me to dust myself off. And then I rode out into the parade, the men not far behind.

Nobody's Favorite

Lorraine M. López

I was born an in-between child to a family from an in-between culture at an especially in-between time. Though bilingual and bicultural Hispanos de Nuevo México, my parents tilted more toward the New World than the Old. Our ancestors immigrated from the Iberian Peninsula to Veracruz and then up from Mexico into what is now the American Southwest prior to the founding of Jamestown. My mother and father, Espiridiana and Espiridion López, considered their forbearers to be Americans from a time before America existed, and though they cherry-picked from New and Old World traditions, they dove into US culture with gusto. Having witnessed the corporal punishment of classmates for speaking Spanish as schoolchildren, they determined that ours would be an English-speaking home and used their first language as "adults-only" code. In terms of diet, though, Mexico prevailed. My mother rolled tortillas by hand; she roasted, peeled, and pureed mouth-excoriating peppers; she prepared frijoles, enchiladas, and caldos on a regular basis. Even so, cultural patterns such as machismo and marianismo failed to work for my assertive mother and somewhat passive father, making my parents outliers in the extended family, distant beyond the fact that they relocated from New Mexico to California before their first child was born in the 1950s.

The second of their five children, I imagine my birth occurred for my parents as an afterthought, somewhat anticlimactic to the brilliant idea that was my older sister Debbie, whose dimply smile and easy charm cast into sharp relief my unspectacular looks and woeful nature. My arrival also provided something of a throat-clearing preamble to the song of joy that was my brother Kenny, my mother's only son and practically the whole point of having children as far as she was concerned. My father, a man ahead of his time in many ways, claimed he wanted only daughters. After Kenny, he was rewarded with two more: Frances, his favorite, and Sylvia, the youngest, la consentida—everybody's darling. In our extended family, especially on the paternal side, naming favorites proved a common practice, so my father made no secret of his preference. My mother diplomatically insisted we were equally special to her, and her pants should have burst into flames with that one. From her moony gazes to the honeyed tones she used to address my brother, anyone could tell she was lying.

My mother also hero-worshipped her firstborn, the tastemaker in our household. After purchasing an orange velveteen chair that caused my older sister to wince, Mom hesitated to buy as much as a dishtowel without first consulting Debbie. My father, far more obvious with his favoritism, often announced at the dinner table that he had "only one girl," whereupon my younger sister Frances would wriggle with delight. A chronic teaser, Dad often tried to make us jealous of one another. Following Debbie's lead, I ignored these mealtime proclamations, but secretly, I was glad not to be his only girl. Yuck. That he failed to get a rise out of me no doubt put him off. Plus, it's hard to warm to a contemptuous child, and I, like my mother, would send many severe looks his way.

Both of my parents and Debbie heaped adoration on the baby of the family. At four or five, Sylvia would slip on a plastic grass skirt left over from Halloween and clip a single strand of pink yarn, about a yard or so, to the top of her pixie-do (for her "long, lustrous hair"). Then she'd bust a move, something between the hula and a somnambulist's shuffle, while singing "*Hawaii, Mexico, Hawaii, Mexico . . .*" at full volume. At this, my mother, father, and Debbie would beam and beat hands together as if Sylvia had just delivered a virtuoso performance at the Hollywood Bowl. "Oh, come on," I'd say. "That's not even a song. She's just shouting the names of two places that aren't even next to each other."

Sylvia, in fact, took on the role of family pet literally, and when not entertaining us in her grass skirt, she pretended to be a dog, crawling around, panting, barking, and wagging her behind (another length of pink yarn—her tail—pinned to the waistband of her shorts). My mother would sometimes place a bowl of water on the floor for her to lap at, and my dad would fling Lincoln Logs for her to fetch. "Good doggy," Debbie would say, patting Sylvia's head. "You are *not* a dog," I'd tell her, worried that this little routine of hers might delay our acquisition of an actual dog, or even a cat. When we finally got a puppy, I was meanly pleased that the noisy nipper terrified my youngest sister, who quickly gave up her canine act.

In those days, I was nobody's favorite, not even my own. "Nobody likes me," I often complained, meaning that no one liked me more than anyone else. "I like you," my mother would say. "You have to like me," I'd tell her. "You're my mother." She would shake her head at this. "I have to love you, not like you, but I do. I like you a lot." No way did I believe that. Back then, I must have had some idea of what I had to do—such as behave in a friendly, rather than sullen, way—to gain favor, but I imagine my younger self, much like my older self, performing a cost-benefit analysis and wondering how being liked, even being favored, could be worth the effort it would take. The grown son of one of my mother's friends once suggested I try smiling. "It won't kill you," he said, and I thrust my tongue out at him.

Still, sometimes it stung that I failed to come first with those I liked best, namely Debbie and especially my mother, who was perfect for me. My older sister now insists our mother was too overbearing, and no one in my family can dispute that Mom coddled Kenny, delaying his maturation. My father's "only girl," Frances often laments the comparative lack of maternal attention she received, and my youngest sister, like Kenny, has been compromised in agency because of an excess of mother love. By contrast, my relationship with my mother landed squarely in the Goldilocks zone. Not too hot, or too cold—it was just right. In fact, she gave me the best gift any parent can offer a burgeoning writer: she left me alone.

Whatever I wanted to do, I could do, provided it was not dangerous. If I wanted to write a play and bully my younger siblings into performing it, fine, so long as no one cried. (Someone always cried.) If I wanted to start a newspaper out on the sunporch and force Kenny, Frances, and Sylvia to work as scribes and then paperboys, well, why not? (More crying.) If I wanted to keep a hen I rescued/abducted from the takeout fried chicken place near school, that was okay with her, too, but again, only on the sunporch. (No live poultry in the house!) For what I had no desire to do, such as household chores, she had a different approach. She would listen carefully to my protests, nodding when my points were compelling. In the end, I still had to wash dishes, dust, sweep, or whatever, but at least my mother considered my arguments, sometimes praising these and urging me to consider a career in law.

After an unpromising start, I also doted on my older sister. According to family lore, on the day I was baptized—gowned in white lace and napping—Debbie leaned into the bassinette to bite my forearm hard enough to break the skin. I no doubt released earsplitting shrieks, and my sister was likely punished, but that was the extent of her antipathy toward me. Barely nineteen months old, my older sister experienced sibling rivalry, acted swiftly, and was done with it. From that time on, we became steadfast allies. Though I am not her favorite (she still adores Sylvia), we continue to share a profound friendship. "In cahoots," our mother would say of us, often frustrated by how we conspired with one another. "Thick as thieves," she called us. Since I was the opposite of sociable, this mostly meant my older sister's handling of our shared household tasks and my alibiing Debbie's made-up excuses for staying out late with friends or going where she wasn't supposed to be. I grew adept at reciting flat-out lies like biblical verses, learning early on what I stress with emerging writers I now teach: details convince. I also knew when to keep my mouth shut. La Tapadera, my mother would call me for holding in my sister's secrets like steam trapped under the heavy lid of a pot.

Nicknames, like favorites, were also prevalent in our extended family, especially on my father's side. My uncle Manuel, with his delectable tawny skin, was called Caramelo by his siblings; a nearsighted aunt became La Ciega; and my father, notorious for following his parents' orders, was known as El Soldado, long before he enlisted in the US Army. Though nobody's favorite and often overlooked, I had not one, but two nicknames. My mother, opposed to nicknaming on principle, granted herself an exception when angry enough to call me La Tapadera. My paternal aunts and uncles gave me my second nickname: La Lloronita. When I discovered this, I, of course, wailed. "I am *not* a crybaby!"

Once, after playing outside on my grandparents' farm in New Mexico, I noticed raised red blotches on the arms and legs of my siblings and cousins. I checked my own limbs and found them unblemished. When I asked a cousin about this, she explained about mosquito bites. Mosquitoes hatched in the nearby ditch had feasted on her and the others, but not a one touched me. Eyes brimming, I stormed off to find my mother, who was chatting with my aunts in the front room. Mom held me close, asked what was wrong. I held up an arm to show my clear skin. "Not even mosquitoes like me," I sobbed. (Years later, in Belize, I learned these aren't the only insects to take a pass on my flesh. I was sitting on a dock with my husband one afternoon, both of us dipping toes in the ocean, when he lunged to his feet and bolted away from the water, a filmy cape of flying insects trailing after him. Sand flies, it seems, don't care for me either.)

That my mother didn't spank me on the spot for crying over *not* being bitten by mosquitoes shows impressive restraint. Sometimes I long to whoosh back through the tunnel of time just to smack my own younger self. But my mother didn't believe corporal punishment to be humane or effective, and she never would have given my father's family the satisfaction of seeing her strike her child, no matter how obnoxious that child might be. My mother read Dr. Spock and A.S. Neill's *Summerhill: A Radical Approach to Child Rearing*; she subscribed to and carefully pored over *Parents* magazine. She concerned herself with our feelings, our self-image, long before self-image was a thing. Only now, when I talk to friends my age about their experiences growing up, do I realize that I had been raised in something quite rare in the mid-twentieth century for any cultural group—a child-centered home.

Despite the coincidence that they shared masculine and feminine forms of the same peculiar first name, my parents had very little in common. One of their few points of connection was their belief that children deserved affection and respect as much as food and shelter. Because of this, they sometimes faced criticism from the extended family for treating us preciously. During one visit, an aunt chided my mother for preventing our paternal grandmother from scouring us with brown soap and a stiff brush in a zinc tub—abuela's practice when grandchildren stayed overnight. But my mother's protest emboldened Uncle Odelio, a rancher married to my father's youngest sister, likewise to refuse having his daughters undergo that ordeal, and our abuela's zinc tub was soon retired to the relief of my cousins, many of whom credit my mother for this. To this day, my oldest cousin Margaret's face softens when she shares her memories of Mom. "No one ever asked me my favorite color or who my best friend was until she came to the house," she says. When still living in New Mexico as a young bride, my mother would take Margaret in her arms and hold her in her lap while talking with her. My cousin, raised by our zinc-tub-child-washing grandmother, claims she will never forget that.

A child-centered home meant that we were more democratic than most families, and since youngsters formed the majority, our entertainment and activities were usually geared to what appealed to us. Once a visiting uncle had the audacity to switch channels to watch a wrestling match, flabbergasting us. Did he not know that we children ruled the television? We complained to our mother, and she said that we had to accommodate our uncle, a guest in our house. When my cousin Benny stayed overnight with us one time, he casually tossed me his keys after supper and told me to get his bags from his car. This plunged me into a deep quandary. In our house, children were not servants to be ordered about. I couldn't bring myself to violate the child-centeredness of our home to act as bellhop for my cousin, barely an adult himself. What to do? If I mentioned this to Debbie, the girl-hero would offer to help me with the luggage. So, instead, I told my mother, and she, in turn, sent my father to bring in Benny's suitcase and shaving kit.

Only one aunt, my father's older sister Luguarda, lived near us in Los Angeles, while the rest of the extended family resided in New Mexico, in and around the small hub city Belen. Like her zinc-tub-wielding mother, Luguarda had a passion for deep cleaning. Though tactful with my parents, she was appalled by the state of our home. To be fair to us, we met the basic standards of good hygiene. We washed dishes right after meals, took out trash regularly, and made beds daily, but clothes, shoes, toys, and books were usually strewn about. Floors often went unswept, carpets unvacuumed, woodwork unpolished; and our large dining room table served as homework central, its mahogany surface piled with notebooks, folders, papers, glue, scissors, crayons, and pencils. We would clear off the clutter for holiday dinners involving guests and eat all other meals at the kitchen table. On the rare occasions that our parents went out and our aunt was enlisted to babysit, she would wander through the house after they departed, muttering, "Filth, filth, everywhere I look," and then set us all to cleaning.

Luguarda had no children of her own, so the concept of a child-centered home would have made little sense to her. Even so, she loved us. I have many pleasant memories of just the two of us riding the city bus down-town for lunch at Clifton's Cafeteria followed by a movie at the discounted matinee price. She appreciated that when I was not blubbering over nothing, I could be a quiet, watchful child, one who listened intently to her many stories, and she was a gifted storyteller. The main thematic question she explored in her tales: Why are people so stupid? This yielded many narrative variations for my aunt and later provided inspiration for the stories I now write. For the longest time, I believed I was my aunt's favorite, but when I mentioned my one-on-one outings with her to my sisters and brother, they chimed in with similar recollections. Somehow, she carved the time to take each of us out on our own, and I, no doubt in a book-induced trance, just failed to notice this.

Like my aunt, my parents soon tapped into stories as a way to keep me quiet and engaged. Before long, they discovered that they could toss a pad of paper and a few pencils my way, the way zookeepers might heave a goat's carcass into a roaring lion's den, and I would fall silent for hours. They also ferreted out that I loved the library—maybe from the way I would charge through the house, whooping as though I had won the lottery, whenever it was time to return and check out books. That, too, became a carrot to dangle in getting me to behave. When I was six, I managed to sign my name in cursive to acquire my first library card, an unforgettably thrilling moment for me. "This is the happiest day of my life," I said, startling the librarian who handed me the small rectangle of card stock.

A graduate student in psychology once told me that second-born chil-dren, often liberated from the responsibilities that hobble their firstborn siblings, have more freedom to explore artistic impulses. But my Internet searches have yet to support this. Instead, I find links to "second-child syndrome" and many articles on rebelliousness and dysfunction in sec-ond and middle children. Still, I like to think being one of three middle children in a largish Chicanx family benefited me, and not just as a writer—but when I was young, I failed to see this and would gripe about going unnoticed. It was not fun to have to share Christmas gifts with my siblings because relatives forgot all about me and had to scribble my name onto gift tags affixed to presents for my brother and sisters. Stupid people, as my aunt might say. Can't they count? How are four gifts supposed to work for five children?

As with my lack of appeal to mosquitoes, I often construed what advantages I had to be disadvantages. Such was the case with the night terrors experienced by Debbie and Frances, both of whom would take turns, every once in a while, waking in the middle of the night, shrieking and drenched in sweat. My mother and father would rush to the bedside of whoever's turn it was, to comfort and calm that sister down. The ruckus usually disturbed my sleep. As I gazed at the cozy tableau of my parents hovering over one distraught sister or the other, I would wonder why I never had dreams that terrible. Had I expressed such negativity during my waking hours that no dark thoughts remained to disturb my sleep? Some nights, before dozing off, I would summon the scariest images I could muster in the hopes of achieving a horrendous nightmare, but then, I'd drift off and dream of talking to penguins or running into Ringo Starr at Safeway. Often I would wake up smiling, even chuckling to myself. One night, I really applied myself and managed to dream of being kidnapped by pirates who stuffed me into a gunnysack. I tried to scream, but my abductors jammed a warm, buttery tortilla in my mouth. My kidnapping nightmare morphed into a tortilla dream. Instead of screaming in the middle of the night, I woke up hungry in the morning.

Before long, weepiness proved unsustainable for me. It was exhausting and caused my forehead to ache. By the time I started first grade, my crying gave way to silence outside my home. With my family, I was chatty and opinionated, annoyingly so, but on my own among people I didn't know well, I rarely said a word, making me all the more forgettable. My lack of speech perplexed my elementary school teachers, and some noted this as low participation on my report cards. One even called my mother in for a conference to discuss the problem. My mother, an educator herself, wasn't too concerned. She trusted that I would "come out of the shell," as she put it, when ready, and probably felt my teachers should enjoy themselves until that time came.

Gradually, I began to see the value in flying under the radar, an idea that first occurred to me when I was young enough for naps, though— slow learner that I am—I failed to take advantage of it for years. One summer afternoon, my mother put Debbie, Kenny, and me down for a rest, but instead of sleeping, we opened the bedroom window and climbed out to play in the backyard. Our voices and laughter no doubt tipped off our mother, who soon appeared to herd us into the house. Though opposed to corporal punishment, she must have been especially furious because she said, "I am going to spank each one of you. Who wants to go first?"

"Not me," I said, thinking, now there's a silly question.

Debbie, my sister-hero, ponied up to get it over with, and Kenny, sobbing theatrically, as if totally unaware that my mother would do no more than play patty cakes on her little angel's buttocks, agreed to be spanked after Debbie. I may not have been more than five at the time, but I was savvy enough to realize that my mother would be somewhat tired and much less fierce after whipping two kids, and besides, anything could happen—earthquake, atomic bomb, Judgment Day—between the first spanking and the third. Sure enough, after my mother finished love-tapping Kenny's behind, the phone rang. She spent a good long while on that call. By the time she hung up, Debbie and Kenny had cried themselves to sleep, so I, too, pretended to be conked out. Through the lashes of my mostly closed eyes, I watched my mother check in on us and then tiptoe out of the bedroom. Forgotten again. Huzzah!

Yes, sometimes it was good to be overlooked, and though it pained me not to be my mother's special pet, I was glad not to be her least favorite. That role fell to my father, whom she regarded as a sixth child—the ne'er-do-well, the worst of the bunch, and a tremendous pain in the nalgas. In the early years of my parents' marriage, before we were born, our mother appointed herself head of the household. There were indicators that—apart from idolizing her only son—she would resist marianismo and reject the role of submissive wife even before they wed. My father, a corporal in the US Army, proposed to her prior to deployment to Europe during World War II. During most of their engagement, they traded letters while he was overseas, and in one, my mother mentioned planning to read *Forever Amber*, a best seller considered racy at the time. When my father wrote back, forbidding her to read such a book, she replied with a one-sentence letter: *Ha ha, very funny!* She had already finished the novel by that time and claimed she was tempted to read it again out of spite, but the story wasn't very good or all that racy.

Soon after the war ended, they married, and my mother quickly pried my father from his brothers/drinking buddies in New Mexico to live in California, where he soon found new drinking buddies. She was certain that her future children would gain a better education and access more opportunities in Los Angeles than in the dusty railroad city that was

Belen. After the five of us were born, she enrolled in classes at UCLA to become a teacher. My mother then taught at a parochial school, and though she never earned as much as my father, she handled household finances. From educational decisions to discipline, she also put herself in charge of all matters concerning us. Mom never said, "Just you wait until your father gets home." If she had, we might have sighed with relief, as Dad would more likely be amused than offended by our transgressions. Besides, he was usually up to much worse, his behavior far more irritating to my mother than anything we could dream of doing.

The conflict that defined my parents' marriage split our household, creating a divide in which Debbie and I found ourselves on opposite sides. She was a loyal Dadian and I, a staunch Mamista. We had no names for these factions back then, and I have only recently begun to consider our former alliances this way. The Mamistas included me and my brother Kenny, both of us utterly devoted to our mother's cause. As Mamistas, we valued order and responsibility. We expected people to show consideration by not returning from work drunk and then passing out on the living room couch. We also wanted others, namely our mother, not to have to drive in rush hour traffic to the Water and Power on Flower and Ducommun in downtown L.A. to pick up a spouse from work on days when said spouse would not show up because he was drinking in some bar, usually the Dugout near Dodger Stadium, with friends. We, personally, preferred not to sit in a hot station wagon waiting fruitlessly with our mother for up to an hour before heading home, again through traffic, enduring a stream of strangled curses—*como fregado . . . pinche idiota . . . qué mierda . . . debería ir al infierno*—along the way. We especially had no desire to be awakened late at night by un pendejo boracho staggering into the house, and we had little stomach for the slanging that would ensue the next morning.

The Dadians—Debbie and Frances, that is—failed to share this perspective. They supported the belief that people, especially adults who provided for the household, were entitled to do as they pleased and that they did not deserve to be harangued for this. The Dadians, though aggrieved by our mother's tirades, would—like Dad himself—wisely remain silent, sympathetic expressions stamped on their faces during these, while Mamistas would cast accusatory looks at our father, though, truth be told, we felt a bit sorry for him, too. Sylvia sided with neither the Mamistas nor the Dadians. Like Switzerland, she remained neutral, steadfastly pretending to be too young to understand what was going on.

After skirmishes, the two factions would rally, among ourselves. In the Mamista camp, my brother and I would counsel our mother not to put up with our father's badness. Kenny, as a young child, would often plead with my mother to "dee-voh-wiss Daddy and may-wee me." While I scoffed at his proposal as ridiculous, and not even legal, I would encourage Mom at least to consider separating from my father, taking me, of course, along with her. Although my father, like my mother, largely left me alone, I was not a fan, and I much enjoyed the sense of calm that blanketed the household when he was out and Mom was not screaming at him.

My father would not talk back to my mother or say anything against her to us. On top of being slow to anger, he truly respected her. One of the few things that managed to irk him was when we would carelessly use the female singular pronoun to refer to our mother. "*She,*" he'd say. "You do not call your mother *she.*" Most days, he would come straight home from work, sober, and pile us into the car to head for the park in order to give our mother a break. On weekends, he'd haul us to the zoo, the beach, or a museum to grant her even more time on her own. We'd return to find the house still wrecked and Mom with a book; she would spend those days reading—not only child-rearing books, but novels by Chaim Potok, Taylor Caldwell, and Irving Stone. Our father also spared her the heavy housework. He would scrub the floors with steaming water and Pine-Sol. He washed windows, swept steps, and hosed down the front porch. Nowadays when I see a man rocking a Baby Bjorn or pushing a stroller, I think, *what a piker.* Dad could manage all five of us on outings, without any form of child conveyance.

Nevertheless, I remained a committed Mamista for years; nothing could sway me to take his side, at least not until my mother's heart surgery, after which my father became her overnight and weekend caregiver, scarcely sleeping yet still working full time for much-needed medical benefits. I was married by then, working and taking classes to earn a teaching credential. Only when I spent the night to spell my father did I discover how hard it was to care for Mom and make her as comfortable as possible. In her last months, after diabetes claimed both her legs, we all swooped in to help. Debbie, though she had children of her own, might as well have moved back home during that time; she was there nearly every day. Yet our father continued shouldering most of the work, tenderly nursing my mother until her death. I began calling him *dear Dad*, in an un-ironic way, and once I jokingly told him, "You know what? You're *my* favorite. My favorite father." He looked away, nodded. "Yeah," he said. "I know that."

My mother, my father, my beloved aunt Luguarda—all three are now gone. Only one of my family favorites remains: Debbie, my sister-hero. She and Sylvia are now social workers for the same agency in Los Angeles, often channeling our mother to comfort the neglected and abused children they interview. An elementary school teacher with three sons, Kenny hasn't been the only male in his household for over twenty years. Frances works in banking in Northern California. Like Debbie and Sylvia, she and I have grown quite close over the years. This past spring, we took a trip to Oregon and had a fine time together, with minimal squabbling.

While in Portland, as we strolled through the Lan Su Chinese Garden, Frances reminded me of when I moved in with a boyfriend soon after graduating from high school. "That really upset Dad, remember?" she said. "He didn't speak to you for a year."

"Really?" I said. "A whole year?" Back then, my mother had been so offended by my moving-out plans that she insisted I accompany her to the depot to pick up relatives who would be arriving for my graduation, so I could tell them myself that I would soon be "living in sin." I said something like, "Sure, no problem." She called me a sinvergüenza and drove out on her own to the depot. During that visit, we never mentioned living arrangements for my first year of college, and Mom got over her disappointment with me. *This* I remember keenly. Decades later, among the lotus trees and jasmine with Frances, I had little recollection of my father's reaction.

She paused on the path to give me a moist-eyed, searching look. "That must have hurt."

"Some things can be pretty hurtful," I said, aware of how his silence would have deeply wounded her. Had it registered, such shunning might even have caused me some distress. But I have my doubts. Since we shared no special fondness for one another, my father's cold-shouldering barely rippled in my consciousness. That I was unfavored rendered me immune, even oblivious to his disfavor.

(Or else, I am truly La Tapadera, a lid too heavy for lifting to see what might be bubbling in the pot.)

While my parents, my aunt, and my siblings provided a solid platform for me to construct myself as a person, as a writer, I now see being nobody's favorite as another contributing factor. In fact, this granted me resilience, some imperviousness to rejection essential to the writing life. Critic Ralph E. Rodriguez points out that marginalization does not have to be an unproductive state for an author. The background is not necessarily a site of degradation, as it offers distance necessary for a more comprehensive viewpoint. That is to say, I am certain that I perceived much more from the sidelines than would have been visible to me in the limelight's glare. Being overlooked and sometimes forgotten altogether endowed me with the freedom to lose myself in stories I read and find myself again in those I write. So let Kenny endlessly gleam as the apple of my mother's eye, Frances always remain my father's only daughter, Debbie forever everyone's Super Girl, and Sylvia the perennial family pet. I—La Lloronita, La Tapadera—now embrace my dearth of cuteness and low-level charisma, as surely these have been among of my greatest gifts.

Coda

I sometimes volunteer at the Greyhound Bus station with a group that welcomes Central American immigrants in transit, awaiting court hearings to determine whether they can remain in this country for humanitarian reasons. We decipher tickets to make sure travelers transfer to the right buses, hand out snacks and bottled water, and offer toys to their children. Recently, I worked the station alongside a co-volunteer named Ana. We both interacted with one young girl heading north with her father, providing her fruit and a granola bar, along with a coloring book and box of crayons. Just before getting on the bus, she raced over to Ana, wagging a cell phone with a cracked screen. She took a few selfies with Ana and gave the phone to me. At first, I thought she wanted a selfie with me, but I should know the story of my life by now. She had changed the setting, so I could photograph her with Ana from a different angle. I snapped a couple of pictures and handed the phone back. After reclaiming it, she flung arms around Ana—one last hug before rushing off to board the bus.

Elote Man

David Dominguez

I stomped down the gutter with shovel in hand. I crushed leaves, aluminum cans, and water bottles with my Thorogood Wellingtons as I removed sod along the curb of my new house. Somewhere under the grass there was a leaky pipe, and the lawn along my tree-lined street yellowed as the summer heat hovered above the San Joaquin Valley. My pride wouldn't let me ask any of the gardeners working up and down my neighborhood for a little help. So no time for road trips to the beach. No bucket teeming with cracked crab. No beer to wash it gloriously down. I held my breath and said a prayer each time I hit a rock with the shovel because I feared it might be the PVC pipe. But in the back of my mind, I enjoyed the extra trips to Home Depot and even saw a maintained sprinkler system as a mark of manhood. No professional gardener would touch my yard.

Finally, I had unearthed thirty feet of pipe. More worry filled my heart as I asked myself whether that was a city waterworks employee watching from that nondescript pickup parked at the end of the block. Had a neighbor ratted? Who needed the mailman to deliver a fine? A cold slap for using the water on the wrong day of the week. "Whatever," I said aloud. "I'm my own man," I exclaimed and turned on the sprinkler line. Muddy water filled the trench, and I couldn't see the leaks. I turned off the line and fell to my knees on the curb, winced when I landed on a pebble, and said another prayer as the dirt soaked up the water. I took out my handkerchief from my back pocket—a blue handkerchief with white stars—wiped my forehead and peered into the tree branches above my head. Squirrels leaped from branch to branch deftly as they scurried toward completing their chores. Dried leaves fell on my head. "Whatever. I'm my own man," I shouted at them. "I've got it all under control," I yelled as I shook my fist at them.

With my hands, I scooped water out of the trench and finally ran back to the valve and shut it. I walked up and down the curb using the tip of my shovel to remove leaves, roots, and gravel from the trench as the earth soaked up the water. The pipe was cracked in several places, especially around the sprinkler heads, so I took out the Rhodia 3" by 4" tablet I keep in my back pocket for such occasions and started my Home Depot shopping list with a Pilot Metropolitan fountain pen in the chrome finish—also kept in my back pocket. As I wrote down *pipe, joints, cement,* and *pipe saw* in my best cursive handwriting, a neighbor I had yet to meet pulled up beside me. She looked me up and down, rolled up her window a few inches and said, "Hey, how much do you charge?"

"Excuse me?"

"How much do you charge to mow lawns?"

"I don't charge anything. I live here."

"Oh, sorry, I just assumed."

Above my head, the squirrels laughed at me and jumped from tree to tree. More dust and bits of dried leaves fell in my face as I looked up through the splintering sunlight and sneezed. *How much do I charge? What the heck?* I mumbled as I fell to my knees and extended the tape measure down the length of the pipe and along the curb, and as I measured the pipe and made my notes with the Pilot, I thought about my dad. I thought about the many weekends we spent working together in the yard. . . .

I remembered the time he showed me how to use the red-and-yellow McLane edger. First he handed me his key ring, showed me which key to use, and said, "Open the shed and take out the gasoline can and the edger." I took the key ring, still warm from his pocket, unlocked the deadbolt, and opened the shed. Above my head, I saw wasps crawl in and out of their nest between the shed's 2' by 4' frame and the corrugated steel roof. I repeated my father's words—*gasoline can, edger*—and feared nothing. "I'll take that, Son," he said and pointed at the gasoline can. "You bring the edger to the driveway." We walked through the gate. Me first. My dad second. Our stride and the sway of our shoulders falling in perfect unison among the shadows of the magnolia branches. When we reached the driveway, Dad unscrewed the gasoline tank and the gasoline can. Both were empty. "Come on," he said. "Bring the can. Tighten the nozzle back up. We need to fill it across the street. Here is a dollar. You give it to the attendant when we get there." I followed my dad down the street. I expected to cross at the light. Instead, we jaywalked. "Get ready," he said, and when we crossed, our strides were long and slow. I felt like a man at work.

"We need gasoline," I said to the attendant.

"Okay," he said and winked.

"You want to fill it?" Dad asked.

"Yes," I said.

"Then unscrew the gasoline can, take the nozzle off the pump, jam it in there, and fill it up. Be careful. Try not to spill it."

I filled the can three-quarters full, slowed down the flow of the gasoline, and when it was completely filled, tapped the spout against the can and watched the last few drops trickle into the can.

"All right, good job. Put it back on the pump. You want a Pepsi?"

We crossed the street. I felt one gallon of gasoline pull at my shoulder, bang against my leg, and smash the insides of my fingers. But I didn't care. I was jaywalking and drinking a Pepsi with my dad.

In the driveway, I popped open the vent cap, unscrewed the nozzle, pulled it out of the can, flipped it, and screwed it back onto the can. "Here, let me help you, Son," my dad said. He unscrewed the edger's gasoline cap and helped guide the nozzle into the tank as my ten-year-old body strained against the weight of the fuel. Once I had filled the tank, I put down the can, unscrewed the nozzle, turned it upside down, and screwed it back into the can. Then, I closed the vent cap.

My dad nodded *good job* and said, "Remember, that blade will slice off your foot."

I looked at him with all the courage a ten-year-old could muster and said, "I understand, Dad."

"Ok, then, stand behind it and pull the cord. You can do it, Son." I could smell the yard work in his orange T-shirt. I loved that smell, and I longed to smell like that too. "You can do it, Son." I leaned forward and twisted my shoulder 180 degrees and pulled my elbow back as far as I could, and the edger started right up. "Ok, now you push in the choke and open the throttle," he said pointing to the red throttle lever. "To lower the blade, you release this lever here, and then, you lower the blade." Puffs of smoke rose above the Briggs and Stratton, and I inhaled the smell of the gasoline and wiped my forehead, and said, "Okay, Dad."

"You'll need a pair of pliers to turn it off, so here, put these in your back pocket. Those pliers belonged to your Grandpa." I put the pliers in my back pocket and watched my dad lower the blade and edge the lawn along the driveway. Orange sparks flew into the sky and hovered among the gnats.

"Dad?"

"Yes, Son." Dad raised the blade and closed the throttle so we could hear each other talk.

"Mom said you two worked in the fields when you were younger than me and that you picked cotton and grapes and that at the end of the day you gave the money to my grandparents so they could buy beans, rice, and flour. She said sometimes all you did was gnaw on bones or an old tortilla and that there was no allowance. Is that true?"

Dad laughed and said, "Yes. But don't forget that we only got one pair of shoes a year and that if we jumped in a ditch and they were washed away, we were out of luck and had to make shoes with twine and cardboard."

"Why did you do that?"

"Do what?"

"Work in the fields when you were younger than me?"

"I had to help my family, so I did what I had to do."

"Am I helping my family?"

"Yes you are, Son."

"How?"

"Well, you are helping dear old dad clean up the front yard," he said and pinched my cheek between his thumb and index finger.

I nodded, opened the throttle, lowered the blade, pushed the edger, and watched the orange sparks fly off the blade. Pride filled my heart as I said to myself, *I gotta do what I gotta do.*

After I finished my notes, I clipped my tape measure to my belt and slipped the Metropolitan and the Rhodia tablet into my back pocket. I got into my truck and headed for Home Depot. At the first red light, I stopped beside a landscaper with an orange water cooler strapped to the back of his truck. I rolled down my window because I wanted to hear Vicente Fernandèz sing from the cab and waited for my moment to join the performance as if I were a mariachi singer:

Con dinero

Y sin dinero

Yo hago siempre

Lo que quiero

Y mi palabra es la ley. . . .

The gardeners nodded at me, and I nodded back as the light turned green. *See there*, I said to myself, *I'm a real Mexican*, and felt good about myself as I wheeled a cart into Home Depot and loaded it with supplies. I grabbed a bottle of Pellegrino sparkling water from a fridge and a bag of Flamin' Hot Cheetos from a wire rack and thought, *See there. Spicy Cheetos with Lime. I'm a real Mexican taking care of business. Maybe I'll install sprinklers on the side. Why not?* My legs felt sore, so I tried to shake out the stiffness, but when my knees started to click and grind, I felt a little nauseated and longed for my other work—reading and writing at my desk.

As I stood in line, I listened to the cashier speak to all the Mexicans in front of me in Spanish. I heard accents from northern Mexico, and I heard accents from Mexico City. And as I waited my turn to pay for my pipe, joints, saw, and cement, I gathered together all the words that shaped my Spanish vocabulary. I gathered them together as if they were family members I saw once every ten years, great uncles and aunts I longed to hold as if holding them might link me to my ancestors now that my grandparents had passed. I practiced conjugating *estar* because that verb, my reliable friend, along with a gerund, always helped me get by. . . .

"Qué haces?"

"Estoy trabajando."

"Ándale pues."

But instead of speaking to me in Spanish, the cashier spoke to me in English as she ran the bottle of Pellegrino across the scanner.

"How are you, Sir?"

"I'm fine. Thank you."

"Good. Have a wonderful day."

And there you go. This college-aged girl with tattoos up and down her arms, a ring through her septum, and good manners had figured me out in a flash. Was it the spicy Cheetos with lime? I felt as if I had been deprived of my identity. Should I have grabbed the pork rinds? The Funions? The Ruffles Queso? I should have grabbed the Ruffles Queso. I felt the obreros staring against my back and cleared the register. I stopped short of the door, opened my Pellegrino, and enjoyed a few gulps of the ice-cold sparkling water. I watched the line of customers and the cashier as I drank my water. But I still felt deprived of my true identity, so I took out my Rhodia tablet and my Metropolitan fountain pen and wrote myself a note: *Go to swap meet and buy a belt with* URES, *my great-great-great-grandfather's birthplace, carved into the leather.* Very well. I had a plan. These men coming through the line with *Micho-acán* branded into their leather belts would see *URES*, and so would the cashier. And we'd exchange manly nods, including the cashier, and speak to each other in Spanish about our days, and after work, we'd meet at a karaoke bar and sing Vicente Fernandez songs all night long. . . .

Con dinero

Y sin dinero

Yo hago siempre

Lo que quiero

Y mi palabra es la ley. . . .

Whatever, I said to myself, and stormed out of Home Depot, but not before I caught the end of an eight-foot pipe on the doorframe, dropped my bag, and spilled the pipe joints across the floor. Two mexicanos walked around me as I gathered the joints. "Que güey," I heard one of them say. *Whatever*, I thought to myself, and headed for the truck.

After I returned from Home Depot, I laid the new pipe alongside the old pipe. I used my handy new pipe saw to cut it and felt a sense of pride as I removed it. I sat cross-legged in the grass and laid the brittle pipe across my lap and unscrewed the sprinkler heads and risers one by one and lined them up beside each other in the grass and took out my handkerchief and cleaned the threads. As I stood up, my knees cracked, my lower back tightened, and my shoulders ached.

I wanted to go inside and watch the Dodger game on MLB TV. I longed to sink into my grandpa's sofa chair, turn on the TV with the remote, and allow the natural light falling through the windows to swirl around me. I wanted the volume to be set low so that the game took on a meditative quality as I watched Dodger blue round third base. I wanted to watch the game from the first pitch to the last pitch without feeling rushed or guilty. I wanted to enjoy Santitas tortilla chips with salsa and Tecate and lime and Himalayan salt. I wanted to sink into that chair and remember my childhood and the years I played Little League baseball. I wanted to replay in my mind 1983—the year I stole forty-four bases and nothing else in the world mattered each time I slid into second base, stood up, dusted off my knees, and glared at the catcher, who was still discombobulated as he adjusted his chest protector and his mask.

Instead, I sat back down and put together a new sprinkler line with the sprinkler heads, risers, side-outlet elbow joints, PVC pipe, T-joints, and cement. Before I dropped the new line into the trench, I used my shovel to scoop out more dirt so I would have plenty of space to adjust the height of the risers and sprinkler heads. I used the shovel my dad had given me—it was my grandfather's shovel. The shaft rattled inside the socket, and the shoulders were nearly eaten through by rust, and every time I used it I picked up a splinter or two. But I used it anyway because I longed to feel that connection to the men in our family—because that connection, and this work with my hands, work that started under a shower of orange sparks, filled me with pride.

As I swabbed the joints one by one with cement and slid in the pipe, a turquoise and primer-patched Ford Aerostar pulled up to the curb. The driver-side door creaked open, and out walked a woman who was about 4'5". Her features reminded me of the campesinos, who I watched pick strawberries in Watsonville one afternoon when I pulled to the side of the road and stretched my fingertips into the fog, hoping the cold bite might wake me as I drove home from my great-uncle's funeral. She walked up to the front door and looked over my work as she squinted, and after she knocked, my wife appeared, and they gave each other a big hug. But as the door closed, I heard them both laugh so loudly that for a moment I couldn't hear the wind chimes that hung from the patio eaves and soothed my wracked nerves whenever I felt anxious to finish a job and to finish the job right.

"Honey," my wife said. "My friend Esperanza wants to know how much the gardener charges and why doesn't my husband do it?"

"Very funny," I said.

"Esperanza, this is my husband."

"Nice to meet you," I said.

"I'm so sorry," she said.

"That's okay," I said.

Truth be told, it wasn't okay. I'd had enough excitement for one day, so I decided the sprinkler line could sit and cure for twenty-four hours. I swept the curb and the sidewalk, wheeled out the green waste bin, tossed chunks of sod into it, and put my tools in their proper place in the shed and in the toolbox on my workbench. I walked back to the front yard to make sure I hadn't forgotten anything, smiled, and thought to myself, *Ah, it's been a good day after all. The sprinkler line is almost done, the yard is cleaned up, my tools are put away, and tomorrow I'll know right where to find them. And I did it all with these hands.* I held my hands up against the sunlight, half serious, half making fun of myself. I felt like an Aztec warrior offering his sword and shield to the gods. *No professional gardener or fancy sprinkler installer will set foot on my property.* I walked up the driveway and walked around my wife's car. Pride continued to swell because I had just leased a luxury SUV for my wife. I remember how I stood in the showroom and said, "I want my wife to drive a nice car. I want one luxury vehicle in this family." So the sprinkler line was almost done. My wife's car sat in the driveway, and on my desk, a stack of essays waited to be graded, which also filled me with pride because my students were writing about Longinus's *On the Sublime*, and I was certain that somewhere among the pages of their essays I'd find a *thunderbolt* striking the page.

I went to the garage, grabbed a clean rag and the bottle of tire shine I keep in its special place above the tool bench, and returned to my wife's SUV. I squatted down like a frog, and the muscle memory I developed working at the car wash for six years came right back. First, I polished her rims with the rag, especially between the spokes, where the brake dust had settled. I stuffed the rag into my back pocket and felt that extra sense of confidence that I used to feel when I was seventeen years old and the tips were collecting in my pocket. I grabbed a clean sponge from the box of auto detailing supplies I keep in the garage, went back to the car, and sprayed the sponge with the tire shine. Then, I glided the sponge over each tire. I started with the sponge just touching the wheel rim and finished exactly one inch beyond the tire's edge. I stood back and slowly walked around the car. I studied the wheels and the tires, used the rag or the sponge to spot check my work, and felt good about who I was. Perhaps I wasn't my great-great-great-grandfather, a Yaqui Indian, who came to the United States with a mule team. Perhaps I wasn't my great-great-grandfather, who was a blacksmith. Perhaps I wasn't my great-grandfather, who was a preacher and a violinist. Not even my grandfather, who worked in the fields and the San Francisco shipyards, nor my father, who by the age of six battled hornets' nests and picked grapes and contributed to the family's monthly income. But at least I could replace a sprinkler line and clean up a set of wheels and tires with my own two hands.

Just then another one of my new neighbors pulled up to the driveway and rolled down the passenger-side window. His blue BMW hummed in the summer breeze. I cleaned my hands with my handkerchief and smiled. I thought I might invite a few neighbors over for a barbecue and a few beers.

"Hey," he said.

"Hi, my name is . . ."

"Hey, how much do you charge?"

"What?"

"Yeah, to detail. Hey, how much do you charge?"

"What are you talking about? This is my car. I live here."

"Oh. Hey, sorry, Man," he said and drove off.

That evening, after a long hot shower, I stared at myself in the mirror as I filled up the sink with water so I could shave. *What gives a person the right to ask me how much? If I had been a white dude fixing a sprinkler line, would it had made a difference? And what made that cashier think I don't speak Spanish? Not brown enough? Not dirty enough? And what if some white dude had been cleaning his wheels and shining his tires in the driveway? Would that have made a difference? I'll tell you how much I charge. . . .* I thought as I shaved the black stubble from my cheekbones.

I put on my favorite pink Tommy Hilfiger polo shirt, my favorite pair of Levi's, and my Levi's canvas belt, and I slipped on my favorite Birkenstocks.

"Babe, let's go get a taco. I'll get the baby ready." Our daughter picked out her Wonder Woman outfit. My wife pulled back her blond hair and made a ponytail and put on a summer dress, slipped into a pair of pink flipflops, and away we went. Walking down the block, I inhaled the summer air and thought to myself, *It's been a good day.*

As we approached the discount shopping center, we scanned the parking lot to see which food trucks had already parked. We saw pizza, gyros, mac-n-cheese, dolma, hamburgers, gelato, shawarma, and tacos. My daughter's eyes grew big when she heard the elote man honking his bicycle horn. We found him walking his tricycle between the food trucks. His tricycle was loaded with cotton candy; duros; shaved ice and syrups; bottles of lemon juice, Tapatio, Valentina, and Chamoy; strawberry, guava, mango, coconut, and bubblegum paletas; and lime, jamaica, tamarind, mandarin, and pineapple Jarritos sodas.

We asked for elote smothered in butter and parmesan cheese. I stood there holding one elote in my fist as if it were feeding the sky and waited patiently for the other two while my wife picked out sodas and our daughter screamed for cotton candy. *Today is a good day after all*, I said to myself, knowing full well I was prepared to spend a hundred dollars at the elote cart. *Today*, I announced to myself, *I replaced the sprinkler line, detailed my wife's tires and wheels, and took my family out to dinner at the elote cart. Today was a good day. Who cares about how much I charge? Who cares whether or not I look like a real mexicano? I can work with my hands like my ancestors, take my family out for elote and Jarritos, and then go home and grade essays about Longinus's* On the Sublime. *Today is a good day.*

At that very moment, *Today is a good day*, I heard, from behind my right shoulder, a woman say, "Hey, Elotero, give me some corns." At first, I ignored it. I figured that couldn't possibly be for me. So I went on my way waiting happily for our elote. But then I heard the woman making demands within my personal space, so I turned around, and sure enough she said, "Hey, Elotero, give me some corns." She raised her eyebrows at me and nodded toward the cart. My first thought was, *Learn English. It's "corn," not "corns."* But before I could formulate thoughts beyond grammar, my wife had spun around with an index finger extended like a switchblade and said, "My husband is not the elote man. . . ."

We walked home. As my wife and daughter ate their elote, I thought, *What a coincidence. I just looked up the etymology of the word* hey. I had recently told a student not to address his professor with, "Hey."

"What's wrong with it?"

"It's just rude," I said.

But at home I could not stop thinking about his question. So I looked it up in *Webster's*. To my surprise, *hey* could be an expression of joy. *That's not right*, I said to myself. So after my daughter and wife had gone to bed, I snuck over to the computer. I felt ashamed: an English professor looking online for the etymology of a word instead of just knowing it. I found *The Online Etymology Dictionary*, which said, "hey (interj.) c. 1200 as a call implying challenge, rebuttal, anger, derision; variously spelled in Middle English *hei, hai, ai, he, heh*. Later in Middle English expressing sorrow, or concern; also a shout of encouragement to hunting dogs." And there you go. That's what stuck in my mind as I slipped into my grandpa's chair and turned on the television, *a shout of encouragement to hunting dogs. Very well, then, I'm a dog.* I flipped through the channels and stopped at ESPN as the opening credits to a *30 for 30* episode hit the screen. As the episode ran through the opening credits, I sat in the dark and thought about my day. I still felt pride in all the work I had done with my own two hands. I could still smell the pipe cement in my fingertips, and my fingernails still had a few grains of dirt. But I could have done without all the guilt over not being Mexican enough. And I could have done without all the anger over being stereotyped five times in one day. *Life is too short.* I pressed Pause, went to the kitchen, and returned with an ice cold Tecate. I opened the can, squeezed lime into the beer, and sprinkled Himalayan salt over the top of the can. I sipped the beer as it fizzed. I pressed Play, and then I heard one of the most beautiful words emanate from the television, "Fernando," and at that moment, I knew the episode I had stumbled upon was a documentary about Fernando Valenzuela—my childhood hero.

I remembered the day my mother brought me home from the dentist after he had pulled four teeth. How he said, "If it hurts, just tell me." And after he had pulled two, I began to feel the pain. I could feel and hear the roots popping, and I told him to stop because it hurt. But all he said was, "Almost done. Almost done." So my sixth-grade mind put itself in a trance the way my mother had told me to put myself into a trance through focus and concentration before I ran the fifty-yard dash on Sports Day at school. I imagined myself camping with my family alongside Shaver Lake. Nothing but the pine, the stars, and the water sloshing against the shore. And after a few more minutes, it was all over, and I was still in this trance until my mother came to get me and took me home. She put me on the couch, turned on the TV, and found a Dodger game as Fernando took the mound. My mother said, "His name is Fernando Valenzuela, and he is Mexican just like you." Then, she laid my head on her lap and stroked my hair.

I adjusted my body and found the sweet spot in my grandpa's chair and thought, *Life is too short. I'll take the pride. But you can have the shame and the anger. Instead, I'm going to be happy with who I am at this very moment. And besides, I'd rather watch Fernando and ask myself—what is he thinking about as he stares at home plate, winds up, and casts his eyes upon Heaven.*

Paco

Stephanie Li

The only time I ever saw my mother cry at the dinner table was when Paco died. I must have been seven or eight years old. When my older brother and I came home from school that winter afternoon, my father told us in a hushed voice that one of our mother's nephews had died. There had been a motorcycle accident. He hadn't been wearing his helmet.

"Who?" I asked. We didn't know anyone who rode a motorcycle.

"Your cousin, Paco."

"Paco?" I tried again.

"The son of your Auntie Lola."

Tía Lola was my mother's eldest sister, a mountain of a woman, who had ten children but said there were twelve because of her two miscarriages. She had eight daughters. As girls, almost all of them had stayed with my parents for a summer in our Minneapolis duplex when Chris and I were young. Lolita was the first of my cousins to make the trip from Monterrey, Mexico, where my mother was born. The youngest of seven, only my mother made her home in the United States after marrying my father. They met in Syracuse, New York, where they had both received their PhDs in pharmacology. When my brother was first born, my parents set up his playpen in their lab, but it soon became clear that they needed help. They didn't have money for a nanny or day care, so Tía Lola sent her third-eldest daughter. In grainy photographs, Lolita hoists my brother on a hip she didn't quite have, smiling as though the baby were her own. At twelve, she had more experience with children than both my parents. During the day, Lolita took my brother on walks around the lake, played with him in the park, and fed him bottles of formula. Every evening my father drove her to Baskin-Robbins, and over the summer she tried everything on the menu.

My father tried again, "Lolita's older brother."

"Yeah, we got that part, Dad," Chris replied. "We know who Lolita is." None of us could say Lolita's name quite right. It wasn't one of the hard names with an *r* we could not roll, but while "Lolita" fell in a perfect drop from my mother's lips, we pronounced each syllable as its own small word. Spanish was always clumsy in our mouths. Nothing like my mother, who spoke her native tongue like a lullaby.

"Who was he?" I asked again. I might have been able to identify all of Tía Lola's daughters, but since when did she have boys, too?

"Don't tell your mother you don't know who he is," my father said, shaking his head. He sighed as though disappointed, maybe in us, maybe in my mother, who had all but hidden her face when we came in the door, leaving my father to do all the explaining. Or maybe the mysterious dead cousin was to blame, so reckless on his motorcycle. I wanted to remember him, but not even the name was familiar.

"Paco," my father continued, "was a sweet boy. He came to visit us once when we lived at Mr. Smith's house on Lake Nicomas. He said it was so well built that we should have bought it." He snickered at the memory. "A good house in the wrong neighborhood. He wouldn't have understood that. Here, I'll get you a picture. You'll remember him then." My father padded across his office and bent to a low shelf where he kept reels of slides. Each was boxed and labeled with the location and date of a trip. He labeled everything with color-block stickers typed in bold on his IBM typewriter. The labels were always perfectly centered, and yet his office teemed with a disorder my mother could barely look at.

Upstairs, she was cooking; she had hardly greeted us when we returned from school. We didn't ask questions, following my father to his basement office, where it felt like we were telling secrets, maybe even doing something wrong. We were not allowed to play here among my father's piles of papers and stacks of journals. His desk was covered in repurposed mugs and canisters holding countless pens of various colors. He had an elaborate system of taking notes that involved different-colored fine-tipped pens that he bought at a local stationery store. They were much smoother than any of my markers, and it was a rare pleasure to draw with them, especially on his desk, which was so wide I could stretch my arm across it and barely reach its midpoint. Usually I would have been elated at a chance to pore through my father's office treasures, but I wanted to be upstairs. I wanted my mother back.

I stared at his can of beautiful pens, waiting for what came next. We couldn't retreat to our playroom with our mother so upset, but there was no place for us here either. Now I realize that my father must have shared our anxiety to claim something of our mother's sorrow. Maybe he was even glad that we were there to join him in this confusion. He wasn't sad and wouldn't pretend to share my mother's grief. We didn't need to be sad either. Even now I don't know what to call the strange disquiet of witnessing someone else's sadness. No word in Spanish or English for that.

"I don't think he was in Monterrey when we last visited. Your mother said he's been living in some other town for quite a while," my father explained as he sorted through a recent reel of slides. "He's not in any of these." He reached for one of their thick wedding albums. "He'll have to be in here, though."

My father flipped through the pages I knew well. My parents holding bites of cake to one another's mouth. My mother's hair pulled back so tight it looked straight. My four grandparents lined up with grim expressions. They were seated next to my Tío Delfino, the most handsome of all my uncles and the one who spoke the best English, but even his charm could not elicit more than a few polite sentences. Though both my father's parents were born in the United States, their families came from Hong Kong. Many of the wedding guests had never seen a Chinese person before. All four of my grandparents blessed my parents' wedding, but no one could hide their bewilderment. My father, "el chino americano," was a mystery to my maternal grandparents. He wore mismatched socks and mangled every Spanish word he tried. Before he watched his youngest daughter set out for her new married life in the United States, Papi Fino reminded my mother that this was always her home and she could come back. In a time when divorce was still a scandal and the vows of the Church represented a covenant with God, this was a weighty declaration. She only returned to visit, but I grew to understand that my grandfather's pronouncement held true. Though she made my home, our home, and even shared it with us, her own was somewhere else. Most days I could ignore this. Most days she belonged entirely to us.

"There!" he exclaimed, "I found him." My father held a group photo. I recognized my uncles and aunts—Tío Chuy with a dark mustache, Tía Lola holding a tissue to the edges of her eyes. The cousins were harder to discern, everyone a child or teenaged version of the adults I knew.

Something was familiar in their faces, but nothing I could express. "Do you recognize him now?"

I studied the picture closely. There were two young men I could not identify, one with light curly hair, the other dark brown.

"It has to be either him or him," my brother concluded, pointing at the two mysterious figures.

"That's right," my father replied. "Those are Auntie Lola's sons, Mario and Paco."

"There's two of them?" I asked.

"Yes, she has two sons. You've met them both, but they're older, so we don't often see them. I am not sure Mario lives in Monterrey either. I think your mother said he moved to Texas or was thinking about it."

"Where did Paco live?" I asked, carefully trying out the past tense.

"Your mother knows," he replied.

I took the picture from his hands. Suddenly I had two new cousins, except that one of them was already dead.

"Which one's Paco? Can you figure it out?" my father asked as if the picture were now a puzzle to be solved.

My brother and I stared at it intently. Both young men smiled widely. The one with light hair stood on the end with his hand held out. The one with dark hair looked off to the side. They didn't look like brothers. They didn't look like Tía Lola either. My mother's family was a universe I could never master. My grandmother was called La Negra because of her dark skin, but her first son was born with blue eyes, or as she said, "los ojos de Jesus." Despite this range, I knew we were the strangest of all. When my father first visited my mother in Monterrey, her nieces asked him if he could see out of such tiny eyes. Later, I wondered if they thought the same of me.

"That one," I decided, pointing to the cousin with lighter hair.

"Is that what you think, too?" my father asked my brother.
He shrugged. "Sure."

"No, that's Mario," my father replied as if we had just lost a game. "This one is Paco." He pointed to the dark-haired cousin.

"That's the dead one?" I asked. Suddenly the young man in the picture looked sorrowful, his eyes cast to a further horizon.

My father took the picture back and studied it again. "Yeah, I'm pretty sure. I mean it has to be. I guess we can ask your mother. But later."

Though my father left the wedding picture on the counter in the kitchen when we went upstairs for dinner, he didn't ask my mother which one was Paco. He didn't ask her anything. She spooned stew and mashed potatoes on our plates, then ate with her back hunched, not looking at any of us. We sat in silence. I was dimly aware that I should acknowledge her loss somehow, but I had no words to communicate that. And I feared that anything I said would be an intrusion or a mistake. She was an island unto herself, as distant and mysterious as the photo of Paco or who we thought was Paco.

She was in that picture too, along with my father, who looked anxious to be done with the picture, the party, the whole wedding. My father was always instantly recognizable in Mexico pictures. Even if he didn't look exactly the same—sometimes thinner, and in the wedding photos a band of surprisingly thick hair covers his head—the angle of his slouched back and a slight space between him and everyone else, as if he has just taken a small step backward, indelibly marked him as my father. But not my mother. In the family photos, she looked not just younger, but like she could be another mysterious cousin and not my mother. In nearly every picture, she smiled like she was living in the moment she wanted forever. The Mexico smile.

It was the look I came to both love and dread during our annual trips to Monterrey. When Tío Chuy first saw us coming out of customs, he roared with laughter and lifted my mother onto his shoulder. She giggled and spoke too fast for my grade-school Spanish to understand. And when we finally arrived in my grandmother's house, circled around the kitchen table, she spread her arm across the back of Mami Lola's chair, a gesture that seemed to say, this, at last, was her home. The tight line of her shoulders loosened, and she fell against her mother. She never leaned on us like that.

Throughout dinner, the three of us spied on her between mouthfuls of food. We each glanced quickly up at her then at each other, then down again. I marvel now at how similarly the three of us reacted to her loss, or were my brother and I only imitating our father? Say nothing, make no eye contact, sit still until this passes. Once or twice my mother sniffled or made some noise in her throat, but it was quiet and changed nothing. At last, she pushed her chair from the table and walked out of the kitchen.

My father mumbled something. I thought she was mad because we had been spying on her or because we hadn't said anything. Usually we greeted our mother with a kiss—first thing in the morning, and first thing when she picked us up from school or came home. With my father we were more careless. He complained that in Mexico it took hours to say hello and goodbye to people, but that was one of the parts I liked best about our visits. We could be held tight and passed to the next relative with no time to answer questions about our lives in the United States. My father tolerated these excesses with a stiff grin. At home his hugs were all elbows, crinkled with the newspapers he folded against his arm. When I pressed against him, I could feel his gaze someplace else.

Now it was my mother who kept her distance, and I had not been brave enough to approach her myself. I knew of no way to make this right. Most of her dinner was still on her plate, and briefly I thought she would be back because otherwise who would clean everything up? The question brought a sense of panic. I didn't know how to wash dishes, and I wasn't sure my father did either. I couldn't picture what would happen next. We would have to sit at the table until she returned and released us, flung us back into the familiar routine of TV, bath, and bedtime.

My mother spent much of the evening on the phone. I listened at the doorway of the kitchen though I could not understand anything she said. I was waiting less for her to get off the phone than for her voice to change back to English. It never did. It only went silent, and I sat with my knees tucked into my nightgown, wishing she knew I was there but afraid of getting caught. She stayed in the dark of the kitchen for a long time. I thought she might be listening for me, waiting for the creak of the floorboards as I returned to bed. Paco had come and gone or gone and come but was now gone for good, and a part of me was glad. We needed her back. I returned to my room and the feel of cold sheets against my legs.

I knew she would not attend the funeral. There was no money for such a trip, and had my mother dared to broach the topic with my father, he would have noted that Paco was not really a close relative. Rather than bear that heartache, I am sure she didn't even mention the possibility. For once, I was glad that we didn't have more money.

In the morning, everything was just as before. There was a cup of orange juice for me, a glass of milk for my brother, cut fruit served in small bowls, and toast waiting at the table. We didn't talk about Paco. His life and death had vanished. The wedding picture my father found was gone. We didn't talk about dinner the night before. There was school ahead, piano lessons, and plans for the weekend. My mother had polished our shoes and promised a special snack after school. Everything felt safe again.

Years later, I learned that Tía Lola's youngest son died in San Luis Potosí, a city in central Mexico I lived in for a summer during college. When I walked the downtown streets, I wondered where he might have died. I followed motorcycles around sharp corners and down alleyways as if my vision alone might prevent them from disaster. Had there been a lot of blood? Was it instant, or did he die in a hospital? Were any of our family members with him? How did his body make it home? Paco moved to San Luis Potosí because of a religious group. Though a devout Catholic like both his parents, he was described as something of a mystic. He trained to be an architect but was not quite grounded to the earth, my mother said. After he died, some of his former companions began the process of having him consecrated as a saint. No one in our family was involved. Once when I asked Tía Lola about it, she brushed off the question. "What does it matter what they call him if he's never coming back?" she asked. I thought she would be proud to be the mother of a possible saint. She pressed her lips through shiny eyes, and I understood that there was nothing that would make her more proud of her son than she already was. I told her how beautiful I had found San Luis Potosí, the cathedral, and central plaza. She nodded and looked away.

Though I had no memories of Paco, nothing but a picture I had mis-identified, he became part of my story of Mexico, the place I am from but not from. Paco is the cousin who died before he had been born in my consciousness, a sorrow that disrupted a single childhood dinner and triggered my anger at not having the courage to embrace my mother when she was in pain. But, of course, those are not the parts of the story I came to tell.

At dinner parties or receptions, when people asked about my Mexican family, I found myself mentioning Paco. Yes, a huge family, of course everyone's Catholic and dozens of cousins, really dozens. I even have one up for sainthood! And instantly, I had everyone's attention. Wine glasses tipped back, someone nudged in closer. Sainthood? Really? Is that possible? How bizarre! Does that really happen? You must be kidding. What miracles has he performed?

But in fact, I knew none of the details. After patiently listening to my inane description of San Luis Potosí, Tía Lola spoke about her son, not his death, nor his possible canonization. None of my listeners wanted to hear about a quiet boy who felt the grace of Jesus and was called to join a monastic group hundreds of miles from his home. That was a story I couldn't tell because even now I hardly know it.

The Hole in the House

Sheryl Luna

I didn't like men, after having been gang-raped by my stepfather and his friends. I didn't even remember the rape for many years, only that I wanted to get as far away from his hatred of me as I could.

So when in 1983 my parents divorced, I was long gone. My stepfather, an abusive jerk, left after having an affair with a woman he worked with at the time. This left my mother, who had not worked for twenty years, in a terrible predicament. It is an old story, but my mother was and is childlike. She enjoys animated movies, loves to go out to eat or watch comedies. She dislikes what she would call the evil of the world. She sees the world to this day in black and white. People are either good or bad. She trusts no one because as she says, "I have been taken advantage of too much."

My stepfather had adopted me, but he was always emotionally, physically, and sexually abusive. My mother stood by quietly, uncertain how to find her voice. My mother, like me, has spent a lifetime learning to find her voice. She is still learning to speak up for herself, for her own needs.

In 1983 she was unreasonable. During the divorce, she would not sign the papers for an entire year, certain my stepfather would return. She said, "The only thing I want is the house." She said this over and over like a mantra or a prayer. She didn't care about his pension or all the money he had saved up for years. She only wanted the house. She envisioned our family—what was left, my brother and sister and I—living in the house together. She wanted to have a place for us to return if things went badly.

I had left town to go to college at Texas Tech University. I had fled my stepfather's verbal abuse as soon as I could. He would always say, "I can't wait until you're eighteen and on your own." So in a sense, I felt it was my obligation to leave, that there would be no parental love. Yet I was eager to leave, adventure, and succeed. I imagined myself succeeding and wealthy, but I never imagined myself married.

My mother was devastated by the divorce, as were my sister and brother. I was not surprised and honestly felt it was good riddance. Since I was at a university, I was unaware how much my family was suffering. I was too wrapped up in myself to care. I was in survival mode, working hard in the college cafeteria to pay tuition. My stepfather sent seven hundred dollars toward my tuition. I was surprised and grateful, but that was all the help I would receive. I was soon on my own again. I realize now he may have done it out of guilt over the divorce and the abuse. But I doubt it. He was always extremely selfish. Even as he died, he was selfish. He wanted what he wanted when he wanted it. He had no regard for the feelings of other people. He was the quintessential narcissist. During the divorce he called me his stepdaughter and told the judge he had paid for my education, a blatant lie.

While I was in college, his new wife called me and demanded to know why I never called my stepfather. He was apparently hurt that I didn't call him. I suppose my brother and sister, out of their anger, did not call him either. The man was full of contradictions. Maybe he wanted to make up for the gang rape, for the sexual abuse. I will never know because he died in 2008.

My mother hadn't worked in twenty years and suffered for years jumping from menial job to menial job. She barely made ends meet, and apparently my stepfather was not paying child support. My brother and sister were almost eighteen. My mother was losing it. I imagine her screaming at my brother and sister as she had sometimes done when my father wasn't around. I call him my father because he adopted me when I was two years old. The damage was irreparable; the wounds would haunt me a lifetime.

My mother did the best she could working at a high school cafeteria, a vacuum factory, a 7-Eleven, and at the local university's athletic department as a secretary. To this day she says she was run off that job by a woman who wanted her friend hired. In any case, she had many other jobs through the years. The Renault she drove continually broke down. My sister rebelled and stayed away from home as much as possible. My mother expected my brother and sister to help pay the rent. I sent her two thousand dollars of my student loan, which to this day she does not remember. She was living in a fog, a nightmare of twenty years of dependence on an abusive white man.

When I was younger I remember him punching her in the arm one night. She had a large round bruise on her arm for weeks. One night I heard him raping her. She was in pain. I could only imagine what was happening. As I stayed in my bed, I berated myself for my fear, for my inability to stand up to him. I was ashamed. I was angry, but I stayed in bed through the whole ordeal. The next day I asked my brother if he had heard anything the night before, and he said no. I couldn't imagine how he could not have heard what occurred. At this time, I couldn't remember my own rape. Everything for me was a fog, and I was angry with the world.

I was constantly in trouble in middle school. I ran with my cousins and spray-painted the school, stole motorcycles, and broke into people's houses. My parents had no idea. Once we got caught being out, and my cousin Joe said we were running away. Instead of getting in trouble, we were forgiven.

In college, I took up causes for the poor and for Latinos. I felt the full pressure of prejudice in Lubbock, Texas, where I went to school. Even though I didn't have a Latino last name at the time, people were rude, saying, "Go back to Mexico," or slamming coffee down at the table at IHOP. I had my hands full, coping with trying to pay for college, trying to understand prejudice, and finally coming to the realization that I was a Latina.

My stepfather demanded that Spanish not be spoken in our home. He said, "People in this country should speak English." There was no room for my mother's bilingualism. He hated my grandmother, who mostly spoke Spanish. Even though we lived along the border, I was unfortunately taught to despise my own kind. It was in college when I came to the realization that my family's culture mattered, that my stepfather was cruel and ignorant.

Meanwhile my brother and sister were plotting their escape from my mother's fog. Her mental illness raged; to this day she argues that she has no mental illness, but having been gang-raped in high school, she likely has post-traumatic stress disorder. When my stepfather left, her world was falling apart. I told her, "Why don't you sell the house?" but she was stubborn. She just knew we kids would return to her and to El Paso someday. We never did. I did come back for a three-year stint in the

MFA program for creative writing–poetry, but El Paso had no jobs. El Paso was poverty, and this is one reason I believe my mother struggled as she did. The city is on the US–Mexico border, and a majority of the jobs are low paying.

My mother is a short woman at 5'2", and after my stepfather, or "daddy," had left, she lost fifty pounds. She was thin and gaunt and sad. She was depressed for ten years, and she still thought he would return to her, but he never did. For some reason she had idolized the man, worshiped him despite his abuse. The more she missed him and pined over him, the angrier I got. I would not return to complete the MFA for seventeen years. I felt I despised my mother. I saw her as weak, as dependent. I thought to myself, "I will never let a man rule over me." But in reality, I would never let any man near me. Sure, I had the occasional relationships, but they were always short lived.

My mother had taken to having roommates so she could afford the house payment. Years of house payments were still left. I couldn't persuade her to sell. My brother had inherited my stepfather's antique cars, a 1927 Chevy and a 1932 Buick. My mother stayed, she says now, because my brother's cars were there. But I know she also held out hope that we would return. We never did, other than my stint at the University of Texas at El Paso's MFA program.

My mom and I were both a mess. I also went from job to job, and I never had a sense of calm or satisfaction. It was as if I were searching for some Truth with a capital *T*. I fell prey to a religious group that some people consider a cult. It was called the Great Commission, a hard-core evangelical Christian group of wounded souls seeking perfection and salvation. The balm of eternal life kept them going. I too experienced being "born again," and I was again living in a fog, a blissful fog, but still a fog. This occurred in the mid-1980s, when I was in my early twenties. I went with the group to Washington, DC, and found myself in the awkward position of having to preach to people on the subway and on the National Mall in front of the Capitol. I remember meeting a Buddhist. He was calm, gray bearded, and smiling the whole time I tried to save his soul. Surely, he needed to see I was right, but something inside told me that this evangelism was pushy and a tad self-righteous. The Buddhist sat on a park bench smiling and nodding and simply told me that he was happy as a Buddhist. In a soft voice, almost a whisper, he said, "I don't mind not having eternal life."

"You'll go to hell," I said, mortified. I was in work boots, dirty jeans, and a light blue T-shirt, as we had done yard work during the morning.

"I'll take my chances," he said with a grin.

Maybe in the end, I didn't believe there was a hell, but I sure wanted to believe there was a heaven. Years later I would wish there was a hell as I remembered what my stepfather had done to me when I was eleven or twelve years old, but at the time, I was searching for clarity, for meaning, for absolute answers in a world that mystified and horrified me. Trauma had left me believing in original sin. We were all bad at the core, I thought, and therefore we were in need of salvation, but in the end, the self-righteous attitude of many of the church members left me uncomfortable. I wanted to have my faith my way, and many Christians would not tolerate that, including my family. It is still a battle today in which I struggle in my relationships with them. Wounds that run deep lead to a need for answers, and religion provides them. My mother to this day cajoles me to pray, and she did indeed suffer for years, and she reminds me she suffered for years, and that God, and only God, pulled her out of it.

One summer when I was in college, my mother's roommates stole her jewelry and wrecked the house. One day a drunk driver drove right into the house. My mother had spent her money on helping me out after a car wreck, and she didn't have the house insurance to get the hole fixed. She was angry with me too. I had been home for the summer and caused an accident on I-10. The car was impounded, and she helped me get it out. She says now that's why the insurance never covered the cost of repairing the hole in the house. She covered it with plastic bags, and there it stood open for years and years, a hole about two feet by four feet. I'm surprised more things weren't stolen. My mother was not well. I was not well.

I visited her another time, and she screamed at me to get a job as soon as I got home for what I considered summer break. I wanted to get a job but not the first few days I was home. She was enraged. I was furious. I left town in a hurry. It was one of the worst decisions I've made in my life that I have come to regret. I left her to her own resources, which were not good. She was nervous, agitated, and depressed all at the same time. I was all about taking care of myself. I have mixed emotions about those events to this day, but the fact is my mother was and is an adult.

She decided to attend community college, which I was thrilled about since my stepfather had refused to allow her to enroll in classes. She got some money from a Pell Grant and began to learn about her culture, her life. Classes in sociology and psychology helped her come into her own strength, but it would take years before she would gain some confidence in herself. It would take many, many disappointments before she would feel better.

Her car kept breaking down, so my sister gave her an old Chevy, and this was my mother's salvation. She still remembers how this saved her from taking the long bus ride to the university, which she attended after graduating from community college.

All through her college attendance, the hole remained in the house. It was symbolic to me, the way our family was bereft and empty: we were all lost, and our family was broken. One summer I returned home to find that our old dog Wimpy was covered in fleas. Black streaks ran up and down his back, under his belly, behind his ears. I was mortified. How could she have let this happen? I was leaving town and begged her to buy a flea collar. She says she did. I hope this is true. My mother was not able to function. She was later trying to take care of her mother, and she seldom spent time at home. I am not sure if the dog had died at that point or not. Now I realize my mother's illness affected her ability to function, not to mention El Paso's horrible job market, but she still refused to sell the house.

The house represented my stepfather to me. I suppose that's partly why I didn't want anything to do with it. Bad memories were persuasive, and by this time I had had some flashbacks of sexual abuse. I was angry with my mother for not having been aware of what was going on at home.

My sister, however, was the angriest. When she was in high school, she came home to an empty house. My stepfather and his girlfriend had loaded all the furniture and valuables onto a truck. She was furious. She never forgave him. To this day she has little patience with my mother, who is still childlike and has an innocence about her. My mother believes in Jesus and eternal life; she prays and attends church. She is always on my case about my needing to pray. Both my sister and brother have found solace in their faith, yet they remain unhealed and in denial about the abuse we suffered as children. My sister's temper is sharp and quick. Anything my mother says causes a rant, a rage. My sister is in inconsolable pain about our parents.

I think my sister's rage is wrapped around the suffering that occurred after my stepfather flew the coop. After a bout with breast cancer and having raised five children, my sister has little patience with my mother, who was emotionally unavailable for years. My sister is unforgiving in her rage. I tell her in time it will heal, that our mother is childlike and had three brain traumas as a child, which I believe have hurt her cognitive abilities. She was hit by a car and did not receive medical attention in one instance. In another instance, she was hit by a baseball. She graduated from college after ten years of struggling, but she could not pass the teacher certification test. Today she is a substitute teacher, and a damn good one. I think my mother has a learning disability, as I do. We both have attention deficit disorder, which makes it difficult sometimes for us to communicate and socialize. My sister is angry that my mother was weak, but my mother was actually strong and persevered.

She lived in dire poverty for years struggling at jobs, which hurt her self-esteem. She was often fired or left out of frustration and weariness. The hole remained in the house for at least seven years. When she finally sold the house, the hole was there. The new owners fixed the broken bricks with new ones, redid the yard, and painted the house. My mother had experienced a flood that had ruined her carpet, among other things. Finally, when she was about to sell the house, my brother showed up to retrieve his cars and help her move, along with my uncle and cousin.

Her stuff was in storage while she looked for a smaller house that would be easier to take care of. The house on Colt Lane appeared dilapidated when she finally sold it. The white paint on the wooden garage door was peeling off, and the white wooden fence that surrounded the house was leaning heavily toward the bridle path. The neighbor's horses seldom walked there anymore. She didn't get much money for the house. The neighborhood was rural. People had chickens and goats, and one neighbor had a giant green-and-blue peacock. But our house was an eyesore, a remnant of the appearance of a happy family. Its condition of ruin matched the condition of our family. We were all scattered across Texas, and we rarely spoke to each other.

My mother found a smaller house. She says that when she looked at the house and was trying to make a decision about buying it that a bird sang, "Jesus, Jesus." She saw it as a sign and bought the house. She lives there to this day, aging and alone, except for her sisters, who live in El Paso. She often talks about that bird's song and how much she loves her tiny house. Her new house has a carport. It is painted beige and white. Its bricks are light brown. The house is lovely, and the neighborhood is often peaceful. Yet, some neighbors who have rented a HUD house sometimes get loud and play Mexican music full blast into the night. Once some boys were throwing rocks, and one hit her front door. But overall, she loves her new home and seems to have recovered from the need to hold onto the past.

She ended up getting her Social Security benefits early because she was desperate for money. She receives less money than she could have if she had waited until full retirement age. She at least got money from his Social Security. Call it karma.

My stepfather had died afraid in a Pennsylvania hospital. I've decided I don't want to die the way he did. I want to face death on my own terms, with peace and acceptance. He died a terribly painful death, fearful and desperate. He died of a rare lung disease. He had also been a heavy smoker for many years. My brother and sister rushed to his side, but I refused to deal with him. Yet out of guilt I sent a card. Why, I don't know. I simply wanted to forgive him. He had torn our family apart from the beginning with his rigid rules and unforgiving attitude. He, unlike my mother and siblings, did not believe in God. In my opinion, he was afraid of love, afraid of kindness. He saw the world as a place of combat and acted accordingly. He was an authoritarian, and at the hour of his death he had no control. My brother says he brought my stepfather to Jesus and that he is in heaven. Fat chance, I still say.

His early death led to my mother's financial salvation since she got his Social Security benefits. My mother helps me now that I am receiving Social Security disability benefits for mental illness. My mother still refuses to go to therapy or get any kind of psychological help, but unlike my sister, I have come to see my mother as a wise matriarch, as a leader and healer. She still suffers from bouts of depression and loneliness, but overall she is thriving, and her house is in fine shape. The yard is immaculate with green grass, a pecan tree, and blueberry plants.

I believe in karma, in the reversals of grief and loss. We may not see it, but we all create our own destiny, whether it is bitterness or thankfulness. My mother is still bitter at times when she looks to the past and sees so much injustice. She recognizes her inability to cope, yet she was a caregiver in the end to my grandmother, and she is in a sense a caregiver to me. I wish my sister could see how much my mother has changed, but she cannot. She still sees the childlike innocence and grows angry. "Let go," I want to tell my mother, my sister, and myself. The past is gone, and there is so little time.

Letter to the Student Who Asks Me How I Managed to Do It

José Antonio Rodríguez

Dear Student,

Sometimes you sit at the front, the reading space a hall with spring-hinged seats, or a small classroom or a large auditorium, one with rising semicircular rows of tables and swivel chairs. Always you are timid but curious enough to ask during the question-and-answer session at the end of the reading some variation of how did I become a writer. Because you've already gleaned, from my predominantly autobiographical poetry and prose and my chatting in between pieces, the basics of my past—the Mexican village, the poverty, the journey to the Texas border, the parents' focus on education, the love of reading and the classroom—I know your question is not about that, not about the mechanics of the craft, not about the discipline of the draft.

Here's something like what I usually say:

I stumbled around a while, came to writing late, went off to study it. And kept writing and submitting and believing I had something important to say.

Here's what I don't say:

I'm not always sure how I did it, or what that means exactly.

* * *

Which is to say, finding myself living in that great metropolis of youthful energy that is Austin, Texas, in my mid-twenties, the last time I was so naïve as to think I could leave my past behind. I am working with the FBI, that very FBI, as a contract linguist, which is a fancy name for transcribing and translating mostly taped phone conversations of suspected criminals smuggling drugs. I'm making okay money, which to me is amazing money because it is more than my father ever made. I'm feeling like the embodiment of the American Dream, which feels like both an embrace and a repudiation of my Mexican parents' dream for their children. An embrace because I feel I've escaped the poverty they lived, the one I, too, lived. I've made good on their ultimate objective: to have their children work indoor, kinder, climate-controlled jobs rather than outdoor jobs in the sweltering heat of South Texas. And I've lived a law-abiding life, never bringing shame upon the family. And a repudiation because I left my parents' side, because I didn't marry and father children, because I left to find a way out of the gay closet in that city where I hear being gay is not so bad.

* * *

Which is to say, I stopped going to church a long time ago.

* * *

Which is to say, believing I have escaped unscathed because I'm enrolled in a weight-training class now and flex for the mirror and pay my own rent and eat out regularly. I dream of a boyfriend, though I'm not sure how that'll happen, because I've never held a man's hand. Still, this feels like a kind of reinvention, now that I'm on my own, introducing myself as Joe rather than José, ever since a sixth-grade teacher suggested it. It's been so long, it feels natural.

Which is to say, joining a gay men's social group sponsored by the city to teach the community about safe sex that holds gatherings in an old, remodeled house in south Austin. I read about it in the *Austin Chronicle*. One Christmas party comes with a sexy Santa on a couch with whom you can take a photo. I'm reminded then of those sweet Santas from elementary school, their welcoming lap and the Polaroid and warm feeling inside. One group meeting comes with the group leaders brainstorm ways of increasing the group's numbers, and one of them, slim with a toned body and visible ab muscles that I'd noticed at a recent pool party, says, I don't mean to be a jerk but I think the reason the group used to be bigger is that the members were hotter. I realize then how often I sneak glimpses of his beautiful body in spite of my best efforts not to and that he probably notices. After that meeting, I go less often.

* * *

Which is to say, one day in my therapist's office I begin to tell him how much I resent the machista culture of Mexico that broke my mother's spirit, coercing her into a loveless marriage of submission to her husband. How many times had she reminded me how children brought her ever more suffering? How her children ought not repeat her mistakes? I feel very American when I share this with him, a relative stranger, aware of how focused I am on my individual well-being, aware too of how taboo it is to talk about one's Mexican family this way, not just criticizing its quirks or occasional slip-ups but labeling it fundamentally misshapen, wounded. I like my therapist with his sandy blond hair and honest smile and his soft-lit office with the tan sofa and the purple quartz by the window. I also know we come from different worlds when he mentions in another conversation that a twenty-thousand-dollar inheritance is not a lot.

* * *

Which is to say, money makes me uncomfortable; the desire to conserve it a discomfiting necessity, I think because I grew up without it, necessitous, anxiety a constant with money.

* * *

Which is to say, becoming vaguely aware of the American middle-class definitions of what count as healthy relationships and how much these may be determined by, or at the very least influenced by, socio-economic circumstances. By money. I have been good at learning from my mostly white teachers and applying what I can to my life with an asterisk. I begin to suspect, though, that my complete assimilation into middle-class (?) (white) American culture is impossible, unless I lock my past away forever.

* * *

Which is to say, no adult ever told me explicitly to hide my immigrant status at school. One day you simply find yourself in the classroom staying quiet and growing small every time the classmate sitting next to you asks another classmate where they're from.

* * *

Austin, it turns out, doesn't seem to be teeming with potential boyfriends. At the office, my coworker in the cubicle next to mine is a former pastor

. . . or minister . . . or something . . . I think. I'm not sure, but he likes to refer to God as the world's supreme judge. Or Jesus. I can't keep it straight. I don't like going into the office. As the weeks pass by, I become convinced that I am a subpar translator and sooner or later the FBI will find out. I go to bed fearing that I will mistranslate something that will result in an innocent person going to jail. Even worse, I nurse the suspicion that I am not the upright citizen that the FBI requires me to be. In the back of my mind, I wonder that this may have something to do with my being in the closet to everyone in the office. After years of doing this job, having passed a battery of tests and a polygraph exam and a very thorough background investigation, I decide to quit and find something else. Something less intense, less secretive, less something.

* * *

Without a job, I spend increasing amounts of time alone in my one-bedroom apartment in the northwest corner of the city, mailing out résumés and cover letters for job postings I find online, avoiding the creeping suspicion that I don't really want to be hired, that I'd rather stay in my bedroom and avoid the world altogether. I'm living off my savings and sporadic temp jobs. Days go by without much of any contact with another human being. I notice I'm eating less. I feel alien. One day, after several months, I get called in for a job interview as an administrative assistant to some important man at the University of Texas. It's an old campus building that reminds me of my old high school with the off-white walls, the fissured ceiling panels, the equally sized fluorescent light panels. The man's office is large, riddled with stacks of files and folders and books. I've never had a male assistant, he admits with a half chuckle in his plush executive chair. I smile. He says, there would be some traveling with me to Mexico, hence the need for Spanish. I assure him nothing is a problem, even as I doubt that I am qualified for this job, never having been an assistant before. There must be protocols for every type of interaction between me and him and everyone he comes across as part of his job. There must be rules for every type of document, rules that I don't know. Baby steps, I tell myself. Your savings won't last forever, I tell myself. Great health benefits, even if the salary's not great. Smile, I tell myself. After the meeting someone at his office calls me, he'd like to offer you the job, come in Monday morning for your first day. Good, I breathe in. The specter of something resembling homelessness begins to dissipate.

* * *

Which is to say, when I'm idle at a red light I imagine the person with the "Will work for food" sign at the end of something like a shift, shuffling away into the blur of traffic.

* * *

Which is to say, when Monday comes I show up on campus and wait in the hallway, a few feet from the man's office with its brown door closed. Eventually a woman comes over to tell me the administrator will not be in today, that I should come back the next day. Inside I sigh in relief. My anxiety lessens with every step I take away from that office, that building. The next morning I sit at the edge of my bed and call in, I'm sorry but I can't take the job. Then I hang up and know with certainty that I have a problem. I can't seem to do what so many people do every day in every corner of the country—feel insecure about a job, dislike it, perhaps even hate it, and still go to it every day. I don't feel so American then.

* * *

Which is to say, I continue keeping a journal, like the therapist suggested, and writing little nothings in it, thoughts on the day's ebb and flow, the objects I've touched, the flower garden park east of downtown, the memories that revisit me—my mother weeping in the living room of my childhood, my father smoking on the front porch.

* * *

Which is to say that when my funds begin seriously dwindling, I leave Austin and move back in with my parents in McAllen, weighing... twenty? Twenty-five pounds less? I'm beginning to forget what it means to sleep well. I can't remember when my pants didn't slip easily past my hips. I can't remember the last time I felt like a winner. Still, my parents welcome me with open arms, big dutiful Mexican arms, even when I don't know how to feel properly human. Maybe this is what it means to fail at the American Dream.

* * *

I miss having money to take myself to the movies as often as I want. Two hours of forgetting.

* * *

Which is to say, I stumble around from one job to another—phone interpreting for car dealerships and utility providers whose English-speaking representatives need to contact Spanish-speaking clients, freelancing as a translator of legal documents, substitute-teaching in different grade schools. One day, a room of energetic seven-year-olds, another day a room of defiant adolescents who remind me of my high school bullies. During one phone interpreting shift, I'm on the line between an electrical utility rep and a customer who is late on her payments. If you don't pay the outstanding balance, we will cut off your electricity, he says, which I then say in Spanish. But I have a baby and his milk in the fridge will go bad, she says, her voice cracking, which I then repeat in English. I'm sorry but we can't help that, he says, which I must repeat in Spanish. I sit in a chair in my bedroom, leaning over the landline phone on the bed for lack of space, the window blinds open to the searing Texas sun. Another day I get into an argument with someone at a local attorney's office who is unhappy with the accumulated cost of my translating dozens and dozens of their documents into English. They're not sure they're happy paying the total fee, even though they agreed to the per-page fee. Another day, a high school student whose class I am subbing refuses to leave the room when I grow tired of his repeated distractions and back talk. I don't remember there being so many security guards when I was in high school.

* * *

Which is to say, I think I am haunted.

* * *

Which is to say, I am running out of options, a voice in my mind suggesting a return to school, to the university twenty minutes away, the same one I went to after high school, that place where I used to feel more confident, where I used to feel safe-r. And didn't I always love books? Were they not a reliable refuge?

* * *

Which is to say, I resist the voice because it feels like regressing. I resist because I wanted so badly to be the American Dream with the home and office job and financial security, which I was told was the gateway for all other securities. I resist because I needed to be the thing that redeemed my mother and father's suffering, their sacrifices. So many,

I can't even count them. I should be making money now, like my high school friends surely are, I tell the bathroom mirror. I should be confident and self-assured, and hasn't it already been over ten years since I graduated from high school? Going back to school feels like a retreat, I tell the mirror. Going back to school feels like being broke again for even longer. And still.

* * *

There is a familiarity with being broke, counting every dollar twice, constantly reviewing every small calculation into a kind of numbing, almost into a kind of being.

* * *

Which is to say, one day in May of 2004 I find myself in a conference room of the local university library along with a professor and about a half dozen other students. The class is an intensive weeklong poetry workshop with six- to eight-hour days, the first course in the master's program in English to which I have applied and been accepted, using the money I've earned from the big document translation gig. (The attorney decided he'd go ahead and pay me the translation fee after all, my first and last job for him.) I'm not sure what I'm doing in the conference room, thinking I might be able to write something resembling poetry, something that might speak of the beauty and pain that seem to shadow me. Still, I am comforted by the room's clean and level surfaces, its recently vacuumed carpet, its quiet dignity. A steady shiver of anxiety reverberates through me, but the anxiety feels different from usual. I think this is not an anxiety of dread but of possibility. This feels like hope, I think.

* * *

Which is to say, the professor—older, soft-spoken, and sitting at the head of the table with that easy authority that I find compelling and mysterious—asks us to introduce ourselves briefly. When it's my turn, I say without thinking: "My name is José," the first time I have introduced myself as such in so many years, and it feels like a beginning, reclaiming the name my parents gave me in this American space. I know then with rare certainty that I will never again introduce myself as Joe. This moment doesn't feel like a retreat but rather like a restart, a recalibration.

* * *

What a gift to concern myself with stressed and unstressed syllables for a few hours.

* * *

Which is to say, I love cool clean spaces because they are the opposite of the spaces I grew up in, even if I struggle to feel *of* these cool clean spaces. It is one thing to be in a space, another thing to be of it. Sometimes I think I've been looking all my life for that space to which I will feel kindred.

* * *

Which is to say, every ending is also a beginning, if you wait it out long enough. I no longer believe I escaped the past unscathed. In fact, I know that I didn't, that I carry the past with me, that we all do. And that the trauma in it haunts me and that to ignore that, to pretend it away, won't work. But that if I find meaning in it, if I learn from that meaning, this too can be beauty.

* * *

Which is to say, writing feels like building a home with words, the foundation and the frame and all the other layers of complexity. And in this home I house everyone I've been, everyone we've been—Mexican, American, man, woman, straight, gay, solvent, broke, saved, damned, loved, rejected, acknowledged, neglected, homed, and un-homed. We labor so hard at belonging.

* * *

Which is to say, years later when the publication date for my memoir, February 16, 2017, was approaching, I became nervous about what it would mean to my mother, the second most important character in the book after the narrator. She doesn't understand any English, exclusively Spanish, so she wouldn't be able to read it. But still. Part of her life was in the book, and besides, she might hear details from my siblings, most of whom had said they planned to read it. One day, she and I in her backyard chatting about the plants' beautiful blooms, I stop us and say, Mom, the memoir is about to come out and in it I tell many experiences, beautiful and painful. My siblings will read it and they may approve or disapprove, but I have made peace with that. What I want you to know is that I wrote it from a place of love; I think the point was to explore—and to tell the world—the ways in which poverty deforms and contorts the body and the soul, el cuerpo y el alma, even as beauty still finds ways to shine through the sweat and the grime, the ways in which poverty damages . . . las maneras en que la pobreza lastima. . . .

There was a pause then brimming with so much unspoken between us through the years, our eyes meeting, searching for a way to reach across, for the words to end that sentence. What all did poverty damage? I think I wanted to say even us, me and you, madre mía, mother of my heart. Strong mother. Wounded mother. Or something like that that I couldn't articulate.

Then she said, Todo. Everything.

The truth of that one word, uttered then without regret or recrimination, as real as the walls erected around our vulnerable hearts. The wind rustling wisps of her once red curls, now mostly grey. My hair now thinning. The late afternoon sun falling gently over us, casting soft shadows, hers moving in union with the sway of her long white skirt. The tall bougainvillea, with its bouquets of fuchsia, witness beside us.

Had we not done our very best under the pressure of forces beyond our control, forces that shaped and deformed us? But I will tell them, Mother, tell it all, the hunger, the shame, the hurt and the beauty, those moments that save us.

I nodded softly in agreement, then leaned in and embraced her. Briefly. Then we went back to her well-tended plants, the vibrant flower its own celebration, because that was all we could do.

* * *

Which is to say, whatever I may have managed I did as a way out of that sadness that is mine and not mine alone. And where others have found a measure of peace or rest or belonging in romance or family or career, I have found it in the page and its utterance, something like this space with you.

Sincerely,
José

 Poetry

The Last Time I Went to Church

José Antonio Rodríguez

My father's body was in a casket
Up there near the altar. Near the light,
I've been told.

The last time I went to church,
My oldest sister asked me why
I didn't weep—not when I got
The phone call, not when I entered
His room, my mother and my aunt silent
As candles, not when I lifted his body
From the bed to lay on a stretcher
Bound for the funeral home
And clumsily banged his head
Against the narrow door frame,
Not when I thought then of the last hospital
Night, the timbre of his weeping—
Each sob smaller than the last,
Each it seemed both lament and deliverance—
After countless sleepless nights.
No more, he said, no more.

Not when I sat at his bedside then
And held him, turning his shoulders
Until he said you're hurting me. A reminder
Of the ripples of our lives' days
Hardly ever interrupted by touch.

The last time I went to church
I told my father, who I'm told
Surely must have been sitting next to me
and free of pain,
I'm so sorry about the door frame.

Duty

Sheryl Luna

I watched my grandmother's frailty
lifted, my mother's arms beneath her shoulders.
She was no invalid, no mindless forgetting,
sharp as a teenager in a tight red dress.
I want to clarify her dignity until the end,
her early poverty as a sibling of twelve children
kept her honest. Her tongue cursing
at us all out of a strange love.
Yet she would make us bean burritos
and chicken with mole every visit.
She would slip me a twenty-dollar bill,
or a ten or a five even though she had little money.
My own mother is aging in El Paso, and I am selfish
in Colorado. She limps with a bad knee
and sciatica. There is a guilt at my refusal
to be selfless. I leave it to my brother
and assisted living. I have become too
Americanized from early on,
my white stepfather demanding
obedience and English only.

Self-Portrait in the Year of the Dog

San Antonio, Texas, December 1970

Deborah Paredez

It's nearing the end
of the year and the woman who will be
my mother is pushing
stickpins through the eyes
of sequins and into Styrofoam globes
until each coated orb ornaments
the tinseled tree. Her body
is full of the curled question
mark that will soon be
my body. The woman who will be
my grandmother is biding time
at the five-and-dime stockpiling
supplies to fill my mother's idle
hands. All along she's carried
me low—
    how I've known
from early on to position myself
for descent. When I enter
this world, I'll enter as Hecuba
nearing her end: purpled
and yelping griefbeast,
my mother's spangled
handiwork.

Why You Never Get in a Fight in Elementary School

Octavio Quintanilla

In this country,
everything about you is foreign
and no one likes the look of scarcity.
You want to tell them
that when you draw a river
on a piece of paper, a fish
always jumps out of it
and you are always ready to catch it
as it leaps out of the page.
You are the fish and yet you are not the fish.
You are this: a kid, and the home you knew
begins to fill with water.
There goes the chair where your father sat
to eat his dinner by the light
of the kerosene lamp.
There goes the only memory you have
of your mother's feet.
You want to tell them that the ocean
where you stand on is not an ocean.
It is your new country,
where your body will be lifted
by all the ways of missing someone,
lifted by all the sounds.

Jarcería Shop*

Sandra Cisneros

A breakfast tray please. For my terrace.
In the morning I invite the bees
To raisin bread with lavender honey.
Don't worry, there's always
Enough for everybody.

I'll take a few of those *carrizo*
Baskets, strong enough for a woman
To haul a kilo of fresh oranges
From the Ignacio Ramirez market.
As if. I usually send Calixto,
my handyman.

And a palm fan.
Add an *ocote* stick or two.
For the fire I'll never ignite.
Solo de adorno, of course.
To amuse the spirit ancestors!

Can you bring down
That papier-mâché doll?

---

*Esto del Dicc. de la Real Academia Española:
jarcería ,
f. Méx. Tienda donde se venden objetos de fibra vegetal.
Una palabra muy antigua, ya casi no se ve.

Dressed in her best underwear.
I had one just like it as a girl.
No, I don't have kids.

A *comal* would be nice
To reheat my evening *tamal.*
Only a comal gives it
That smoky flavor.
I don't know how
To make tamales.
Why bother when
You can buy them
From the nuns.

A *molcajete*. Maybe.
A cool bird
Bath for my yard.

Ay, and *ixtle—*
Maguey fibers
Hairy and white as
The grandfather's chest—
To strop the skin raw in the shower.

My outdoor sink,
With ribs like a hungry dog's,
Could use a step stool stone
That dances a *danzón,*
And an *escobeta* scrub brush
Cinched tight at the waist
Like a ballerina.

Please deliver a fresh *petate*
With its palm tree scent
For my bedroom floor.
In the old days they were
My ancestors' coffins.

And that ball of *metate* string.
Might as well.

Plus a lidded straw basket
To store the plastic market bags
The colors of the Mexican
Tianguis

Sky turquoise,
Geranium coral,
Jacaranda, amethyst,
The tender green of
The paddles of fresh *nopal.*

A cotton hammock
Wide as a market woman,
So while I sleep
The pepper tree can bless me.

Six *carrizo* poles
To hang the new curtains
Made from *coyuchil* cotton.

I came for a cage
For my onyx parrot;
A goodbye gift from my agent
Attached with a warning:
Don't move south.

Los abuelos,
Who couldn't read, fled
North during the revolution,
With only what
They could carry in *un rebozo.*

And here I am at fifty-eight
Migrating in the other direction
With a truck hauling my library.

I live *al reves*, upside down.
Always have.
Who called me here? The spirits maybe.
A century later. To die at home for them
Since they couldn't.

And for my cobbled courtyard,
Your best branch broom
With a fine *shh-shh*
Like the workers who sweep up
Saturday night on Sunday
Morning in el Jardín.

And, a bucket.
To fill with suds.
For the simple glory of scrubbing
Mexican porch tiles
In my bare brown feet.

When I feel like it.
On my housekeeper's day off.

To set the grandmothers
Grinding their gravestone teeth.

Garden of Gethsemane

Diana Marie Delgado

I am repairing silverfish
on a station of the cross

when Jesus pulls me onto his lap.
Someone sees and he leaves

through the screen door
with a slam, shouts *liar.*

—I hide my nakedness
inside his belly,

a thatch of olive fields
where my father walks

around in boxers,
waiting for my mother

to fry him potatoes
with a black eye.

On one side of his face
where hope is written

a speck of me appears
that he never sees.

Can you forgive that?

You're tired of your life,

Octavio Quintanilla

so you buy a small house in South Texas.
      Before you buy the house, you get arrested for drinking and driv-
ing.
You go to jail for three days till your older brother, finally, bails
      you out.
He tells you not to worry, that he knows someone who knows
      someone
who knows someone.
Everything will be okay.
You won't lose your driver's license.
You won't lose your job.
      It's all about knowing someone who knows more than you.
Then you tell him that maybe you shouldn't have bought the house,
that you're tired of living the way you do.
Divorce was invented for a reason, he tells you,
that maybe she'll respect you a hell of a lot more knowing you had
      the guts
to cut her loose.
But you are not sure of anything.
So you think of the story of your parents falling in love.
(You had to come from somewhere, right?)
They have three children and you're one of them.
The third one died as a baby.
      The two times your mother talked about it, you wondered
how a person can live with such sadness and keep it all
to themselves.
Sadness like an unhealed bone.

Like a splinter in the iris.
But back then, all you wanted was to be alone,
so sometimes you'd write yourself into a story
as a nine-year-old boy building a tree house.
You wanted to tell your parents that you were old enough
to leave their town, that their appetite
was not big enough to keep them all alive.
It was just a thought.
You never wrote this down,
and you never finished the story.
The town was small like the heart of a flea.
The town was dry like a scab on a knee.
In the story you write years later,
your older brother bails you out of jail and tells you he knows
  plenty of people,
that it's all about knowing someone who knows someone,
for you not to worry.
You won't lose your job, he says,
you'll keep your driver's license,
keep your house.
He has no way of knowing that you're still trying
to climb out of the tree house
you never finish building.
You're still trying to convince yourself to leave
your parents' small town.
What if you leave and there's no way back?
No one there to give you directions?
No one there to remember you and point a finger
to what you wanted
to forgive?

The Soul

Diana Marie Delgado

Great-grandmother,
bowlegged and already blind
was out back killing chickens,
when in the nearby distance,
we saw a white horse
running up and down
the mountain,
and without saying it
knew it was her soul.

 **Fiction**

Dutiful Daughter

Diana López

Juanita stepped into the outpatient clinic at Spohn. She wore scrubs, but she wasn't a doctor or nurse. She didn't carry a stethoscope. She carried a tray with needles and tubes, and that was okay because orderlies didn't carry anything. Maybe she wasn't a doctor or nurse, but she wasn't an orderly either.

She was a phlebotomist. She liked saying it, *phlebotomist*. Her parents liked saying it too, but only because they couldn't. Not really. They tried, but they didn't try very hard. They were proud that Juanita's job wasn't as easy to say as "waitress" or "maid."

At first, Juanita thought "phlebotomist" was spelled with an *f*, but when she learned it was spelled with a *p*, she straightened up a little. Lots of medical jobs were spelled with *p*—podiatrist, practitioner, pediatrician. Other jobs started with *p* but not the *p* sound—psychologist, physician, physical therapist. Originally, she wanted to be a forensic scientist, which *did* start with the letter *f*, just like it sounded, but she didn't think she could graduate from college, then graduate again, then do rotations, then take a national exam. She went to Del Mar Community College instead, and she didn't have to graduate or do rotations or take a test for the certificate. It was a three-month program, twice a week, at night.

"Hi, Juanita." This from the client care specialist, the CCS. She didn't need college for *her* job. "I got the order for the lab," she said, holding out a form.

The patients in the lobby glanced up, saw Juanita's tray, and flinched. She could tell they understood her job now even if they didn't know her official title, "phlebotomist." Lots of people didn't know that word, but they knew other words. That's why when she first stepped into the clinic, Juanita pretended. She wore scrubs, so it was easy. In those few seconds before the CCS or someone else called her out, the patients, she hoped, had spotted her and thought "There's the doctor," but since she was young, if they'd thought, "There's the nurse," that was okay, too.

Juanita grabbed the order, then stepped through swing doors to a hallway lined with examination rooms. A chair was there and a scale. Even now a patient stood on it while a nurse, a *male* nurse, fiddled with the weights.

"I'm looking for Mr. Jefferson," Juanita said.

The man getting weighed said, "You here to take my blood?"

"Yes, sir, if you don't mind."

"Of course, I mind." He smiled as he said this, teasing.

The nurse wrote down the weight, then asked Mr. Jefferson to sit, then put the blood pressure cuff on his arm. "I'll be done in a bit," he told Juanita.

"That's okay," she answered, but she was bothered. Why'd *she* have to wait? The nurse wasn't going anywhere. This was his post, but she had two more stops before going to the lab. Sure, this nurse needed a college degree for his job, but he was fat, probably because he didn't move enough. Nurses shouldn't be fat. They shouldn't smoke or drink or eat doughnuts, either. She tried peeking at his badge to see if he was an RN or LVN, but he was turned away.

The cuff got tight on Mr. Jefferson's arm, then started to hiss as it deflated. Juanita wondered how it worked, what the top and bottom numbers of the blood pressure meant. It wasn't part of the three-month program at Del Mar. Maybe that's why she had to wait, because she didn't know stuff like this.

The nurse wrote more numbers on Mr. Jefferson's chart and said, "All yours," but he didn't leave. Just took a step back. Juanita peeked at his badge again—LVN, no big deal, though obviously *he* thought it was. She couldn't worry about it. She had work to do. She grabbed a purple top and a red top. Then she twisted a needle into the Vacutainer tube.

"How much blood do you need?" Mr. Jefferson asked.

"Just a little," Juanita answered.

"You call that 'a little'? I don't think so. You're a regular vampire, aren't you?" He laughed when he said this.

"I'm not a vampire. More like a mosquito."

This made him laugh even more.

She lifted the armrest, flat and broad like a cutting board. She propped

Mr. Jefferson's arm on it, tied the tourniquet over his bicep, and tore open an alcohol swab. His eyes got wide, but he didn't say anything, not even about the cold alcohol or Juanita's taps on his vein.

"You're going to feel a little prick," she said, getting the needle ready. Then, winking, "Just like a tiny mosquito bite."

She wasn't lying. She had "the touch," no pain at all for most patients.

There wasn't much to understand about her job, but she knew this—blood was warm; it was not red inside the tubes but a dark, rusty brown. And veins, healthy ones, bounced back, even on the fat patients; veins from patients on prednisone were hard to pin because of excess tissue fluid, which made them float around; veins from drug addicts felt like cords from all the scars. And a good stick meant the blood softly gushed out, while a bad stick meant it came out in squirts. Juanita rarely had a bad stick. She could get blood from a rock. That's what they said in the lab. That's why the other phlebotomists called her when they struck out.

She finished drawing blood from Mr. Jefferson, pressed a cotton ball against the puncture, and secured it with a Band-Aid. "All done," she said.

He inspected the crook of his elbow. "Well, I'll be. You *are* like a little mosquito. I didn't feel a thing." He stood up and followed the nurse to an examination room. "You have a great day," he said before disappearing behind the door.

Juanita smiled. She took a deep breath, the kind that lets you lift your chest and roll your shoulders. She studied the walls with their posters about diabetes. There were type 1 and type 2. It was all about insulin and sugar—no, *glucose*. There was a lab test for that, the glucose tolerance test. It meant drawing a patient's blood three times.

She finished her rounds and returned to the lab. First, to Chemistry, where she left the red tops in a water bath. She'd learned that the water bath was kept at the same temperature as the human body in order to help with clotting. Then she went to Hematology to leave the purple tops on an agitator, a machine that gently rocked because these tubes weren't supposed to clot at all. Finally, she went to Microbiology, where Zang worked. Zang was the nicest person in the lab. Maybe she was forty or sixty. It was hard to tell. Her face looked young, but her hands had lots of wrinkles.

"What're you looking at?" Juanita asked when she saw Zang at the microscope.

"See for yourself," Zang offered.

Juanita sat and focused the lens. "It's gram negative," she said about the pale red organisms on the slide. "They look like . . ." They weren't rods or cocci. This was something new. "I don't know. They look like little beans paired up."

"Very good!" Zang said. "That's exactly right. Diplococci." Then, she whispered, "This patient has gonorrhea."

Juanita remembered her high school health class, the unit on STDs, the pictures that showed the sores but never the tiny organisms that *caused* the sores.

"Diplococci. Gonorrhea," she repeated, studying more closely. She didn't want to forget, just as she hadn't forgotten that strep and staph were gram-positive, purple dots in a line or cluster, and just as she hadn't forgotten that bacteria called *Pseudomonas*—another *p*-word!—smelled like corn tortillas on the petri dish.

Zang leaned against the counter. "You really like this, don't you?"

"It's interesting," Juanita said.

"You could be a lab tech, if you wanted. John over in Blood Bank used to be a phlebotomist. Then he got his license to be a lab tech. Then he went back and became a med tech. He liked moving up, step by step like that. They've got the programs here in Corpus Christi, and the hospital's 24/7, so we could work with your schedule while you went to school."

Juanita thought for a moment. On the counter was a case of slides and, at the sink, a row of bottles for the Gram stains. By the hood were petri dishes and inoculation loops. She knew that in other rooms were pipettes and centrifuges and protein electrophoresis machines—so many instruments beyond the items of her phlebotomy tray.

"I always wanted to go to college," she said. "In the beginning, I wanted to be a forensic scientist like on *CSI*, but I could settle for a tech. I'd still be working in a lab."

"There you go," Zang said. "Come here. I've got a moment."

They went to the computer, looked up the requirements. Juanita could go to Del Mar again, this time for two years and for a degree. She'd have to do rotations and take a test, but if John in blood bank could handle it, so could she.

Zang printed out application forms. "They probably want you to apply online, but I like to do paper copies. I'm old-school."

Juanita took them, looked at the questions. She could answer every one.

After work, she headed to the Molina where she lived with her teenaged brother and her parents. *Still lived*, she thought. She took the Greenwood exit. There weren't any woods, and the grass wasn't green, and neither were the weeds. There was a Whataburger and KFC, but most of the restaurants were mom-and-pops, and a lot of businesses were this-and-that types, what her brother called "hybrids"—a car wash *and* a pet store, a tire shop *and* a taquería, a laundromat with dryers for clothes *and* hair.

"I know it's strange, but this 'hood was good enough for Selena," Juanita said, defending out loud, though no one had objected because no one else was in the car, a *used* car, a ten-year-old Honda Accord.

She got to the house, idled out front, and honked, so her mom could open the chain link fence that blocked the driveway.

Her mother ran out, cellphone to ear. She unlatched the gate, leaving it open after Juanita drove in, all the while talking to someone.

"Yes, yes, she's got a good job," she heard her mother say as they stepped into the house. "At Spohn," her mother continued. "She wears those medical pajamas like the doctors. She had to go to college."

All of it was true, but listening, Juanita felt like a fraud. When her mom hung up, she said, "I didn't technically graduate. I got a certificate, not a degree."

"Aye, mija," her mother said, "what's the difference?"

But there *was* a difference—between certificate and degree, between LVN and RN, between phlebotomist and med tech. Still, she couldn't blame her mom for not knowing or not *wanting* to know because Juanita *also* pretended, and not just about *her* job but about her parents' jobs, too.

When people asked, she said her father worked at a school and because she didn't want to sound like someone showing off, she added that it was an elementary school. That's where she left off, like a giant fill-in-the-blank on a homework page. She hoped those nosy people concluded that he was a teacher, or better, a principal. "He's been twenty years with the district," she'd say, thinking that twenty years should be enough for someone to move up. The twenty years was true. The moving up was not. Sometimes she felt guilty for lying, but then she reminded herself that she hadn't lied, had only *implied*, and couldn't be responsible for whatever conclusions people drew, yet hoping they drew the ones that had her father in front of students and faculty, wearing a suit and being called *Mister* Arriaga, or *Doctor* Arriaga, anything but Joe, which is what they called him—the administration, the faculty, the secretary and attendance clerk, the kids, even those in pre-K.

The truth? Her father was a custodian at Barnes Elementary on the other side of town. To get there, he turned on a street called The Mansions, and even *that* was a lie because there weren't any mansions, just as there weren't green trees along Greenwood. The Mansions was lined by rows of townhomes, each unit narrow and tall. Maybe the neighborhood near her father's school was better, but maybe it only *seemed* better because there weren't any mattresses or sofas out front.

Juanita wasn't ashamed of her father. He was a good, hardworking man. He had keys to the school. He was the first to open and the last to close, and if there was an assembly or PTA meeting, he stayed, making sure the ladies were safely in their cars because he was old-fashioned and never understood why some got offended when he held open a door or offered to lift their heavy boxes.

He cleaned the school, and there was honor in that. Sometimes things broke—water heaters, dishwashers, copy machines—and he fixed them. Juanita once asked, "How'd you learn to fix those things?" and he'd said, "Pues, I just know," as though he'd been born with the handyman knowledge the way he'd been born knowing how to breathe and suckle and cry.

Her mother babysat but when people asked, Juanita said she ran a day care, though it was really a *night* care because the parents in the neighborhood worked the registers at Valero or the front desks at Motel 6. They dropped off their children with sandwiches or Campbell's soup for dinner. Juanita's mom fed them, made them brush their teeth, and put them to bed. She bought air mattresses, called them an "investment." In the morning after the children left, she propped the mattresses against the wall. They'd be firm for a few days, but eventually the air leaked out and the sheets slipped off.

Sometimes, Juanita looked at those deflating mattresses and saw her own self losing air and sinking.

But not today. Today, she sat at the dining table and worked on the forms for Del Mar. Meanwhile, the doorbell rang, then rang again. Soon, four children were fighting over which DVD to watch. Then her brother got home and dumped his backpack on the couch. He wore earbuds. He *always* wore them. He nodded at Juanita, and that was extent of their conversation. Then her father came home, kissed the top of her head, tousled her brother's hair, and pretended to be el Cucuy for the children.

Meanwhile, her mother heated the cans of soup, placed sandwiches and carrot sticks on paper plates, and microwaved ribs leftover from a weekend barbecue. Everyone grabbed dinner except for Juanita, and when they asked her about it, she said, "I need to finish these forms first."

"And what forms are those?" her mother wanted to know.

"For school. I'm going back to Del Mar, so I could get promoted, be a lab tech. It's only two years."

"Two years! That's a long time."

"It's really not."

Her mother glanced at her father, so he could add his "pesos y sesos," as they liked to say, a family joke. He was chewing. Then he wiped barbecue sauce from his chin.

"What's wrong with the job you have now?" he finally asked.

"Nothing, but it could be better."

"Better? How? You make good money, right? You have benefits."

"I could make *more* money." She hated saying this because it wasn't about the money. She wanted to be a professional, but how could she explain this to her parents? "Maybe I could buy my own house."

"And live *alone*?" her mother asked. "What's wrong with *this* house? You have your own room."

"Don't you *want* me to move out?"

She glanced at her brother, hoping he'd add *his* pesos y sesos, but he hadn't heard anything because of those damn earbuds.

Her mother reached over to stroke her cheek. "Juanita, honey, you can move out when you're married." Then she went back to her plate as if that gentle touch settled things.

Juanita glanced at the kids. They were sitting on the floor and eating at the coffee table while watching a cartoon. Some princess was singing. One of the girls sang along. An hour ago, these kids were fighting, but now they were calm, all because her mother chose the DVD herself. Maybe she touched their cheeks, too, and that was that.

But Juanita wasn't a kid, even though her name implied it. How she hated her name, hated *hearing* it, how it was the official name on her birth certificate. She tried going by Janie one time but it offended her parents. Then, she tried Juana, but they were still offended. "You're our Juanita," her mother had said. "That's the name you got baptized under. When you go to the Lord, you'll be Juanita. How will He know who you are if you say something else?" So she went by Juanita to please her parents, but it irked her.

"You know," her father said, taking a sip of water before continuing, "you work at a hospital. Maybe you can find a nice doctor to marry."

"Those doctors are hard to catch," her mother said. "But, mija, maybe you could marry a nurse. What do they call those man nurses?"

"Just 'nurse,'" Juanita said.

"¿De veras? That can't be right."

Juanita straightened the papers. She'd finish them in her room later, with the door closed. "I know you mean well," she said, "but I'm going back to school. I'm going to get a degree this time. Nothing's going to stop me."

"But—" her mother tried.

"I don't want to hear it," Juanita said. "I'm going, and that's that. Now let's just eat in peace," and because she didn't want to sound disrespectful, she added, "please?"

She went to her room to leave the papers, but she came right back, served herself a plate. Her parents stared as she took her seat.

"We're just saying," her father insisted—would these people ever stop?—"We're just saying that going to college is hard and expensive, that you don't need to go because you already have a job. We only want you to be happy the way *we're* happy, okay? Yes? *Now* we can eat in peace."

Arguing was pointless. They'd had this conversation before when she was still in high school, still with her boyfriend Richard, still dreaming—not about Del Mar but about a *real* college, a *university*—about living in dorms, walking through quads, eating at eclectic cafés, her laptop open before her, her feet propped on a backpack heavy with books.

After dinner, she went to her room and got to the forms just like she promised herself. She needed to submit her transcripts, too, because the certificate program hadn't required them but the *degree* program did.

That was fine, even desirable, because she'd had good grades in high school. Not great, but good. She made As and Bs, mostly.

She knew the importance of a GPA because her senior year had been about college. *Richard* had been about college. It's what they talked about—going away and escaping Corpus Christi. He kept saying, "I need to escape. I need to escape," and *she'd* said he made it sound like a prison, and *he'd* said, "Not like a prison but like a land of lotus eaters." At first, she didn't get the allusion but then she remembered reading the *Odyssey* in senior English, how the lotus eaters were happy to laze around, and it made sense because no one in Corpus Christi moved, because even though her parents had their own house, it was in the neighborhood where they grew up, where Juanita grew up, and Richard, too. He never needed a car. She'd walk to his house, and they'd sit at his dining table with college applications, filling them out while his parents watched 20/20. Then, he'd walk her home, holding her hand or putting an arm around her shoulder, kissing her on the dark porch of an empty house that was always for sale. He'd say, "Someday, we'll have our own place for this," and she'd dream about an artsy loft in Boulder, Colorado. She'd never been there but she'd seen the brochures. "Yes, yes," she'd whisper, "when we escape."

But her parents had all these objections.

"Why so far when there are schools right here?"

"Where are you going to live?"

"Do you know how expensive it is? It's not just about paying for school. You have to support yourself, too."

Juanita looked into it, the costs. It was true. Everything was so expensive, but she wouldn't give up. She was going. She'd find a way.

Then her mom said, "Mija, it's very competitive. You have to be real smart to go to a university."

"I *am* smart," Juanita insisted.

"Well, you're not dumb. That's not what we're saying."

When Juanita had looked to her dad for support, he'd said, "Those big cities . . . they're dangerous, especially for young women like you."

And Juanita had said, "Maybe, but you can't protect me forever. I'll figure it out. You'll see. You'll be proud."

Only she didn't submit her applications, and the deadlines came and went.

Richard, meanwhile, headed to U of H. When he first left, they Facetimed every day, then a few times a week, then once a week . . . maybe. Then they sent texts every now and then. At some point, they just started clicking "likes" on Instagram. Then Juanita stopped liking his posts because she didn't want him to know she was still interested. She had this fantasy that he checked to see if she had "liked" him and that it stung when she hadn't, but she knew it didn't sting because he kept smiling. He kept freaking smiling, and with his genuine smile, not the fake one.

She knew the difference. He kept taking selfies with people—with *girls*. She didn't know them, *any* of them. She tried to not be jealous, but it was hard. Even the ones who weren't pretty were smart enough, *brave* enough, to go away to school. They would always have that over Juanita because she was a lotus eater, just like her parents and grandparents and everyone else stuck in Corpus Christi. But she wouldn't be a lotus eater anymore. She was going back to school. She would do things step by step, just like John in Blood Bank.

The next morning, she placed her application on the passenger seat. She'd take it to the admissions office after work.

Her shift started at five, so she could get samples in time for the techs who came at seven. She liked the early hour, though it meant waking the patients. Luckily, most were gorked out—that's what she called the heavily drugged or dying.

She had a Ms. Garcia first. She tapped at the open door, then announced herself. "Hello. Good morning. I'm Juanita Arriaga from the lab. I'm here to take your blood." She switched on the lights, checked for movement. Ms. Garcia stirred. "I hope you had a good evening," Juanita said as she approached. No answer, so when she reached the bed, she gently took Ms. Garcia's wrist to check the identity band. This roused her. She opened her eyes but only halfway, and since she stayed gorked out, Juanita narrated. "The doctor ordered electrolytes. Lucky for you, that's just one tube. I'm placing the tourniquet on your arm now. You're going to feel something cold. It's just the alcohol. Now you're going to feel a little pinch. Everything's looking good. I'm going to remove the tourniquet. Needle's coming out now. That wasn't so bad, was it? Here's a cotton ball. Keep your arm bent for a while. Okay, you can go back to sleep." But Ms. Garcia had slept through the whole thing. She'd probably wake up and wonder how the cotton ball got there.

Juanita repeated the procedure eight more times for eight more patients. Some were alert enough to say "Good morning," their breath like foul geysers, so much stink from so few words.

She hated confronting the smells of sick, unwashed people. At least, when she was a lab tech, she wouldn't have to go into rooms anymore. She wouldn't have to see those arrangements of roses, carnations, and daisies withering and dropping their leaves. She wouldn't have to walk by people squirming or pacing in waiting rooms, or worse, nodding off from the fatigue of so much waiting. She wouldn't have to hear the code blues and alarming beeps of heart attacks or step aside for the doctors—doctors who didn't run like on TV—doctors who walked but walked fast and importantly, tucking loose strands into surgical caps or snapping on latex gloves, all the while forcing Juanita to the sidelines so they could save lives, and later, accept the grateful hugs of the saved.

When she was a lab tech, she could stay in the lab all day. She wouldn't miss any chisme. She wouldn't have to hear about interesting cases after the fact, like the ovarian cyst that was as big as a football or the man who had spinal fluid dripping from his nose.

She couldn't wait. Two years wasn't a long time, but it was.

She had an order for a woman in oncology. Juanita knocked on the door, announced herself, and when she stepped in, she saw Beth Jimenez. She wasn't the patient but the woman at the bedside. Beth and Juanita had been in the same high school Spanish class, and they had always paired up for the conversational part of their lessons, laughing because their Spanish was awful despite their last names. That was the only class they shared. Beth was an AP student. She graduated in the top 5 percent and got accepted to the A&M in College Station, not the one in Corpus Christi.

"Beth? Beth Jimenez?" Juanita said as if she were unsure.

"Juanita, is that you? What are you doing here?"

Instead of answering, Juanita held up her tray.

"You work here?" Beth said. "You're a nurse?"

Juanita paused to let the possibility live a little. Then, "No, I work in the lab."

"Wow. I remember how you always talked about those medical shows."

She hadn't. She had talked about *CSI*, but she didn't correct her friend. "Yeah, well, I'm not a forensic scientist, but I like my job." She put her tray on the counter and started gathering equipment. "Looks like we'll be running a CBC and a liver panel today."

She hoped Beth caught the "we" and inferred that it meant Juanita plus the others in the lab. It wasn't exactly a lie, since Juanita'd be the one running the tests soon.

The old woman in bed said nothing, so Beth gently shook her. "Abuela," she said, "Abuela, wake up." She snapped her fingers in front of the old woman's face. "She's on all these medications," she explained.

Juanita nodded, then she spoke, too. "Ms. Jimenez? Ms. Jimenez, can you wake up for a moment? My name is Juanita Arriaga. I need to collect a blood sample, okay?"

The woman stirred. "I hear you. I hear both of you. Do what you need to do, just let me keep my eyes closed. The light, it bothers me."

"Okay," Juanita answered. "I just want to make sure you're aware of what's happening."

"I'm aware, mija. Yes. You're a good girl."

As she lowered the bed rail, Juanita asked Beth if she were still at A&M and if she liked College Station.

"I'm not there anymore. I hated it. Felt lost. Too many people at that university. And going from dorm to class, all the buildings, all the navigation. I felt so lonely. Really struggled to make friends. I guess I'm too shy. That was part of it. I just felt invisible there. Gave it one year and then transferred over here. It's much better, and I'm back with my parents, which saves me lots of money. Can't wait to graduate and have a real job like you. I work at IHOP right now. Do I smell like syrup? I swear, everything smells like syrup."

Juanita couldn't believe it. Beth was one of the smartest girls in school, and here she was, back in Corpus Christi and working at IHOP. Yes, she'd be graduating, but from the local university, which wasn't the same as going away to school. Still, it was a step up from Del Mar.

"I bet you love living on your own, huh?" Beth said. "Being independent?"

"Oh, yes," Juanita replied. Then, because she didn't want to show off, "I mean, I just live in a one-bedroom, but I'm saving money for a house and hopefully moving soon."

"With Richard? Are you guys still together?"

"Yes. I mean, no."

"No way! What happened?"

"Nothing major. I mean, we were in high school and then we grew up."

Beth nodded, even though she never had a boyfriend as far as Juanita knew.

"Ms. Jimenez?" Juanita said. "I'm ready to draw your blood. You still with us?"

The woman nodded, so Juanita started the procedure. She tied the tourniquet. She rubbed the alcohol. She unsheathed the needle. Problem was, the woman was old. She didn't have muscles anymore, and she'd lost weight from the chemo. Her veins rolled. Usually, this wasn't an issue.

With her free hand, Juanita would pin the top and bottom areas of the stick, but she couldn't clamp these veins. They kept rolling. She missed, but instead of taking the needle out, she tried inching it over. Ms. Jimenez cried out and flinched, making the needle slip.

"I'm sorry," Juanita said.

"Ow! Ow!" the woman cried, her eyes still closed.

Beth rubbed her shoulder. "It's okay, Abuela. She's just trying to do her job." And to Juanita, "They always miss on the first try."

Juanita nodded, but she was embarrassed. She wasn't like the other phlebotomists. She was better.

She set up again, tied the tourniquet, rubbed the alcohol, unsheathed a new needle. This time, Beth watched every move. The old woman moaned even though Juanita hadn't poked her yet. Mysteriously, her hand started shaking.

"Are you sure you know what you're doing?" Beth asked.

"Yes, I know what I'm doing," Juanita snapped, and she stuck the needle to prove it, a hard jab, which caught the vein but also went *through* the vein. A hematoma started to form and the old woman cried, "¡Me duele!" Juanita pulled the needle out, grabbed gauze, and applied pressure.

"You hurt my grandmother," Beth accused.

"She flinched," Juanita said. "If she holds still, I can get the sample." She peeked beneath the gauze. The woman wasn't bleeding out but her arm was purple now. The technical term was "subdural hematoma," but most people called it a bruise. "I'll try her other arm."

"No, you won't," Beth said. "We'll get someone else."

"No, I got this."

"I want someone else to try," Beth repeated. Then, softer, perhaps to be polite, "Please?"

Questions could be answered, this one with a simple yes or no. Juanita could apologize again, insist, but she hesitated, and the opportunity slipped away.

She gathered her phlebotomy tray and left without a word. At the lab, she'd have to admit she missed a vein. It happened sometimes—not to her but to others. She wouldn't lose her job. They wouldn't even write an incident report because no one cared—not really.

The rest of the day was routine, and busy, too busy to check in with Zang. After work, Juanita walked to her car. She had to park across the street. It meant waiting at a light. When the walking man signal came on, she stayed on the curb, waiting for the countdown, crossing only when the five-second mark flashed. And she took her time. Cars had to wait, but no one honked. They were amazingly patient at the intersections of Corpus Christi.

When she stepped into her car, a dozen mosquitoes flew in, too. She slapped at them but they were hard to catch with their unpredictable flight patterns and habit of settling in the crevices. So she waited for them to land on her arm, start sucking at the blood, those fucking little vampires. One found a vein on top of her hand, the same one she used when the patients' arm veins were shot. It bit her. She watched it get sluggish from so much drink, and then she slapped it, leaving a spot of blood and the black smear of its body.

She glanced at the Del Mar application on the passenger seat, her neat handwriting. How silly to write it out when everything was done online nowadays. She could always go online to apply. She didn't have to go to the admissions office today. There were other days—tomorrow or next week. And the Internet was 24/7. She could apply at three o'clock in the morning if she wanted. No need for all these papers, no need at all, so she picked them up and used them to wipe off the mosquito and the blood.

Melancholy Baby

Severo Perez

Every day, seven days a week, rain or shine, fifteen-year-old Oscar Buscoso rode his bicycle to Zarzamora Street to wait for a truck to toss a bundle of newspapers on La Poblanita Bakery's sidewalk. When the bundles hit the pavement, Oscar and Harry Poole, a red-headed freckled-faced classmate, pounced, cutting the cinching wire with a pliers and either rolling or blocking the newspapers for delivery.

Across the street from the bakery stood the stately Our Lady of Mount Carmel Church and Little Flower School. Oscar finished folding his newspapers and loaded his bike bags.

Harry shook his head. "Why are you doing it?"

"He's wrong." Oscar mounted his bike and peddled away to throw his route.

* * *

Tenth grade should have been an easy slide for Oscar. He'd breezed by for eleven years; now every part of his school life was coming apart. His trouble began in the spring semester, when an austere Spanish priest entered life at Little Flower School. Father Luis was there to provide religious instruction once a week for one hour. Unlike the parish Carmelite discalced priests, who wore brown robes and sandals, he dressed in a black suit and a black shirt with a clerical collar. While clean and ironed, his sleeve cuffs were frayed, and holes in his elbows had been neatly patched. His strong Castilian accent contrasted with the Irish brogue spoken by the nuns. Gaunt, and not much taller than some of Oscar's classmates, his outstanding physical feature was his generous aquiline nose.

In the fall of 1956, the enrollment of St. Teresa of the Little Flower, a parochial school in Westside San Antonio, Texas, was roughly 350 students, with one classroom for each grade, kindergarten through twelfth. For most kids, the transition from junior high to high school at age fifteen was a big-deal rite of passage—not so much at Little Flower School, as it was called. For the tenth graders, high school was the same room they'd used the previous year.

Boys wore khaki uniforms, and girls wore brown skirts and white blouses. With only a few student departures over the years, Oscar had known most of the teenagers in his class since kindergarten. Rita Sue Hinojosa, Harry Poole, Eddie Martinez, and Joey Caulfield were his closest friends.

Throwing a newspaper route had given Oscar a unique view of the community. He knew which customers paid promptly for their subscriptions and which wouldn't come to the door when he came to collect but complained to the newspaper if he stopped delivery.

He had grown up near this stretch of Zarzamora Street, bracketed on the north side by Handy Andy Super Market and the white neighborhood and on the south side by the disreputable Lerma's Nite Club and the Mexican barrio. In between were Our Lady of Mount Carmel Church, Little Flower School, La Poblanita Bakery, Sanchez Cleaners, the fire station, the old ice house, and Hurtado Brothers Iron Works. This in-between neighborhood was a mix of working-class Mexican American families and working-class white folks. His grandparents and other relatives lived nearby.

Sister Bartholomew, his teacher for most of his tenth-grade classes, had encouraged Oscar to enter into discussion with Father Luis. "This is preparing you for an adult understanding of our faith," she told him. Not that Oscar was ever shy about speaking up. His questions were usually intended to elicit a laugh from the class. Sister Bartholomew allowed them because he was never malicious and occasionally his questions enlivened a sluggish lesson. She had no reason to believe that would be a problem.

There was a religion textbook they were required to read. On the first day, Father Luis told the class that they shouldn't simply accept what was in the text. "Question everything," he said. "Question even me."

Father Luis then proceeded to drone on for twenty minutes in torpor-inducing accented English about Pope So-and-So, St. Augustine, and St. Thomas Aquinas. Since the material was all in the textbook, most of the class tuned him out. After finishing the background to the Catholic faith, which he apparently had committed to memory to the horror of

Oscar's classmates, Father Luis opened the textbook and proceeded to read out loud in the same listless monotone. "God is good. What He creates is good."

Oscar's hand shot up. Father Luis appeared appreciative to get a question so early. So did the class. Rita Sue, his latest crush, sat in the next row. She gave him a look as if to say, "Thank you."

Oscar stood. "If what God creates is good, why does He create bad things?"

"There are many things that are mysteries," Father Luis said. "God does not create bad things."

"What about polio?" Oscar pushed on. "Cancer. Malaria. Plague. They're all bad."

He motioned for Oscar to sit down. "Later," he said. "We will get to that in the future."

"God is everywhere," Father Luis continued. Wait, that was something Oscar had been thinking about.

He raised his hand, and stood again. Father Luis nodded, pleased to see the enthusiasm, not so pleased at the interruption.

"If God is everywhere, why is there a candle on the altar? Where is God?" A chuckle went through the class.

"This is not a joke," Father Luis warned. "Questioning must be serious."

"Father, I am serious. Does God have office hours?" A bolder chuckle followed.

Father Luis's eyes flashed, probing for the snickering offenders. Oscar was saved by cool Eddie Martinez and the class clown, Joey Caulfield. Eddie and Joey were having a balance-your-chair-on-two-legs contest. Eddie's chair slammed the floor with a loud thud.

Father Luis made them stand. Joey's pudgy, somewhat disheveled appearance was a lost cause for the nuns. He couldn't sit or bend over without his shirt pulling out from his trousers. His scuffed shoes were a disaster. Joey could make fun of himself but didn't take well to being teased.

"You are no shining example of a Catholic student," Father Luis said.

"You're not so sharp yourself," Joey shot back.

"What was that?" Father Luis stared at Joey. "Look at you. You are a disgrace." He looked up as if to say, "Help me, Lord."

"Don't turn your nose up on me; you'll scratch it on the ceiling," Joey mumbled loud enough for everyone to hear. Naturally, several boys laughed.

Father Luis zeroed in on Joey. "For next week, you will copy in long-hand from the book Chapter 12 about respect. Failure to do so will mean an F for the semester." Joey realized he'd gone too far. "I'm sorry, Father," he muttered, and sank back in his chair.

Cool Eddie Martinez disappointingly slouched and apologized, which got him off without punishment.

Father Luis continued with his lecture as if Oscar had never spoken. The distraction gave him time to think. Examples and arguments spun in his mind.

The following week when Oscar expected Father Luis to allow time for discussion, he'd come prepared. However, Father Luis now lectured about the soul and free will.

"Free will decides our fate. The choices we make will make the difference in our eternal life."

Oscar raised his hand. Father Luis paused and reluctantly nodded.

"What about a human without free will?" He recalled a comment Sister Perpetua made in biology class.

"Everyone has free will," Father Luis replied with certainty.

"In biology class I heard about a baby born without a brain," Oscar began. "Sister Perpetua says the child has no intention of dying. It is fed and wears a diaper, but it doesn't think. If it can't make choices, does it have a soul?"

"All humans have a soul."

"If . . . it has no brain and can't exercise free will, does its soul go to heaven?"

"It depends if the infant received the sacrament of Baptism," answered Father Luis.

"What if it wasn't baptized and it dies?"

"The child will then remain in purgatory." Father Luis answered.

"That's doesn't seem fair, I mean, it has no choice. What about the parents?" Oscar persisted. "They're poor. Why would God do that to them?"

"God may be punishing the parents or teaching them a lesson," he said.

"So a soul is condemned never to see heaven, through no fault of its own, in order to punish the parents? I thought that was why he created hell."

"God has his reasons. They are not for us to know." Father Luis raised his palm to Oscar as if he were stopping traffic.

"But . . . how does that make God good?" Oscar asked.

The silence in the class was palpable. Father Luis paced.

"There will be no more questions." Father Luis asserted his authority. "God is good. That is your answer."

The clashes evolved into a weekly incident. Whatever the subject, Oscar couldn't stop asking questions. By the third session, the situation became acrimonious.

"Father, if it is a mortal sin to eat meat on Friday, a mortal sin to purposely miss Mass on Sunday, and a mortal sin being so bad that if one were to die without absolution, the condemnation to hell would be instantaneous. How are those sins equal to murder?"

"That is why our souls must be kept pure at all times," Father Luis replied.

"But if Confession is supposed to cleanse the soul, why do Catholics have to do kitchen duty in purgatory? Will there be Protestants in purgatory?" Half the class laughed; the other half read the expression on Father Luis's face.

Oscar's classmates may have been on his side at first. Rita Sue and others groaned when he asked, "What is God made of? Is he like the ether that can carry sound waves? Or is he like abstract nouns, as in honor and glory?" Harry Poole raised his arms in mock surrender.

Father Luis related his frustrations to the school authorities. "You're being obstreperous," Sister Bartholomew cautioned.

"He told us to ask questions. And he never answers."

"Be respectful. He's a priest." Sister Bartholomew may have tolerated Oscar's impudent comments in her class. On this issue she was inflexible. "Stop the nonsense!"

The following Saturday morning while standing under the awning waiting for the newspaper delivery truck, he looked across Zarzamora Street to his school and church. Heavy rains had gouged potholes in many of the low spots where Woodlawn Creek overflowed its banks.

The route manager drove up to La Poblanita Bakery and called Harry and Oscar to the car. Because of the rain, the delivery truck would be an hour late. Car tires hissed on the wet pavement. Oscar felt drawn to the church. He darted across Zarzamora Street.

"You going to pray?" Harry called after him.

"Nah."

He entered the church, touched his forehead with holy water, and genuflected before he took his seat in a pew. He hadn't come to pray. Little good came from that. Prayer had done nothing for his acne or his grades. He had prayed hard for his friend Isabel not to die when she went to the hospital. He never saw her again. The priest at her funeral said she was now running around healthy and happy in heaven.

In the cool stillness, footsteps and voices echoed. A lone woman wrapped in a black shawl murmured repetitive *Ave Marias*. A monk in a brown robe and sandals genuflected as he crossed in front of the altar, his wooden rosary beads clicking with every step. He carried a wet mop. The roof had leaked. Oscar had been here numerous times, yet details he had taken for granted now appeared amplified.

The pews faced a spacious vaulted semicircular recess. A marble altar anchored a twenty-five-foot-high sculpture of a cloud with St. Teresa ascending into heaven. The Virgin Mary, with the Holy Child seated on her lap, reached down for St. Teresa's hand. Joyous angels and cherubs circled. Still higher, the focal point of the sculpture was the disembodied head of a crucified Jesus staring out from the center of a gilded sunburst.

Oscar had always felt secure inside the church. Outside, he had very little that gave him cultural prestige. He had worn thick corrective lenses since he was six. He couldn't participate in any type of sport that involved a moving ball. However, inside the church he had earned real recognition. Three years before, Sister Gregory, the principal and also choir director, selected Oscar for the solos. At fifteen, he could still sustain high notes without his voice cracking. In the natural echo chamber of the church's nave, he would let loose in Latin on "O Salutaris Hostia" and "Tantum Ergo." His solos at Christmas services were "The First Noël" and "O Holy Night." When he sang, he felt suspended in the music. He suspected his future as a soloist was coming to an end. Sister Gregory was trying out younger boys with voices not on the verge of change. They would likely be doing the solo performances in the fall.

When Oscar exited the church, the truck had already dropped off the bundles. Harry was nearly finished rolling his newspapers.

"Just shut up in class," said Harry, loading up his bicycle bags. "I think Father Luis is a joke. But, I'm not going to poke him. Why do you?"

"I can't help it," said Oscar.

The following week, Oscar was at it again. He stood and asked, "Is God like Santa Claus, all knowing, but unlike Santa, unknowable?"

"Santa Claus? You would compare God to Santa Claus?" Father Luis sneered.

"How is the invention of Zeus, or any god, different than the invention of a mythical character like Santa Claus?"

"God is not mythical," said Father Luis fiercely.

"I didn't say he was, but what happens to a good person who doesn't believe in God? What happens when they die?"

"You either believe, or you don't believe. There is no middle ground. Outside the church and its teachings, there is no salvation. Now, sit down." That was supposed to have ended the discussion. Father Luis paused to find his place in the text.

Oscar sat, his brain still spinning. "How much of God is real and how much is invented?" he blurted.

Father Luis put aside his book. "Come to your feet. Get up here. Now. Bring your textbook with you," demanded Father Luis.

Oscar stood and awkwardly passed his classmates. He turned and saw twenty ticked-off faces.

"If you think you know more than the textbook, teach the class," ordered the priest.

"I don't know more than the book," said Oscar.

Father Luis glared, "Then read. Open to Chapter 7, and read."
Oscar believed the priest expected him to beg, apologize, maybe cry. Oscar couldn't do it. In that anxious state his visual limitations kicked in. His eyes skipped around the page. He'd lost his place. The word "predictable" came out "peedicable." The class tittered. He grinned. He didn't do it on purpose.

That's where Father Luis pinned Oscar to the wall. Every time he fumbled the text, which was nearly every paragraph, the priest forced him to read the entire passage from the first line, often several times, before he allowed Oscar to move on.

Rita Sue looked up at him in pitying disapproval. Harry Poole wouldn't look at him. Joey Caulfield, his last remaining ally, mouthed, "Give it up."

Mortified, Oscar couldn't stop. He read on.

The next chapter was about the worst sin a human can commit. Oscar thought of genocide, since he recently read about Anne Frank; and it wasn't murder, incest, or rape, evil things he'd read about in the newspapers he delivered. He and the class learned the worst sin a Catholic can commit was suicide, because from suicide there is no salvation.

Oscar couldn't help himself. "May I ask a question?"

Father Luis closed his eyes and exhaled an irritated, "Yes."

"Does this mean a terrible criminal can kill hundreds of people, then repent on his death bed; and he might eventually get into heaven, as long as he doesn't commit suicide?"

"If the contrition is true, in a long time, yes. He can achieve salvation." Father Luis answered.

As Oscar read on, the text said that the symptom for suicide was melancholy.

Father Luis stopped him. "That is pronounced *meh-lawn-ka-lee*."

This word Oscar knew. "It's pronounced *melon-collie*."

"*Meh-lawn-ka-lee*," Father Luis corrected.

"No, Father, it's *melon-collie*." Oscar almost felt embarrassed for the priest.

"*Meh-lawn-ka-lee*," Father Luis demanded. "Read the entire section again."

Oscar paused. He looked out at his classmates' faces. They hated him for making them witness to his self-inflicted humiliation. Oscar closed his eyes. In the best voice he could muster he sang,

"Come to me my *meh-lawn-ka-lee* ba-ya-by.

Cuddle up and don't be blu......ue."

The class burst into raucous, sustained laughter. Eddie fell off his chair. Harry slapped his desk. Joey hooted the loudest. Rita Sue didn't want to laugh but couldn't help herself. She hid her face.

Father Luis's face turned a deep poisonous red. He pointed to the door.

The incident occurred a few weeks before the end of the spring semester. Sister Gregory, the school principal, informed Oscar's parents of his behavior. She advised it would be best if he didn't return for the fall term. Oscar assumed his parents thought the change of schools was for the best. They never said a word about it to him. For the last three weeks, Oscar was sent to the library when Father Luis came to teach religion.

* * *

Oscar had lived in this Westside neighborhood all his life. He'd been in the Scouts with the boys and had crushes on the girls. His parents had been married in Our Lady of Mount Carmel Church. He was baptized, confirmed, and took first communion there.

Through the years, Oscar had participated in all the school's activities and numerous church obligations. He took his turn as an altar boy at eight years old, getting up at 4:30 a.m. and catching a bus in the dark to serve 6:00 a.m. mass. He wore a canvas belt and sash and did his duty as crossing guard on busy Zarzamora Street. All that was history.

In the fall, Oscar took a bus out of the barrio into an entirely different neighborhood to attend Thomas Jefferson High School. The enrollment was over 1,500 students. Oscar went from knowing everyone to knowing no one.

Since his schedule had changed, he could no longer maintain his paper route. He passed on the job to his younger brother. As the months passed, he had no reason to return to Zarzamora Street and Little Flower School. He soon lost touch with his school friends Joey, Eddie, Rita Sue, and Harry.

Even though his questioning about God was earnest, it hadn't been easy. He'd had eleven years of Catholic indoctrination. Oscar recognized that people found security and comfort in religion.

He could argue with Harry and Joey, "If the story of creating the earth in six days is a myth, how can the rest be true?" That was the line Joey and Harry wouldn't cross. One side of the line required little effort, just unquestioning faith and overlooking numerous contradictions.

When Oscar's ninety-eight-year-old grandmother died, the priest said she was now in heaven happily dancing with her husband. She wasn't. Oscar's 105-year-old grandfather was sitting in the first row. The mourners laughed. Oscar thought about the conceit that there was happiness and frolic after death. It might comfort some, but Oscar questioned how the priest knew that for a fact.

That was the last time Oscar set foot in Our Lady of Mount Carmel Church. He had once believed that the proof of God's existence was in the magnificent basilica. Looking up at the ceiling he noticed tobacco-brown water stains caused by the recent storms. The church, with all its fine architecture, stained-glass windows, splendid altar, and a candle burning continuously, was only a building. A few months after leaving Little Flower School, Oscar concluded he was an atheist.

Mundo Means World

Octavio Solis

There I was, sitting on the porch taking in the Saturday morning rays in my pajama pants and T-shirt, nursing a cup of Mom's café con leche with the light buzz of my doobie taking hold. The grackles with their oil-slick wings scattered as Louie-Louie rolled by in his royal-blue Chevy Impala with the mag wheels and chrome bumpers, like he always did on weekends. Only this time he pulled into the driveway. That sleek machine next to my car reminded me that no matter how I customized it with a cherry-red Earl Scheib paint job and new tires, my Gremlin would always be a Gremlin. There went my buzz.

Louie-Louie sat in his car with his sunglasses on like the Prince of Low and waved me over to him. He never got out of his ride if he could help it. Some people thought it was laziness on his part and rude too, and some even wondered if he had legs at all. But I knew better. That Impala was Louie-Louie's throne, and as long as he sat on it, he was king. Why would he abdicate that when there was enough daily shit in this dusty old town to make us all feel provincial? I slipped into my flip-flops and sauntered over all cool and easy.

¿Que onda, Louie-Louie?

Nada-nada. How about you, bruh?

I'm cool.

Been too long, ese. You high?

Just a hit. Keep it down. My mom, sabes.

I'm hip. How's your sister doin'?

Still married.

I don't see it lasting.

Like a lot of the guys that called themselves my friends, or camaradas in the jargon of my time, Louie-Louie took an undue interest in my sister Mickie. It didn't matter that she was already married and had a four-year-old kid to show for it. He was waiting for the day she'd come to her senses and ride off with him to some romantic getaway like Carlsbad Caverns. Like that day would ever come.

Mundo, I need you to do me a solid.

A what?

A favor, bruh. I need your help.

For what?

Without taking his eyes off me, he reached under the seat and whipped out something wrapped in newspaper. He laid it in my hand and by the weight of it, I knew it was trouble.

What's this?

Just for a day. Watch it for me.

I peered through a slit in the paper and saw the shiny blow-hole of nasty looking right back at me.

This is a gun, ese. What the hell am I gonna do with a gun?

Nothin'. Just put it away and forget about it. I'll be back for it tomorrow.

What's going on, ese? Is this your cuete? What've you done?

Nothin'. Look, Mundo, I'm asking you to fucking do me this solid, and if you don't want to, then fuck it, I'll find someone else. But I thought you were mature enough for this shit. How old are you, twenty-one, twenty-two?

Eighteen.

Eighteen? Fuck it, I'll see you later.

He started to take it back, but I moved my hand away. I didn't realize that I had done that. Something about the heft of it, the blunt unpredictable weight of it, felt good against my abdomen, and that's where I kept it.

Just kidding, ese. I'll watch it for you.

He smiled. Like an idiot, I smiled back exactly the same way.

Orale, Mundo. That's my bruh. You my rock-steady bruh. Later.

He turned up the music in his car and shifted it in reverse.

Is it loaded? I asked.

Louie-Louie gave me his over-the-sunglasses look and said, Say hi to Mickie for me, bruh.

* * *

Louie-Louie used to be Luis Gutierrez, and he used to work for my dad's tree surgery business back when Dad was still married to my Mom. But sometime after Dad left home and later the state, Luis got mixed up with these other people who worked in used car sales, which we all knew were fronts for money-laundering operations—and just like that, he's Louie-Louie, and his shirts look cheap and he smells of cologne and he's putting a gun in my hand. I didn't like the way he called me bruh either, like it would endear me to him instead of making me feel like an article of women's underwear. But the fact that he entrusted this hardware to me, that said something about how the world seemed to be gearing up for me.

I closed the door to my room, turned up the music on my stereo, and decided I wouldn't even look at it. I'd put it in the closet under all my old *Famous Monsters of Filmland* magazines, leave it there until tomorrow. But before I knew it, I set the package on the bed, on my knees like a supplicant peeled back the newspaper with my hands shaking, and readied myself for the sight of it. Suddenly, everything in the room blurred out except for a single revolver, Smith & Wesson .45, stainless steel burnished to a matte finish, with a black grip finger-grooved for easy handling. I peered into the cylinder and found a bullet nestled in each chamber. I held it gingerly, shifted it from hand to hand and nursed that heft in my palm, aimed it at my graduation picture on the wall, at the whole tribe of graduates in my senior class panoramic, feeling the faintest voice whisper right into my fingertips the word yes.

I heard my mom making noise outside my door, so I wrapped the cuete in its paper and buried it deep between my magazines in the closet, right by the blunt I'd lit earlier. I needed a long, steaming shower. Standing there in the tub with the hot soapy water running down my legs, I looked at my sad skinny body and the not-quite-adult machinery of my sex, frail and incomplete. Only then did I realize that my hand was still gripping the gun, even if the gun wasn't there at all.

After I toweled off and combed my hair, I heard voices in the kitchen. I opened the door and called out, Amá! You talking with somebody?

Sí, mijo, she bellowed back. Mickie's here. She's gonna watch the house while I'm at work.

Hey, carnala! I shouted to her.

Hey, Mundo! Get dressed so you can say hi to Bruno!

Bruno was the aforementioned four-year-old fruit of my sister's loins and my nephew, but his real title was holy fucking terror. This little brat had a mad knack for ferreting out whatever meant the most to us and leaving it in a shambles. He once found a set of my great-grandma's diamond earrings and disposed of them in such a fashion that we found one of them deep in the bowels of the washing machine and the other deep in the bowels of Bruno himself. Needless to say, the shit he got into made us get into it too.

Bruno's here?

Yeah. Isn't he in your room?

I frantically wrapped a towel around and ran to my room and when I opened the door, there he was, holding that stainless steel three-inch barrel in his tiny toddler fingers. He was a striking boy with long lashes and deep green eyes, but his head already bore the scars of too many tumbles down stairs and out of trees. I dropped the towel and his gaze went straight to my groin, and that was distraction enough. I snapped the gun out of his hands and quickly pushed him out. No way that pinchi cuete was staying in the house now.

* * *

To keep it hidden, I put on my denim jacket and shoved the hardware barrel-first into the waistband of my pants. I flashed past Mom and Mickie with hardly a word and got in my car and drove. I didn't know where I was going, but I hardly cared. I headed down Alameda past the old motels and my old elementary school and the many used car lots that were only just sprouting along both sides of the avenue. I was raised along this old highway and connected to its low-rent charm, but now it was starting to turn. Into what, I couldn't say back then.

I stopped at the light and waited for my green with the other cars around me. Los Tigres del Norte from someone's radio bled into my car, and that's when it happened. The same smooth little whisper that had earlier coursed into the whorls of my fingers spoke up a little louder now, saying

Look at him.

I froze. Again I heard it.

Look at him.

I turned to the driver in the pickup next to me. An older guy in a Diablos baseball cap with a cigarette buried in his mustache.

In that brand new troca. Fucking music. He thinks he's el mero-mero.

The guy caught me looking and stared back like he's about to laugh 'cause I'm in a fucking Gremlin. I wanted to turn away but the voice said,

Nah, man. You got this.

And I did. Some kind of force hardened my look and the guy blinked and the light changed and he turned away and then he was gone. The car behind me honked, and the voice whispered

Take your fucking time. You are the man.

* * *

I stopped at the Sonic and had a burger for breakfast while I thought about where I should go next. El Paso is a big sprawling city with hardly nothin' to do but stay out of the heat. So I cruised around for a few hours, me and Pink Floyd and the .45. I drove through the serious streets of El Segundo Barrio, where no doubt some of the rough vatos standing on the corner were anchored with similar heft. When they turned their blunt grackle eyes on me sitting low in the saddle, I gave them the stern look of brotherhood. At first they looked affronted and I could almost see their spines stiffening, but then their hard Indian looks softened as they gave me their cholo salute, that lazy upward nod of the chin, and I went on my way at the speed of chill. Out of nowhere I thought I should stop by and see Lisa Morales at her parents' house just for the hell of it, and the voice in my waistband said yeah.

Lisa lived in this quiet residential neighborhood where everyone keeps their grass trim but the summer burns it yellow. All the Mexicans there think of themselves as upper middle class and look down on us in the Lower Valley, but I know for a fact they got all their fine imported furniture at haggled prices from the Mercado in Juárez. Lisa's family were very cool, though; they weren't into throwing airs and shit. Every time I went, her mother regaled me with her good home cooking.

Que surprise, Mundo! Come in, ya acabamos breakfast, but we got some bacon and pan dulce left over.

Está bien, señora. I just had a bite.

Lisa! Raymundo's here! Ándale, sit down.

I settled into her father's La-Z-Boy with the worn arm rests, which out of respect I'd never done before. It wasn't lost on Lisa. When she appeared in her shorts and tank top looking real fine, fingering her shag-cut hair, she stopped and smirked at me.

What are you doing? That's my dad's chair.

I know.

Her mother brought me a plate of ground chorizo and tortilla anyway, then Lisa and I talked in the living room about the highlights and lowlights of the previous night. Lisa had gone to a wedding dance with some guy who tried to force himself on her. He'd unzipped his pants in the car and tried to push her face down into him. I told her she deserved a better class of dude. I told her I'd bust his ass for her. She just laughed. I really liked Lisa Morales, but she didn't think of me as boyfriend material. She tells me everything that goes on in her life: the likes, dislikes, the secrets that claw at her young girl heart, the dark yearnings that run through every teenager who's tired of the burden of being chaste. It was easy for her to share those thoughts with someone who was afraid to admit that he was growing tired of the burden too. Only now there was this other burden, an even deeper secret, digging into my crotch like a finger.

Wanna walk to the park with me? she asked with those kissable lips.

The gun whispered in my pants, fuck yeah.

Sure, I said.

* * *

In that oppressive border heat that turns the sky almost white, we made our way down the block to the small park with the playground. All along the path, we talked, fell silent, then talked some more. Sometimes as we walked side by side, my hand would brush against hers light as a web, and that was enough for me.

Not this time, it whispered.

We sat in the swings while we talked about our plans for after high school. She was looking into a nursing career, and I told her she'd be good at it. She asked me what I wanted to do after graduation, and I said, college, I guess, but I didn't really know what that meant or whether it was even possible. I didn't want to think that far ahead. I couldn't think of anything except those long brown legs of Lisa's and that way she had of saying nu-uh, like it was a jingle for her own show or something.

Then while she was looking at some little kids playing soccer with a Wiffle Ball in the scrappy grass and weeds, the gun whispered trouble into me.

Turn around and kiss her. She wants it.

I swiveled sideways in my swing and faced her. What, she said.

Nothing.

No, Mundo. Tell me.

I just know you can do better.

So can you, the gun said.

I will, she said.

You will too, the gun said.

I got all the time in the world, she said.

World? That's you, loco. Mundo means world. El Mundo. You are her world, said the gun.

And when the right dude comes, I'll know it, she said.

See? She wants it.

I was about to say how every song in the radio lately seemed to be about her and how I couldn't keep my mind on my Algebra II homework and how I really needed to kiss her on the mouth, but she abruptly interjected.

Check it out.

We looked in the direction of the parking lot and saw a car pulling up. It was the guy with the zipper, tall and built like a biker, his curly hair teased into an Afro. He was all smiles, coming right for us. Lisa didn't look too pleased.

Sangrón. Wait here, Mundo. I'll handle this.

She knew I wasn't the type of guy to make a scene, which is to say she knew I was a coward. They stood far off in the stumpy withered grass saying stuff I couldn't make out, except something about dropping over to say hi and something about another chance. I sat in the swing making circles in the sand with my foot, trying not to look, but sometimes I would and I'd see him taking her hand and her pulling it away. Some grandma sitting on the bench watching her kids going up and down the slide squinted once in my direction and turned away. I thought for a minute it was 'cause she heard the gun laughing.

Almost without knowing it, I got up and strode right up to Lisa's side and stood there. For a second, the guy glared at me from under his Afro, then smiled all conceited and shit.

What it is.

What it is is you, said the gun and me.

Lisa tensed up when she saw how I was acting. Mundo, she said, this is—

I know who this is, we said. This is the guy who can't keep his pants zipped up.

Mundo!

The guy chuckled like it was the funniest thing he'd heard that day.

Pos, guess what? You can't treat my friend like that.

Like what?

Like some tramp. You can't do that, ese. Lisa's class and you got no business with her.

Mundo, stop.

How would you know, puto, he said.

'Cause I know Lisa like you don't, puto.

I'll kick your ass.

Try it, fuckhead.

Mundo! I mean it!

And he pushed me with three fingers, just three fingers, and I reeled back and almost fell. I took a shallow breath and like another heart pumping all kinds of courage and rashness and heat into me, filling me up with the here and now, blurring my vision of everything but the clarity of the time, the gun howled me right back into his face.

Push me again, I said. Go ahead. Push me again . . . *bruh.*

I don't know what it is, how some people know. Maybe they got an instinct for it, maybe they got a scent for gunmetal the way some mutts smell the meanness on another dog. Maybe he saw my fingers already wrapped around that invisible grooved handle and sensed my power to make it real. The guy looked intently into my eyes and snarled, fuck you. Then he backed off and threw her a look.

Some buddy you got here, Lisa. By the grace of God he ain't dead. See you tonight?

Lisa could barely speak.

Yeah. Sure. Ten.

Right on. Then to me as he walked back to his car: grace of God, puto, grace of God.

I was stupefied, not so much by my crazy newfound nerve, but by this instant pact between Lisa and the guy.

You're going with him?

Lisa, red in the face and burning with tears, shoved me as hard as she could screaming, What the hell are you doing? Idiot! Fool! I told you I got this!

But are you going back out with—

Yes! What do you care, shithead? Who made you sheriff all of a sudden?

She shook her head in disgust and stomped off back to her house. The kids and their grandma at the playground were staring at me. I stood there, throbbing with unspent purpose, feeling like I was gonna shoot my jizz right through the barrel of Louie-Louie's gun.

I did, it said. I made you sheriff.

* * *

It's a poor man's therapy for us to drive blind all over town, burning off gas while we let our minds churn and drift and reel along to the music on the radio. Steering around from red light to red, we feel like we're in control of something when we don't even know where the fuck we're going. We look for counsel in the faces of strangers and in the chance graffiti on the walls, the scrambled layers of gang tags, symbols of devotion, and fading mercantile signage. They seem like portents or maybe encrypted formulas for fixing the shit that has us by the throat. We want out of this dullness, the heavy dullness of this life, but when we find it, when we feel a trace of the sting of living fully, some of us retreat into our droning cars and ride the mazes of our making. Like I was doing in my little cherry-red Gremlin.

All afternoon, I was thinking about Lisa and how she kept ten paces ahead of me all the way back, her long shadow just out of reach of my shoes. I was thinking how she might never let me come over again and how the rest of the school year would be ruined by that. I was thinking about how I almost told her right before she went inside that I had a gun, and how that might have changed anything at all. But mostly I was thinking about the gun. And how it spoke to me. How it goaded me toward this other stronger Mundo, a Mundo less afraid. This was the ballast that kept all of us unstrung vatos from being swept away by the gales of change. Lisa would hate me from now on, but she'd tell her camaradas all about how I stepped up to this guy and how he backed down and they would know it too, and that made me smile. I was somebody to respect. I glanced at the passenger seat and saw the gleaming steel barrel flare its own dirty smile back at me.

I stopped to tank up my car and get a Slurpee and then at the last minute, I didn't get the Slurpee, but a six-pack of beer, and I didn't get carded. That was my experiment. Could I command the respect of the world with Smith & Wesson at my side? And the answer, my friends, was fuck yes.

I drove up to Scenic Drive on the mountain, stopped at the overlook, and drank my beer there. Looking down at the divide between Juárez and El Paso, marked by the concrete channel that used to be a great river, hemmed in for its own good, I took in the dimensions of this new Mundo. There wasn't anyone around, so I walked to the crags at the edge with my brew and in the waning red of sunset, took out the gun and aimed it directly at the point where I thought my house was. Somewhere out there, an invisible bullet was streaking through the window and into the heart of a dope who still saved all his monster fan magazines.

Night fell and I was still on the crag. All the beer was drunk and the air suddenly cold. And still nobody there. I wanted to talk to someone, to demonstrate my deft handling of this firearm, to declare to la gente what a badass cabrón I had been in the park. I needed them to see how different I was now. But nobody came. Occasionally, headlights would approach, then ease on past. I sat on the hood of my Gremlin crunching up the beer cans and getting pissed. I tried to listen to the radio, but the songs weren't about her anymore. I took a wizz on a rock and slung Spanish curses at the lights of the cities below and the black monolith mountain behind. Then I put that cold pinchi cuete right up against my cheek and cried. I cried at the injustice of Lisa Morales. How could she go back to that guy? How could she be mad at me after all we'd shared? Doesn't she see that it's me she wants? Then in the pitch blackness, I heard

She don't.

What?

She don't see it.

No, huh?

You have to make her see it.

Should I?

About time, Mundo.

I wiped the snot off my face and got in my car. My hands shivering on the wheel. My teeth rattling. The whole time the gun was humming some song. I don't know what song. It was pretty, though, and sad. When I got to Lisa's house, the gun said to park it around the block. So I did. Then I walked all casual up to her house and almost knocked, but the gun said not to. It said to go around the side to her window, or don't I know which room is hers? I said I did and I went. I looked in her window and there was Lisa, sitting on the floor talking on the phone to a friend. Or maybe the guy, said the gun.

Yeah, maybe him.

Bet he's got his zipper down.

Probably does.

She's gonna see him soon.

Yeah. At ten.

You can put a stop to that.

I should too.

So what are you waiting for?

How?

You know how, loco.

You mean, this?

You got it.

I looked down at the gun, and it felt so light now. All that weightiness of before was gone. It almost billowed in my hand. I raised it gently in the air till my arm made a straight line between my right eye and hers. My heart was stamping in my chest.

Mundo means world, I said.

That's right.

I am the world.

The whole world.

All the time in the world. That's what she said.

Yes she did, murmured the gun.

I nodded and slowly lowered my arm. I stepped back from the window and let my weak legs carry me back to the car. I put the gun in the glove box and drove home. Somewhere along the way, I threw up all over myself but I stayed focused on the sudden vividness of everything. The oil refinery along Trowbridge lit up at night shimmered like a crystal palace through my tears. I came home to a dark and quiet house, took a shower and lay awake in bed for hours after, deaf to everything but the long wail of the Southern Pacific rolling in. That and the comforting snores of my mom sleeping.

* * *

Next morning Louie-Louie pulled up and found me cleaning out my Gremlin. He didn't even shut off the engine. He sat in his car with those sunglasses on and summoned me with his smile. I threw the rag in the pail and popped open the glove compartment, took out his .45 wrapped in crisp newsprint, and put it right in his waiting hands.

What you washing that piece of shit for? You selling it?

Nah, I like my Gremlin.

No shit, he chuckled. Well, you ever wanna trade it in, I'll get you a good deal, ese.

I'll keep that in mind.

Thanks for the solid. It wasn't no trouble, was it?

I shook my head. I told him about how Bruno got his hands on it, and we had a good laugh about that.

I owe you one, he said, 'cause if you knew the reason I had to unload it on you—

But I raised my hands and cut him off.

Honestly, dude, I don't wanna know. Just take it away.

Louie-Louie gave me the sidelong gaze of the Prince of Super Low and slipped the gun from its swaddling. It looked like a cannon in his small childlike hands.

Mundo, I'm serious, bruh, he said. When are you gonna figure out the Life According to Gun?

I shrugged like an eighteen-year-old is supposed to and said, Bruh, I got all the time in the world.

Border as Womb Emptied of Night and Swallows[*]

ire'ne lara silva

I followed you here. I'd follow you anywhere. My father said it wasn't right. That we had it backward. That it was the woman who was supposed to follow her husband. But that never mattered to me. I'd never do anything that would keep us apart. What I am is yours. I am yours even when you are away. When I am alone. I am yours for as long as I breathe and even after. I am yours for as long as you want me.

Memory brought you here. Brought us here. Your history is here. Your family. Your parents and grandparents and great-grandparents. Your siblings and nieces and nephews. When we were in Ithaca, all you could talk about was how much you missed them. How much you missed this land and the endless horizons and the wind and the heat and the sunsets and the rose-colored fog in the morning and the sugar cane burning and the river and driving to South Padre Island and the roasted corn and the shaved ice with syrup and El Pato's and the botanas and the chorizo from San Manuel and the taquitos de trompo served with frijoles a la charra and baked potatoes and the cabrito al carbon on the other side of the border. You missed everything, even the scent of the air and the heat of the nights and the feel of the earth. To you, the Rio Grande Valley wasn't simply a place on a map—the name itself was an incantation. Earth and sun and magic all at once.

I promised you I'd follow you. To love you is to live here. The palm trees lining the highways and the fruit-bearing trees in the orange groves and the mesquites everywhere all whisper your name to me.

Most nights, when you're at work, I go for long drives. On the freeways where all the lights blur, the access roads when I want to see things pass

*after a line of poetry by Rodney Gomez

by more slowly. Interstates, state roads, county roads, farm-to-market roads, connecting one town to the next. Some towns hardly more than a city-limits sign, two houses, and a gas station. Some nights I turn onto caliche roads, counting the lights of trailer parks, surprised suddenly by what look like little houses with parking lots and too many cars. Some of them bars without permits, most of them brothels. I sit at truck-stop diners, drinking cup after cup of coffee. I have something sweet. Pancakes. Or pie. Or cake. Then more coffee until I can bear to go back out again and devour the miles. Windows open and the road screaming past. Everywhere I see roadside descansos, wooden crosses piled with plastic flowers and ribbons and beads. All the tattered and bright colors of someone's grief.

Some nights I listen to the radio, and then I'm almost happy. I shout-sing along. Doesn't matter what it is—Top 40, country music, the songs I remember from the nineties, the Cure, the Cranberries, new and old Tejano, Michael Salgado and Intocables, and old conjuntos, Los Relampagos and Los Tigres del Norte and Los Cadetes de Linares looping over and over again.

When the whispers began, I tried to outrun them, first on the treadmill then at the university track. I tried weights. I tried punching the bag in the garage. I tried jerking off. I tried drinking. At home and then at the bar down the street. And then at the icehouse on the far edge of town. I thought about going across the border to the bars in Reynosa or Progreso, thought about how it wasn't safe anymore, thought about how, even on good days, it pissed me off to deal with the border patrol and the checkpoints. I didn't grow up like you—I wasn't used to their omnipresence, to the constant questioning of my citizenship. I thought I might take a swing at one of them if I was drunk. So I stayed away from the bridges that would take me across. I stayed on the roads. Listened to the wind and the music.

I'm always home by the time the sun rises. Early enough to shed all of my clothes and warm our bed and for my eyes to become bleary with sleep before you arrive. I hear your car park in the driveway, hear your keys at the door, hear you make tea and drink it in the kitchen, hear the groan when you take off your shoes. And you sit there for a bit and breathe. And when you come to bed, I greet you with open arms and hold you tight. You tuck your face into my neck, and I breathe in the scent of your hair. And you tell me about your day. Sometimes we laugh.

Sometimes we cry. And we lie there, breathing together until the alarm goes off, and I have to leave you, get showered and dressed, go to work. I sleep enough, I guess. I stay awake all day. I sleep on the nights you're home with me. The rest of the time, it's an hour here, an hour there. I start awake, find myself patting my own chest, feel a phantom warmth smaller than the palm of my hand over my heart.

Unlike you, no one's life depends on how awake I am. I don't love my job. But it's a living, and sometimes that's enough. I took it when we moved here and you were starting your residency. I sit in a cubicle all day, looking over reports, checking numbers and names, comparing endless streams of data for eight hours. The phone never stops ringing with people calling to ask me questions. For lunch, I walk over to the taqueria next door. Sit in the corner by the jukebox, back to the door, and eat my enchiladas while I take in the music. The waitress brings me limonada without having to ask me. There's a streak of grey in her hair. She calls me, "mijo," asks after you, and always tells me to get some rest, that I'm too young to have such tired-looking eyes. I pat the hand she puts on my shoulder and tell her in Spanish that I know that my mother, from the other world, would thank her for taking such good care of me. The name tag on her ruffled Mexican blouse says, "Altagracia." You've never met her, but she knows all about you—how we met, your family, your job, your favorite foods, what we've done every weekend and every holiday for the last five years. She adds the "ita" of affection to your name, calls you "la Raquelita," and I don't doubt that she'd greet you like a long-lost daughter if you ever walked in through the door.

On the way back to my little beige cubicle, the urracas make their harsh cries, wings moving this way and that, dark eyes following my steps. I think of you when I see them. You love their cacophony. Their quick eyes.

I've never told you, but I loved a boy once. Loved him for his dark skin and the sadness of his eyes and for the way he dug his fingers into me when he held me. He was also from here and knew the sounds of all the birds. He taught me their names, their cries, their songs. Not just owls and crows but palomas and urracas and golondrinas and garzas and ruiseñores and chachalacas and cenzontles. He taught me the silhouettes of golden eagles and vultures, roadrunners and bob white quails, by tracing them over and over on my skin. I hardly had to say his name,

Abel. I'd just cry out like a grackle the way he'd taught me, and he'd turn to look at me.

We met the very first week of our first semester in college. I didn't tell my father about him. He didn't tell his family about me. Before he ever said the word *love*, he said, "If they knew, my brothers would fight over who'd put the bullet between my eyes." Neither of us went home for Christmas break— his family in Texas and my family in Nebraska were too far and too poor for them to come visit. Spring came and went. Our last night together, he wept in my arms. I called him every day that summer, left messages with a woman who only spoke Spanish. He never called me back. Eventually, she started to hang up when she'd hear my voice, and then the number was disconnected. When fall came, I went back but he didn't. I couldn't sleep. I'd wake up screaming, wake up calling for him. With time, the silence froze something inside me, but the bird songs stayed with me. I took to staring out an open window, even when winter came, even when the temperature dropped below freezing and there were hardly any birds in the sky.

It was because of him that I learned to love you. I knew your name before I ever spoke to you. Had seen you in class a dozen times, seen you talking to your friends, seen you across the room at a party or two. I'd even thought you had beautiful eyes. But I'd never talked to you—until the day I passed by you with your friends and heard you describing the urracas you loved, how they swarmed and flipped and wheeled in the sky above the grocery store parking lots back home. Thousands every evening. All of those splintered wings and their deafening sound. Your voice was filled with such longing. Later that afternoon, you were sitting alone at one of the cafés on campus. I decided to approach you, ask you something about a class assignment. We ended up deciding to meet over pizza to talk about our papers. We shut the place down; I walked you back to your building and then walked home in a daze.

Since then, my heart has belonged to you only. But that first night in South Texas, when you were introducing me to your parents, I heard the cenzontles and they made me think of him and I felt a little less like a stranger. I knew the names of the birds. Their songs already lived in my bones. And I knew your home could be mine.

I graduated but stayed with you because I refused to risk what we had to distance. I worked until you graduated too. We moved to California while you went to med school. I worked while you studied. And then the pull of the Texas border became too much.

I'd lived with the whispering for a while before I thought to mention it to you. We were sipping coffee with our pan dulce, both of us reading at the kitchen table. You lifted your head up for a second, tilted it like a bird, and gave me an odd look. You turned away without saying anything. I knew what it meant when your face turned to stone and your silence swallowed everything. There were things you wouldn't discuss, and if I insisted, you'd go to the small unadorned room farthest from our bedroom. You'd said it'd be your hobby room and double as a guest bedroom, but it didn't even have a bed in it. Just a single chair. The first time I found you there, your eyes were closed and you were silent, shaking and shaking in that chair.

I didn't bring up the whispering again, even when it started to follow me everywhere. For the first few years, I only paid attention to it at night when I was alone. It followed me to work and when I went jogging and when I ran errands. It was there when I was with you, growing so loud I could hear it even when we were with your family— the cacophony of voices, music, TV, children, and pets unable to drown it out entirely.

I started driving at night when the whispering stopped being whispering and became distinct voices. Men and women and children. Sad, angry, happy, lonely, lost, demanding. In English and Spanish and languages whose names I didn't know. Sometimes it seemed like they were praying. Reminiscing. Weeping or laughing or screaming or whimpering or calling out for someone who never answered. Sometimes I can barely understand what they're saying, but the voices grow louder and then fade and then grow louder again. And sometimes I go suddenly deaf— the voices and all the sounds of the world gone. And it feels as if my insides have been scraped at, leaving parts of me raw that should never be touched.

I haven't spoken to them. I don't even know if they know I can hear them. I imagine it would be worse if they were trying to get my attention. If every plaintive cry began with, "Antonio, Antonio." Almost every night, I drive, keeping my eyes on the road, letting the wind and the music drown out the voices. I drive until I'm so exhausted I sleep even with all their voices booming and ricocheting inside my head.

I'm not imagining them. I'm not losing my mind. They're real. I've never heard the voices of the dead before, but I know that's what they are. I want to tell them they have the wrong guy. They're not my ancestors. My family never passed through here. Not this land, not this river, not these roads, not even this sky. Why did they choose me when they could choose one of their own? Someone born and nurtured on this land, someone taught to speak, sing, pray here? I don't know what they want. They're not asking for my help. They just gather around me as if they're moths, and I'm giving off some light I don't know how to turn off.

I have deaths curled inside of me. Layered and limned with my grief. I lost my mother when I was little, my brother soon after I met you, my grandparents after we married, some friends, and now, too, our daughter. None of your people have died. Your parents, your grandparents, your great-grandparents, all of your sisters and brothers are still living.

I know our daughter was your first death. But you won't call it that. Never born, you said, only sixteen weeks. As if that wasn't enough time to start thinking of names, to imagine how she'd have your water-straight hair and your dimples. "Socorro," I'd breathed against your barely rounded belly. Before you told me, I'd dreamt of a little girl riding on my shoulders, a little girl with my mother's name. I heard her laughter and felt her tiny hands in mine.

I dream her all the time. Small enough to fit inside the palm of my hand—my little ruby-hearted girl. Perfect tiny limbs, fingers, toes. Her little belly. Her little arms. I wait, breathless, to see her eyes open, but they never do. Her flesh a rosy color. The tremendous pulse of her heart pulsing through her entire body. Sometimes I look for her when I'm awake. I get lost in our house wondering why I can't find the nursery. I wake up thinking I hear her crying.

You won't speak of it. I've never seen you cry. But sometimes something moves over your face that reminds me of the ocean, and I know you're thinking of her. If I stay silent, you'll stay in the kitchen but move to stand by the sink. Your mourning place. You keep your face turned away from me. And if I stand behind you and wrap my arms around you, you'll lean against me but push my arms up so that they are wrapped around your shoulders instead of your waist. It doesn't matter. I'm here if the day comes that you need to cry. I'm here even if that day never comes.

The first time we made love, I tasted my own tears on your skin. I didn't know who else to go to when they called to say my brother had died. A car accident. No alcohol, no drugs; he just took the curve too fast and spun out of control. No seatbelt. Died instantly when he burst through the windshield. My little brother Armando gone, just like that.

Tears were streaming down my face when I knocked on your door. You led me to sit on your bed then crawled into my lap and wrapped your arms and legs around me while I sobbed into your neck. Even now, all these years later, when my lips are on your skin, I can still taste those tears. Or perhaps I am tasting yours, all the tears you've never released, restless oceans pushing up against the surface of you.

It would have been simpler if I could have convinced you when the voices were only whispers. Or when it was only voices, because then I started to see their faces in my dreams. And then when I was awake. Shadows inhabiting all reflective surfaces. The bathroom mirror, the kitchen stove, my coffee mug, the car windshield, storefronts, anywhere, everywhere. All of them strangers. Sometimes they seemed to be looking at me. I learned to ignore them, learned to avoid focusing on their eyes, their mouths.

I went with you because it was your family's tradition to go to the Shrine in San Juan on Sundays. We arrived first and waited on the sidewalk until your parents and grandparents and siblings and cousins arrived. There were hugs and kisses and handshakes and shoulder thumps in greeting. At least thirty of us when we started walking toward the Shrine. Palm trees and oak trees and acres of green grass. Concrete beds of overflowing flowers. It was always beautiful and grand. I would have preferred the outside grotto at the San Juditas Tadeo church that you and I went to when we wanted to pray, but your family preferred to get dressed up and come to the Shrine. I kept you close to me, my hand spread across your back, my thumb touching your bare skin. The sight, scent, touch, taste of you made the voices recede. I didn't know why it worked that way. If it was because you didn't believe in such things, if it was because you dealt with life and death every day, if it was because we had always been each other's refuge.

I took your hand as we climbed up the steps. You gave me a worried glance when the first step inside the building sent a jolt through my entire body. I held your hand too tightly, but I managed to nod. You seemed reassured. The sound of trumpets, violins, guitars, and guitarrones filled the altar space and then rose in a wave toward us. The music sent the voices colliding into each other, rendering their words unintelligible. We took our seats in the pew. An intense brightness filled my sight, until I couldn't tell where one thing ended and another began. The line of mariachis became one blur of blue with shining metallic streaks. The priest's face and hands merged with his robes. Even the Virgen de San Juan on the wall—the blue of her dress wavered, as if it were water reflecting sunlight rather than wood and turquoise paint.

Only her face was as I remembered it, dark and serene. Her eyes black and radiant. When it was time to kneel, I looked to her, looked only to her, and prayed with my heart in my throat:

Milagrosa, make it stop. I can't do this. One man can't contain all of this. Can't channel it. I will lose my mind if this goes on much longer. What do I do, Virgencita? Any moment now, they'll learn my name and then their voices will never stop. I can barely sleep. Barely work. All I hear is them. I am not strong enough to bear this. To hear them. To carry them. Help me. Please help me.

The voices and all the colors came crashing back as soon as we stepped through the doors of the Shrine. I put both hands to my head, unable to take another step. Spikes of pain. You wrapped your arms around me as if you feared I was dizzy. I heard your parents saying my name. You made our apologies and took me home. I leaned my head back and closed my eyes, the voices too close, too urgent when you weren't touching me.

The house was dark and cool. You put my arm over your shoulders and took me to our bedroom. I shrugged off my guayabera after you unbuttoned it. Took off my undershirt. Shoes and pants. Laid down on top of the comforter in my boxers. You were gone for a second but then came back with a cool compress for my eyes.

I took hold of your wrist, "Don't go away, lie down with me." I heard you slip off the strappy sandals and the salmon pink dress you'd worn. Earrings and bracelets and rings clacking onto the night stand. I sighed when you lay down on your side against me, and I felt the long bare expanse of your skin. The voices gentled.

"Antonio, what's wrong? What's happening?"

It wasn't the time to tell you. It was too late. There was too much and too little to tell. It would have been different if you'd asked me when it was just whispering. "Just let me hold you, Raquel. I feel better when I hold you," I kissed your temple, and you sighed when I pulled you on top of me, wanting to feel not just your skin but your weight on me. So that I could pretend you'd never leave our bed. That I would spend the rest of my life like this, your body on mine holding the voices at bay.

I slept for the first time in days. When I woke, you'd already left the bed. We had dinner, your eyes dark and worried the whole time. I didn't know what to tell you. The voices were too loud, and the light was so bright I kept wincing. Before you left for the hospital, you brought me a glass of water and painkillers. "We're talking about this when I get back, Antonio," you shrugged with one last helpless look before you picked up your keys and opened the door to the garage.

I don't know if I slept or not. If it was one hour or many. The bathroom mirror showed me a man with swollen eyes. Beard stubble. Sweat-drenched hair. Alone with the voices. With the faces. They kept whispering my name. Over and over, in looping chains, so that the *o* at the end merged with the *A* at the beginning, creating a new name for me. A name without end.

I shoved on my sneakers and headed to the garage, passing by the kitchen counter where a single religious candle burned. The Virgen de San Juan. I touched the cool base, watching the light flicker and flare across the dark room. I remembered my prayer, the blurring colors, the sharp pain I'd felt. I leaned forward to read the prayer on the back, but the only words I could distinguish were, "the Way of Life which gives meaning to moments of sorrow." There's always a candle burning on the counter—a second one always lit before the first goes dark.

The voices left me unable to think, but it had all become habit. Car door. Ignition. Garage door. Windows down to let the hot air out. Warm wind poured in. I didn't know where I was going. I just wanted to go fast. Fast so that the wind was louder than their voices. A few turns and a couple of miles between our quiet neighborhood and Highway 107. And I saw their faces everywhere I looked, under the streetlights, in the headlights of oncoming traffic, in the rearview mirror. I refused to look at them, didn't want to see their mouths shaping my name— oantonio-antonioantonioan. . . .

I'm not in Edinburg anymore. It's dark out here. My foot presses harder on the gas pedal. The radio seems louder, all fluttering accordions and rolling drums. Other towns pass in quick-lit blurs. I stop reading the city-limits signs. I turn and turn and turn on impulse. I stop reading the signs that tell me how many miles it is to San Antonio. How many miles to South Padre. North. South. East. West. One and then the other and the other. Where I go doesn't matter, only that I *go*. I don't want the city, and I'm not going to the beach. That much I know. It's not the ocean I want tonight. The night smells different now—more earth, more green. Finally, it's cool enough that the earth has begun to release the day's heat. The scent is what life would smell like if life didn't depend on blood.

The voices are getting louder. I turn up the radio. I barely brake turning onto a caliche road. Don't slow down even though the road is uneven and narrow. I want the wind to tear me away. I imagine a cyclone whirling on the road, tossing up me and the car and all the faces, all of us spinning and spinning until we're flung away from each other and into the silent sky.

I hear it right away—the small sound. Much softer than the voices, the wind, the music. It's not calling my name, but I know it's meant for me. It's mine. It's so dark here it's hard to make out where the turnaround is. Barely enough reflectors to keep the tires off the grass. And then I floor it. As fast as I can go, following the soft sound. Sometimes I think I see animals in the shadows. Sometimes I see people, their faces too bright, surprised by my headlights at this hour of the night. The city-limits signs come and go again. If I'm thirsty or hungry, I don't feel it. If I was tired or sleepy, that's gone too. I'm listening as hard as I can, entering the ramp for the freeway, swerving around eighteen-wheelers and cars and pickup trucks.

It's not as if I'm responding to my name. Or your voice. It's almost like something I felt in those first delirious months of falling in love with you. As if I could feel you thinking of me when we were apart. As if something of me was twisting and pulling against something of you. That's what this was. A pull on my insides, as if something was threatening to unravel if I didn't listen, didn't respond, didn't follow.

The wind was changing. A slight coolness. The scent of sweet green things. I pull over on the side of the road by brush and mesquites. Hope that my car doesn't draw the attention of the Border Patrol. I walk in the dark. For a long time, constantly scanning every direction. But there's no one to stop me. Only one light on the sign at the entrance. No security. My feet know the way. I've been here a hundred times. Raquel and I were here only a few weeks ago, protesting the wall they want to build here. The wall that will desecrate one of the last few wild places. The branches of the trees move serenely in the wind, as they have moved, undisturbed, all their lives. Even though there's hardly any light, the little neon orange flags marking a line on the ground are as obscene as they are in full daylight. I fall on my hands and knees, the voices swirling around me, and start pulling the flags out of the ground. The earth is soft beneath me. The earth is solid. I can hear the river. Smell it. The trees are wide shadows, more alive than I am. But I know what's possible. Remember how horrified I was the first time I saw the endless concrete of the California–Mexico border. San Diego so green and so blue and then the roads to Tijuana and the shock of towering walls— the earth burned, razed, salted. Pale dead earth as far as the eye could see. The lights. The Border Patrol trucks. The uniformed men with guns.

Here in this natural place there is no concrete. There are no walls. Only these little orange flags marking death, death, death. In this darkness, I can't see the faces, but the voices are growing louder. You can feel it here, a shuddering under the skin. How the river here connects to the river everywhere. How the river carries hopes and dreams and losses and anguish. How the river is both water and blood. How the earth here weeps and sings at the same time. How it longs to be like the quiet earth elsewhere. And I understood that the voices were telling their own stories and the stories they'd been trusted with and the stories of this land that no longer had a voice to speak them. And my story was one of those stories. The faces had been witnessing, telling my story, braiding my story into all the stories that lived in this earth, connecting me, making me theirs.

There's a sudden dip I don't see in enough time and I go sprawling. End up on my back and only realize when I see the blurring stars that I'm sobbing. I couldn't hear myself over the voices. Couldn't feel my chest with the flags in my hands. The voices sound like they're sobbing too, but it's only my name, on loop, on loop, on loop, drumming at my temples.

The small sound is constant.

And then the wind stops. And then the voices stop. Completely. They stop completely.

I am alone.

No, not alone.

It wasn't fog that had slowly crept toward me but a mass of shadowed figures. There was the rushing of wings and the silhouettes of birds in flight. And the soft sound, louder now that the voices were gone. I could feel it under my skin. I wiped at my eyes with both hands, and knew I was streaking my face with dirt.

He was whistling the song of the golondrinas and cradling something I couldn't see. My eyes were busy devouring his face. He looked exactly as I remembered him, hardly a day older. He smiled at me the way he used to smile at me, his eyes crinkling the way they'd always crinkled.

"Abel," I breathed.

He was so close, impossibly close. And I closed my eyes the way I'd always closed them when he was close. His lips on mine. Impossibly light. Impossibly soft. And I leaned into him the way I'd always leaned into him.

"Antonio," he whispered, drawing back, "Here, I've been taking care of her for you."

And the small sound filled me. She wasn't crying, wasn't whimpering. She was humming. She was so tiny in my hands. As beautiful as she'd been in my dreams. My little ruby-hearted girl. She opened her eyes. As wise and black as yours. Her little hand tried to grasp my fingertip. I held her up to my cheek, humming the lullaby my mother had hummed to me. And the small sound became a large sound, a thunderous sound. Her body, tiny and powerful, rumbled with it. And my hands warmed and started to radiate a golden light. And even in the blanket she was swaddled in, I could see her ruby light flashing like a jewel through her skin. Her heart beating fast like a hummingbird's.

I don't know how long I stood there holding her and looking into her black eyes. It was still dark when I heard Abel's voice again.

His voice was soft, "Come back whenever you want. We've been telling your story. Your mother and brother are almost here."

I stared at him. He held out his hands. I didn't want to give her back, but I knew we were running out of time. He held her delicately, reverently, as the light of her dimmed.

"One of us will always be waiting here for you. We'll teach you how to live with the voices."

In the night, the birds wheeling around us were almost silent. I stood there, watched their shadows draw away, watched the darkness lighten bit by bit.

The voices returned, but this time I didn't fight them. And somehow, though they were still loud, it no longer hurt. I walked and walked. Trying to understand what it meant to let them in, to let them flow through me, to feel like I was walking with one foot in this world and the other in theirs. Soft earth, soft light, soft river. And underneath it all, the small sound. Alive in me.

It's okay, Raquel. I can tell you everything now. Or at least, as much as you can bear to listen to. I know what I am now. I am a bridge. The voices will always be with me. And it will be my work to listen to them—while I work, while I live, while I love you, while life moves forward. And when you're ready to see our Ruby, I'll bring you here.

There's nothing to fear. Everything is here. Abel. Our little ruby-hearted girl. Soon, my mother and my brother and all my lost ones. Here amongst the wind and the trees and the river. The voices and the light and the humming. And the birds. All the birds.

Family Unit

Rubén Degollado

Here it was. I was outside this house at a place called the Hidden Villa in Cannon Beach, Oregon, on my spring break. Just me and this old white dude named Tom at his front door, with him blinking fast as if he could not believe what I had just said to him, as if I were speaking Spanish. Even though I didn't want to get all racial about it, that's how I read his expression. Throwing out the *r* card had been hard for me not to do since I had gotten off the plane in Portland and the only people brown like me had been the ones mopping the floors and emptying the trash cans. It seemed like each person I spoke to about my job as a teacher along the border wanted to ask what I thought about the wall and kids in cages. I mean I protested, had a #NoBorderWall sticker on my car, and was as pissed off as everyone else. And even though I wanted to take a break from that because it was my vacation after all, out here in Oregon, however, I found myself leaning toward being Chucky Chicano, Mr. Activist, Mr. Wave My Flag, Mr. Speak Spanish to the Workers Whenever He's Got the Chance. If asked now about the walkouts, my undocumented brothers and sisters, I would have proudly said that my family didn't cross over the border, but had the border crossed over them.

Anyway, this was not the point of me standing there in Oregon of all places, even though I was tending to dwell on it. Fight it, hey, fight it, I kept telling myself. I was standing in this wooden doorway painted white much too long ago because of my beautiful wife Evelyn, because this was where she wanted to spend our spring break.

With the way Tom stood at the door, blocking me from looking inside, and talking to me condescendingly with get this, an English accent of all things, it was hard not to think like that. This wasn't just your average gringo entitlement, this was your from-overseas gringo entitlement, the old kind where gringos not only expected the best for themselves, but also told you what was good for you. I had not seen this version since I had been in the Army, stationed in Germany. Over there, they were masters at it.

"I *said* I would like Unit Five." The volume of my voice surprised me. My teacher voice only sounded normal when I stood in front of my classroom, pointing my chalk at my eighth graders, trying to make a point about how we should always be mindful of our civil liberties and those of others, that this class was based on those principles.

"You mean the one on the end? You know that's a *family* unit, right. It's for families." Again with the condescending, with the pinche white colonialism. I wanted to say that my people crossed a river, yes, but his ancestors crossed a whole pinche ocean.

Again, I was overreacting, but this guy was killing me. He was really shitting the stick. "Yes the one out *there*," I said and pointed across the green, green lawn and past the arbor where Evelyn was sitting in the rental car waiting for me. I didn't even want to look at her face right now, as she would probably know that this was *not* going well, and because I had told her that the reservation was a sure thing, that it was in the bag, no hay problema, that it was a done deal. If Evelyn thought she had to get out of the car to give me backup, this trip would be all over. Evelyn would get results like she always did, but it would be good night for me, adios muchacho. I just waved and gave her the thumbs up like it was all good. Evelyn just kept looking at me, no smiles, no encouragement. Those ass-kicking brown eyes of hers had to fight themselves from rolling.

Tom flipped through this black binder with crinkly pages that had gotten wet too many times. With the sun right on him at this time of the morning, the hoods of his eyelids were purple, actually purple, fluttering with the effort of looking at the bright pages of that binder. I could see the question with each of his movements: Why does this couple want to pay for a family unit when those are more expensive and there are only two of them I can see? I heard the rental car door open and shut behind me. He looked past me, out to the car to make sure it was still just the two of us, as if maybe there were more of us hiding underneath the car or in the trunk, like we were Mexicans trying to sneak into a drive-in movie. Evelyn stood by the front of the car, stretching her legs, and cracking her knuckles. Her brow was pushed down, and I couldn't tell if it was from the bright morning sun or because she thought she had to put me out of my misery. This was going to be bad if I didn't fix it. I looked at her, and she gave me that smile with no teeth showing, the smile teachers give kids who've complained to their parents about them, the one that says I am acknowledging your existence, but that is all you get, cabrón.

"Mister," he said and paused. Here was another thing. I had to pronounce my name *every* time since I'd been out here. It makes you tired.

"Izquierdo, but you can call me Seferino." I said and let it roll out Chicano brown and proud. I wasn't playing that today, wasn't about to say, *Is-scared-o* so it would sound better to his ears.

"Yes, yes. My apologies, I can't seem to find anything, which doesn't necessarily mean that you didn't make the reservation. It just means that I can't find it. I guess these things sometimes happen."

I had to say, "Yes they most certainly do." He was right, and these things did happen. How many times had I lost my grade book or students' assignments underneath all the piles and piles of papers on my desk at Nimitz Middle School?

It was clear he was getting frustrated as the pages started flying and he started to breathe harder through his nose. These sounds did not belong on such a fresh quiet morning where it was cold in the shade, where I did not warm up until I stepped back and felt the sun on the backs of my legs. A morning that was nothing like home and reminded me more of Germany, where I had been stationed in the Army. We could have gone anywhere else for spring break, and I had even priced out the Bahamas and Las Vegas, but Evelyn had insisted on coming here. She had chosen Oregon because they had lived there when she was very little and they were migrants. She wanted Unit Five because that is where her father had brought them one time to spend the weekend, and she wanted to relive this happy family memory. *Why do I want to go somewhere hotter than Texas? Seferino, please.* I had not thanked her for choosing Oregon, for choosing this place that could be hot and cold on the same day at the same exact time, that had mountains (other than Mt. Hood, she called them all hills) and old trees. Before Evelyn, I never in all of my imaginings would have thought that I would be in Oregon. And if we could get past the microaggressions, it would be a lovely place.

I decided to take a different approach with this man, because this was going to get ugly if I did not get that room. You see, it all hinged on this.

"Well, since you can't find it, is it okay if we just stay there tonight? I mean is anyone else going to stay there? I am certain that I made the reservation, but the mistake could have been mine. I do remember speaking to you, but perhaps we didn't solidify things. Tom is your name, right? Perhaps it would be okay if we got that unit, Tom."

"Yes, but I don't remember talking to you, and I have a memory for these things. This is most disconcerting. I don't know if anyone else is going to stay here. It's just that I might get some drop-in that's a family, and I would hate not to have a family unit available for them, as Unit Five is the last one I have. You sure you don't want to stay in one of the other units? They're very spacious for a double, and they also have the kitchenette. Surely you see the predicament this puts me in."

Though some men I know would tell him the whole story of what this trip and what that room meant, start crying about all their problems and their reasons, this Tom did not deserve it. He was no compadre at all. Some other men I knew, the ones who had been raised without shame, were out there with things like this. I would like to say that it was a thing only gabachos did, but the one time I'd gone to an ACTS retreat, I'd seen Mexicans darker than me cry and talk about all of their struggles, their hardships, their secret sins (always pornography), the promises they would try their best to keep. They shared these things with men they did not even know as though they were on daytime TV or in the confessional booth. These men would blubber and tell this complete stranger Tom that they wanted Unit Five because their wife had requested it, that they really needed to make their wife happy on this trip, that everything needed to be perfect, that if it was not perfect their remaining days together could be in jeopardy. Then these malcriados would tell them why their marriage was in trouble, things they had done and said, the terrible thing that had happened to them. They would be hanging out there with it for everyone to see, even if it was none of their business. How do you tell someone all of this? If you've been raised right, and understand that family business is for family only, you don't. At least, you shouldn't if you have any respect for yourself. Instead, you do what I did.

"How about we do this?" I said, and got out my credit card. "How about I pay for Unit Five now with my credit card and give you cash for the deposit."

"But I can't find the reservation," he said. This Tom, he was all about the rules, all about what could be found in that black binder.

"I know, I know, but it will be all right. The deposit you can keep regardless."

I handed him my credit card wrapped in two hundred-dollar bills I had ready for something like this, even though I had mostly done it for fun and had not expected to actually use it. My compadre Omar would laugh about this when I got home, about me paying a mordida on this side of the border, all the way in Oregon even. "You take this and get the receipt ready, and I'll get the bags down from our car." I handed the credit card wrapped in the bills like Tom was just another Aduana officer I was paying to get through the lines quicker. Tom looked at the money and raised his eyes too high on his forehead and for too long, like the Aduana knew not to. He then tried to act like nothing was out of the ordinary, but those purple eyelids could not lie.

"Oh well, I suppose we'll be fine like you say. Don't anticipate many families today, being the middle of the week and all. I'll just go and get the key." He walked back into the house, a living room darkened by thick brown curtains covering tall windows.

Tom came back out with an old school slip for me to sign and said, "Well, as you know it's a family unit so you have your choice of two double beds. You could even use the sofa bed if you were so inclined."

"I think we'll cross that bridge when we get to it," I said and laughed while I signed, despite this being something a Mexican would never say or laugh at. You can make innuendo about women all day long as long as it's not about your wife or mother. That one is a deal breaker. I threw in a wink too. *If I were so inclined.* I would have to remember that one.

* * *

Evelyn had a list for everything. On this trip alone, she had made three lists that I knew of. She had a list titled "Going Away," which detailed all of the things we would need for the trip, things we would need to do before we left. Of course, the things "we" had to do before we left, usually meant things *I* had to do. Evelyn's lists were not just for responsibilities. She also had lists for fun. For this trip to Oregon, she had a list of places where she wanted to eat, divided between "Bite to Eat," "Sit-down Fancy," "Nice," and "Sort of Nice" restaurants. She also had a list of things she wanted to see, like the Astoria Column, Multnomah Falls, Haystack Rock, this American Stonehenge she did not know the official name of, and the Devil's Punchbowl. All of these things she had seen when she lived here as a child with all six of her brothers and sisters, years back when her parents had moved to the Pacific Northwest for the crops and later stayed to work in a nursery for a few years. Her father called Oregon the "Cielito Lindo" he now thought of when he heard the mariachi song of the same title. From the days we had spent driving from the Gorge through the mountain pass to central Oregon, I saw what my father-in-law had seen all those years back.

The first thing on Evelyn's list for the coast was "Walk On The Beach." We were doing this now, and it was nothing like standing on South Padre Island or Corpus Christi and looking out over the water. I had never seen rocks that big and we had not even seen this Haystack Rock up close, but it was out there and it looked like a mountain to me. Families with little kids, families with dogs, and couples alone walked along the beach with us now. Some of them wore fleece sweaters or vests. I had a T-shirt on, and any time a cloud covered the sun, I got a chill and wished I had listened to Evelyn when she told me to bring a sweatshirt. Who brings a sweatshirt to the beach? As soon as the cloud went away and the sun was shining on me, I thought I could handle it.

Another item on Evelyn's list of things to do was to put her feet in the ocean and see how long she could stand it. This was something Evelyn had done as a child with her brothers and sisters. I had no idea what she meant about the ocean being that cold until now, as I stood there without my shoes on the wet sand. If the sand was this cold, what was the water like?

I said, "You go first."

"What, are you scared?"

"No, I just want to see you. Just see how it goes."

"Whatever, big gallina. Just watch and learn." With this, she walked into the water past her ankles and shut her eyes.

The foam washed over her feet and went up to where her pants were rolled on her ankles.

After a minute or so, I said, "Is it cold yet? Can you stand it?"

"No really, it's not that bad. Just come closer and check it out."

Evelyn's eyes were still closed, and I hesitated. I thought she was going to kick cold water on me.

"Come here, hold my hand and enjoy this with me."

The water washed over my feet, and it felt like needles. I didn't know how she had already been standing in it for a few minutes and she was okay. It was killing me. It was worse than when I was young and my cousins and I would walk to the McAllen public pool in our bare feet so we wouldn't have to worry about anyone stealing our shoes. Our feet would burn up and blister and we would watch kids who went without shoes all summer walk on it like it was nothing.

I reached out for her hand, and she grasped it harder than she had in a while. "My brothers and sisters and I used to hold hands when we were trying to see how long we could stand it. We could always stand it longer when we held hands. I don't know if it kept our mind off the pain or what, but it was somehow easier. All seven of us holding hands in a chain, and we were so strong and could take anything."

I closed my eyes and said, "I know what you mean." It was true, I found it easier not to think about the water. It was Evelyn's hand in mine, the contours of her palm, the tightness of her grip. Then, without wanting to, I thought of us taking the classes at the hospital. I saw Evelyn walking around the room with a handful of ice in her hands. The ice was meant to prepare her mind for pain, for focusing on other things or embracing it, telling herself that this was a good pain, that her body was doing it for a reason. I remember feeling helpless, not able to hold the ice for her, just walking around the room with Evelyn, telling her to breathe, rubbing her back, looking at the faces of the husbands, each of them as helpless as me.

I opened my eyes to focus on where I was at now. She kept walking out and the water was getting deeper. I tried to pull away from her, but she held me tighter.

"Come on," she said.

"That's okay. I think I've had enough of this."

"Fine then," she said and pulled away.

"What are you doing?" I didn't like the sound of my voice. It said, *Don't do anything crazy. Please come back.* I wasn't okay with sounding like that.

"Come on now. Don't be a chicken-livered ninny." When Evelyn was in a good mood, she did this thing where she talked like a cowboy. She would say, *Oh that's a bunch of hooey*, or, *Go on now, git!* She did this mostly on Friday nights when we were getting ready to go dancing at the Tejano Saloon, which we hadn't done in a while, since way before we took this trip. She'd be putting on her pair of ropers and squeezing into those jeans she only wore on a Friday night, and she'd say, *Now I'm all gussied up and rarin' to go.* However, there was something different in her voice now, as if this Evelyn here was making fun of the Evelyn who used to say those things.

Evelyn was up past her ankles in the seawater, and she was going deeper. I was wishing she had her ropers on, as I was afraid she would step on something sharp. She dipped in all the way up to her thigh as she got close to the rock. I felt a twinge in my throat. I wanted her to say something, to make a joke and let me know she didn't plan on going any deeper. Evelyn just kept walking into the water, but now she was moving away from the rock, deeper out to the water beyond.

I said, "Evelyn? *Evelyn?*" I knew I sounded afraid for her, but I could not stop myself from sounding like some overdramatic woman from a telenovela. I tried to think of something funny to say but came up with nothing.

I smiled at an older woman who had been playing with her grandson nearby, picking up rocks and putting them into a bucket. She gave me a smile, but it was tentative. She could tell something else was going on. The grandson beside her wore green rubber boots with frog's eyes on the tips, and a yellow raincoat. The boy's hair was a red I had never seen before, a red I could only describe as cinnamon. I stepped between him and Evelyn to keep him out of sight, but I knew it was too late. They had both seen each other.

Evelyn moved out farther, and I made up my mind to go out after her if she did not turn toward the rock. She stopped in the water with her face turned away from me, and I wished I could see her expression. The water was up to her hips. She lowered her head. I felt a hand light on my arm.

"Is everything okay?" The grandmother said. She held the boy in her arms. The old lady had one gray tooth and green eyes that were younger than the rest of her.

"It's all fine," I said. "She's just remembering."

"You go get her out of that water. It's not good for her to be getting that deep without a wetsuit. She could get sick. She can go remember somewhere else." I didn't even mind the white lady maternalism because she was right.

When I turned back, Evelyn was climbing up the rock. I breathed.

I called to her across the water. I said, "Don't those things hurt your feet? I'm not sure that's such a good idea."

"What things?"

"You know those sharp things stuck on the rock." The word was there, but I could not think of it just then. All I could think about was Evelyn walking out deeper and under.

"Barnacles, Seferino. Do you mean barnacles?"

"I guess so. Be careful, you're going to cut your feet if you're not careful."

Evelyn seemed to know where to step to avoid the sharp parts, but she knew her limits. She sat down on a lower part of the Haystack and didn't go any higher.

"I didn't bring the camera," I said. "I should get a picture of this. I guess I could use my phone."

"Don't worry, we'll come back tomorrow and take some real pictures."

"I guess I'll just have to take a mental picture."

We were walking back on the sand when I said, "Is it always cold like this? I mean the sun is out, but it's still cold." I could not think of anything else to say.

"You think it's cold? I've been through colder. One time we came out when there was a winter storm, and you should have felt it then. The cold got up into our clothes and didn't leave until we were sitting by the fire our dad had made out of a bundle of wood he had to buy because he had forgotten to pack any in the truck. He blamed us girls because we were always rushing him when we came to the coast because we just couldn't wait."

When we got back, we went about the business of getting ready for bed in silence, all about the task at hand as if it were a work night. I knew better than to ask her if she was okay or talk about what had happened in the water. If she were on her way back to being okay, my question would definitely make her take a U-turn back to where I didn't want her to be.

The sheets were cool on my bare legs as I waited for Evelyn to come to bed. I thought of joking with her like I sometimes did, how she was like a little grandma in there, putting all of her creams and lotions on just to come to bed. The door to the bathroom opened, and I imagined the next few seconds. How she entered the bed would tell me everything. If she jumped on the bed and landed on her knees, we would make desperate love, no words or kissing or looking at each other, just she and I taking everything from each other. Or she could slide in next to me and put her hand on my chest. If this were the case, we would make slow wordless love, and she would be looking into my eyes the whole time. Or, as had happened every night the last few months, she would slide in and immediately lie on her side, facing away from me and tell me to have a good night. The expectation would be for me to leave her alone, let her sleep, kiss her head, pat her shoulder, and fall asleep on my side of the bed.

Evelyn turned off the light in the restroom and opened the door. In the available light, I could see that she wore her long-sleeved nightgown, the one she saved for those nights back home when we had a cold front. She lay on the bed and got under the covers next to me. Just as I thought she was about to settle in and turn on her side, she stayed on her back. This was something new, an in-between gesture I did not know how to read. I turned to her and put my hand on her ribs, my hand heavy so I would not tickle her. Also, I made sure to go no lower than this. Evelyn's eyes were on the ceiling, and she would not look at me. Her skin warmed to my touch, but she did not hum like she did when she was inviting more.

I said the only thing I could.

"I love you too," she said.

"You tired?" I said, which was our language for "Do you want me to leave you alone and go to bed now?"

"Yeah, I'm *kind* of tired. It's been a long day for me." This could have meant the decision to make love was up to me, but I didn't want to guess wrong. I wanted her to want it as much as I did, and I wanted to be sure.

"Okay baby. You sleep now." I tried my best to say this without defeat or frustration or resentment, anything that would make her feel guilty, which often made it hard for her to sleep.

I began to pull my hand away, and Evelyn gripped it and moved it down. Her belly was soft and yielded to my hand as if my hand was always meant to be there. This is what I had thought the first time I had touched her face, those years ago when we had a daylong date at South Padre Island, that my hand matched her face perfectly, my palm on her chin, my fingers curling up to her cheek. And all of those years ago, when I knew I would marry her, I thought that we would have many children like our own families, all three of my sisters, my thirteen tíos and tías on the Izquierdo side with all of their children and their children, Evelyn with all of her brothers and sisters. Now there was just us two and always would be, me wanting to reach down through her skin to fill that space in her belly that would forever be empty. Evelyn's breathing changed, and I knew that she was asleep and that her sleep was a happy one. I kept my hand on her belly and as soon as she fell asleep saw something like a smile on her face. At least I had done that.

* * *

When I walked out the door in the morning, with Evelyn still sleeping, Tom was watering his plants and flowers, the fine mist rainbowing across the lawn.

"Good morning, Tom. Say, do you know where one of those drive-through or walk-up espresso stands is?"

He seemed confused by my question. "Just thinking about which the best one is. What are you looking for, Seferino?"

"I don't know, just a place to pick up coffee. Get one of those Mexican mochas I've heard about."

"Somewhere to sit a while or to just get it and go?"

"Get it and go," I said and motioned my head toward our unit.

"You should go where I go, but I don't want to send you too far. It's on the other end of town, and by the time you walked back, it'd be cold. Don't want you to go to the Haystack Bakery, either. They have great pastries, but their coffee's for shit. Too weak, like drinking tea. You could go to the new one that just opened, the one with the Italian theme, all the dark colors and the paintings, but you're going to be paying for all that ambience, and the coffee's just okay. The baristas aren't hard to look at though. You should go up to the main street, take a right, and just after a women's clothing store, you turn the corner and there you should get a decent cup."

"Thank you, Tom. I appreciate that. Enjoy the rest of your morning."

"You too, buddy."

"Sounds good, friend. And Tom?"

"Yeah, buddy?"

"We are a family."

"I'm sorry?"

"Evelyn and I. Yesterday you said that Unit Five was for families. She is my family and I am hers."

Tom said, "A nation of two. That's what Vonnegut called it. I get it, buddy. Enjoy the family unit and enjoy it as long as you're here."

I nodded at him, and walked down the hill.

The dog walkers and joggers were the only ones out on Hemlock. Why would you do that on vacation? I thought. Once Mr. Arrambide had asked me if I wanted to start jogging on the track before school started, and I had told him the only time I ran was when I was being chased. Otherwise, it just wasn't worth it.

When I got to the little coffee shop, I was not impressed. This was not a sit-down kind of place unless you wanted to sit on patio furniture and look down at old linoleum. A college-aged girl was behind the counter, behind plastic-wrapped muffins and scones, glasses filled with prewrapped biscotti and licorice. She must have been at least six feet tall, a basketball player that would have towered over any of our players in the district. She was tall and dark and had dreadlocks, which I had never personally seen up close. She could have been Mexican, Asian, Hawaiian, or Native American. It was impossible to tell, and I didn't want to be that guy who actually asked.

"How's it going this morning?" she asked with big white teeth and a space in between the middle two.

"Oh it's going," I said and immediately regretted my tone, as I had told her too much. It was like those Monday mornings with students when you told them too much with your tired, sagging body, your eyes that would not look at them. If you stood up there like that, you let them know you were not having a good morning or week or life and you were just begging for them to ask you more. Some of them asked you more because they didn't want to do any work that day, and others asked because they cared, because they were the type who would come to visit you after they had graduated.

"What can I get you?" she said. "What can I get you that would make sure it's going *well* and not just going? I'm up for the job," she said and rolled up the sleeves of a long-sleeved shirt she wore underneath a puffy green vest. Here was something new, not just a question into why I was not feeling great, but a solution.

"I would like two Mexican mochas, both mediums and one of them without the espresso. I know that sounds crazy, a mocha without the espresso." I thought to explain how Evelyn had talked about these Mexican mochas from Oregon for years, had wanted us to have one together for so long, but could no longer stand the taste or smell of coffee for herself, even now that she was no longer pregnant and never would be. I thought to tell this girl how Evelyn had been looking out the plane window somewhere between San Antonio and Portland and had said, *I could have one without the espresso and I bet it would still taste great and not upset my stomach.* I also thought to tell her how I had thought this Mexican mocha was a perfect example of cultural appropriation and gentrification, but I decided to leave it.

I said, "A mocha without coffee. You must think that's a contradiction, huh."

"Actually it's not. I make them all the time," she said over the steamer and went about the business of smacking the grinder lever to fill the handle and tamping it down. This was loud and fun to watch, and I started to understand why else this had once been on Evelyn's list, this experience of watching someone else make coffee for you.

"How hot do you want the Mexican mocha with no espresso?"

"Regular temperature, I guess. Why do you ask?" It was a strange question.

"Because if it's for a kid, I don't steam it for as long. Kids don't like it so hot. Is it for a child?"

My voice could not find itself, lost somewhere between us. Finally, I managed to speak in a voice that sounded like it belonged to someone else, as though I were standing nearby listening to the conversation, wanting to hear the words that came next.

"It's *because* of a child," I said. The girl stopped the dance of her hands, turned her head sideways, and looked straight into me, waiting for me to continue.

The Surprise Trancazo

Helena María Viramontes

That August Saturday afternoon in 1940 began with V. Rocha returning home from work, navigating the plotted assemblage of Chavez Ravine trails with five lucky dollars in his wallet and female possibility spacious as the sky. Lost in his own calentura of party planning, he had ignored the nearby wrangling of barefoot baseball players, a combustive debate of children's voices rising, *But you did, No I didn't, You skunked us,* as he climbed the deep-grooved runoffs that ruptured the dirt paths, feeling grateful for the long-legged eucalyptus and undulating palms that had shaded his walk up the neighborhood hillside.

A winding ascension of wooden clapboard houses sprang forth from the blazon-baked boulders like the clusters of wild beavertail cacti, stunted mesquite here and there, and ashy sage bushes that bustled like stalwart barnacles. Uneven pathways threaded each house after house in crisscrossing loops, hillock gulches, and sharp corner bends where tufts of thicket grasses had thrived between rusted tools salvaged for metal scrapping, where overgrown cattail weeds sprouted from beneath old tires hoarded for recycling.

On that same August day as V. Rocha continued up the road, neighbors tied wet strips of cloth to fan turbos for relief from a sweltering Los Angeles summer, and rows of potted mint and manzanilla seedlings in shortening tins withered in the feverish afternoon heat. A fine dust rose as he mounted the hillside, tomcats thrashed dried corn husks in front of him, and a pair of straggly mutts sniffed at his lunch pail. He passed a patchwork of yards quilted together by beds of verdolagas crimped in darkest kale green, chrysanthemums para los muertos, and wild geranium blossoms, with staunch spires of lilies nurtured for church altar ofrendas. By the time V. Rocha had made it to the hill's high ridge, the shirt under his loose jumper was soaked with sweat and the last stranglehold of sunlight seemed to grip his neck with a bracing burn.

The porch terrace of the Rocha home afforded a panoramic southern view. Darting finches, mournful crows, and squat pigeons often vied for space on the wobbly porch railings as if they perched on the boughs of a special tree. To the west of La Loma, the San Gabriel mountains delayed the sunset, and to the east the sunrise descended upon the basin as if businesses and buildings and everyday lives had rolled down into the desert architecture of arroyos, settled into the unholy alchemy of fossil bedrock and steel. From the north, the tower of Los Angeles City Hall skewered the horizon, and a low-hanging plateau of thick vaporous clouds lingered over the basin just like the ashen smoke of Chumash fires once did, carrying in its spiraling rise the aroma of fowl and, no doubt, the vibrant scent of maize roasting.

On said Saturday in August, unbeknownst to V. Rocha as he dragged his tired clunky work boots across the house's low threshold, a radiant vermilion had smeared the face of heaven and the lacunas between New Chinatown, Placita Olvera, Little Tokyo, South Central Avenue, and Boyle Heights began to slowly coalesce under such flooding darkness, the splashy neon billboards scarcely visible, the warped luster of the marquees' blinking bulbs like sunken specters.

V. Rocha's younger sister, Guadalupe, partially hidden behind tall stacks of magazines, cropped with her mother's sewing shears a *National Geographic* cover featuring the magnificent redwoods as snippets of kindling tumbled from the oilcloth table onto the gray planked floor. From the houses she cleaned, she had collected discarded magazines for their spontaneous color and trimmed their picturesque pages so the deep coffee brown of the Buick Drop Dead Coupe, the dazzling glossy yellow fields of tulips, and the turquoise backdrop of the ads for Bile Beans could be fashioned into geometric patterns and then glued to the clapboard walls of their rasquache house that Guadalupe believed, down to the very fingernails of her soul, was in dire need of decorative wallpaper. V. Rocha's boots stomped heavy, shuddered the wooden plank floor, making the table quake, which caused the butter knife in her jelly jar of homemade paste to totter.

—Hey Rocky, Guadalupe said to her older brother laconically, pausing her work to pull her hair back, rearranging hairpins to hold up a swirly brunette bun—Are you gonna take me dancing? Jokester question, they both knew, she was to spend another week grounded for sneaking out with Lulu. She fanned herself with a snowcapped Himalayas cover, her gold hoop earrings swaying as the small table radio's cloth speakers throbbed to the beat of the Ink Spots' "Maybe." She had been lip-synching enough to irritate him.

—No muelas, he replied without extravagant conviction, in no mood. He wasn't crazy about the song either; like a lullaby it was too swoony to tirar chancla.

—*Maybe* . . . Guadalupe sang mournfully.

Beneath the kitchen sink, which was hemmed with a floral pattern curtain, their mother had hung a green towel and bucket from a single nail for washups. Above the sink was a newly installed water spigot. V. Rocha placed his lunch pail on the table, unlatched the door jamb of the leaking ice box, its bottom tray overflowing and puddling the floor (it was his sister's chore to empty), and chipped an ice nugget, crunched half between his teeth, using the other half to swipe his neck for a welcome chill.

He rested his damp sweaty shirt on a chair across from Guadalupe, shed his jumper uniform, and unlaced his boots to roll off his socks, tested their longevity with a faint sniff.

—Your feets stink like a sock-hop!

—Qué mitotera, mop the floor more better! He was dutiful, not wanting a fight with his mother. Not tonight. But what an ingrown toenail his sister was.

—Chale! Can't you see I'm busy? Guadalupe gestured indignantly at the stack of teetering magazines. She continued with a louder refrain: *Maybe you'll sit and sigh / Wishing that I were near, then.*

V. Rocha twisted the spigot, and the new pipes pinged and banged in laborious drama, the water finally spurting abruptly like a nosebleed, a tainted muddy stew clearing to a clean gush. Scrubbing with soap and cloth, he swiped his neck and pits and then palmed his spade beard around the curvature of his jut jaw, lifted a handheld mirror near the spigot for self-reflection, a front tooth prominently missing from his full smile. He filled a mason jar with water and carried it to the back bedroom to begin the sacred ritual in the matter of dressing. Guadalupe remained too busy trying to use the last of the daylight before the dusk disrupted her perspective, too preoccupied with dabbing clots of flour and water onto the flaming orangey red Lucky Strikes cutouts, to say what she often said—*You better leave my stuff alone*—to V. Rocha, much less notice the ice box puddle expanding on the floor.

In the corner water closet, there was an open window the size of a shoebox above the new toilido, and after V. Rocha had entered the single bedroom with his mason jar of water, he plugged the iron's cloth electrical cord to the one bare ceiling lightbulb. He then swept his hair using Guadalupe's forbidden brush and spritzed his puro patada pompadour using Guadalupe's forbidden hair spray. A cigarette clasped between the corner of his lips, V. Rocha stooped behind an ironing board, sprinkled water from the mason jar onto salmon-colored peg pant leg, then meticulously pressed the tapering seams of his zoot trousers with the point of a heavy hot iron. Clad in a clean white tank-tee, the inked tattoo across his forearm, his long blue boxers billowing close to the elastic sock garters that squeezed a pair of thin, spindly pale calves, V. Rocha would look up from his smoky, steamy, concentrated ironing effort to see from the bedroom window the newly constructed and highly stylized Navy and Marine Corps Reserve Armory compound. Framed by the window, the Art Deco–designed Armory smacked of a glossy fashion magazine cover, not a warehouse built for scores of sailors and soldiers while on furlough in Los Angeles. So far from the Angels, the hot iron angrily hissed on contact, so close to the Armory.

From midnight to dawn and full clock spin again, the uniformed servicemen dressed in regulation Army wool tight olive-drab trousers or sailors in their bell-bottoms with Navy watch caps worn "squarely on the head, parallel to and one and a half inches above the eyebrow" bolted like stallions out of the Armory corral in a hurried attempt to get as far away as possible from reminders of monotonous seas or isolated desert camps and into the theaters, ballrooms, cabarets—good-time promises of downtown L.A. The uniforms clocked the dirt pathways of Chavez Ravine back and forth 24/7, and in their rush, they trampled through the twisting trails of the three hillside neighborhoods. They crunched their dress shoes around the small homes of the Palo Verde neighborhood to get to Casanova Street; or staggered up Bishop's steep lupine networks of gravel inroads, heaving and sweating, when they returned from a club, bar, or restaurant all-nighter on Central Avenue. They overstepped yards of La Loma's vegetable gardens, short-cutting to Solano Drive to get to New Chinatown streets to throw back cocktails at the Rice Bowl, order chop suey at the popular Golden Pagoda. And worse than scaring the chickens or releasing the goats, worse than waking the dogs, was their brazen drunken habit of thrusting their hips, wagging their tongues to smack loud kisses at the chicas sitting on porch steps washing after-church menudo bowls, enamel tina buckets between their knees; hey there, you know you want it, *moo-cha-cha*, flirt-singing *sen-your-ritas*…(beat) *to me* (punchline) to the teenaged girls who were snapping and hanging bed sheets on T-poles on laundry days; cat-calling, *here kitty kitty, here wet pussy puss*, at younger ones watering hierba buena sprigs, lavender and lilacs out front. The neighborhood boys wanted to slap white right off their faces, fathers and brothers to tirar guantes with these disrespectful bolillos. Mothers and aunts reciprocated contemptible glares, threatening rolling pins with each sucio provocation.

V. Rocha sat all the way to 35th so as not mess his sculpted pompadour on the Yellow Electric Car's ceiling, but chanced wrinkling his handsome salmon-colored trapos. The cable currents sparked and buzzed the Y-Car forward, and it struck in him a curious awe similar to that of watching a single aeroplane machine flying overhead. Every time the Y-Car commenced or made a turn, the webbed cables sizzled above, and V. Rocha felt as if his muscles were cords receiving electric jolts, his veins zapping with acute vitality. Once he disembarked, he pulled out his handkerchief, rebuffed his shoes to a glassy shine, straightened the collar of his pearl white shirt, and then began his strut through South Central Avenue, knees bent and legs kicked in long calculated strides, as if he skipped every second tie of a train track, as if he marched to a hustle all his own, puro chingón.

The sweet fragrance of barbecue molasses and busy lard from round-the-clock eateries disguised the exhausts of speeding convertibles, honking carrumflas, manned rickshaws, of lonesome uniforms in search of hookups, sweetheart couples in search of privacy, friendly groups in search of good times. Every mestizaje, you name it, you'll see it, sought out the jazz nightlife of Central Avenue temptation surround-sound coming from all those club joints spilling bootlegging light into the darkness of night, all that amplified Lindy-hopping, upbeat bones breaking, bass sounds of whatever depression mood, bipolar American jives pumping every which way. The music drowned out the street-corner preachers croaking damnation or the soulful sorrow-sighing old women outside the doors of the undertakers; one smacked a tambourine firmly as if slapping breath into a newborn, the others joining in a wantful inharmonious pleading, their hats wreathed in artificial sunflowers, fake cherries shimmying, their charitable singing raw like the raking zinc rasp of a washboard, a repetitive grieving reframe of backbone cracking. Hock joints closing, club fronts hopping, pool balls clopping, *what's your pleasure, cue sticks or drumsticks*? Soup-kitchen lines, unemployment lines, seen-better-days face lines, tattered and frayed cuffs of a once-upon-a-time dressy shirt, sooty palms pleading for change, jostling the styling sequined customers lined up at club entrances or exiting the grand movie theaters. Discordant disarray of laughter like instruments tuning before a major concert, this was Saturday night digs just beginning to gas out on Central Avenue, in the hot August of nineteen hundred and forty, just beginning to grease up to Charlie Barnet's big band Redskin Rhumba pouring outside Lincoln Theatre—and V. Rocha wanted it all: the music, the mitote, the movida, the mota, and he gave in completely a chanclazo a todo dar to the full swing pachangas at the Orpheum Theatre on Broadway, *Jumpin' in the Groove, Cee Pee Johnson Orchestra* flashing on the marquee; or tapping to all that rhythmic refrain, to all the Last Word Café's exuberant tracalada. Or feeling rhapsodic pressure throbbing in his ears at the Downbeat Room, V. Rocha twisted and raked, his veins sizzling like the trolley cables, his legs kicked it fierce all night long, his zoot coattails spinning, his shoulder pads bouncing, his dancing knob-toed calcos smoldering atop the axis of the zing-zang world, the soles of his soul—you got it—*smokin'*.

Afterward, V. Rocha struck a statuesque pose against a Windsor five globe lamppost on the corner of South Central Avenue and 42nd, toe-tapped to the beat percussions, digging the most outta the bebobbing piano riff, Hot Lips Page's cool trumpet shrrrrreeddddiinng the summer night's mood. He couldn't afford the Club Alabam's cover charge, but no law against standing outside to absorb Bud Freeman's onda, the orchestra bones pulling in and blasting out the club's doors, a clunky plug of Big Kick Plain juicing his mouth. At the Dunbar Hotel nearby, platoons of Negro soldiers in sharp shined uniforms broke out with bam-booming flourish to seek after-hours, and it was time for V. Rocha to return to Chinatown Broadway and climb Solano Street a second time. Wreathed in a fog of grifa buena, in his own upbeat calentura, he strutted home, taxi drivers passing him without a second look, a single matchbook in a trouser pocket strumming his thigh—*Margarita "Marcy" Martinez* written in parochial school script taught by nuns, the curvature *m* reminding him of her beautiful pair of melónes. *Remember me*—all those *m*'s so inviting, ay carajo! His back aching as he bent to kiss her goodnight, face dance with his short baby-doll, her address below with the words, *near ELAC, the green house.* V. Rocha quickened his gait, convinced the swiftness would shorten the week.

But on this Saturday night—a Sunday morning to be exact—South Central Avenue had thinned out, and V. Rocha hadn't noticed Trouble *with a capital T* following him, three stragglers, liquored clobbered crackerjacks, their white Navy watch caps aglow as bleached bone does from desert floor, overtalking one another and then overtalking over his shoulders, all of them, three sheets to the wind.

—Ain't he cute? one of the sailors said, another blurting —I'm fuggin' star-vince, the third bracing a storefront locked grid in alcoholic vertigo. V. Rocha ignored the heckling and kept his strut, showing no outward expression of concern, already missing one front tooth from an old school fight and not about to ruin his trapos throwing chingasos with three pendejos. But his nonchalance didn't stop the sailors from closing in closer anyway, nipping at him, pitch-pulling his coattails, slam dunking the pads of his shoulders, believing in their own patriotic immunity, marinated in cheap cologne, juiced up on homebrew, righteous blood crackling through their plumbing.

—Stop it right 'ere, cocksucker. This from the fat broad-chested gordiflón. V. Rocha halted and then spat, and his jut jaw clenched; he surveyed the patas saladas, studied the three muscular but very boozy swab jockeys. The drunkest one said:

—Go bac to Mex-c-go.

—Fuck off, V. Rocha replied, with edged malice —Is that enuff Mexico for yous?

—Sho' us resspeck….Sangrón, the middle one said.

V. Rocha shook his head in a "say-it-ain't-so" gesture to the güero güerinchi. This sailor's a homeboy, a vato trying to pass, trying to impress his buddies, V. Rocha was sure of it.

—What did yous say? V. Rocha admonished —Don't jive me cuz yous with these boy scouts!

V. Rocha kept one hand weighted inside his trouser pocket, jingling assorted change, mind swirl debating, the matchbook *m*'s restraining the urge to crush their mugs. *No way José,* Marcy had said when he brushed the swell of her breast, its melon-moist ripeness, her body damp after all that dancing, a hint of fragrant gardenias, could be jasmine smudged on his palm, bending over to reach that face, those lips, ay carajo! Right outside of the Last Word Café she told him, *not now, not here,* looking directly up at him with those chestnut eyes laced in caked blackish mascara lashes, *maybe later,* reaching to place a finger over his lips, *if you're good.*

—Ay shit, ese! V. Rocha said, over his shoulders, wanting to stay good—Just get back to your booze, I ain't looking for nothin'.

In the blackout wake-up, sparkled flames followed a fuse from his toes to his thighs, his balls, his chest, and then the explosion like fireworks from behind his eyes, shrapnel pieces piercing inside his skull, one huge pulpy, swelling consciousness, the chilled concrete awakening him, his beard and his hair already spongy, blood soaked. His bloodied gummy mouth tasting of metal, his tongue pushing against his teeth, Big Kick Plain a buffer to the clobbering drunken kicks. A confusing savage rampage, ears bleeding, lip double sized, V. Rocha converted his pain into ferocity, blocked a shoe and thrusted it forward, hauled himself up, slipping on his own blood, one eye already swollen shut, swung cabronazos, his knuckles bruised and ballooned, the maddening mongrel LAPD siren frenzy scattering the sailors. V. Rocha's zoot trapos shredded now todo desmadrar, his face all fucked up, his brain scrambled like papas, police batons whacking him behind his knees into kneeling submission, hands behind his head, his arms now torqued painfully behind his back for the handcuffs, pinchi chota, a trail of blood to the cop car, punctuating asterisks on the pavement like footnotes. Forget the hospital, forget the judge's gavel banging the case closed; guilty of disorderly conduct, public intoxication, possession of illegal substance. Booted to boot camp, floated to boat ride, *Return to Sender* from Marcy Martinez, her loud rejection written in her beautiful calligraphic nunnery script on his unopened letters.

Mujeres Matadas

Daniel Chacón

I saw her standing on the stage. She had short hair, dyed orange, and she was in her twenties, looked like a Latina. She was tiny, too. As the other band members were setting up their equipment, she played some riffs on her guitar, her fingers playing lead, but no one could hear her because her amp was unplugged and because of the music the club blasted on the loud speakers. She wore a lot of rings, but they didn't seem to slow down her fingers, and they blurred up and down the neck of her guitar.

I don't remember the name of the band, but along with the girl guitarist there were three boys. Two of them were skinny kids who looked alike: Hard rock T-shirts and jeans, long silky hair to their waists, like miniature versions of Robert Plant in his *Song Remains the Same* days, only their hair was black, panther black. The drummer was a fat white kid. He looked white, but he was probably a light-skinned Chicano. As he put his drums together, he seemed like he was breathing hard through his nose, like he was out of breath.

"Hey, Viejo. Ready for some rock and roll?" said the girl. She was standing right next to me at the bar, paying for her beer, but she was so small I had to look down.

"Rock and roll!?" I said. "I thought this was a Neil Diamond tribute!"

She smiled and said, "Have fun," as she walked back to the stage, back to her guitar. She was Mexican, probably from Juárez. Her accent was strong.

Now her amp was plugged in, and she was testing her guitar with some rock riffs, "Iron Man" by Black Sabbath, "Wish You Were Here" by Pink Floyd.

The fat drummer was warming up too, pounding out some beats, and in spite of his large mass he was fast, his arms blurring as he pounded those drums. The two skinny boys were on guitar and bass, and that was the band: two guitars, a bass, and a drum set.

The way I liked it. That was all you needed to play rock and roll, any rock and roll, death metal, heavy metal, Black, gothic, whatever kind of rock you like, just four instruments and vocals. One of the skinny boys set his guitar on a stand and grabbed the microphone and said, "One, two three."

The girl came in on the guitar, a death metal beat, *fffoo fffoo fffoo fffoo*, and then the drums came in and the bass, and it was loud, and it was good, and the boy clasping the microphone started singing into the cup of his hands, and like a lot of death metal voices, his was raspy and loud, indistinguishable from other voices of death, just another instrument like the guitar, loud, distorted. Who could tell what he was saying? Together the guitar and the voice were like roars, and it got to me.

I liked it.

Kids started running into the mosh pit, and they ran around in circles, young, plump and skinny kids, running in both directions.

And when I say kids, I mean, in their twenties. Kids to me. Boys and girls to me.

They ran so fast, around and around, as if frenzied by the music, and as they passed each other in opposite directions, they brushed against each other, almost slamming into each other, but not quite. It wasn't violent like other mosh pits I had witnessed (and participated in), but cute, like children playing in a field. And this was El Paso in the twenty-first century, so almost all the kids in the club were Mexican kids, Latinos, Chicanos, whatever term it was they used to indicate themselves. I had lived the last thirty years in L.A., and although there were a lot of Mexicans and other Latinos here it was different, if only because white people on this border city were not just the minority—they were rare. There were a lot of light-skinned Latinos in El Paso, blonds with blue eyes and freckles on their cheeks, but they were more likely to speak Spanish than English, and even if some of them may have felt themselves superior to indios, they were still Mexicans.

I walked closer to the stage, because I wanted to get a closer look at the band. The girl was "in the zone," as they say, her eyes closed as her fingers slid up and down the width of the neck, playing *one, two, three —one, two, three* and then subverting it with a hard *one* and a hard *one* and a hard *one, two, three* again.

The boy on vocals put the mike on the stand and picked up his guitar. He took over the rhythm that the girl was playing, and she started on lead. Her fingers fluttered fast, like locusts over rows of wheat fields, and people yelled and whistled. I couldn't help it. I whistled. She was that good.

I must have been standing there for a while, my body moving to the music while my mind wandered into a labyrinth of memories and thought, because suddenly the music was over.

The boy told everyone their CDs were for sale, and then the bar manager came on stage and said the next band would be called "Dead Gabriel."

I went to the bar to order another drink. On stage, the girl was rolling up her chord, and I think she looked over at me and winked. The fat drummer was carrying his stuff off stage, like a little boy taking his toys home. I gulped down my whiskey and ordered another one.

Finally I was feeling a little happy drunk, energetic drunk. I wanted to hear more music, more intensity. I didn't want to let my mind enter my mother's house, the dark windows, the dusty wooden floors, or the wooden shack in the back, where the only light came from when the doors were pulled open and the sun shot in and shone on the piles of junk, stuff my mother hoarded over fifty years. A bike from my youth covered in dust and cobwebs hung on the wall, and I wondered how long it had been in that same spot, and how long would I have to stay here before I was able to get rid of all the stuff, sell the house, and go back home to my wife and dogs. I found myself hoping that the next group would be good, would play so hard it could spill me all over the floor.

I joked with the bartender about making it a better drink next time, and he did, pouring me a healthy shot that looked like a triple. I had to bend over the bar to sip at the rim of the glass, just so I wouldn't spill whisky all over my trembling fingers. I thanked the boy and tipped him well.

"So what did you think, old man?" She was standing there at the bar. I could barely hear her because of the music they played between bands, loud death metal en español.

Machete en mano

Y sangre india

"Sounded like a bunch of noise to me," I said.

She laughed and pointed at me and squinted her eyes. "You're a liar. You liked it very much, I think."

"Seriously. You play well," I said. "You were great."

The boy brought her a beer. She took a drink.

She looked at me, then walked over to me. She had dark green eyes.

"Can I sit here?" she asked about the bar stool next to me.

"Yeah, of course," I said. I even backed up my stool to give her a bit more room.

She climbed up the stool and straddled it like it was horse. Her cheeks were thin, sunken in, like you could imagine the shape of her skull. She took a drink of beer. Looked at the label, interested in everything. She had long fingers with rings on almost all of them. "You like this kind of music?" she asked, indicating the song on the speakers.

I recognized the band, a death metal group from Mexico.

"Brujeria's all right." I said.

She raised her eyebrows, as if she were impressed with my knowledge.

"Do you know what they are singing?" she asked.

"Matando güeros."

"¡Qúe chulo!" she said, surprised. "You know the music even!"

"Not bad for an old, man, huh? What's your name?" I asked.

She took a cocktail napkin, wrote something on it, and slid over to me. It said *Mari(a)*.

"How do you pronounce it?" I asked.

She shrugged her shoulders. "You tell me, Viejo."

She looked at me as if she wanted to tell me something but was unsure, but then she said it, leaning in a bit.

"Look, I just want you to know that I'm just being friendly, okay? I wouldn't get the wrong idea, you know? I'm not into old men."

I nodded, held up my right hand, showing her my gold band.

She took a drink of her beer, looked at me, and she said, "You remind me of my uncle. That's all."

"Who's your uncle?"

"He's dead."

"Sorry."

"Juárez," she said, as if that explained it all.

The drummer came by and stood in front of Mari(a)'s stool. She introduced him as Beto. Then a few of their friends came by, and now a bunch of them were chattering and laughing, me in the middle of them like a chaperone. She said, "Hey, guys. This is my uncle. He came to see me play."

Everyone referred to her as Mari(a) and to me as "sir."

Beto asked me what I thought of the music.

"Prefiero rancheras," I said. "Vincente, música así."

Mari(a) was the only one who laughed at my joke, and she punched me on the arm.

Dead Gabriel was the best band of the night. From Austin, the lead singer was a black kid with so much energy he ran around the stage in short bursts, his voice pure rage. He had a 1970s style Afro, like Billy Preston, the round of it blurring as he moved his head. His voice vibrated on the walls, on the floors, on my arms, and in their best song of the night, I realized what made him so good was that it was *his* voice, death metal style, but with clarity and precision.

Let the dead
Bury their dead!
Let the dead
Bury their dead!

As if pulled by their force, Mari(a) and some of the kids and I got up off our stools and walked closer to the stage, so we could look up at them, sway with them, raise our fists with them. We even started to jump up and down. Every now and then Mari(a) and I looked at each other and mouthed, "Fuck!"

Jesus said
Fuck the dead
Let the dead. . .

And then they were done
We stood there.
"Wow," she said. "They were good."
We walked back to the bar, and I bought us both another drink.
"So why do you like death so much?" she asked. "We don't see too many . . ."
"Old people? How old do you think I am?"

"Fifty," she said.

"On the nose," I said. "And you, María?"

"Twenty-two," she said. "So what do you like about death?"

I thought about it, looking for a canned response in the shelves of my memory, but I remembered that I had never been able to find an answer. One time my wife walked in on me when I was working on my computer in my office at home, the death metal blasted so loud I didn't hear her come in. I thought she was at work, but she walked in on me, and when I looked up and saw her standing in the doorway, the sunlight shooting in, she looked down on me as if she had caught me masturbating. I turned down the music. "Is everything all right?" I asked, standing up.

"Why do you like that crap?" she asked.

I wasn't able to answer her. I said, "I just like it."

"But why?" asked Mari(a). "Why do you like it?"

"It's evil," I said.

"That's why you like it?"

"I mean, I'm not into Satan or anything like that. I sometimes even go to church. Sometimes. Mostly for my wife's sake, but when I'm there, I feel it. God is real, and if I'm going to be on anyone's side, it's God's. It's just . . ." I took a drink of my whisky. "Sometimes you need to feel the opposite."

"So, do you want to see something really evil?"

"What do you mean?" I asked, looking at her as if horns were about to sprout from her head.

"Do you like Black?"

"Black metal? Like Gongoroth?"

"Darker. Real evil. I could show you some bands."

I laughed, wondering what she thought would be evil. I had been in town for a few weeks, and I had seen almost every metal show that I could. What could she show me? And as I watched her face look at me as if she held a secret, I remembered how young she was, how much she hadn't yet experienced.

I looked around the club at all the kids. "They try to be dark around here," I said. "In the mosh pit they run around in circles high-fiving each other as they pass, like kids playing 'Ring around the Rosies.' No one ever gets hurt."

"Is that what you want to see?"

"No, that's not the point. It's just such a friendly release of energy, like a mosh pit in heaven. In California, I've seen mosh pits where . . . people let go. Their rage."

"Well, anyway, I'm not talking about El Paso." She straightened up. "I'm talking about Juárez. There's some underground clubs."

"Juárez? I thought the clubs were dying over there. That's what I read. Many of the businesses are moving to El Paso, you know. Restaurants. Nightclubs. They're all moving here."

"I said underground."

"In Juárez?" I wasn't sure if I believed her.

"I'm talking hardcore Black, tío. *Negro* Metal. Maybe you would not be able to handle it," she said, her accent so strong she sounded like a foreign actress, like Penelope Cruz, even though she wasn't a Spaniard, but a middle-class Mexican. "It will not be so comfortable as here."

"I don't know. I've seen some petty evil things in my life. Maybe some of them *you* would not be able to handle."

"Okay, tell me," she said.

"I used to live in Mexico City."

"So please tell me your dark adventures in el DF."

An image popped into my head, a murdered woman in an alley, behind some garbage cans, stray dogs sniffing around her body, but then I remembered that the image wasn't something I had seen in real life, but in a book I had read when I lived for a year in Mexico City.

"Do you want to go or not? I'll take you there."

"Isn't Juárez a bit dangerous right now?" I asked.

"What isn't dangerous?" she said. She took a drink from her beer bottle. "All these guys in the band I play with. They won't go. They're too scared."

"But you're not?"

"It's my home. I will never be afraid to go home. The place I'm talking about is like a guerilla movement. They set up in some abandoned building. They play, and then they move on."

"You're making this up," I said.

"Trust me. You can take me. I don't have a car."

"You want me to drive in Juárez?"

"There's one on Friday. Wanna go?"

"I don't want to drive," I said.

"Don't be such a gringo. You'll be fine."

"Even the US government warns citizens not to go to Mexico, especially Juárez. It's the murder capital of the world."

"Oh, so you are very sure that you do whatever the US government tells you to do?"

"Not, that's not it."

"Do you want to go or not?"

"I don't want to drive. I got California plates. I'll get carjacked."

"You know who's playing at this event? Las Mujeres Matadas."

"The murdered women?"

"They are an all-girl, black-metal group."

"That's . . . that's unusual."

"They'll give you nightmares."

I took a zip of whisky, and I was drunk by now, and had it been Friday, I would have said, Sure, let's go. Instead I said, "I'll think about it."

"You can pick me up at 8 p.m."

"Where do you live?"

"By UTEP."

"Are you a student?"

She nodded, and suddenly I felt that all this was innocent after all, that she was bluffing, that if anything, I reminded her of her uncle and that reminded her of Juárez, her *Amor por Juárez*, and she just wanted to imagine going into the city, going back home. She was just a bourgeois kid.

"Gee, I haven't asked this in a long time," I said. "What's your major?"

"Philosophy," she said.

"Figures," I said.

She handed me a piece of paper with handwriting on it, and at first glance, I didn't recognize an order to the letters and numbers, not even the symbols, as if it were written in some ancient language, some secret code—and my heart skipped a beat. But then my eyes adjusted, and I saw that it was her address written on a cocktail napkin, "2199 Prospect. #3. 79902."

And a little note that said, "8 p.m."

* * *

When I was in high school, we used to cross into Juárez at night, a bunch of us kids ready to party and lose our minds, and we were so skinny and light with youth that we floated across the bridge like naughty angels and stumbled back like the happy dead. We did dollar tequila shots and drank bottles of beer, and sometimes we paid ten bucks to get into club that had a deejay and a barra libre, and we drank so much beer and sweet, blended drinks that our bellies felt full and some of us barfed just to make more room.

Drunk and together with our crazy friends, a bunch of us would skip our way down Avenida Juárez to a taco place and stuff our mouths and tummies with greasy meat and cheese wrapped in a stack of corn tortillas as we drank cans of Tecate. Little street kids would come to our table begging for money and food, and we bought them bottles of Fanta and gave them dollars and quarters and tacos stuffed with meat. We were only teenagers, years away from the legal right to drink on the other side of the bridge, but in Juárez, we felt like adults.

The city was our playground, a nighttime labyrinth of possibilities, and because we were full of hormones, we used our freedom to make-out in public, feel each other up at the clubs, at dark tables or in underground hallways that led to the bathrooms. Some of us had sex in the bathroom stalls, and when it was over, we did lines on the backs of the toilets.

This was when Juárez was safe, or so we believed.

Turns out that it was never safe.

But we were safe, or we felt like it.

Even when we passed by Juárez police on our drunken-boat walk back to the bridge, back to our side of the border, as the cops looked at us, sometimes shaking their heads at us, we continued to laugh and talk loudly, sometimes yelling so loud at each other it was like we wanted everyone to hear us, wanting others to witness our youth.

Some of the girls with us walked back in short skirts and high heels, and the men standing idle on the corners watched them as they bent over to take off their shoes, carrying them by the straps, walking barefoot across the concrete screaming, *Woo!!!*

But that was then, when Juárez seemed safe.

Or safer.

There were always stories our parents told us in order to warn us about the dangers of getting drunk in Juárez, which is how the fact of the murdered woman first came to our attention. There were stories, rumors, about a girl missing, a girl walking home from the factory, a girl from Michoacán, from Sinaloa, Veracruz, Quintana Roo, and then there were sporadic articles in the *El Paso Times*, the bodies of girls on the sides of barren hills, dead girls found only because their young hands were spotted sticking out of garbage heaps, as if trying to grab on to something, or an ankle would be coming out of a mound of dirt and rock, girls barely approaching puberty, their bodies mutilated, all of the parts being uncovered little by little, until we saw the whole horror of it, the numbers adding up, the murdered women, the murdered girls, the authorities pretending that there was no problem or they were doing something about a small problem at most.

And now there were the drug wars. Now Juárez had the dubious distinction to be called the Murder Capital of the World, and women and girls were still disappearing, a lot of them, sixteen-, seventeen-year-old girls.

When Mari(a) and I drove into Juárez on Friday evening, there was still sun enough to see. It looked pretty much the same to me, pharmacies and liquor stores and restaurants, the only difference being the army trucks full of young Indian soldiers carrying automatic rifles. They were patrolling the streets, parked on busy intersections, short Indian boys holding rifles taller than them as they stood in parking lots of strip malls, boys too young for facial hair.

Since the drug wars had started, every time I had come back to El Paso to see my mother for some matter of her estate or health care, I avoided Juárez. This was my first time here since I was thirty years old, about twenty years ago. I remember I was right out of law school, my first year working with a firm in L.A., the job I always dreamed of having, the city in which I had dreamed of living. I was staying for a few days with my parents. My dad was still alive then, and I was helping him with some paperwork, the company where he'd worked for forty years trying to deny his retirement. I filed papers. I studied documents. One night I walked across the Santa Fe Bridge and into downtown Juárez. I drank some beers at the Kentucky Club, which was full that night with a mixture of Júarenses and El Paso people. After a few beers, I wandered through Boys Town, where I slipped into a place called Pigalle. I sat at a table by myself and watched the women at other tables surrounded by men and bottles of beer, the ladies laughing and controlling the hands of all the men groping them, like octopus women. I wasn't married then, and I must have been looking for something, because when a plump woman walked in with big lips and wearing a ridiculously small outfit, I stared at her. She knew I was looking at her, and she looked at me, smiled, and winked. I rose from my table.

Juárez.

It wasn't until we entered deeper into the city, away from the border, that I saw how different the city had become during wartime. On intersection light poles, on the sides of buildings, on stone fences, there were posters and fliers with the pictures of young girls, posted there by their mothers, ladies who were doing all they could to get their girls back, Lupita Perez Montes, Esmeralda Monreal, Nancy Muñoz, Ayudanos buscarlas.

I was afraid to be in Juárez in my car in the impending night, but somehow having Mari(a) next to me in the passenger's seat made me feel safer, maybe because she wasn't afraid.

Much of the businesses were boarded up, weeds growing out of the cement in the parking lots, and many buildings had been demolished and stood in piles of rubble as though bombs had gone off.

"Fucking sad, you know?" she said, looking at piles of rubble on a corner, a building that used to be a mini mall. "I used to fucking shop there, man," she said, shaking her head as if she couldn't believe it. We drove onto a narrow street lined with dentist offices and tailor shops and discount stores, then a few larger stores full of people going in and out. We passed by a storefront with big display windows onto the street, and inside, behind a barrier of sandbags, was a soldier, pointing his rifle at the street, at us, as if the enemy might drive by at any moment.

We passed the Hotel Juárez, a corner building with a facade of turquoise-colored tile, like it might have been pretty fancy a long time before. Maybe when I was a teenager, sneaking in and out of Juárez with my friends, that hotel was luxurious; maybe it had a ballroom with gilded walls and a chandelier.

The deeper we drove into the city, the more abandoned it seemed, and the angrier Mari(a) seemed to become. "Fucking men!"

I didn't argue with her.

"You know what really fucking pisses me off?" she asked. "Turn here."

I turned where she asked me to, and we drove down an abandoned road with nothing on the side but dry land and rock. A housing development appeared up ahead, one of those suburban tracks with an entrance and a sign. It was a new development, the houses modern with two stories and the garages pushed up front. Each house had a small yard and big double doors.

But the homes were empty. If they weren't boarded up, they were abandoned, the windows busted out, doors knocked in. Some of the houses had debris all over the front yard. Some of them had spray paint across the garage doors, ¡Sálvanos! and other, more profane, expressions.

"Stop," she said, and I braked in front of a house that wasn't boarded up but that had signage all over warning about keeping away. "Keep away" signs were everywhere: spray painted on the walls, posted on stakes in the yard, written on the door.

It hadn't worked. The place looked pillaged.

"That's my house," she said. "Or was."

I drove around for the next hour or so, wherever she told me to go, and although I was scared at first, I kind of just forgot where we were, and I just followed Mari(a) until it got dark and we found ourselves driving down a two-lane road out of the city. Nothing lined the road. We could see some lights in the distance, buildings somewhere far off, and in the distance, sirens wailed. We could see the El Paso star burning on the black mountain, but all else was dark, and we could only see what the headlights lit up in front of us, the white lines coming at us.

Mari(a) said, "Here, you want this?"

She held two red pills in the palm of her hand.

"What is it?" I asked.

"What do you think?"

She told me to pull up to a cluster of buildings, which looked abandoned, surrounded by a chain-link fence. The gate to the parking lot had been torn off. "Here?" I asked.

The buildings reminded me one of those old insane asylums in the country, where they used to give electric shock treatments.

I took the pills from her palm, but she said, "Only one. The other one's for me."

I threw it in my mouth and swallowed, and she handed me a bottle of water.

"Give it about twenty minutes," she said. "Come on."

We heard the pounding coming from inside the building, which used to be a factory. The double metal doors were closed shut, and on it was written Peligro! No Ingresa, and I could feel the bass pulsing from the other side, as if it might blow the doors off.

There was a man at the door in a dark suit and tie who looked like a Secret Service agent. He even had a wire in his ear. When he saw us coming, he stood before the door, and when we got there, Mari(a) opened her palm and held a red poker chip. The security man nodded, and he turned to open the doors.

He grabbed both door handles with both of his big fists, and he pulled hard with a single jerk.

We watched the doors fly open like the wings of an angel, revealing a nighttime sky scattered with stars and a moon as big as the sun.

The force of the music seemed to lift us to the middle of the floor, surrounded by hundreds of young people, boys with long hair, girls with black makeup. The stage was empty except for some people setting up for the next band. People were standing around, drinking, yelling into each other's ears. The music was blasting from the speakers, and a few boys were in the mosh pit, forcefully banging against each other.

The song playing sounded like industrial noise, a repetitive whip.

Frrrrom.

Frrrrom.

"This place used to be one of the biggest maquiladoras in Juarez," Mari(a) yelled into my ear. "A lot of the murdered women worked here in this very spot."

"It's huge," I said, looking around. It seemed the size of an indoor skating rink, high ceilings, with metal beams running across it. In the middle of the floor, separating the room, there was a counter, where maybe there used to be machinery for an assembly line. Now the Juárez kids were standing on it, drinking, moving to the beat. "This is the last place some of the girls saw before they were murdered," she said.

Frrrrom.

Frrrrom.

"And the company bus," she continued, "picked them up right outside, but they dropped them off downtown. And they walked home alone."

I looked up and saw that part of the ceiling was falling in a giant chunk, and outside the moon was falling from space onto the floor, and I covered my head as if that would protect me from the debris all over my shoulders.

"It's kicking in, isn't it?" she asked.

"Maybe."

"I'll be right back," she said.

"Where are you going?" I said not wanting to be left alone, but she vanished into the blur of bodies, and I had what must have been a vision: lights came up and the music stopped and I saw the factory in full production, the whack of the machines, the buzzing of the saws, the women standing on the assembly line. Two European men in suits stood in an open door and watched one of the girls who worked walking into the bathroom.

Frrrrom.

The music stopped, and the voices rose around me like dark vines.

I don't remember how long I walked around that dead factory, in and out of the past and present. I don't know how many groups played that night. I remember lights, I remember the moon shattering on the floor, and I remember a mosh pit where shirtless young men rushed into each other, a fist, a head butt, and I remember that they carried more than a few boys out on stretchers, and I remember the announcer walking on stage, the lights blasting from behind him, and he introduced the next group, Juárez natives, "Las Mujeres Matadas."

The crowd exploded when they walked on stage, five young women, some of them wearing outfits like factory girls—dirty smocks, white lab coats spattered with blood—and a few of them wore Catholic schoolgirl skirts that were ripped and soiled and bloody. All their faces had makeup, as if they were zombies, white face, blood dripping from the eyes, and then they started their music and it was so hard and fast that I jumped up and down on my feet, and I'm not even sure at what point it occurred to me that the guitar player was Mari(a). She was wearing the Catholic schoolgirl skirt, but she didn't look sexy, didn't try to; she looked dead, murdered, angry as hell.

She had on skeleton makeup, a cross between black-metal style and the calaveras of the Day of the Dead, and she had a Frida Kahlo–style scarf on her head.

Odio por Juárez
Pa' esos hombres
es odio por Juárez

Mari(a) stepped forward and played lead, those fingers running back and forth like the legs of tiny people, the notes so fast and intense it felt like fleeing from the light of a nightmare you can't remember, the crowd growing in frenzy the quicker her fingers moved, and all the other girls were watching as her guitar screamed pain and anger. It opened something in me, and I walked in.

I don't remember what I did in there, but the landscape was pulsing with rage. I saw faces, bodies piled, lights glaring, shovels and picks, rocks and dirt, and a kid's bicycle covered in sand. I saw my mother's body shriveled up under the covers, her eyes closed.

The band kept playing. I don't know what really happened or if it was the drug or if it's my memory now that I try and recall that night in Juárez, my perceptions of reality filtered by ego and past experience. I don't remember what I did while the Mujeres Matadas screamed for justice, for love of Juárez; I only know that I must have been inside that place for a while. And I remembered another song they played.

It was a black-metal version of a Talking Heads song, "Life During Wartime."

This ain't no party
This ain't no disco
And I ain't fucking around.

Then they were done with it.

Mari(a) became Mari(a) again. She was out of breath, her chest moving up and down, but she was happy, not laughing and smiling, but fulfilled, as if the clouds broke open and the sun blasted her in warmth. She held her guitar like a rifle, and then she looked above the silhouette of heads that was the crowd, the lights shining in her eyes. She didn't look for me, didn't want to know what I thought of her performance. It wasn't about me. In fact, after it was all over and the lights came on and people left, I would look for her but wouldn't find her. The security men in dark suits would tell me to leave, and I would drive back to the border alone that night, figuring she must have left with some of her friends. But for now she was on stage shrouded in sweat and applause. She turned around and looked at the other Mujeres Matadas, all of them sweaty and done with it, too, all them carrying instruments like weapons after the battle.

As the crowd whistled and yelled for them to play another song, as the motion around them blurred into a dull-colored background, the women looked at each other, the light in their eyes holding them together like a star.

The Astronaut

Matt Mendez

Carlos stayed buried under the covers when the baby crawled into his room. He came at night, like the year before and every year Carlos could remember. He picked the baby up and nestled him beside his chest. Outside his window were the stars and moon, hanging fat and round in the sky. The baby didn't make a sound; without eyes its empty sockets looked as hopeless as the copper mines where Apá worked. He had told Carlos about them, described the pitch-black darkness and how it was swallowing him, little by little, every day. Apá lived somewhere in Arizona and sometimes called late at night trying for Amá. Him all drunk, all want. The baby had no tongue, no skin or muscles or organs, and was made entirely of brilliant white bone.

The baby was his brother.

"You'll only be alone for a little while, mijo," Amá yelled from her room. "Think you can handle that?" She was getting ready for work, but Carlos could also hear her talking to the dead, her finishing the ofrenda she put together every Día de los Muertos. She was whispering to Nana, *her* Amá, who died from cancer two years before. And to Estela, her big sister who ran a red light and crashed, the wreck happening when Amá was only a girl. Amá whispered to her baby, too, telling him all the things he would have become, had he only been born alive.

The baby wrapped his cold bony hand around Carlos's pinky. *Had* he been born, the baby would've been his mirror image—minus the scar along Carlos's belly and torso, a long fleshy worm inching up from his bellybutton and stopping just between his nipples. The scar was born the day Apá left his Buck knife unattended on the coffee table. Carlos had slowly pulled the folding blade open, pausing halfway to make sure no one was watching.

His parents had been arguing in their bedroom as he snapped it the rest of the way open. The sound, metallic and secure, satisfied him, just as it must have satisfied Apá when he used to robotically open and close the same knife while watching TV alone in the living room. Blood had appeared briefly as a thin red line across Carlos's belly and chest before drooling down his crotch and legs and puddling around his feet. Apá moved away after that, deciding to spend the rest of his life crawling deeper and deeper into the earth.

Pulling the blanket tighter over him and the baby, Carlos remembered how things had been when they'd shared Amá's belly. They were two astronauts floating in space, Amá's faraway voice a kind of Mission Control meant to lead them home. But then one night, or maybe it was day, Carlos could never tell, he felt hands slip around his body, pulling him away from his universe. Panicked, Carlos reached for his brother, but he was gone. Amá's guiding voice was gone too.

"Carlos, promise you won't do anything crazy? I just talked to your tía Alejandra. She's on her way."

Amá emerged from her bedroom dressed in her waitress uniform—black, grease-stained slacks and polo—her apron, filled with straws and loose change, flung over her shoulder. She walked over to Carlos and plopped down on his bed. The expression on her face, tired and with an unhappy smile, was exactly how she'd looked in the moments after he'd been born.

"I don't do crazy things," Carlos said. "I do tests."

Carlos wanted to find his brother, to bring him home. Amá leaned over and squeezed Carlos tight, her body inches from the baby. "Well, don't do any tests tonight . . . just watch some TV until your tía gets here."

Amá's altars were what brought the baby back year after year, and Carlos wondered if Amá could feel the little skeleton snuggled underneath the blankets, just inches beside her leg. When Carlos had tried splitting himself like a cell, he couldn't get past the anaphase stage and onto telophase, the final part of mitosis. Looking back, he was glad that division didn't work, that making another Carlos wasn't what anyone wanted.

"Did you finish the ofrenda?" he asked, already knowing she had.

Amá's altars were beautiful. The usual clutter of her dresser, crumpled receipts and mail, envelopes opened and ignored, replaced with bouquets of roses: white and yellow and red blooms cut and set in old jars. Sacred Heart velas flickering. The photos of Nana and tía Estela, and other dead faces Carlos didn't recognize, gently slid inside picture frames Amá painted by hand. And then there was the food, plates of cut strawberries and chunks of pomegranate, along with homemade pan tornillo, each delicately portioned under each photo.

"I finished the altar last night," Amá said. "And I promise I won't be too long. I'll be home before you even wake up in the morning."

At the center was a porcelain statue of La Virgen de Guadalupe. She was fixed over the image of his brother, over the sonogram inside a baby-blue frame. Carlos was also in the picture, one of the two indistinguishable blobs floating in the cosmos, part of the ofrenda.

"You always say that," Carlos said. Amá rubbed his hair into his face. If Carlos didn't know better, he might think she was being playful.

"Promise me, mijo. No jumping through mirrors looking for other dimensions. No digging up the courtyard looking for mines. And no cutting yourself in half. I need you to be . . . *normal*."

"I *am* normal," Carlos said, moving his bangs so Amá could see his face, but, like always, she avoided looking at him and instead gazed toward the open door of his room. "I promise, Amá."

"And *you* always say that," Amá said getting up to leave. "And please don't go into my room."

"Don't you wish you could see Hector again?" Carlos asked, using his brother's name.

Amá looked back at him, now standing in the doorway. "One day," she said. "I will. . . . we both will, just not today."

"I can find him," Carlos said. "I know where to look now."

"You're making me worry."

Carlos could see the uneasiness creasing in the neat lines around her eyes. "Don't worry, Amá. I'm all done with tests."

"I love you, mijo" Amá said, pausing for a moment and then looking at the clock on the wall. "I gotta get going." Amá blew him a kiss and then rushed from the room without looking back. If she had, she would have seen the little skeleton crawling out of the blankets.

Her altar had brought the baby back, if only for the night. Carlos watched as his brother struggled to flip onto his back, his mouth open, grunting or crying, but all his effort made no sound. Carefully turning the baby over, Carlos wrapped him in a blanket—he weighed almost nothing—and carried his twin to Amá's room, where he placed him at the center of her bed and sat beside him.

Carlos had already set everything up. Outside he'd propped a ladder against the back wall of the apartment building, ready to be climbed all the way to the roof, where he'd stashed his sneakers and a jacket. He'd read that outer space was cold, though he didn't remember it that way.

Kicking off the blanket with his little bony legs, Carlos knew the baby didn't have long. He studied the ofrenda. Every Día de los Muertos his brother came to him only to again disappear, leaving Carlos to spend the rest of the year searching.

He took a bite of the pan tornillo. The bread was soft, and he watched as a crack spiderwebbed across the baby's forehead. He took another bite and then had the strawberries. The top of his brother's head collapsed like a hollow egg. As Carlos finished off the pomegranates, the bones of his brother's hands and feet separated and fell uselessly beside him, his arms and legs disembodied. He watched as the pile of bones crumbled into dust, as they always did.

Carlos had never touched the offering meant for his brother before, but now he understood that these were his fruits too. That Amá's altars were also calling to him. He grabbed the baby-blue picture frame and gently pulled the sonogram from inside. He studied the image, the two blurry smudges sharing the one black circle. Outside the desert sky looked just as dark, the scattered stars embedded in the sky like precious stones waiting to be mined. Carlos climbed out of the window and scaled the ladder, climbing from his second-floor bedroom all the way to the roof. Below, tía Alejandra was pulling up to the apartment, her parking crooked in her space.

"Hi tía!" Carlos waved as his aunt climbed out of her car, freezing and then looking for the voice calling down to her. "I'm up here. Tell Amá that I'm going to find Hector."

"Stay right there Carlos," tía Alejandra said, slamming her door shut and then running toward the building. "Don't move from that spot."

The North Star glowed by the Big Dipper, shining brighter than normal. That's where Hector had to be. Carlos cinched his tennis shoes and zipped up the jacket, making sure to slide the picture of him and his brother inside the breast pocket. As he walked to one end of the roof, he could hear tía Alejandra, already inside the apartment, yelling for him not to do anything crazy. Carlos took off in a dead sprint, his eyes fixed on the sky as he raced across the length of the roof and then planted his foot right before the edge, leaping into the air.

Below him was the world he knew. Where the living needed the dead. Tía Alejandra's voice faded away as cold air whipped against his face. Never looking down, Carlos focused on the brightest spot in the sky, lifting off higher and higher and toward the light.

About the Editor

Sergio Troncoso is the author of *A Peculiar Kind of Immigrant's Son* (2019), a collection of linked short stories on immigration. The first story in that collection won the Kay Cattarulla Award for Best Short Story. Troncoso also wrote *From This Wicked Patch of Dust*, which *Kirkus Reviews* named one of the best books of 2012 in a starred review. The novel won the Southwest Book Award. Troncoso wrote *Crossing Borders: Personal Essays* (2011), winner of the Bronze Award for Essays from *Foreword Reviews*. He is also the author of *The Nature of Truth* (revised 2014), hailed by the *Chicago Tribune* as "impressively lucid." *Publishers Weekly* called his first book, *The Last Tortilla and Other Stories* (1999), "Richly satisfying," and the book won El Premio Aztlán Literary Prize. His work has appeared in *New Letters*, *Yale Review*, *Michigan Quarterly Review*, *Texas Monthly*, and *CNN Opinion*. He has served as a judge for the PEN/Faulkner Award for Fiction and the *New Letters* Prize for Essays. A Fulbright scholar, Troncoso is president of the Texas Institute of Letters and teaches fiction and nonfiction at the Yale Writers' Workshop. His novel *Nobody's Pilgrims* is forthcoming in 2021. Visit his website at SergioTroncoso.com.

About the Contributors

Francisco Cantú is a writer, translator, and the author of *The Line Becomes a River*, winner of the 2018 Los Angeles Times Book Prize and a finalist for the National Book Critics Circle Nonfiction Award. A former Fulbright fellow, he has been the recipient of a Pushcart Prize, a Whiting Award, and an Art for Justice Fellowship. His writing and translations appear in the *New Yorker*, *Best American Essays*, and *Harper's*, as well as on *This American Life*. A lifelong resident of the Southwest, he now lives in Tucson, where he coordinates the Field Studies in Writing Program at the University of Arizona.

Oscar Cásares is the author of the story collection *Brownsville* and the novels *Amigoland* and *Where We Come From*, which have earned him fellowships from the National Endowment for the Arts, the Copernicus Society of America, the Texas Institute of Letters, and the Guggenheim Foundation. His writing focuses on the US–Mexico, where he grew up and his family began to settle as far back as the mid-1800s. His essays have appeared in *Texas Monthly*, the *New York Times*, and the *Washington Post* and on National Public Radio. He teaches creative writing at the University of Texas at Austin.

Daniel Chacón received degrees from California State University, Fullerton in political science and English. He received his MFA in fiction from the University of Oregon. The author of seven books of fiction—including *Kafka in a Skirt: Stories from the Wall (2019)*; *Hotel Juárez, Stories, Rooms and Loops*; *The Cholo Tree*; and *Unending Rooms*—Chacón has won the Southwest Book Award, American Book Award, PEN Oakland Prize for Fiction, and Hudson Prize. He founded and hosts the literary radio show *Words on a Wire* and is currently chair of the Bilingual Creative Department at the University of Texas, El Paso. Visit his website at SoyChacon.Wordpress.com.

Sandra Cisneros is a poet, short-story writer, novelist, essayist, and visual artist whose work explores the lives of Mexicans and Mexican Americans. Her numerous awards include a MacArthur Fellowship, the National Medal of the Arts, a Ford Foundation Art of Change Fellowship, and the PEN/Nabokov Award for Achievement in International Literature. *The House on Mango Street* has sold over six million copies, has been translated into over twenty-five languages, and is required reading in schools and universities across the nation. A dual citizen of the United States and Mexico, Sandra Cisneros earns her living by her pen.

Rubén Degollado's fiction has been published in *Beloit Fiction Journal, Gulf Coast, Hayden's Ferry Review, Image,* and the anthologies *Bearing the Mystery, Fantasmas,* and *Juventud.* He has been a finalist and has received honorable mentions in contests at *American Short Fiction, Glimmer Train,* and *Bellingham Review*'s Tobias Wolff Award for Fiction. Recently, his debut novel, *Throw,* was published by Slant Books and won the Best Young Adult Book Award from the Texas Institute of Letters.

Diana Marie Delgado is the author of *Tracing the Horse* and the chapbook *Late Night Talks with Men I Think I Trust.* She is the recipient of numerous grants, including a National Endowment for the Arts Fellowship. A graduate of Columbia University, she currently resides in Tucson, where she is the Literary Director of the Poetry Center at the University of Arizona.

David Dominguez holds a BA in comparative literature from the University of California at Irvine and an MFA in creative writing from the University of Arizona. He is the author of *Work Done Right* (University of Arizona Press) and *The Ghost of César Chávez* (C&R Press). His poems have appeared in *Miramar, Crab Orchard Review, Poet Lore, Spillway,* and *Southern Review.* In addition, his work appears in *The Wind Shifts: New Latino Poetry; Bear Flag Republic: Prose Poems and Poetics from California; Breathe: 101 Contemporary Odes;* and *Camino del Sol: Fifteen*

Years of Latina and Latino Writing. Dominguez teaches writing at Reedley College.

Alex Espinoza earned his MFA in fiction from University of California at Irvine. He's the author of *Still Water Saints* and *The Five Acts of Diego León*, both from Random House. His newest book is *Cruising: An Intimate History of a Radical Pastime* (Unnamed Press, 2019). He has written for the *Los Angeles Times*, the *New York Times Magazine, Virginia Quarterly Review, Literary Hub*, and NPR's *All Things Considered*. The recipient of fellowships from the National Endowment for the Arts and the MacDowell Colony as well as an American Book Award, he lives in Los Angeles and is the Tomás Rivera Endowed Chair of Creative Writing at University of California at Riverside.

Rigoberto González is the author of seventeen books of poetry and prose. His awards include a Guggenheim Fellowship, a National Endowment for the Arts Fellowship, a USA Rolón Fellowship, and an American Book Award. His memoir *What Drowns the Flowers in Your Mouth* was a finalist for the National Book Critics Circle Award in Autobiography. Currently, he is professor at and director of the MFA program at Rutgers–Newark, the State University of New Jersey.

Reyna Grande is the author of *The Distance between Us* (2012) and *A Dream Called Home* (2018). Her other works include the novels *Across a Hundred Mountains* (2006) and *Dancing with Butterflies* (2009). She has received an American Book Award, El Premio Aztlán Literary Prize, and the International Latino Book Award. In 2012, she was a finalist for the National Book Critics Circle Awards, and in 2015 she was honored with a Luis Leal Award for Distinction in Chicano/Latino Literature. She has written about immigration, family separation, and language trauma for the *New York Times, CNN*, the *Dallas Morning News*, and *Buzzfeed*. Visit her website at ReynaGrande.com.

Stephanie Elizondo Griest is a globetrotting author from the Texas–Mexico borderlands. Her five award-winning books include *Around the Bloc: My Life in Moscow, Beijing, and Havana*; *Mexican Enough*; and *All the Agents and Saints: Dispatches from the US Borderlands*. She has also written for the *New York Times, Washington Post, VQR*, the *Believer, Orion*, and *Oxford American*. Her distinctions include a Henry Luce Scholarship to China, a Margolis Award for Social Justice Reporting, a Hodder Fellowship at Princeton, and a Lowell Thomas Travel Journalism Gold Prize. She is currently Associate Professor of Creative Nonfiction at the University of North Carolina–Chapel Hill. Visit her website at StephanieElizondoGriest.com.

Stephanie Li is the Lynne Cooper Harvey Distinguished Professor of English at Washington University in St. Louis. She is the author of five books, including the award-winning *Something Akin to Freedom: The Choice of Bondage in Narratives by African American Women* (SUNY Press, 2010) and *Playing in the White: Black Writers, White Subjects* (Oxford University Press, 2011). Her work has also appeared in *Callaloo, American Literature, SAIL, Legacy*, and *SAQ*. She is currently working on a book focused on postwar white life novels.

Diana López is the author of *Sofia's Saints* and middle-grade novels such as *Lucky Luna* and *Confetti Girl*. Her short fiction has been featured in several anthologies and journals, including *Her Texas: A Collection of Poetry, Image, Story, and Song; RiverSedge*; and *Sycamore Review*. She is assistant professor of creative writing at the University of Houston–Victoria.

Lorraine M. López teaches in the MFA Program at Vanderbilt University. Her first book, *Soy la Avon Lady and Other Stories*, won the Miguel Marmól prize for fiction. Her second book, *Call Me Henri*, was awarded the Paterson Prize for Young Adult Literature. López's short-story collection, *Homicide Survivors Picnic and Other Stories* (BkMk Press), was a finalist for the PEN/Faulkner Prize in Fiction in 2010 and winner of the Texas League of Writers Award for Outstanding Book of Fiction. Subsequent publications include two novels, *The Realm of Hungry Spirits* and *The Darling*. López's most recent publication is *Postcards from the Gerund State: Stories* (BkMk Press).

Sheryl Luna's *Pity the Drowned Horses* (University of Notre Dame Press) received the Andres Montoya Poetry Prize. *Seven* (3: A Taos Press) was a finalist for the Colorado Book Award. Recent poems have appeared in *Poetry, Taos International Journal of Poetry and Art,* and *Huizache.* She received the Alfredo del Moral Foundation Award from Sandra Cisneros and was recently inducted into the Texas Institute of Letters. She's received fellowships from Yaddo, Ragdale, Canto Mundo, and the Anderson Center.

Domingo Martinez is the *New York Times* best-selling author of *The Boy Kings of Texas* and *My Heart is a Drunken Compass. The Boy Kings of Texas* was a finalist for the National Book Award in 2012, a Gold Medal winner of the Independent Publishers Book Award, and a nonfiction finalist for the Washington State Book Awards. *The Boy Kings of Texas* is currently under option with House of Heath for a potential series on Showtime. His work has been featured in *Epiphany Literary Journal, Seattle Weekly, Texas Monthly,* the *New Republic, Saveur* magazine, and *Huizache.*

Matt Mendez grew up in central El Paso, Texas. He is the author of *Barely Missing Everything,* his YA debut novel, and the short-story collection *Twitching Heart.* He earned his MFA from the University of Arizona and lives with his wife and two daughters in Tucson, Arizona. Visit his website at MattMendez.com.

Deborah Paredez is a poet and performance scholar. She is the author of the critical study *Selenidad: Selena, Latinos, and the Performance of Memory* (Duke, 2009) and of the poetry volumes *This Side of Skin* (Wings Press, 2002) and *Year of the Dog* (BOA Editions, 2020). Her poetry and essays have appeared in the *New York Times,* the *Los Angeles Review of Books, Boston Review, Poetry,* and *Poet Lore.* She is the cofounder of CantoMundo, a national organization for Latinx poets. Born and raised in San Antonio, Texas, she lives in New York City, where she teaches creative writing and ethnic studies at Columbia University.

Severo Perez grew up in a working-class neighborhood in Westside San Antonio and graduated from the University of Texas at Austin. An award-winning filmmaker, playwright, and writer, for over forty years he has produced works for PBS, corporate sponsors, the educational market, and network and cable television. His feature film adaptation of the novel *. . . and the earth did not swallow him* (1994) by Tomás Rivera won eleven international awards, including one for Best Director and five for Best Picture. His first novel, *Willa Brown and the Challengers*, is historical fiction based on the real-life African American aviation pioneer, Willa Beatrice Brown. *Odd Birds* is his second novel.

Octavio Quintanilla is the author of the poetry collection *If I Go Missing* (Slough Press, 2014) and of several limited-edition chapbooks of visual poetry, including his most recent, *Wasted Time/Tiempo Perdido* (Alabrava Press, 2019). His writing has appeared in numerous journals, and his visual work has been exhibited in the Presa House Gallery, Southwest School of Art, and Equinox Gallery. He holds a PhD from the University of North Texas and teaches Literature and Creative Writing in the MA/MFA program at Our Lady of the Lake University. Currently, he serves as the 2018–2020 Poet Laureate of San Antonio, Texas. Visit his website at OctavioQuintanilla.com.

José Antonio Rodríguez's books include the poetry collections *This American Autopsy*, *The Shallow End of Sleep*, and *Backlit Hour*; and the memoir *House Built on Ashes*, finalist for the PEN America Los Angeles Literary Award and Lambda Literary Award. His work has appeared in the *New Yorker*, the *Nation*, *POETRY*, the *New Republic*, *McSweeney's*, and the *Texas Observer*. He is a member of the Texas Institute of Letters, CantoMundo, and Macondo Writers Workshop, and he earned a PhD in English and creative writing from Binghamton University–SUNY. A Mexican immigrant from South Texas, he teaches in the MFA program at the University of Texas Rio Grande Valley.

David Dorado Romo is a writer, musician, and historian who specializes in borderlands and transnational studies. He is author of the award-winning *Ringside Seat to a Revolution: The Underground History of Ciudad Juárez and El Paso, 1893–1923*. Romo is codirector of the Museo Urbano, a public history project based in El Paso. His historical essays and editorials have appeared in *Texas Monthly*, Mexico City's *Nexos*, the *Texas Observer*, and the *Los Angeles Times*. He is currently writing a book about propaganda and intelligence on the US–Mexico border during World War II. For this project he has conducted research in archives in Germany, Mexico, and the United States.

ire'ne lara silva is the author of three poetry collections, *furia*, *Blood Sugar Canto*, and *CUICACALLI/House of Song*, and a short-story collection, *flesh to bone*, which won El Premio Aztlán Literary Prize. She and poet Dan Vera are also the coeditors of *Imaniman: Poets Writing in the Anzaldúan Borderlands*, a collection of poetry and essays. silva is the recipient of a 2017 NALAC Fund for the Arts Grant, the Alfredo Cisneros del Moral Award, and the Gloria Anzaldúa Milagro Award. She was a Fiction Finalist for AROHO's 2013 Gift of Freedom Award. Her website is at irenelarasilva.wordpress.com.

Octavio Solis is a playwright, director, and fiction writer whose works have been produced in theaters across the country since 1988. His fiction and short plays have appeared in the *Louisville Review*, *Catamaran Literary Reader*, *Chicago Quarterly Review*, *Arroyo Literary Review*, *Huizache*, and *Stone Gathering: A Reader*. His new book, *Retablos*, is published by City Lights Books and recently won the 2019 Silver Indies Award for Book of the Year from *Foreword Reviews*. His new plays, *Mother Road* and *Quixote Nuevo*, premiered in 2019. He is a Thornton Wilder Fellow for the MacDowell Colony and a member of the Dramatists Guild.

Helena María Viramontes is the author of the novel *Their Dogs Came with Them* and two previous works, *The Moths and Other Stories* and the novel *Under the Feet of Jesus*. Named a Ford Fellow in Literature for 2007 by United States Artists, she has also received the John Dos Passos Prize for Literature, a Sundance Institute Fellowship, a National Endowment for the Arts Fellowship, and a Spirit Award from the California Latino Legislative Caucus. Viramontes is Goldwin Smith Professor of English at Cornell University in Ithaca, New York, where she is at work on a new novel.